SPACIOUS SKIES
AMBER WAVES

THE GODS ARE BASTARDS | BOOK 2

D. D. WEBB

All rights reserved. No part of this publication may be reproduced, stored in a retrieval system, or transmitted in any form or by any means electronic, mechanical, photocopying, recording, or otherwise without prior written permission from Podium Publishing.

This is a work of fiction. Names, characters, places, and incidents are either products of the author's imagination or used fictitiously. Any resemblance to actual events, locales, or persons, living, dead, or undead, is entirely coincidental.

Copyright © 2026 by D. D. Webb

Cover design by Joe Wilson

ISBN: 979-8-89539-034-4

Published in 2026 by Podium Publishing
www.podiumentertainment.com

Spacious Skies Amber Waves

CHAPTER 1

"You can't do this to us!"
"It's *murder*!"
"He'll drop us all down a well or something!"
"There have to be laws about this kind of thing!"
"Don't you have a bleeding *heart*, woman?"
"*Children!*" Professor Tellwyrn shouted in exasperation. "You were told on the first *day* that you'd be graded primarily on field work. If you want to put up a fuss about things that aren't going to change, that's your lookout, but do not act as if you've been put upon without warning."

Tellwyrn stepped off the staircase, cutting diagonally across the grass about three-fourths of the way down the mountain, with the girls of Clarke Tower trailing along behind her. Ruda, Teal, and Fross kept right on her heels, exchanging glances and gearing up for another round of complaints; the others followed a bit more sedately. Each student was carrying a well-stuffed backpack, and not everyone was fully awake yet. Most of them weren't used to being up before the sun.

"It's one thing to know something's coming, theoretically," Ruda ventured at last. "This is last-minute panic. As in, 'holy shit, they're actually going to send us out into the goddamn wilderness with an idiot from another dimension as a tour guide.'"

Tellwyrn actually laughed at her, not turning around, and lengthened her stride. The line stretched out as the girls made varying degrees of effort to keep up. They remained mostly quiet, though, for the rest of the trip down. Their professor had cut a path that avoided the town, depositing them at the base of the mountain beyond its edges. The boys and their guide were already there waiting for them.

Toby smiled and waved; Gabriel appeared to be asleep standing up. Upon their approach, Professor Rafe turned and threw out his arms as though offering the world a hug, beaming delightedly.

"BEHOLD!"

"We're gonna fuckin' die," Ruda said.

"Ten points, Punaji!" he crowed, pumping a fist in the air. "But pace yourself. And remember, people *do* have feelings."

"We," she repeated, "are going to fucking *die*."

"Yup," said Gabe. "Can we just do that *now* and save ourselves a hike?"

"All right, enough," Tellwyrn said flatly. "Admestus, go wait up ahead."

"Aw, but I was gonna make a speech!"

"You can speech while walking. *Go*."

He turned and trudged away, shoulders slumped in an exaggerated pantomime of dejection. Naturally, this did not set a very fast pace.

"*Now!*" Tellwyrn shouted. He shuffled faster, taking off at a near run, still with his arms hanging limply and head down.

"Are you *seeing* the problem, here?" said Ruda.

"He has no respect for rules!" Fross added shrilly. "Not even basic standards of civilized behavior! I don't think he even gets how to—"

"Enough," Tellwyrn said flatly, with enough force that they all fell silent. She tilted her head down, staring at them over the rim of her spectacles. "Admestus Rafe has created a limited anti-death potion."

There was a moment's silence.

"That's impossible," Ruda finally scoffed.

"Wait, anti-death?" Gabriel paused to yawn, scratching his head. "Isn't that just, y'know . . . medicine?"

"Miss Punaji, you seem to have done some out-of-class reading," said Tellwyrn. "Care to take this one?"

Ruda scowled at her, but answered grudgingly. "Medicines are made to treat specific problems. An anti-death potion is just that: it prevents *death*. If you take one, anything that would cause death just doesn't affect you."

"Huh," Gabe said, then blinked owlishly. "Wait . . . how's that even work?"

"It fucking *doesn't!*" Ruda exclaimed. "It's like eight different kinds of tautologically impossible. It's a *myth*, like the Philosopher's Stone."

"Actually, Philosopher's Stones are real," said Professor Tellwyrn, "but the empire tends to disappear people who have them, since manufacturing gold on any significant scale would implode the economy overnight. But back to the topic at hand, yes, anti-death potions are *quite* impossible; they violate several physical and magical laws. And yes, Admestus Rafe created one."

She let that sink in for a moment, panning her gaze around them. Several of the assembled freshmen still barely looked awake, but they were all quiet now and paying attention. "Your professors at this University were offered employment here because they are the best living practitioners of whatever art they teach," she went on at last. "They were *not* selected for their academic qualifications." She glanced over at Rafe, who was now standing on his head, facing the Golden Sea. ". . . or social skills. The exception being Professor Yornhaldt, who *is* one of the greatest teaching mages alive, but honestly, I hired him to be a calming influence on this place. Regardless, before you start getting uppity, be aware of who you're dealing with, and why they deserve some respect."

"Well, that's all well and good," said Fross. "I mean, he's good at alchemy, and that's very impressive, but we're not doing alchemy on this trip unless someone gave me the wrong assignment parameters, which I'm gonna be *really* mad about if that's true because that's a mean thing to do to someone. We're basically doing wilderness survival with miscellaneous other tasks and maybe someone who's good with alchemy and doesn't have the most basic social skills isn't the best choice for keeping eight students alive in the depths of a huge, endless magical prairie?"

"Ah, but that's *not* his job," Tellwyrn replied, holding up one finger. "It's *yours*. This is something of a dry year; ordinarily I have a much bigger freshman class to deal with. However, even just the eight of you are a force to contend with. You've heard a lot about the dangers of the Golden Sea, and what you've heard was not exaggerated, but keep it firmly in mind that as long as you don't fall to backstabbing each other, *you* rank high among those dangers. Follow Juniper's lead on outdoor survival issues and Trissiny's in combat situations. Let Shaeine and Toby handle any negotiations that you need to do. You'll be fine."

"And the rest of us are what, chopped liver?" Ruda asked sourly.

Tellwyrn grinned at her. "You each have a valuable role to play, as anyone can attest who's tried to play a game of chess without pawns."

"Oh, fuck you."

"While Professor Rafe *does* have some friends and contacts out in the Golden Sea which may prove useful to you, all of that is secondary." Tellwyrn laced her fingers together in front of her stomach, looking smug. "He is there to watch you, not watch over you, and report back on your performance pertaining to the core classes in which you'll be given credit for this outing: history, combat, magic, and herbalism. In short, you're going out there to deal with people, fight things, contend with local magical forces, and make use of native plants. Your assignment, kids, is to have an *adventure*."

"That's just idiotic," Gabriel groused. "This is the twelfth century. *Nobody* does that anymore."

"I kind of want to," Juniper piped up. "It sounds like fun!"

"In a sense, yes, a journey into the Golden Sea is a journey into the past," said Tellwyrn. "You're accustomed to living in a settled, civilized world, full of mortal laws and the institutions that enforce them."

"Um, excuse me, but—" Juniper began.

"*Except* Juniper and Fross," Tellwyrn amended. "The point is, the Golden Sea is a patch of land where such things have never taken hold, and likely never will, nor can. Testing yourself in such a state of existence will give you a firsthand idea of what life was like for your ancestors. More to the point, it will give you the opportunity to strengthen and harden yourself as *they* had to, merely to survive. There is a trade-off, students, for living in a comfortable world of *systems*. You gain numerous assets and advantages from being part of an advanced society, but you are denied the opportunity to develop the toughness and inventiveness that people in less abundant eras must. I intend to see that you go out into the world with the advantages of both. I'm setting you up to *win at life*, kids. Kindly stop bitching at me about it."

"I would rather you didn't use that word."

"Oh, give it a rest, Trissiny." Tellwyrn sighed. "Anyhow, we are done here. There's your guide . . . the skinny man now doing cartwheels in the grass . . . and there's the Golden Sea. Off with you; try not to get killed, don't stab each other in the back. I'll be up here enjoying some peace and goddamn quiet."

"Does she know there are other students on this campus?" Gabriel asked as Tellwyrn turned to go.

"Shh," said Ruda, grinning. "She's making a dramatic exit. *Respect* the exit, man."

Rafe must have heard them approaching, assuming those ears of his weren't merely decorative, but he didn't turn around until the eight freshmen came to a stop right behind him, several dropping their backpacks to the grass. He stood, silently, staring out into the Golden Sea.

"We live in fishbowls," the alchemy professor intoned quietly. A soft wind blew across the prairie, making his golden hair shimmer along with the waves of tallgrass, both gleaming in the orange light of a new sunrise. "Our lives are ordered, structured, safe. We are fed, provided for, housed, and in return, our labors go to sustain the grand machine of civilization. It makes us healthier . . . in some ways stronger. More secure. But we forget, sometimes, just who and what we are. And so, my children, we embark on this voyage into the great beyond, into the last of the wilds, where there will be no one to catch us when we fall. We will live as animals, as savages. We will *live*. I say unto you . . ." He slowly raised both arms from his sides, extending them fully as if to embrace the prairie itself, and drew in a deep breath.

"BEHOLD!" shouted nine voices in unison.

Rafe turned around to face them, grinning broadly. "See, this is why I love you guys. You *get* me."

"You're not that complicated, man," said Gabriel.

"All right, kids," the professor said, suddenly brisk and all business. "Grab your satchels and your asses; we are *out* of here! Let's go grub around in some dirt. ONWARD TO GLORY!"

He took off at a run into the prairie, not even turning to see if they were following.

"Yup," Ruda said fatalistically. "Everybody remember that I called it. We are going to fucking die."

He was the first one off the coach when it rolled to a stop, but held the door open for the other passengers politely. Eager as he was to get the hell out of that hot, dusty, rattletrap prison, good manners were important. Webs and Sweet had both hammered that lesson into him over the years: Without manners, a body was likely to piss off the wrong people and alienate all the others. No way to do business.

The man in the cheap suit smiled politely at expressions of thanks from the old army officer and the aging lady in the severe gray dress, and then much more warmly at her young charge. He didn't quite dare go any further, though she was a lovely little piece, and had been shooting him increasingly daring grins all through yesterday. Poor girl was too sleep-struck to carry on their silent flirtation now; he was the only one who hadn't managed to nod off during the overnight ride. Ah well, nothing could have come of it anyway, though he did treat himself to a long appraisal of her rear as she collected her luggage and made her way into town.

His suitcase was the last to be handed down. The discourtesy of it rankled, even as it suited his purposes; he wanted to pause here and get a good look at Last Rock before getting down to business.

A wooden footbridge arched over the Rail line from the coach stop, which was the only thing on this side of the line from the town itself. This was where the road was, and for some damn fool reason the imperial survey had decided the Rail was of more import to the town than the means of transportation favored by honest folk since time immemorial. Not that he was honest folk, but it was the principle of the thing. He could have made this journey in minutes rather than days had he taken the Rail, but he had ridden that damnable contraption once before, and it had been plenty. How anybody got out of it without broken bones was a mystery to him.

    He accepted his suitcase from the driver with a curt nod and turned away, noting the man's clenched jaw at the lack of a tip and not caring. The guy would be on the road again soon and he'd never see him again, so why waste the effort, or the coin? Settling his hat over his slicked-back hair, he set off for the footbridge.

    The mountain was an awe-inspiring sight, especially with the University clinging to its peak, though he couldn't see that as well from this close up, what with the angle of the mount itself. Still, the University wasn't his business, at least not directly. His firm orders were to stay the hell away from it.

    Crossing the bridge, he made his way right for the first tavern he saw, a place with a sign proclaiming it the Ale & Wenches. Sounded like his kind of spot.

    Inside, the A&W was asleep, as all reasonable taverns were at not nearly long enough after sunrise. A groggy-looking boy was busy sweeping the floor and raised his head to blink stupidly at him as he entered.

    "Mornin'," the man said politely, tipping his hat. No telling who this kid was or who he knew; no use getting off on the wrong foot, though the Big Guy knew the little shit looked like he didn't have two brain cells to rub together. "I'm lookin' for a place to stay for a spell. Got any rooms to let?"

    "Uh . . ." The kid blinked and stared at him, and the man repressed a spike of aggravation. Really, this was no worse than he'd expected from this little cowpat town on the very edge of nowhere. "Uh, rooms're a silver piece a night, or five fer the week. An', uh, I'll need a name."

"Jeremiah Shook," he said, still polite despite the rising urge to slap some of the stupidity out of the boy. "And if it's not too much trouble, maybe you can help me find a friend of mine I'm lookin' for. Heard she was settled around these parts. Name's Principia?"

At that, the kid straightened up, suddenly a lot more alert. "You know Prin?" Oh, he wasn't just alert. He was *alarmed*.

Thumper permitted himself the luxury of an honest grin, not caring how it seemed to unsettle his new acquaintance. This was the place, all right. Maybe, just maybe, he'd be able to have a little fun with this job after all.

From her perch atop the church steeple, Principia was higher up than anything in town other than the scrolltower; as such, she was the first in Last Rock to experience the sunrise that morning. It illuminated her and her perch from the east, warm orange light causing the crystalline coating of the ankh atop the structure to burst into radiant life, then sliding progressively down the steeple, doing interesting things to the subtle highlights in her black hair. Even looking north as she was, it would have been half blinding to a human. Her eyes, of course, had no trouble.

She leaned back against the steep shingles, arms folded across her chest, heels resting on the tiny lip at the base of the steeple. Wind blew errant locks of her hair loose from the tight ponytail into which she'd pulled it, but she ignored this. It wasn't strong enough to affect her balance.

The elf watched, face intent, as the small column of people set out from the base of the mountain, heading into the Golden Sea. They weren't setting much of a pace; it took hours for them to vanish over the horizon. Still she stood there, motionless as a gargoyle, as the wind faded, the day heated, dew turned to steam, and the ruddy glow of sunrise turned into the steadily hot glare of day. Not until the town had come fully alive did she finally move. Even her elven eyes could no longer see the students.

Principia leaned her head back, momentarily looking up into the bright blue sky, and sighed softly.

"Keep her safe. Just for a while longer. Please."

She kicked herself carelessly forward, dropping down to the sloping roof of the church, slid down its shingles on her heels, and plummeted to the alley below, where she landed as silently and gracefully as a cat.

Whistling, she strolled off down the street, returning greetings from her fellow townsfolk with her customary insouciance. Just a pretty young woman without a care in the world.

CHAPTER 2

It quickly became apparent which of them were accustomed to hiking, and which were not. Very rapidly the sun climbed, the air heated, and the more indoorsy of the students began to struggle with the erratic pace Professor Rafe set as he darted back and forth, picking plants and frequently shouting gleefully about them. Juniper, likewise, would sometimes rush away to investigate something growing, but little that they found made much of an impression on the other students. The Golden Sea was a featureless plain stretching in all directions, with not so much as a shrub to break the shimmering monotony. The variety of grasses to be found was limited and of interest only to their resident herbalist and dryad. For the most part, the rest of the freshman class were preoccupied with the heat and their aching legs.

Around the time the sun had risen high enough to banish the colors of dawn and turn the sky crystal blue, they came to a sudden halt when Gabriel let out a yelp.

"The mountain!" he shouted, facing back the way they'd come. "It's gone!"

"Nonsense, it's right where we left it," Professor Rafe said easily. "*We're* gone."

"Wh— I *know* we're gone, but we've barely been walking an hour! That mountain is freaking huge; we should still be able to see it from here," Gabriel snapped.

"Oh, you worry too much," Rafe said, grinning easily. "Like you said, it's huge. I'm sure we'll find it again when we need it. For now, further up and farther in!"

"Are you *nuts*?!" Ruda shouted. "The Golden Sea shifts around and changes, everyone knows that. We've been shunted off to fuck knows where! How the hell are we gonna get back?"

"I'm sure something'll turn up," their professor said breezily, turning back around and strolling off. "Come on, that's why it's called an adventure! Get into the spirit, Punaji. Now keep a lookout for any interesting geographical features, kids. We'll wanna stop pretty soon to rest our legs and have some breakfast. Sitting down in standing tallgrass is kind of a pain, much less making a fire."

"I knew it!" Ruda pointed at him, turning to glare around at the others. "I fucking *called* it. The moron's led us out here to die."

"Then we shall die as heroes!" Rafe bellowed, already ten yards distant. "ONWARD TO GLORY!"

"Shut the fuck up, you asshole!"

"If I may?" Shaeine raised her voice only slightly, but it was sufficiently enough out of her normal register that both Ruda and Gabe stopped and turned to look at her. "Do you recall Professor Tellwyrn saying in our first class that there is a geas upon the University that prevents outsiders from knowing its true name?"

"Yeah, what of it?" said Ruda.

"There is more to it than that. Initiates of the Ultimate University can always find it from the Golden Sea. The general rule of navigating the Sea is that going uphill leads one farther in, while going downhill leads toward the edges."

"Wait, there's a hill?" Gabriel looked around, then lifted one of his feet and checked under it, as if expecting to find a squashed hill beneath his boot.

"The incline is very slight, but it's noticeable," said Trissiny.

"Look to the east or west."

"Moving laterally is . . . effectively random," Shaeine went on, "in terms of where the Sea will put you. For most people, exiting the region may mean departing at any point at its circumference, but we will always come back to Last Rock."

"Oh. Okay." Ruda slowly let out a breath. "That . . . would've been nice to know a little earlier."

"Yup!" said Rafe cheerily, coming back to join them. "And since our resident pixie is clearly an ice elemental and not an exposition fairy—"

"Excuse me, but those are a myth," Fross interjected.

"—you can assume that Shaeine came by her knowledge the old-fashioned way, by braving the wrath of Grumpypants McPonytail to access the library. Which you could *also* have done, had you been arsed to do the slightest of prep work before swaggering off into one of the world's most dangerous wildernesses. This is what we in the biz call a 'teachable moment.'" Grinning, he pointed a finger at Ruda and pantomimed squeezing a clicker with his thumb. "Zzzzzap! You're dead."

"Up yours, Twinkletoes."

"Wait, who's Grumpypants McPonytail?" Fross asked.

"The librarian," said Gabriel.

"I . . . Wait, what? The librarian's name is Weaver. I'm *positive* it is; I pay close attention to him. He said he was gonna put me in a bottle and use me as a lamp if I got frost on the books."

"Grumpypants is his nickname," Rafe said solemnly, "a hard-earned moniker that gives due credence to his vast contributions in the field of being grumpy."

"Oh." Fross buzzed around in a circle a couple of times. "Should . . . should I call him that?"

"Yes!" chorused Rafe, Gabe, and Ruda, wearing identical grins.

"*No*," Trissiny said firmly, dividing a hard look among the three. "Don't make fun of her. How would you like it if someone set you up for that kind of rude awakening?"

"Oh, pishposh," Rafe said cheerily. "How do you think Arachne welcomed me to the staff?"

"I am so confused," said Fross, drifting lower in the air.

Toby cleared his throat loudly. "Since we seem to have stopped anyway, how does breakfast sound to anyone else?"

"Remember what I was saying just now about camping in the tallgrass?" Rafe said condescendingly. "We can do that if you really *want*, but honestly, it's a recipe for getting really itchy even *before* the bugs start climbing up your clothes."

"*Bugs*?" Gabriel squawked, jumping to the side and looking down under his feet again.

"I remember, thanks," Toby said patiently, then pointed off to the group's right. "How's that?"

Visible above the shoulder-high grass about thirty yards away was a flat-topped outcropping of stone. Its surface was irregular and slightly angled, but looked large enough to hold them all comfortably, and more besides. It had definitely not been there a moment ago.

"Ha-*hah*!" Rafe crowed. "Brilliant! Good eye, Mr. Caine. Your quick thinking has saved us all a raging case of ass grass! ONWARD TO BREAKFAST!" He charged off toward the rocks, flailing with both arms to push tallgrass out of his way.

"I *still* say we're gonna—"

"Oh, give it a *rest*, Ruda," Trissiny said sharply, and stalked off after Rafe.

The pirate lifted her hand and scratched her head, peering quizzically after her roommate. "What's with her?"

"Dunno," said Gabe, following the paladin. "Don't care. Imma go sit down."

The lowest end of the flat rock was about chest high and had a convenient pile of tumbled stones on one side that enabled them to scramble up without difficulty. Rafe commented, as he set up a fire, that this boulder was probably a piece of the same mountain on which the University sat, hurled into the Golden Sea millennia ago by the explosion that had half sunken the plateau. His pupils were mostly disinterested—only Gabriel was paying him any attention, and that was not to anything Rafe was saying, but to the fire he'd set up by liberally coating a handful of tallgrass stalks in oil from a vial he'd taken from his belt. They burned as hot and steadily as a stack of wood.

Rafe sang off-key in elvish as he fried bacon and eggs. He and his cook fire were set up on the tallest part of the rock, and also the only completely flat one. The eight students sat in small clumps along the long, downward-sloping surface, positioned mostly facing west to keep the sun out of their eyes. Even without being blinded, there was no escaping the heat. None of them wanted to be anywhere near the fire.

"Aren't you hot under all that?" Teal asked, sitting down beside Shaeine, who as usual when outdoors, kept her hood well up. "I thought Professor Rafe gave you sun oil for your skin."

"He did. I don't like to complain," the drow demurred. "The heat I can suffer; without the shade of my hood, I'm afraid my eyesight is rather poor in this level of illumination. At home, I'd thought being out in the sun would be like walking in the agricultural caverns, with their sun crystals. I'm afraid they do not do justice to the real thing."

Teal nodded, a smile tugging at her lips. "So . . . aren't you hot under all that?"

Shaeine shifted slightly. ". . . extremely, yes."

"Oh!" The bard sat bolt upright, then clapped a hand to her face. "Oh, *damn* it, I'm sorry . . . I meant to do this before we set out, but I overslept and then it just went right out of my head. Hang on." Pulling over her backpack, she pried one of its smaller compartments open and withdrew an oblong leather case. "Here. I got this for you in town. It was gonna be a surprise . . . just, ahem, a more timely one. Sorry about that."

Shaeine took the little case carefully and flicked it open with her thumbs. Nestled inside was a pair of rectangular eyeglasses, made of smoky black glass.

"They're enchanted," Teal said a little nervously. "Should protect your eyes from the glare, even though they won't cover your whole face, obviously. It seems to work for Natchua. I thought the rimless ones were more your style, though . . . Oh, and the rubber coatings for the earpieces are detachable, so I got the ones in dark red and green. Awarrion colors, right?"

Gingerly, Shaeine unfolded the glasses and slipped them into the depths of her hood. After a moment's adjusting, she lowered the cowl of her robe, revealing her face; her white hair glowed under the full sunlight. The dark glasses made her look oddly rakish, in contrast to her serene demeanor.

"Thank you, Teal," she said softly. "This was extremely thoughtful."

Teal grinned delightedly. "You like 'em?"

"I do. Very much." She smiled in return, an expression that was just a perceptible hair warmer than her usual polite smile. After a moment, Teal cleared her throat and glanced away, biting her lower lip.

"Well, it'll at least help out here. Honestly, I don't know how you've been managing in Ezzaniel's class. You'd think a school this rich would have a gymnasium; why do we have martial arts on the lawn?"

"I have managed with my eyes narrowed to slits, actually. It is less than optimal, but allows me to preserve some vision, at least. And I am accustomed to using other senses to compensate."

"Wait, wait, hold up," said Ruda from a few feet away, craning her neck to look around Teal at the drow. "Are you telling me that on our first class, you fought me to a draw with your *eyes closed*?!"

"Not *closed*," Shaeine clarified. "Narrowed."

The pirate groaned and collapsed backward onto the rock. "My humiliation is complete. I should give Papa back the sword and become a fisherwoman."

"Or," Shaeine said gently, "apply yourself in Professor Ezzaniel's class and return home a better warrior than you left."

"No, no." Ruda placed her hat over her face and waved a hand dismissively. "It's all over. I'll just lie here and wait for decomposition. Clearly, I do not even deserve a proper burial at sea."

"Now, help me out here, 'cause I can't always tell," Gabriel said, grinning. "Is this *ironic* self-pity, or do you actually need your diaper changed?"

"Arquin, if my legs weren't so fucking sore, one of 'em would be halfway up your ass right now."

"Whoa, girl, let's save that for the third date," he said, grinning, then barreled on before she could reply. "I like your vest, by the way. I don't think I've seen you in that before. Is it armor?"

Under her long coat, Ruda wore a tight, midriff-baring vest of sturdy leather, embroidered sparingly with blue thread to offset its obviously utilitarian design. "Yeah," she said without looking out from under her hat. "It's armored."

"Well, I should point out that it leaves your tummy exposed. Y'know, the part that has all your vital organs?"

"Just because you *can* point something out doesn't mean you should, Gabe," Toby remarked.

"Well, what can I say." Ruda shrugged. "I'm a creature of style. I'll be the swankiest disemboweled corpse in the group."

"Oh, don't listen to her," Juniper said cheerfully, "she's just funning you again. That's for support."

"June," Ruda said, a note of warning in her voice.

Gabriel blinked and cocked his head. "Support?"

"Yeah!" the dryad bubbled on. "We're gonna be doing a lot of physical activity on this trip, probably, and Ruda's pretty busty. Breasts actually get *really* uncomfortable if you just let 'em bounce around. Like, even painful, for the bigger ones. They're just glandular tissue and a coating of fat, with a lot of nerve endings, so they need some artificial structure to avoid getting hurt."

"*Really?*" Gabriel said, grinning broadly. Across from him, Toby sighed.

"Juniper," Ruda said more firmly, sitting up and adjusting her hat.

"Yup!" Juniper went on blithely. "Well, not *mine*, of course, but I don't really have the same kind of nervous system you guys do. Also, my internal structure is more . . . well, that's kinda off the topic. She's probably fine with a good brassiere most of the time, but when we're gonna be out—"

"*Juniper,*" Ruda said sharply, finally getting the dryad's attention.

"Hm?"

"Remember when you asked me to warn you when you were talking about things that aren't for polite company?"

"Uh, yes?" The pirate stared at her evenly. Juniper gazed back, nonplussed. "... what about it?"

"I think she means you're doing that now," Fross piped up.

"What? I . . . Wait, *really?*" Juniper frowned. "You don't talk about *breasts* in public?"

"Not as a rule, no."

"But that's just *crazy*," she protested. "Boys love breasts. Even the gay ones. Girls, too. *Everyone*, just about! It's pretty much a universal positive. Everybody can gather together and bond over breasts. Nobody doesn't like them!"

"She speaks wisdom!" Gabriel proclaimed, his grin having reached almost Rafe-like proportions. "This is a profound revelation of truth, and society would be better for everyone if the whole world accepted Juniper's understanding."

"See, he gets it!" The dryad nodded enthusiastically. "Gabe *definitely* loves breasts."

"It's true," he agreed.

"And he could really benefit from an open discussion of the subject, too. I mean, *I* like being roughed up a bit . . . Well, heck, I like just about everything . . . but I'm concerned for the first human girl he sleeps with, if he's not a bit more gentle."

Gabriel's smile slipped. "Uh, wait a second, Juno . . ."

"I mean, really, you don't seem to grasp that that's *one* scenario where you want to suck on something without trying to suck it *off*, y'know?"

Ruda fell back to the stone, howling with laughter.

"Wait, stop!" Gabriel waved his arms frantically. "I changed my mind! I'm with Ruda, now. *Inappropriate*! Subject closed!"

Juniper blinked her eyes twice, glanced back and forth between him and Ruda, then sighed, her shoulders slumping. "Aw, man . . . I can't say *anything* right, can I?"

"Aw, c'mere, you," Ruda said cheerfully, getting up and going to sit down beside the dryad. She threw an arm over Juniper's shoulders. "You're an adorable little numbnut, y'know that? Don't ever change."

"Thanks, I'll . . . try not to? Oh, but I don't *actually* have nuts. I'm not literally a tree, you know."

"So noted."

"Also, nothing on me is numb."

Ruda grinned diabolically at Gabriel. "So I hear."

"Students! Companions! Fellow adventurers!" Rafe waved a spatula at them from the top of the rock. "BEHOLD! I give you the glory that is EGGS AND BACON! And also beans."

"We have to *what?*" Gabriel exclaimed.

"Hunt!" Professor Rafe cried exultantly, stomping ahead of them through the tallgrass. It was late midmorning and several of the students were as worn out and hungry as they'd ever been at the end of a long day. Rafe had finally settled down and set a more reasonable pace, after he ran out of things to show them. It hadn't taken long; there was a starkly finite number of grass species to be found, and after the flat rock on which they'd paused for breakfast, the Golden Sea had stubbornly refused to yield any more interesting geographical features.

"None of us knows anything about hunting!" Gabe complained.

"At least one of you does," Rafe said cheerfully, glancing back over his shoulder. "And really, Gabe, you might wanna let someone else get the next round of whining. I admire your enthusiasm, but we're all here to learn! Well, *you're* all here to learn. So maybe you set up camp and, say, Fross can whine and gripe about everything."

"Um, is he serious?" Fross asked nervously, fluttering along just above the tallgrass. "Is this humor? I don't really have anything to gripe about."

"Why the hell didn't you bring enough food?!" Gabriel bulled on.

"*Because*, princess, the whole point of this outing is for you lot to try your hand at keeping your butts alive in the howling wilderness! What, you think I should have brought along a butler to set up a pavilion each evening? Have your meals catered? Maybe with an orchestra and dancers, yes?" Gabriel fell to cursing under his breath; Rafe laughed at him and went on. "The eggs you just ate were all I brought. We've got beans, jerky, hardtack, and tea. That is *it*, boys and girls. From this point on, you wanna eat, you best damn well find something *to* eat!"

"We could stay stocked up on protein by grazing as we go," Juniper said brightly. "There's *lots* of bugs in this grass."

During the general outpouring of groans at this suggestion, and Juniper's confused response, Toby shortened his pace slightly, falling back to walk beside Trissiny, who'd appointed herself rear guard.

"You seem to be in your element," he commented.

To her horror, she felt a flush climbing up her neck. She blurted out her response before it could take hold in her face. "Well, it's not my first hike, by a long shot. I mean, we didn't do a lot of *walking* for its own sake, but, yeah, Sisters in training do cover wilderness survival. It's pretty important for those who plan on going into the Silver Legions. It's not really my *thing*, per se. Not that I mind it." *Oh, goddess, Trissiny, shut up,* she commanded herself silently. "I guess, yeah, I'm maybe a little less *out* of my element than the others. Well, some of the others. I don't mean you! I mean, I don't know what kind of training you have." *Shut! Up!*

Toby, fortunately, laughed softly. He had a nice laugh; it made her feel included, not mocked. "The walking doesn't bother me; Omnist monks keep pretty fit. The sun definitely doesn't, of course."

"Oh, right, yes. Omnu. Sun god, that makes sense." *What is going on*?! she berated herself. *When did I forget how to hold a conversation?* This had been the first time they'd talked alone in weeks. She didn't remember it being this *awkward* before. Of course, the last time had been before the . . . incident.

Toby nodded. "My complexion is too dark to burn, ordinarily, anyway, but it is nice not to have to worry about sunstroke. It's the little things that make a paladin's life bearable, eh?" He smiled at her sidelong; she couldn't help smiling rather foolishly back.

"I know you have that aura of serenity you can use . . . I didn't realize Omnu . . . Well, actually, now that I open my mouth I'm remembering I have no idea what I'm talking about. I don't know *what* Omnist paladins get."

"Don't you have any special perks? Like, an aura of command or something?"

She had to laugh at that. "Do I *seem* like I have an aura of command?"

"Well, yes," he said frankly. "I'm not the only one who's noticed, either. Honestly, I suspect that's why your roommate seems to butt heads with you; I don't think she likes authority very much."

Trissiny didn't know what to say to that. The silence began to stretch, feeling heavier with each passing second; almost frantically, she grasped at the first thing that came to mind. "Well, it's not a divine gift, but apparently I'm a general in the Imperial Army. I mean . . . automatically, by default, all Hands of Avei are. They didn't tell me about that at the abbey . . . Mother Narny probably didn't want it to go to my head. I, uh, had a kind of awkward encounter with your new roommates, when I ran across them. Apparently, they can't even talk to me unless I say 'at ease' first."

At that, he laughed again. She could listen to his laugh all day . . . "Yeah, they mentioned that. Rook's got a case of hero worship going for you, I think."

"Really? Isn't he the one who looks rumpled even when he's not?"

"Hah, that's a pretty good description! Well, it's like I said: aura of command. If it's not a gift from Avei, it must just be you, then." He smiled at her, and she felt another blush rising. Trying to conceal it, she moved a hand over her ear as though tucking away an errant strand of hair. There was none, of course; her braid was firmly in place. "You manage to make an impression, whatever it is. People either want to fight you or respect you."

So far, so good . . . If they could just avoid the bad subjects . . .

"Is that why you've been avoiding me?" she heard herself ask quietly.

. . . why, brain? What did I ever do to you?

He lowered his eyes, silently watching the grass ahead as they walked. In front, Rafe and the other students carried on their banter; the voices washed over the two of them, finding no purchase.

"I wasn't sure you'd want to hear from me," he said finally. "After my best friend started a fight with you over nothing."

Trissiny was so surprised she almost stopped walking; she did stumble slightly, hoping he didn't make anything of it. *Toby* felt awkward? After being chewed out by Tellwyrn and then Avei, enduring jabs from Ruda, it had come to seem to her that everybody blamed her for what had happened. She didn't quite know how to explain this to Toby, however.

"You mean, you don't blame *me* for that?"

Well, that worked.

He looked up at her, his expression pensive. "Well, not really. I got the full report from Gabe himself; he insisted the whole thing was his fault. Actually, he feels pretty awful about it." He hesitated, as if reluctant to say what came to mind next, but after that short pause continued in a low tone that almost sounded deliberately soothing. "Knowing Gabe, I suspect he's been too awkward to apologize properly. I can promise you that *is* awkwardness, Triss. He's not just being stubborn. I bet if you made the first move he'd practically grovel."

"I . . . I see," Trissiny said woodenly. She did *not* want to talk about Gabriel. Not generally, certainly not with Toby.

His soft laugh had a bitter undertone. "Some peacemaker I am. Ah . . . sorry, ignore that. I don't mean to put any pressure on you. Especially after Gabriel did."

"You're not responsible for Gabriel."

"I sort of am, though. I mean . . . no, technically, I'm not, but I *feel* that way. I've always kind of . . . looked out for him. Well, we did for each other. It really kills me that you guys don't get along . . . He's like a brother to me, and you're one of the most admirable people I've ever met."

"People have to make their own mistakes," she said vaguely, still trying to suppress a blush by force of will. He really found her admirable?

"The thing is," he went on quietly, "Gabe is . . . I think he'd be just about the best person I know if he would just *think* before acting or opening his mouth. You really haven't seen what's he's like, deep down. He works hard to do the right thing, and he's a great guy to have your back. He's just . . . well, a little reckless, I guess."

"Being thoughtless isn't a charming personality quirk on anyone," she said stiffly. "For a half demon, I'd say it qualifies as a real *problem*." Did they *really* have to talk about this?

"You're not wrong," Toby said solemnly. "And I'm only just starting to realize that. He's always been just Gabe to me. We grew up together, and . . . well, maybe I have a blind spot there. It never occurred to me before that he might actually *hurt* someone."

Trissiny held her silence. She didn't trust herself to say anything that wouldn't offend him.

"GUYS!" Abruptly, Professor Rafe rushed over to them, scattering the other students in his abrupt change of course. His expression was even more maniacally gleeful than usual; Trissiny felt a sudden urge to kick him in the shin. "Guysguysguysguys! C'mere, come over here, you gotta see this!" So saying, he charged off to the left of the group.

"Onward to glory," Toby muttered, and Trissiny shot him a grin.

Rafe left a trail of mashed tallgrass leading to a patch of leafy green stalks that towered over them. He skidded to a halt, leaving the freshmen to meander in behind him. Flinging both arms wide, he actually hopped up and down twice in excitement. "BEHOLD! A wonder of the Golden Sea! A marvelous plant! A gift from the very gods themselves! CORN!"

For a moment, only the rustling of the breeze in the grass could be heard. A hawk cried in the distance.

"You rushed all the way over here to show us *corn*?" Gabriel said in disgust. He had moved more slowly than the others in responding to Rafe's enthusiasm and now stood at the rear edge of the group.

"Hell yes I did!" Rafe crowed. "Corn is *awesome*."

"Um," said Teal, "this . . . this is *cultivated*. Look, it's planted in neat rows. And the patch is almost square."

"Isn't it great?" their professor gushed. "Ooh, and it looks about ripe, too. Everybody grab an ear. You've never tasted corn till you've had it *right* off the stalk."

"Or," Ruda said loudly, "*or*, we all back the hell away and get outta here before whoever's ballsy enough to *farm* in the Golden goddamn Sea comes back and finds us fucking around with their corn."

"Uh, yeah," Gabe said nervously. "About that . . ."

Everyone turned to look at him, and the group shied away as one. An elf had appeared out of the tallgrass.

She wore a simple buckskin shirt and trousers, bleached nearly white and decorated with uneven vertical streaks of brown and gold that blended with the surrounding tallgrass. Similar markings were painted on her face, and dark strands were dyed through her honey-blond hair. The camouflage was nearly perfect; even having stepped out of the grass into the cleared area around the cornfield, she seemed almost to fade into it.

The cleverness of her garb wasn't what held their attention, however. In her right hand was a wand, the tip of which was pressed against Gabriel's throat.

CHAPTER 3

Jeremiah Shook pushed open the swinging doors of the Saloon with both hands and stepped inside, pausing just past the threshold to sweep his gaze around the room. Scattered at tables and the bar, men in the rough garb of laborers and cattle hands looked up at him curiously; he nodded once to the room at large, then stepped inside and made his way to an empty table. A few pairs of eyes followed him until he sat, but most turned back to their drinks, conversations, and card games. His dark suit was of a more moneyed cut than most of them wore, but not by much.

He could afford better, but rarely bothered. In his line of work, clothes tended to get mussed pretty quickly.

"Nice entrance," said the waitress, sidling up to him. "Classic. You're a fan of cowboy fiction, I take it?"

She was mocking him. Bile rose in his throat; he pushed it back down, giving her an easy smile. "Tell me honestly: How many out-of-town visitors feel the need to do that at least once?"

"Pretty much all of 'em," she said with a grin, "but you've got them mostly beat for self-awareness. What'll it be, stranger?" She was an elf, a pleasingly slender little piece with sharp features and almost childlike eyes, but where elves were almost always some shade of blond, her hair was a glossy raven black. He'd eat his boots if there were two women of that description in a town this size, but the proprieties must be observed.

"A wanderer like me is compelled to keep simple tastes," he said, a rueful grin camouflaging his use of Guild codes for the sake of the onlookers. "At least, till I get settled in and figure how well my business will fare in this town."

"So, cheap whiskey, then?" She winked, but her smile was sympathetic. "You're in luck; Last Rock is kind to wanderers. They bring us most of our custom, after all. The welcome's warm, and the drinks are . . . substantially less awful than they could be." Her reply covered all the Guild countersigns and told him everything he needed to know about the current situation. No current Guild business, no pressure from police. A ripe town; it was ironic that they were both specialists in particular fields and not positioned to begin relieving the townsfolk of their money.

"Cheap, but not the cheapest," he replied. "Upgrade me from 'less awful' to 'not awful,' if y'don't mind."

"Ooh, big spender! Anything in particular you want it to wash down?"

"Just here to drink for now, doll."

"And drink you shall, darlin'. Back in two shakes." She sashayed off; he indulged in a half-moment's perusal of her backside before returning his attention to the room at large. Principia had a cute little tush, but he didn't yet know how well-liked she was in this town. Based on what Tricks had told him of her, he suspected not very, but ogling a woman who the locals held in esteem was a quick way to get on everybody's shit list. Best not to take foolish risks until he had his bearings.

Nobody was even looking at him. In addition to finding out where Principia lurked, he'd taken advantage of his day at the Ale & Wenches to learn a bit about the town. Last Rock got most of its income from the University, one way or another. Quite a few of the students had more money than was good for them, and the townsfolk had grown adept at squeezing it out of them without cultivating any bad blood. Aside from that and the local cattle industry, the town did business largely with passing adventurers. The Age of Adventures might be over, but the Golden Sea still held the promise of riches for the skilled and the lucky. The town saw decent traffic in heavily armed loners heading into the prairie, and in some cases staggering back out of it, and there were tradesmen who made a good living seeing to their needs. He was clearly neither student nor adventurer, and thus of little interest to the men in this room.

"Here we go," Principia breezed, returning and setting a bottle and glass on the table. "Whiskey, and a *clean* glass, because I like you. So tell me, wanderer, what's this business that brings you to our dusty little town?"

"This year, it's alchemy." He set a small stack of copper coins on the table before pouring himself a drink; she deftly made them vanish into her apron. "Cures, minor enhancements, that sort of thing. I've a modest stock with me and the option to send back to Tiraas for more if the ground here proves fertile."

"Oh?" She leaned one hip saucily against his table, folding her arms in a manner that framed her bust. Like most elves, she wasn't particularly buxom, but had clearly selected her dress and apron to maximally accentuate her assets. "Now, would that be real, *effective* alchemy, by any chance?"

"Y'know, that's a fairer question than I might admit in other circumstances," he replied with a grin, taking a sip of the whiskey. She was right; it wasn't awful. "I'm not ashamed to say I've peddled a few vials of snake oil in my day; a man has to make a living. But in the end, there's no future in it. The real stuff's where the money is, once you've built up enough of a nest egg to invest in a basic stock."

"There's a town alchemist, you know," she said. "He may not appreciate the competition."

"Mm. Then again, he may not mind. I'm sure we can come to an understanding." Shook sipped his drink again. "There are lucrative but shady concoctions an upstanding local business owner may not want to pass across his counter. Not to mention the kind of characters he wouldn't want to pass 'em to. I'm confident I can keep out of his hair."

"Well, I know the lot of the casual tradesman," she said with a sly smile. "I do a side business in minor enchantments, as well. In a town like this, it's enough to keep me drinking a slightly better quality of whiskey than that."

"Good to know," he said appreciatively. "Fertile grounds after all?"

"Oh, you'd better believe it. Between the college kids and the wannabe heroes, you can always find someone willing to trade his coin and his common sense for a little edge."

"Perhaps we might have business to discuss, then. We are in similar fields after all."

"Perhaps," she purred. "I just know there's *something* mutually beneficial we can find to talk about."

"Hey, Prin, how about this?" rumbled the man behind the nearby bar. "How's about you see to the business I'm actually payin' you for while you're on shift. Table three needs drinks."

"It seems there is a whiskey crisis and only my unique combination of brains and beauty can see justice done," she said wryly, straightening up and tipping him a flirtatious wink. "I will see *you* later, handsome. I'm off at ten."

"Good to know," he murmured again into his glass as she swished away.

He was going half stir-crazy by the time ten o'clock rolled around. There was nothing to damn well *do* in this wretched patch of streets they called a town. Only the two pubs, a bunch of shops of various kinds, and one hotel that didn't offer a public drinking room, preferring to maintain a calm atmosphere for its clientele. Shook stayed the hell away from *that* place while he was in this mood, well aware he might otherwise end up burning bridges he'd not even crossed yet. What kind of frontier town didn't even have a whorehouse?

It didn't help at all that Principia made him wait. He lounged against the front wall of the Saloon, working quietly away at a cigar, while ten o'clock drifted by and retreated further into the distance. Passersby nodded to him, and he nodded politely in return; some gave him curious looks, but he wasn't challenged. Doubtless the locals didn't see much aimless loitering, but clearly they didn't see much real trouble, either. He took his time at the cigar, it being his only excuse for hanging around outdoors, but it would only burn so slowly. If she made him light up another one . . .

Principia finally emerged from the swinging double doors with a splash of panache that made his eye twitch, as if she hadn't a care in the world, nor anybody standing out in the dark waiting on her.

"You're late," he noted, barely keeping his tone under control.

"Ah, ah, ah," she said sweetly, wagging a finger at him. "I'm an elf, a thief, and a woman. That's three separate flavors of doing whatever the hell I want and automatically being right. Shall we?" Slinking up to him, she wrapped herself around his arm, giving him an up-through-the-lashes look that she had doubtless practiced.

Shook drew in a deep, slow breath, forcibly repressing the first five urges that came to mind. Not much got under his skin faster than a woman with an uppity attitude. He flicked the remains of his cigar to the ground and crushed it under his heel before stepping away from the wall and heading at a sedate pace back toward the center of town—such as it was—with the elf clinging to his arm the whole way. Doubtless they looked like any pair of lovers out for an evening stroll.

He glanced about swiftly. Despite the late hour and the general dinkiness of Last Rock, they weren't entirely alone. There was a faint sound of carousing from Ale & Wenches, even though they were several streets from it, and lights on in a few windows. For the moment, they had the street to themselves, however.

"This'n's gone larking after catching the birdsong," he said quietly. "A big bird tweeted of—nf!"

"*Stop* that," she said sharply but in a similarly low tone, punctuating it with a fist to his ribs and very nearly earning herself one in the eye. Principia continued on, apparently heedless of the hazards to her health she was accumulating. "Don't use cant in this town; you'll bring all manner of hell down on our heads."

Shook drew a deep, slow breath in through his teeth, counting to ten as Sweet had instructed him once upon a time. "Unless you have a quiet place to talk..."

"The street is plenty quiet. Oh, unclench your sphincter; you're gonna burst something. Look, you know the three kinds of invisibility, right? *Tell* me you have at least that much savvy." The look she gave him, up through her lashes, was equal parts condescension and amusement.

Right then, he decided he wasn't going to get through this job without smacking that mouth of hers. It was just a matter of when.

"Can't see, don't see, and won't see," the elf explained, as much as calling him an untrained fool right to his face. "You probably think of the cant as a 'can't see,' and you'd be partly right. There are probably a few outsiders who can puzzle it out, but not enough to matter. But in Tiraas, where the Guild is a significant power, it's also a 'won't see.' People hear the word *cant* spoken and know it's time to find some business elsewhere and mind it. Last Rock is *different*. Nobody will pay any attention to two people acting as they expect, but between the damn students and the so-called adventurers, anyone hearing a snatch of thieves' cant has a good chance of figuring out *what* it is, even if they can't follow it. *Then* all hell breaks loose."

He was only listening to her witless prattle with half an ear. A man had stepped out from around the corner up ahead and was ambling toward them on their side of the street. In the darkness, he couldn't make out any details except for the hat and the rattle of spurs, but he shifted his fingers toward the knives hidden in his sleeves. "Shush, girl, let me handle this."

"Here, I'll show you," she said, ignoring him, and then actually waved to the figure ahead. "Evening, Sheriff!"

"Prin," the man replied, tugging the brim of his hat politely, while Shook tensed, ready for a fight. "I don't believe I've met your friend."

"He's an itinerant salesman passing through town," Principia went on cheerily. "I'm gonna take him back to my rooms under the pretext of letting him under my skirt, then slip him a mickey, rob his ass blind, and skip town!"

"Dammit to Vidius, Prin, no!" The sheriff clapped a hand over his eyes, disturbing his ridiculous ten-gallon hat. "You *know* I have to take that stuff seriously. Don't even joke."

"If he doesn't have anything worth stealing, I may even slit his throat!" she said, grinning ghoulishly, and leaned closer to the sheriff, drawing her next word out with relish. "Mmmmm*uuuuurrrrderrrr*."

"No. Absolutely not, the hell with this. I don't have the patience for your bullshit tonight." The lawman swiped a hand across the empty space between them, as if wiping Principia and her companion from existence. "This didn't happen, I never saw you, go *away*. And you, stranger." He paused, leveling a finger at Shook. "I don't care how pretty she is, I don't care if you've never had an elf before and been dreaming of it since before you could shave, *this one* is not worth the trouble. She ain't gonna do anything as gentle as what she just promised, but I guarantee she'll give you a bigger pain in the ass than a joint case of sunburn and crabs. You have a pleasant night, people I don't see."

Principia laughed aloud in evident delight as the sheriff stepped into the street to go around them, steadfastly refusing to acknowledge her any further. Shook glowered down at her, and had to be tugged along impatiently before he continued moving.

"See?" she went on in a more circumspect tone. "I have a rep in this town. People know me, and know what I'm about: shady business, but strictly small potatoes with a side of aimless mischief. I'm seen strolling around in the middle of the night with the new salesman in town, they'll just assume I'm out to bed and/or swindle you. Anybody passes close enough to hear a snatch of conversation, they're not likely to make anything of it, because a snatch is all they'll hear. On the off chance someone *does* overhear a dirty word like *steal*, well, that's just me again, and as the good Sheriff Sanders just demonstrated, messing around in my business is more of a pain than it's worth. *However*, if someone hears the resident ne'er-do-well and the new guy talking in the thieves' *goddamn* cant, *that* will get their attention. They will then go get the sheriff's attention, and it's a toss-up whether he'll then go get the empire or *Tellwyrn's* attention first, and it's equally a toss-up which of those things would ruin our day faster or more thoroughly. So, at the expense of repeating myself . . ." Again, she looked up at him through her lashes, but this time her expression was hard and her voice dropped to a hiss. "Knock it the *fuck* off, newbie."

"Mm-hmm. You about done?"

"I believe that covers the basics, yeah. So, how's about you tell m—"

Despite his original intention to avoid attention, trouble, and people in general, he had allowed her to lead them toward the A&W, where lamplight and laughter spilled out through windows and a set of swinging doors much like the Saloon had. They weren't yet in front of the building, and thus within sight of its windows, and the noise did, he had to acknowledge, provide a little auditory cover. After glancing briefly about the square next to the Rail platform to verify that the sheriff had passed from sight and nobody else was about, Shook grabbed her by the upper arms and darted into the alley between the A&W and the general store beside it. He lifted the elf bodily from the ground to prevent her digging her heels in. She hardly weighed anything.

Principia didn't struggle or protest as she was carted a few feet down the alley, not far enough that they'd be hidden, but not in immediate sight from the street. She did let out a soft grunt as he slammed her back against the stone wall of the general store, then covered her body with his own. To any passerby, they were just a couple necking in a patch of improvised privacy. "Won't see," indeed.

"I'm Thumper," he said in a bare whisper, inches from her pointed ear. "Want to guess why?"

"An homage to your exquisite dancing skills, no doubt," she said lightly.

He lifted her away from the wall momentarily, then slammed her back into it. This time, she made no sound, just giving him an ironic look with a raised eyebrow. This time, too, he shifted his position to place a hand around her throat, and so wasn't fooled by her cool act. He could feel her pulse.

"I'm an enforcer," Thumper breathed. "You *do* know what that is, don't you? Not much of one for cutting purses, jimmying locks, or running cons. Some of those in my line like to crack heads in alleys and collect the Unwary Tax that way. Me? I'm a creature of order. A true servant of Eserion and his Guild. I don't like it when the Guild's business is disrupted, when the Guild has problems. I make problems go away . . . or at least rethink their choices. So the question, Keys, is this: Are you going to be a *problem*?"

"Does Tricks know you're out manhandling Guild members this way?" she asked lightly. "You wanna be careful, *Thumper*, or the Boss might decide *you* need someone to come around and . . . 'solve' you."

"I asked you a question," he said in a mild tone. "I expect an answer."

"I find that expectations are exactly the kind of—"

He drew back just enough to lift his hand from her throat and slap her, then backhanded her face drawing it back the other way. Her head bounced against the wall behind her, those big, pretty eyes going momentarily out of focus.

"Tricks gave me the rundown on you, Keys," he said softly. He lifted his hand again, grinning in satisfaction at her flinch, but this time just brushed the backs of his knuckles over her cheek. "He knows you got yourself assigned to this shithole town to work some angle of your own. Probably something to do with Tellwyrn, since all you're *supposed* to be doing . . . all there really *is* to do in Last Rock . . . is watch to make sure she doesn't pull anything harmful to the Guild's interests. He knows you don't like taking orders, that you fancy yourself above any authority. That is why he sent me, Keys. *I* wasn't brought to Last Rock to carry out an assignment; I came here to give you orders for *your* new one . . ." Thumper leaned in closer, near enough that his breath was hot on her face. ". . . and ride you as hard as I have to, to make sure you fucking *do* it. So I'm gonna ask my question one more time. It's a simple question, for a simple girl. All it needs is one word—yes or no. You're gonna answer the question accordingly. So tell me, Keys. Are you going to be a problem?"

"No," she said quietly. Somehow, the silly trollop managed to fill the word with another dose of her dry, disdainful attitude. He let it pass, for the moment. Plenty of time to straighten her out later.

"Good girl," he said approvingly, stroking her black hair once and enjoying the grimace that flickered across her features. "Then let's talk about the job."

Thumper drew back slightly, granting her a little breathing room, though he kept one hand gripping her upper arm. Keys, evincing some basic common sense for the first time since he'd met her, didn't attempt to pull away from him or offer any further sass. Those blue eyes watched him carefully.

"We've got trouble with Elilial and the Black Wreath," he began, nodding at her when her eyes widened. "Yeah, that's bad. They're not after us, but they're fucking with both the Church and the empire in a big way, bigger than usual. Do I need to explain all the thousands of ways this could cause problems for the Guild? No? That's my girl. The Guild isn't getting involved directly, but the Boss is preparing for a situation in which we might need to, and that means casing. Lots and lots of casing. We need information, and *you* are going to help us acquire it. Right now, the only other player who the Boss *knows* is involved in this is Arachne Tellwyrn. What we know is she's responded favorably to an overture from the throne, and she's personally beaten the hell out of at least one Wreath cell recently. We need *better* intel than that. And since you're not only conveniently on site but have a history with Tellwyrn, you're going to get it for us."

"Tricks is out of his fucking mind," she breathed. "There is no possible good result from screwing around with Tellwyrn. The *only* safe plan for dealing with her is to watch from a circumspect distance and give warning if she starts making noises in our direction. Y'know, what I've *been* doing."

"Actually, as I understand it this was Sweet's idea," he said lightly, "but the orders come from the Boss. So that's what you'll be doing."

"Then you can tell the Boss he's asking for what can't be—"

She managed to brace herself slightly, this time, as he slammed her against the wall again. "In the years you've been farting around out here in the sticks, Keys, you seem to have started confusing the Guild with the law. The Guild does not need to *prove* that you're trying to fuck us over beyond a reasonable doubt; if it knows damn well that you are, that's it for you. You're clever, you're stealthy, you're good at not getting caught. Those are the skills you are being ordered to use. They are *not* skills that will protect you if you decide to challenge the Boss's authority. And since it apparently hasn't sunk in yet, as far as you're concerned..." He leaned closer again, pressing his stubbled cheek against her smooth one to whisper right into her ear, "I *am* his authority. Do the job, Keys."

"I *can't* get close to Tellwyrn!" she protested. "She knows me; I used to work with her back around the Enchanter Wars. She *specifically* told me to stay off her mountain and away from her students. I so much as *try* to snoop up there and she'll fry my ass."

"Well, then," he said, drawing back enough to let her see his grin, "sounds to me like you've got yourself a problem. Ah, ah, ah," he chided, placing a finger over her lips as she opened her mouth to protest again. "I believe that's enough lip out of you for one evening. Let me be clear: You're a Guild member, Keys, but you are not a member in good standing. You're not trusted, or liked. This is an opportunity for you to redeem yourself... or create the opportunity for the Guild to get you out of its hair for good. Tricks expects you to try to run instead of doing your job. That's fine, I'm not to bother chasing after you if you bolt. In fact, I didn't want to tell you this, but he gave me firm orders, so here it is: You wanna pull a runner, you can. You'll be a dark mark, and any Guild member who happens across you can bring back your head—attached or not—to make his own rep, but Tricks isn't gonna bother *sending* anybody to do it. Course, he won't be Boss forever, and elves live a long time, I hear. That'd be a stressful existence for you, waiting to see if each new Boss of the Guild decides to start tying up loose ends. But all that's in the future. Let's talk about the now."

Thumper grinned even more broadly at her; still holding her arm with his left hand, he lowered his right to place against the side of her body at the ribs. She was as compact and delicate as all her race; he could clearly feel the frantic banging of her heart. "If you try to run and I *do* catch you before you get out of town... Or if you continue to refuse your assignment, or if you turn on the Guild and try to bring Tellwyrn or the law down on us, if you *fail* at your task... Or hell, if I find myself less than satisfied with your progress . . . then you're mine, Keys. I have full discretionary authority over this job, and what disciplinary measures need to be exercised." He lowered his voice to a growl, and as he continued, slowly dragged his hand downward, brushing his thumb against the side of her breast, sliding it across her waist and then around to grip a handful of her rump. "In that event, Keys, the *first* thing I'm gonna do is bend you over the nearest level surface, hike up your skirt, and take myself some recompense for the various insults and annoyances you've already caused me. And *then* we will get down to the disciplinary measures."

For a silent moment, he held her that way, staring into her eyes. Her insouciance was gone, but nothing replaced it; she stared back up at him, face utterly blank.

Then, so suddenly that she staggered, he released her and stepped back. "Do the job, Keys. I'll be checking in on you. Regularly."

Thumper turned away and strolled nonchalantly back out the mouth of the alley, tucking his hands in his pockets. He didn't look back at her as he went, not even when he turned left to amble toward the A&W's door and the promise of a pint to wind down the evening. As such, he didn't see the look she directed at his back. If he had, he wouldn't have cared.

He had always had more self-confidence than self-preservation.

CHAPTER 4

Trissiny and Ruda both reached for their swords, but before either had a chance to draw, Toby stepped forward, his hands raised peaceably.

"Good morning," he said politely. "Despite what Professor Rafe was suggesting, we have no intention of disturbing your corn. We don't listen to him as a rule. Would you mind removing the wand from my friend, please?"

"Actually, go ahead and blast him," Rafe said cheerily. "Boy's half hethelax, I doubt he'll even get a sunburn."

"Professor," said Gabriel tersely, trying to watch the elf out of the corner of his eye without moving, "*please* go fuck yourself."

"Hah! Sass and sauciness in the face of imminent zappage! Ten points, Arquin!"

"Sideways," Gabe clarified, "with a hatchet."

"Enough *banter*," Trissiny exclaimed. "Put down the wand, please. Nobody here wants a fight, but if it comes to one, you're *not* going to win."

"Whoa, whoa, everybody just calm down," Rafe said soothingly. "She's not gonna shoot him. She knows Tellwyrn's hunted people down over longer distances for less reason. Also, Triss, when you're scrapping with elves, don't worry about the one you see; worry about the three you don't. Guys, this is my old buddy Ansheh. Annie, dollbaby," he went on, turning to face the elf directly and holding out his arms for a hug. "You never come visit anymore! I was starting to worry you'd been eaten by a swallowgator or disemboweled by a jackalope."

For a tense moment, she stared at Rafe, eyes narrowed but her expression unreadable. Then, her lips curled up in a sneer and she spoke one syllable.

"*Ugh.*"

She did, however, remove the wand from Gabriel's neck, immediately stepping back out of arm's reach. The wand stayed pointed at the ground, for now.

"Well," Gabe said, rubbing his throat, "I guess that's a sign she really does know him."

Professor Rafe said something rapidly to the woman—Ansheh, apparently—in elvish. She replied in the same language, her posture still wary and expression faintly disdainful. The students glanced about at each other as this exchange drew longer.

"Is anybody gonna let us in on the joke?" Ruda asked finally. Rafe and the elf ignored her, but Teal spoke up in a low voice.

"He's getting the news on the region. Apparently, her tribe lives around here, usually . . . Oh, wait, no, they travel through this area a lot. They're nomadic. They're not here now, though. She's scouting the region to check up on patches of crops like this one and to see if . . ." Her voice trailed off and she grew a shade paler. "Centaurs."

"To see if centaurs?" Ruda snorted. "Well, that's good to know. Personally, I hate it when centaurs."

"Don't joke," Trissiny said tersely.

"Listen, Shiny Boots, the day I stop joking because *you* told me—"

"*Ruda,*" Teal said more urgently. "She's right. Centaurs are not a joking matter."

"They are not," agreed Ansheh flatly. The two of them had ceased talking as Ruda grew louder, and now she switched to Tanglish and addressed herself directly to the students. "The presence of a full horde in the region is the reason my tribe has moved on." Rafe started to say something again in elvish, but she cut him off with a slashing gesture.

"Are you not some manner of teacher, Admestus? Then do not presume to 'protect' your students from truth. I will warn you, and them, of a danger in the region as I would any traveler in good faith."

"Are they still nearby?" Trissiny asked, tense.

Ansheh shook her head. "The main horde has moved on, and the Sea has shifted. They are nowhere near. However, there are fresher tracks of a smaller band that may have split off from them, within miles of here. Forty to sixty, maybe. I have three times seen tracks of individuals, doubtless sent out to scout."

"Time? Location? *Direction*, even?" Trissiny insisted.

"You're new to the Golden Sea, little warrior," the elf replied, her face softening into the merest hint of a smile with more than a hint of condescension. "These things cannot be planned for here."

"Then how do you maneuver, or manage not to get lost from *your* tribe?" Toby asked.

"There are ways." Finally, she holstered the wand, then reached behind herself into the tallgrass and plucked two long stalks, one with each hand. The left she held up before them, perpendicular to the ground. "The center of the Golden Sea can never be reached, but one can travel toward or away from it; one can go deeper in, or seek to escape, and the Sea will allow this." As she spoke, she manipulated the other stalk with the fingers of her right hand with amazing deftness, twisting it into a figure eight. "To travel *around*, though, is to travel at the Sea's whim. One place may be next to another place one moment, on the opposite rim the next. A person may never see it shifting, but in the instant you close your eyes, the world realigns around you."

"We know this, thanks," Gabriel said, reaching up to rub his throat again. His expression was just barely on the right side of a glare.

"It is in traveling *around* that one must make accommodations with the Sea itself," Ansheh continued, ignoring him. "You initiates of the *tauhanwe* University tie a rope to yourselves that leads you back home. The Sea allows this because it does not affect the Sea itself, but only how you pass through it. *My* people align ourselves with the will and the way of the Sea. It is kind to us because we are kind to it, because we are *of* it. We trust in it to lead us where we should go."

"The fuck does that even mean?" Ruda demanded.

"It is a thing that is done," said Ansheh, gazing inscrutably at her, "not a thing that is said."

". . . the fuck does *that* mean?"

"The centaurs," the elf continued in the same even tone, "are practitioners of dark magic, of the infernal. They twist the Sea to carry them where they wish to go. It works, until it does not. That is why we are always alarmed to find centaurs where they are rarely seen. Right after the Golden Sea has struck back against their manipulation and thrown them off . . . that is when they are most angry."

Trissiny blinked her eyes twice, then shook her head. The elf's roundabout explanation—or what was apparently meant to be an explanation—made her brain feel the way her stomach did when she tried to digest richer food than she was used to eating. "All right, well . . . Can you tell us *anything* about how close the centaurs are? Any suggestions how we avoid them?"

"They are few, and they are not *here*," Ansheh said infuriatingly. "'Close' means nothing here. You will probably not find them unless you wish to, or they wish to find you. The Sea does not reward their sorcery."

". . . okay, then. Thank you."

Ansheh nodded gravely to her.

"Right, then!" For a few moments while he and Ansheh had been speaking, Rafe had seemed almost concerned. His irrepressible cheeriness was back now, in such force that it made his momentary lapse seem like a trick of the light. "Nothing for it but to press on! We'll either meet centaurs or we won't, and probably not more than sixty."

"*Not more than sixty*?!" Ruda planted her fists on her hips, glaring at him. "I don't even know what the deal is with these centaurs, but if they're hostile, *sixty* is a pretty big fucking deal!"

"Nonsense!" he bellowed. "Bring them on in their hundreds, in their hordes! We shall show them what it means to be, uh . . . paladins, pirates, priests, and whatever-all else! The bards will sing of our triumph for ages to come!"

Ansheh gave him a flat look and said softly, "*Tifau.*" It was one of those words that didn't need a translation to communicate quite plainly. She made three soft clicks with her tongue in a syncopated rhythm, and a shape rose from the tallgrass behind her.

It was horse-sized but built more like a deer, with delicate legs and cloven hooves, and a long tail ending in a graceful tuft of fur. A single, spiraling horn rose from above its eyes. The unicorn's coat was silvery white, but had been painted with vertical streaks in shades of brown and gold; hiding motionless in the tallgrass, it was as invisible as the elf had been.

Fross gasped audibly. "*Pretty.*"

Ansheh placed one hand against the unicorn's neck and then leaped onto its unsaddled back in a smooth motion that resembled water flowing uphill. She clicked her tongue once more and her mount turned to face the endless sea of tallgrass; she looked over her shoulder at them and nodded once, curtly. "We will not be back here in time to harvest. Take as much corn as you need; the rest will go to the crows as the wards fade." Then the unicorn bounded away, making only the most impossibly soft noise as it disturbed the grass in passing. In seconds they were lost to sight.

"Huh," said Gabriel. "After Tellwyrn and Sunrunner, I figured the old stereotype about elven mysticism was bunk. Maybe it's just the wild ones."

"Yeah, no, the stereotype is bull," Rafe replied, grinning. "Don't go expecting any elves you meet to act like that; they'll either laugh at you or shoot you. Ansheh's the biggest drama ham I've ever met. You give her attention, she'll give you a show."

"Also, it may be a bad idea to judge anyone by Tellwyrn's example," Toby noted.

"That, too," Rafe agreed. "Welp! You heard the nice lady with the ears, kids. Since I was just talking about finding food a few minutes ago, let's CORN IT UP!"

"So what's the big issue with centaurs?" Ruda asked after they had resumed their trek. Rafe was again in the lead, and again singing to himself in elvish. Ruda had produced a bottle of bourbon from within her coat and was working at it. Apparently, their professor had similar bag-of-holding enchantments on the pouches at his belt; that, anyway, seemed to be where he was keeping all their supplies, including the corn they'd just picked. "The way you guys reacted, I'd have thought you were talking about Elilial's own brood."

"They might as well be," Trissiny said darkly. "Centaurs are diabolists. That magic the elf was talking about that they use, it's pure evil."

"Oh, everything's evil with you," Ruda said dismissively.

Trissiny drew in a breath and let it out slowly. "How many things have you actually heard me describe as evil? Name two."

"Centaurs and Gabe." The pirate grinned at her and had a long pull of bourbon.

"Honestly, I thought centaurs were a myth," Gabriel said.

"History," said Teal, "not myth. They still live, but only in the Golden Sea, because the shifting geography makes it pretty much impossible to go in and hunt them down. The Sisters of Avei have wiped them out everywhere else."

"Big fuckin' surprise, there!"

"Ruda," Teal said sharply, "the fact that you can't get along with your roommate doesn't mean you get to call all Avenists genocidal maniacs. They're anything but. The Sisters gave up trying to deal with centaurs diplomatically and simply killed them en masse, and *nobody*, not even the Omnists or Izarites, argued with them about it. *That* should tell you everything you need to know about centaurs."

"It is the nature of demons to be unreasoningly aggressive," Shaeine said quietly, "unless the infernal magic that animated them is countered by another force, such as mortal blood." Gabriel sighed, making a wry face, but didn't interrupt as she continued. "Mortals who *practice* that magic can fall prey to the same. My people have seen the like in the Scyllithene drow of the deep dark. There is no thought, no negotiation, often not even strategy. Only hate and violence."

Another brief silence fell, which again, Ruda broke. "Well . . . shit. Good on the Sisters, then. Hell, I kinda hope we meet some now. Wouldn't mind killing a few of those myself."

"You really don't possess a shred of common sense, do you?" Trissiny asked.

"Really, blondie?" Ruda tilted her head back to give her a long look from under the wide brim of her hat. "You wanna start this up?"

"Let us not start anything up, please," Shaeine urged.

Ruda grunted and tilted her head back, drinking. They all watched the level of bourbon in the bottle go down.

"Ruda," Toby said from behind them, "it occurs to me that I always seem to see you drinking something, but I've never actually seen you *drunk*."

"Yeah?" She grinned at him over her shoulder. "Or maybe you've never seen me sober."

"I've been meaning to ask about this, too," Gabriel added. "It's supposed to be a dry University, but I've seen you hitting the bottle right in *front* of Tellwyrn. How come the rules don't seem to apply to you?"

"Diplomatic immunity," she said cheerfully. "It's good to be a pirate, boys. Incidentally, anybody have any clue just where the fuck this guy is taking us?"

Rafe paused in his current song to shout "TO GLORY!" without turning around.

"Wow," Ruda muttered, "I walked right the fuck into that, didn't I. Well, I hope glory's got a roof. We're gonna get rain here in a day or two."

"Wait, what?" Gabriel peered around at the sky, which was deep blue and cloudless. "Maybe you *are* drunk after all."

"Up yours, Hell's Bells. That's your new nickname, by the way. I grew up on ships; don't fucking talk to me about weather." She twisted her mouth in a grimace, then took another drink. The bottle was getting close to empty. "I could tell you more exactly than that, but . . . I dunno how much this place is fucking with my weather sense. There's no decent-sized bodies of water anywhere around, and who the hell knows how it all works when the ground isn't even lashed down properly. Rain's coming, though. Bank on it."

Before anyone could reply, the ground began to rumble.

"What the—Earthquake!" Gabriel cried, reflexively ducking down.

"Shh!" Up ahead, Rafe turned and waved his arms frantically, shushing them as if he hadn't been singing at the top of his lungs moments ago. "SHHHHH!"

Juniper's gasp of obvious delight only added to the confusion, at least until she pointed off to their right. "Look! Look! Bison!"

Carefully, the eight of them crouched low enough to almost hide themselves, peering through the upper fronds of the tallgrass. Fross belatedly fluttered down to join them after being hissed at and urgently beckoned by Ruda.

It was an awe-inspiring sight. The herd stretched nearly to the horizon beyond, but they were passing close enough that those nearest the students were clearly visible, their numbers fading into a deep brown expanse that moved as if with one mind. The bison were running parallel to them, beginning to curve away, but as the freshmen watched, they gradually slowed, coming to a halt and beginning to graze. No longer running, they could be examined individually. Massive, shaggy beasts with huge hammerlike heads surmounted by black horns, each bison was an impressive spectacle. Together in their sheer numbers, they were breathtaking.

"Wow," Gabriel whispered.

"Um," said Ruda softly, "what happens if they all charge this way?"

"Well, then we get trampled," Rafe said cheerfully. "That's not likely, though. So, who wants to go bag one?"

"Every time I think you've said the stupidest fucking thing you can possibly say, you open your mouth again," said Ruda.

"Oh, don't be such a sourpuss, Punaji. Elves hunt these."

"They hunt them with staves, spears, and arrows, while riding unicorns," Teal hissed. "Let's *not* provoke the herd, please."

"Oh, but you were saying we need meat, right?" said Juniper. "One of those would keep us supplied for . . . well, probably the whole trip, assuming we're not planning to be out here more than a week or so. That's about what Tellwyrn said, right?"

"Yeah, well, the fact remains, those are *bison*, there are *thousands* of them, and we are really not equipped or prepared to do any hunting," said Gabriel.

"Lemme see what I can do," she replied, and stood upright, disregarding the hisses of her classmates. The dryad strode forward through the grass directly toward the herd.

"The thing that bothers me most is how we didn't hear them before they were this close," Teal muttered. "If the Sea can drop thousands of bison right on top of us . . ."

She didn't bother to finish. Everyone knew where that thought was going: *Why not centaurs?*

They all reflexively ducked even lower when the herd spotted Juniper and shied away. Those nearest the dryad seemed to move as one organism, the effects of their alarm rippling backward. She kept approaching slowly, though, making a beeline for one specimen standing relatively near. The general consensus of the herd seemed to be that she wasn't a threat worth running from, but they weren't interested in being approached; they began to resume their course at a brisk walk.

All except for the single animal Juniper was approaching. It moved to face her directly, tail swishing behind as it studied her. There was something almost poetic about the way it broke from the herd to acknowledge the dryad's approach; suddenly it wasn't facing the same direction as the others, nor moving along with them. From part of a unit, it transitioned to an individual, shifting its allegiance to the dryad. It did shy backward a few steps as she drew closer, hands upraised, but eventually allowed her to stroke its face.

"Quick bit of trivia," said Rafe, "dryads have an innate and powerful connection with nature. The rest of you, do *not* try to pet wild animals. Especially not ginormous ones with big-ass horns."

"Got it, thanks," said Gabriel. Nobody else commented; nobody tore their eyes from the spectacle before them.

It was a spectacle worth beholding.

The young woman stood before the mighty beast, her green hair and golden skin framed by its dark, shaggy bulk, running her hands over its face, scratching in its bushy mane, stroking along its giant horns. All the while, behind them, the herd was picking up speed, heading away and leaving one of its members to the dryad's attentions. Juniper had crossed her arms, now, for some reason, each hand taking hold of the horn on the opposite side of the bison's head.

When it happened, it was almost too fast to catch.

She quite suddenly untwisted her arms, throwing her weight to one side. The audible *crack* of the bison's massive neck breaking was immediately lost in the *thud* of its weight slamming to the ground. It landed, head twisted at a horrible angle; its legs kicked feebly a couple of times, then with startling suddenness, the creature stilled.

The herd took this as the signal to leave. In the next moments, nothing was audible but the constant thunder of their stampede. Blessedly, they held to their previous course and did not turn toward those watching, but some of the students had difficulty balancing due to the shaking of the ground. Despite their speed, the incredible numbers of the bison meant it went on for some minutes.

Eventually, though, the ragged rear edge of the herd passed, and then they were retreating toward the horizon. As soon as the noise lessened enough that she could be heard, Juniper waved cheerily back at the others, shouting, "I got lunch!"

Ruda summed up what they were all thinking.

"Holy *shit*."

They approached slowly, warily. Juniper seemed as cheerful as usual, and rather pleased with herself. "It's a *lot* of meat," she said proudly. "Like I said, this should keep us set for the rest of the trip. How much storage space have you got in that belt, Professor? Oh, well, Ruda and Gabe have the same kinds of enchantments on their coats; we'll manage. You don't mind helping carry, right, guys?"

"Um. No?" Gabriel offered hesitantly.

"Great! Let's just get this started, then." Stepping around to the side of the felled bison, she pulled back her arm and drove a hand directly into its shoulder, sinking up to the wrist in flesh. Gabe clapped a hand over his mouth and turned away. "Oh . . . oops, I'm sorry. I should've thought first . . . Did anybody want its hide? Cause, y'know, it's pretty *big*, so I guess it doesn't matter where we tear it. I've heard people trade the hides for good money, though."

"I don't think that's important right now," Trissiny said carefully. "We're survivalists, for the moment, not fur traders."

"Great!" the dryad said, beaming. "We can still make use of the skin, I'm sure, but I guess it doesn't matter how many pieces it's in." She grasped the torn edges of the bison's thick hide with both hands and pulled, ripping a long seam open across its side, baring steaming muscle. Gabriel retched and doubled over; fortunately, Juniper didn't seem to be paying him any attention. She sank the fingers of one bloody hand into the muscle and pulled, dragging out a large chunk. Strings of tissue snapped, flicking droplets of blood across her face and upper chest, leaving her with a thick handful of raw meat.

"Um, I always forget details like this," she said thoughtfully. "How important is it to you guys that meat be cooked before you eat it?"

"It's fairly important," Teal said, her voice faint.

"Ah. Well, I guess we'll need to make a fire, then . . ." She pulled off a few strands of muscle and tucked them into her mouth, slurping them up like spaghetti. Gabe, having chosen that moment to look up at her again, immediately turned away. Toby stepped over to drape an arm over his shoulders as Juniper carried on with her mouth full. "Y'don' min' if I do, righ'?"

"Knock yourself out," said Ruda, and finished off her bourbon.

"You've got blood in your hair," Fross noted.

"Yeah, I'll clean up after we're done here," the dryad said cheerfully. In fact, she had apparently opened an artery in her prey and now had blood splattered across herself rather liberally, including dripping from the corners of her mouth. "Doesn't seem much point when I'm just gonna get all bloody again! Now, who's got a knife? Or I can just keep tearing; it's no trouble!"

CHAPTER 5

Sweet waited deep within the belly of the Guild. Off to one side of the training pit, perpendicular to the exit and the door to the treasury was the map room, where waist-high shelves lined two walls, filled with rolled-up or folded maps, which could be spread out on the circular table in the center of the chamber. Above the shelves, every stretch of wall was covered with permanently hung maps. The city, the province, the empire itself, and various detailed portions of each were all depicted. The far wall, before which Sweet stood, was covered floor-to-ceiling by an incredibly detailed map of the city of Tiraas.

Hands folded behind his back, head lifted to study the map, he made an impressive sight from the door, even in his slightly scruffy suit. That was the whole reason he'd chosen this position. Truthfully, he was starting to get a crick in his neck; it was taking longer than he'd expected for those he'd summoned to arrive.

Finally, he thought as the door creaked open behind him. All the doors in the Thieves' Guild creaked; otherwise people would tend to inadvertently sneak up on each other, which could result in . . . accidents.

He turned, slowly, starting with the legs but keeping his face aimed at the map for another second or two; this action acknowledged those entering—initially ignoring them didn't suit the image he wanted to project—while creating the impression that weighty matters occupied his attention, warring with his desire to greet them. Everything precise, everything calculated. When Sweet really began putting on a show, he often ran the risk of becoming distracted by how *good* he was.

Two elves slipped into the room, followed by a glowering Style. They still slipped and crept everywhere, as if afraid they were going to be thrown out; though Flora and Fauna were starting to settle in, there was a process. They had more to adjust to than most of the human Guild members. Dressed in simple shirts and trousers for training, better rested and more well-fed than when he'd first seen them, and best of all, smiling, they'd already come a long way from the two miserable streetwalkers he'd encountered outside the Pink Lady.

Well, aside from certain little details like what they were here to discuss.

"Ladies," he said warmly, coming around the table to greet them. His smile was careful; he needed to be glad to see them, but not too chipper, in light of what was coming. The elves smiled back at him with a lot more enthusiasm. He was, after all, the one who'd not only sponsored their apprenticeships in the Guild but helped them settle in. If not for Sweet, they would still be turning tricks in the Glums. That gratitude was real and counted for a lot. Or so he devoutly hoped.

"I'm sorry I haven't been to see you since you arrived," he went on. "They've got me running all over the city doing the work of three men. How are you getting along? Anything you need help with?"

"We are very well," Flora said, still beaming up at him. "There's a lot to remember, but the work is not arduous."

"Training is good," Fauna added. "Very satisfying. It's good to flex minds and muscles again."

"They have potential," Style grunted from behind them, folding her arms and not relaxing her glare. She was dolled up in an eastern barbarian outfit that was even more revealing than her Punaji phase of last month. It was all boiled leather with brass studs and fur accents; above the waist all she had on was a thick leather brassiere, the kind Stalweiss women were often shown wearing on the covers of penny dreadfuls and pretty much never in real life, because it was a stupidly impractical garment, even in a much warmer climate than the eastern mountains. Some women bared skin to be alluring; Style bared her square shoulders, trunk-like arms, and craggy abs to discourage people from giving her backtalk. It worked.

"I'm glad to hear it. And I mean it. I may not be around much, but if you need anything, you can get a message to me." Sweet let the smile slip from his face, leaving his expression grave. "For now . . . I asked Style to bring you in here because I'm afraid I have some pretty bad news. You may want to sit down for this."

The pair exchanged a glance, but at his gesture, slowly lowered themselves into chairs beside the map table, Fauna pulling one over so they could sit side by side. Behind them, Style pushed the door shut and positioned herself in front of it, then folded her arms and resumed glaring. This earned her a couple of glances from the elves, but Sweet quickly recaptured their attention.

"I know you weren't exactly close, but I thought you should be informed that Missy, from the Pink Lady, died last night."

". . . oh," said Flora when he paused. They didn't glance at each other this time; in fact, both girls looked rather nonplussed.

"I'm afraid it was pretty bad," Sweet went on, eyebrows creased together in his best expression of bishoply solicitousness. "Really quite brutal, in fact. Her digestive tract was strung all around the room, without having been, ah, disconnected, first. There were glyphs of some sort written on all the walls, floor, and ceiling in her blood and . . . well, other fluids. And," he added gravely, "her head was missing."

"How awful," Fauna said, gazing up at him without expression. Her tone tried at regret without much effort. *Oh, the rain isn't letting up. Oh, it's okra stew for lunch again. Oh, Missy was savagely butchered.*

"As per the terms of her will, Rose gets the property and the business."

"That's good," Flora said with a bit more enthusiasm. "Rose cares about the girls. She tried to help us. As much as . . . possible." She trailed off, looking away; Fauna reached over to squeeze her hand.

"I'm sorry to have taken so long to get to you about this," he said sincerely. "I've been out all day dealing with it."

At that, their eyes widened a fraction and they did exchange a glance. "*You* had to deal with it?" Fauna asked, sounding more actually concerned now.

"Well, surely you don't think someone like Missy *actually* left a will, do you?" He gave them a very careful hint of a grin, conveying a touch of gallows humor without undercutting the gravity of the situation. "Putting those girls in Rose's care seemed the best thing I could do for them, since I can't exactly move them *all* into the Guild."

"Ah," Fauna said.

"I'm afraid that little matter took longer than it ought to have, since I wasn't able to give it my full attention. There was the rather more urgent issue of dealing with the imperial interest in the case. Even in the Glums, a murder that, ah, *extravagant* draws official attention. I don't mean to imply that the imps give a damn about anybody living down there, but you just can't have people doing things like that while you're trying to carry on a civilization. It's bad for business, you see." He sighed heavily. "Unfortunately, the whole city's in a tizzy over it now."

"It is?" Flora asked faintly.

He nodded. "The papers got wind of it. Now everyone's in a panic about there being a headhunter in Tiraas."

Both of them stiffened. It was slight, but perceptible. They very obviously did not look at each other.

"Headhunters are a myth," Fauna said tersely.

"That's right," Sweet agreed, nodding. "The official stance of the Church and the empire has always been that elven headhunters do not exist. Just a scary bedtime story mothers use to make their little ones behave. Of course, interestingly enough, Imperial Intelligence somehow knows *exactly* what a headhunter attack looks like, and has protocols in place to deal with it."

". . . they do?" Flora croaked.

"Keep that to yourself, though," he went on. "I probably shouldn't have told you. I am the Church's liaison to the highest level of imperial government; I learn the most *fascinating* things on busy days like today. Let me tell you, it kept me on my toes, working this thing around to keep the imps from busting in here to haul you two little rascals away. Quite apart from the sanctity of our temple, I'm kinda fond of you."

"Now, wait a minute," Flora protested. Both of them had gone quite rigid.

"Don't worry, it's all taken care of. I was able to deflect attention to Rake. Elowe something or other . . . what was his last name, Style?"

"I always called him Treefucker," she grunted.

"I guess it doesn't matter now. He'd been passing information on our jobs to the authorities for *months*. A known traitor is actually a fabulously useful thing to keep around, ladies; you can feed them false intel to throw your enemies off the scent, and when a situation comes up where you need to throw somebody under the carriage— like today—you've got a ready-made scapegoat on hand. So the Guild is down one elf, and I'm sure poor Elowe was more surprised than anyone to learn he's secretly a headhunter, but . . . so it goes."

"We don't have to listen to this," Fauna snapped, leaping to her feet; Flora was a split second behind her. Both of them braced themselves as if for a fight. "You can't just *accuse* someone of—"

"*Girls,*" Sweet said firmly, raising his hands in a peaceable gesture. "Please, *think*. I've just stated I believe you're among the most dangerous creatures in existence, and were doing something unspeakably vicious about this time yesterday. Now, would I put myself in a room with you if I intended to piss you off?" He gave that a second and a half to sink in, then went on in a more soothing tone before they could begin forming more objections. "I am trying to *help* you. Please, sit down."

They did, slowly, looking warily at him, around the room, and at Style, who was still leaning against the door.

"Now," he continued, straightening up and folding his arms behind his back. "I hope you understand the problem we have here?"

The two exchanged another telling look. "We don't have a problem with anyone in the Guild," Flora said quickly. "Miss . . . *That woman* snared us into . . . into utter *debasement*. So she could make *money*. It was personal, and justified. We don't want trouble with anyone else."

"Ah," he said, and shook his head. "I feared not. The issue is . . . How shall I put this . . ."

"You scrawny, knife-eared, pants-on-head, psycho DUMB FUCKING TWATS!" Style roared, stalking toward them. Flora and Fauna again leaped out of their seats, backing against the table. "Do you ever stop to fucking *think* before you act?! This is *not* whatever fucking tree you swung down out of; this is motherfucking Tiraas! Did you *actually* think you could just strew someone's guts around a room like she was a scarecrow and not bring the fucking imps down on you? Down on *all of us*! So help me, if you *ever* put my Guild in this kind of danger again—"

"*Style*," Sweet interjected. "Enough. Please. Mistakes happen, we deal with them. These are apprentices; we'll *teach* them, not box their ears. Girls," he went on, again gentling his tone, "again, please, sit. You're not in any danger here. I *won't* say you're not in any trouble." He put on a more dour expression. "This is exactly the kind of thing we can't just let pass; next time, you could do significant damage to the Guild."

They looked at each other, then spoke in unison. "I'm sorry." He believed it; both looked quite crushed as they slid carefully back into their seats.

"To begin with, I had to spread quite a bit of coin around today. *That* is being added to your apprenticeship debt. If you prove as skilled as I'm confident you will, you're looking at probably an additional year of heavy tithing to the Guild after your elevation."

"A *year*?" Flora said.

"Again, it was *quite* a bit of coin. I didn't add anything for having spent an entire day of *my* time straightening this out, but you should know that next time you force a high-ranking member of the Guild to fix a mess you made . . . well, the consequences will depend on the situation, but they will be significant. Do you understand?"

They both nodded, then lowered their eyes to the ground. Between those big eyes, their pointed features, and the presently downcast expressions, they seemed almost childlike. It was ironic; for all he knew, they were older than he. That, and they had spent last night festooning Missy's entrails around her room like tinsel. From what he'd read about headhunters, in and around his various other tasks of the day, she had likely still been alive for part of that.

"Right . . ." He drew in a deep breath and let it out slowly. "I don't want to make any prejudiced assumptions about elves . . ."

"Can I?"

"*Enough*, Style. But it's obvious you two aren't very familiar with city life. So, I am going to assume you're more comfortable with the world of nature and try to spin a metaphor from that. Girls, you seem to regard Tiraas as a sort of hunting ground, that you can prowl through, strike your prey, and retreat when you're done. That about right?" He paused for them to glance at each other again and nod mutely. "It isn't that you're entirely wrong . . . but the matter is more complex. Hunting is an excellent description of much of what the Guild does, but . . . Well, think of the city as a spider's web. Every touch you make resonates across the *entire* thing. Light enough touches to avoid attracting anything dangerous should be your goal. It grows more complicated from there, however. It isn't just a matter of avoiding the attention of the very large, very hungry spider in the center. There are *multiple* spiders of various sizes, operating at cross purposes; multiple powerful organizations and agendas are at work in the city, and you need to be intimately familiar with each before you go traipsing through their hunting grounds. The Guild is one such spider, one of the bigger ones, and that affords you some protection . . . but only some. You are also competing with millions of other little bugs, all doing the same dance, all trying to hunt one another without growing tangled in the web itself or attracting the attention of the spiders."

"I think this metaphor is getting away from you, Sweet," Style commended with a mirthless grin.

"Oh, shut it. I think I'm doing fine."

"I think so, too," Fauna piped up. "It . . . explains some things. We . . ." She glanced over at Flora. "We didn't think anybody would care.

Nobody ever cared about any of us, or anything else that happened in the Glums."

"And *that* is why you cannot just run around and *do* things," Sweet said firmly. "You don't understand *who* is active and powerful in this city. You don't know *what* they care about, what will or won't provoke them to take action. That's not a criticism, ladies, it's an analysis of your situation, and part of the purpose of your apprenticeship will be to rectify that ignorance. Until you have achieved this knowledge, though, you are two bugs with unusually big stingers that won't do you a damn bit of good if you don't know which are the sticky strands or where the other predators lurk. In fact . . . it's those big stingers of yours that cause us some problems now."

"Can we *stop* with the bug metaphors?" Style groaned.

"Fine, I'll speak more plainly. Flora, Fauna, you're *dangerous*. I promise you, however, that you are *not* the most dangerous things lurking in this city. The Church and the empire both have powers under their control that could crush you. If you act carelessly, if you give them a *reason* to do so, they won't hesitate. And you are members of the Thieves' Guild now; your actions both reflect on us and involve us. Nothing you start up with a rival faction will affect only you. Today you got Elowe killed. That's no great loss; he was, as I said, a traitor. Next time, it could be me. Or anyone else." They both looked up again at that, alarm registering broadly on their faces. "Now do you understand the problem?"

Both nodded. "We won't do anything else without your orders," Fauna promised.

"Let's not be too hasty," he said, holding up a hand. "The worship of Eserion heavily emphasizes a love of freedom; you don't want to be bound *too* restrictively to the Guild. This is a relationship; you're not servants. But *while* you are still apprentices, I will hold you to that promise. And you will *stay* apprentices at least until I—and your trainers—am confident that you don't absolutely *need* to be held to it anymore. Clear?" They nodded again.

Sweet leaned back against the edge of the table, folding his arms and turning his head to speak to them sidelong. "Now, as a rule, the

Thieves' Guild does not dispense death. It's messy, irrevocable, draws *very* persistent attention from the authorities . . . It's a lot of the things we most ardently avoid, is what I mean. However, if there is *one* truth all thieves can embrace, it's that *rules* are not meant to be absolute things. There are times when . . . Well, let me just say that people of your unique talents are useful to have around. Again, I don't want you doing diddly dick out there in my city until I'm reasonably sure you're not going to inadvertently screw the pooch again. To get us to that point . . . it looks like you're going to need a somewhat more refined curriculum of training than most of your fellow apprentices."

"Refined, how?" Flora asked.

"To begin with, you'll be working closely with Style here." They gave Style a very careful look; she grinned back in a way that showed far too many teeth to be friendly. "The finer points of causing pain you clearly have down; she'll teach you about the blunter ones, which are more generally useful to our sort of people. She will *also* teach you how to carry yourselves so as to create the impression you need to for any given circumstance, and I guarantee you'll find no better trainer in *that* art anywhere."

"Your flattery isn't getting you any closer to my bed, Sweet."

"Baby, I quit fantasizing about *that* after you broke that guy's back. Additionally, girls, I am going to break with my usual policy and take you under my personal tutelage." At that, their heads snapped around in unison and smiles bloomed on their faces. "The *reason* I don't take on apprentices is, as I mentioned earlier, I quite simply have too goddamn much to do. You'll get a better idea how I spend my time as we go forward, because if you're going to be underfoot demanding my attention, I assure you, you'll make yourselves useful in the process."

"We will," Fauna promised.

"I know. That's going to mean a change of sleeping quarters, I'm afraid, since it's going to be a lot easier for you to commute to the Guild for daily training than it will be for me to get down here to train you. As such, you will be moving into my home. The cover story will be that you're housemaids; I have a civilian identity to keep up, after all. My butler will show you that particular set of ropes."

"Your . . . A servant?" Fauna asked, frowning. "Can he be trusted with . . . Guild business?"

Style brayed in amusement, earning a pair of annoyed looks.

"Guild business, she says." Sweet shook his head. "Girls, I'm a high-ranking priest of Eserion. I don't employ anybody who's not a member of this Guild in good standing. Don't worry about that, you'll get to know her in good time. For now, I want you to concentrate on training. What you'll be learning from *me* is the subtle art of being a spider. Knowing where the strands are, how to navigate them, pluck them, make the web itself serve your needs. Tiraas is a living thing, girls. She breathes, she feels; she has moods. You have to *romance* her."

"That would be disturbing even if you didn't segue into it from more spider talk," Style said, grimacing.

"I intend," he went on, ignoring her, "for you to gain a sense of perspective. You're going to learn how to get by in this city *without* dealing out death . . . and how to *do* so, if the need arises, with such circumspection that it doesn't come back to bite you—and the rest of us—on the ass."

Again, they exchanged a long glance, then Fauna looked back up at him with a particularly inscrutable expression.

"You want us to kill for you."

"No. *No.*" He straightened, turning to face them directly and staring down with more intensity. "I want you to use your skills for *your own* best interests. As your sponsor and trainer in the Guild, that means my task is twofold: I need to prepare you to do so in this extremely complex world without causing unforeseen havoc, and I need to help you understand why the Guild's interests are your own. Ours is not an authoritarian cult, ladies; the Guild retains the loyalty of its members because it *earns* that loyalty. In time, you'll understand why, but for now, I just ask that you trust me, and trust the Guild, to have your back when you need it."

"Like today," Style snapped, "when Sweet ran his ass ragged all over the fucking town to fix your fucking screw-up, when we should've just given your fucking heads to the empire, gift wrapped."

"My ass is not ragged, thank you," he said wryly. Her words had their effect, though; the elves looked very suitably abashed. "But she's not wrong. We look out for each other here. Now, do you have questions about any of this?"

Flora bit her lip and looked at the ground, but Fauna raised her eyes to gaze at him seriously. "*Eldei Alai'shi*," she said, "what you call headhunters . . . It's a very specific path. It involves . . . bargains, rituals, contracts with powers that . . . What I mean is, there's a reason we're not welcome among our tribe, or any tribe. None of this is done lightly, and there are costs. Whatever happens in the future, you cannot expect us to serve as assassins. The spirits demand purpose, and *challenge*. The prey must be worthy—either because it deeply deserves to suffer, or because it will not fall easily. Preferably both."

"We do not and *cannot* kill on a whim," Flora added, "or none of those . . . men . . . would have survived laying hands on us. We cannot kill for . . . for *business*. It may not be possible for us to serve you the way I think you expect."

"Oh, I don't know," he mused. "It sounds to me like you may be precisely the thing I need." Sweet glanced over at Style; behind the elves' back, she grinned broadly at him. They'd done this routine enough times to have it down pat. Once, he had jokingly suggested that he could be the bad cop for a change; she'd laughed for nearly a full minute, then punched him. "As I said, the Guild doesn't kill lightly. Ideally, not ever. No, there are exceptional circumstances afoot, growing more exceptional faster than I can get a handle on them. I have something specific in mind that your spirits might find to their liking."

"You don't know the spirits," Fauna remarked, and there was both bitterness and sour humor behind her voice.

"Perhaps," he said. "Let them be the judge. Tell me . . . Have you two ever heard of the Black Wreath?"

Again, the two looked at each other, but this time much more slowly. Faces blank, they held gazes for a very long moment, communicating on some level he couldn't grasp. Then, just as slowly, they both turned their heads to face him again. Identical smiles blossomed across their faces.

There was nothing childlike about them now.

He smiled back.

CHAPTER 6

"Finally," Gabriel groaned. "It's about time the Sea gave us something good for a change."

"Oh, you are *such* a whiner," Ruda said, grinning. "This trip has been awesome! So far the Sea has given us free corn and all the beef we can eat." She laughed at his slightly peaked expression.

Carving up, cleaning, parceling out, and preparing the meat from the entire bison had occupied them the rest of the afternoon; Rafe and Juniper had been adamantly against letting anything go to waste, and their thrifty sensibilities had found enough traction among the group that Teal and Gabriel hadn't gathered much sympathy when they'd suggested stopping once they judged enough meat had been gathered.

Drying, smoking, and curing meat were all very long processes, ordinarily the work of days at least, but Rafe, of course, had alchemical shortcuts aplenty in his magic belt. Cheerily announcing that this would count toward their grade in his classes, he handed out reagents, walked them once through the processes involved, and then set the students to preparing meat for storage in a variety of ways while he built another alchemical fire, broke out his frying pan, and cooked up some fresh bison steaks for lunch.

By the time they'd taken a break to eat, their collective desire for food was diminished. Only Shaeine appeared completely unbothered by all the blood and effluvia they'd been handling. Juniper had somewhat spoiled her appetite; once she determined that nobody else wanted a share of the bison's organs, she had been busily snacking while they worked. Watching this had seriously dampened everyone *else's* appetite.

Bison-carving kept them occupied until dusk was closer than noon had been. By then, the bison was reduced to bones, scraps of hide, and various detritus that nobody wanted to touch, no matter how Rafe nattered on about the uses of each bit. Evidently, wasting all that bowstring-worthy sinew offended his elven sensibilities. Juniper had eventually declared, in her cheery way, that nothing left to nature was truly wasted. She'd said this while cradling the animal's skull, which she intended to keep as a souvenir—after having eaten the brain, eyes, and tongue—and was all but slathered with liquid bison.

After pausing a bit longer to clean themselves up with the aid of more of Rafe's alchemy, they had finally continued on their way.

Sunset was far enough in progress that Trissiny, their most experienced trekker, had begun making noises about camping for the night when they came across their next, and hopefully final, surprise of the day.

Now, they stood—or in Gabriel's case, sat in the grass—around a house-sized formation of volcanic rock, which put off faintly sulfur-scented steam, watching the two fae return from inspecting it.

"Safe!" the dryad yelled, waving. She had clearly taken the opportunity to scrub some of the bison bits out of her hair that had been missed earlier during Rafe's alchemical cleaning. In fact, she was drenched from head to toe, her green hair plastered haphazardly to her face. "No elementals of any kind present—uh, that we didn't bring with us. Sorry, Fross. There's a nice little current, and it's old enough that the stones inside the pools are nice and rounded. It's perfect!"

"Also, no curses or undead," Fross chimed in. "No anything, really. I don't think anybody's been here in years, if ever."

"Animals have," Juniper said, "which is how you *know* it's safe."

"All *right*!" Rafe rubbed his hands together gleefully, wearing an even more manic grin than usual. "Hot springs, baby! Kids, you have not *lived* until you've had a soak in natural hot springs!"

"Um, excuse me, but I'm pretty sure I'm alive."

"It's a figure of speech, Fross," Toby explained.

"There's a nice flat area up on top where silt has settled in a depression and there's grass growing," Juniper said brightly. "Not as tall as down here, but it's softer than the rocks and probably safer than camping on the flat ground, where *anything* might come creeping out of the tallgrass."

"Campsite ho!" Rafe shouted. "But first, WE BATHE!"

The rock formation looked like a tumbled heap of dark stone when approached, but as they explored it well enough to gain a sense of its proportions, it revealed itself to be rather like the stump of an old tree in shape. The "roots" of stone spread out in multiple directions, dividing up low areas between them and affording some privacy; a lot of these contained pools of water, the three lowest of which were large enough to swim in, though not deep. They were also, fortuitously, separated enough by the mass of the formation that the travelers could segregate themselves by gender and soak in relative privacy. The broad, flat top of the "stump" was probably another such crater, now inactive for whatever reason. Over the eons it had filled with wind-blown dirt, and then a light carpet of soft grasses and moss.

"This is almost suspicious," Trissiny said, leaning her head back against the rock wall; her utterly relaxed posture clashed with the tone of her observation. "It's so . . . perfect. Like a gift from the gods. I almost can't imagine it not being some kind of trap."

"Anybody ever tell you you're a real ray of sunshine?" Ruda asked lazily from the other side of the pool.

"No."

"Ever wonder why?"

"There's stuff like this all over the world," Teal said. "This planet wasn't shaped by entirely natural forces, you know; lots of things that seem like a part of nature are actually designed for the sake of people. And yeah, a lot of them *are* traps, but there are also quite a few that are gifts. The gods aren't the only powers up there that like people. Anyhow, Juno and Fross would've noticed anything bad lurking around here."

"Probably," Juniper said lightly. While the others were sitting around the edges of the steaming pool, submerged up to the shoulders, she was floating on her back in the middle with no regard for modesty. Teal flushed and averted her eyes whenever she happened to glance at the dryad.

"Paladins can also sense evil, as I understand it," said Shaeine. "You would likely be the first to know if we were in danger, Trissiny."

"For a given value of 'evil,'" she replied. "Demons, undead . . . a few other related things. Sometimes people who've had a lot of contact with them. Things not directly, specifically opposed to the gods can slip by my senses."

"What's that?" Ruda grinned at her. "You mean you're *not* perfect? I am *stunned*."

"Don't you ever get tired of that?" Trissiny asked with a sigh.

"Not so far, but I'll let you know! Sure you don't wanna come in, Shaeine?"

"I am quite comfortable, thank you," the drow replied politely. "The steam is invigorating." She was sitting on a rock formation beside the pool, still in her robes, ostensibly keeping watch over their clothes. The whole time they'd been soaking, she had steadfastly refused to even glance in their direction.

"I just feel kinda bad, you missing out," said Ruda.

"Not all cultures are okay with communal bathing," Teal admonished her. "Don't push. In fact, hell, imperial culture really isn't okay with communal bathing. I'm very privileged to be an acknowledged deviant."

"Now, is it the pacifism that's considered deviant, or the gay?" Ruda asked, grinning.

"Take one of each, I'm feeling generous," Teal said lightly, closing her eyes and shifting down in the water so that only her head was above the surface.

"My culture does, in fact, practice communal bathing," Shaeine said, still watching the horizon, "but only among family."

"Guess I can respect that," the pirate conceded, then playfully sent a wave in Trissiny's direction. "Gotta say, roomie, I'm surprised you unbent enough to be naked in a big tub with a lesbian. Not afraid you're gonna catch it?"

"Ruda," Trissiny said wearily, "would you at least *read* about my faith enough to mock it *intelligently*? Avei has always supported the right of women to love whoever and in whatever way they choose. In fact, I was raised in a barracks among other girls, in a culture that idealized romance among women. I was *thirteen* before anybody thought to reassure me that being attracted to boys didn't mean I was mentally ill."

Ruda blinked. "Well . . . damn."

"This isn't dangerous to you, is it, Fross?" Teal asked, looking up at the pixie, who'd been drifting slowly around above them, riding the updrafts of steam.

"What? Don't be silly, I'm not *made* of ice. I actually kind of like the heat. The contrast is soothing. Sort of almost painful, but in a good way, y'know? Like a really intense thing that kind of straddles the line between good and bad. But no, it's not dangerous."

"Wanna try swimming, then?" Teal suggested. "Or are your wings not built for that?"

"Pshaw, my wings are built for everything! I'll try anything twice. You know, 'cause nobody ever does something right the first time. *Dive bomb!*" With an uncharacteristic battle cry, she buzzed down, plopping into the surface of the water near Juniper.

Strangely, the intense glow that surrounded her seemed to wink out while she was viewed through water. For the first time, the girls were treated to a view of Fross's tiny humanoid figure, white as fresh snow, as she plunged to the bottom of the pool, then fluttered back upward.

Unfortunately, ice had begun forming around her before she got there. Fross broke the surface, lifted off a few inches and fell back, encumbered by the clump of ice in which the lower half of her body was stuck. It expanded rapidly, and soon she was drifting in the hot springs, trapped in a thick, dinner-plate-sized ice floe that steamed constantly as its edges melted and reformed. Her wings buzzed impotently, lifting her no more than an inch out of the water.

"Um," she said sheepishly, "help?"

"Gotta hand it to you, Professor," said Gabriel, relaxing in the steam, "sometimes you *do* come up with a pretty damn good idea."

"Hah! *All* my ideas are damn good, Sonny Jim. You just lack the wit to appreciate my genius. I look forward to the day when you are educated enough to understand the sheer brilliance of everything I've tried to teach you." Rafe paused, then amended, "Well, the day when most people would be educated enough to appreciate it. You . . . We'll have to see."

"Oh, up yours," he said, but without rancor. "Let me just enjoy the steam, and the knowledge that there's a half dozen naked girls a mere few yards from here."

"You do realize Shaeine can probably hear you," Toby noted, fighting a smile.

"And Shaeine knows I'm not gonna go peek. Trissiny barely needs an excuse to stab me in the guts as it is."

"Yeah, how's that coming along?" Rafe asked cheerily, pushing his rubber duck around the surface of the water. The boys had steadfastly refused to comment on it. "Aren't you two supposed to be all chummy by now?"

"Ugh." Gabriel grimaced. "I'm *trying*. She's completely immune to my charms."

"Have you tried a love potion?"

"That's right, Professor. I, a half demon, will slip an illegal mind-altering potion to the Hand of Avei. Just as soon as I want the entire fucking Sisterhood to mount a crusade for my head."

"You have *got* to learn to take a joke, kid."

"I'd be careful with that kind of joke, Professor," Toby warned. "Sisters of Avei consider the use of love potions a form of rape. So does imperial law, for that matter, but imperial law doesn't get quite as . . . *worked up* on the subject as they do. I doubt Trissiny would find this conversation funny at all."

"Bah! I will not be censored!" Rafe brandished his ducky, grinning wildly.

"I think I blew it with Triss pretty hard," Gabe said more soberly. "I've tried to put on a nice face with her and . . . Well, she *tolerates* me. Exactly as much as she did on the first night. It's like . . . she's decided the status quo is perfectly fine and is done with the whole thing. And I wouldn't mind that so much; she's not exactly the most delightful company . . . but Tellwyrn's got a bug up her butt about this. I dunno how long this can go on before she actually *does* chain us together."

"She hasn't done that in years, and it was a much more extreme case," Rafe said airily. "You're probably safe."

Gabriel straightened up. "Wait, she's *actually* done that?"

"Twice, that I know of."

He slumped back down into the water. "Well, fuck. How do you get a grumpy paladin to give you a second chance?"

"Well, there's the usual," Rafe suggested. "Flowers, chocolates, poetry . . . Of course, she's an Avenist, so maybe the still-beating heart of an enemy . . ."

"I'm not trying to *court* her, you lunatic. I just want to get things . . . civil. But I can't have a civil relationship alone. If she doesn't cooperate . . ."

"Aside from self-interest with regard to Tellwyrn," said Toby, "and by the way, Trissiny doesn't have a lot of self-interest . . . Well, this is what I don't get, man. Are you *sure* nothing else happened that night? When we talked about it you emphasized pretty hard that it was all your fault."

"Come on, why would I lie about *that*?" Gabriel muttered, looking out toward the horizon.

Rafe lowered himself into the water so that it covered him up to his nose, eyes darting back and forth between the two boys.

"It's just . . ." Toby frowned, obviously choosing his words with care. "When I talked to Teal and Shaeine, they both said you asked them not to discuss it with anyone else. Taking all the blame for some mutual fight doesn't sound like you, but neither does going that hard at the Hand of Avei in the first place. I can't help feeling like there's a piece of this story missing."

"Oh, it's not so complicated," Rafe said breezily. "A man can endure all manner of slings and arrows from the world at large, but when they come from a pretty girl he knows he can never, ever have? That shit's *personal.*"

"Oh, *ew,*" Gabriel spat. "Don't even joke, man. I'd sooner stick it in a termite nest."

"You stuck it in a dryad, which for *you* is considerably more risky."

"Quite aside from Trissiny's personality, what there is of it, she's a twig! A brawny twig. I like *curvy* girls."

"Again, let's remember that Shaeine can probably hear us and dial this back a bit," Toby said. "And my concern stands. I'm not trying to give you a hard time, Gabe. I'm . . . worried."

Gabriel lowered his eyes from his friend's concerned face and sighed. Long seconds passed before he spoke.

"Well, now that I've had time to think about it . . . I sort of had it all worked out in my head. It was going to be *different* here. Better, y'know? It was the University, run by Arachne Tellwyrn, famous anti-hero or antivillain, depending on which stories you listen to. No more black-and-white, gods-vs-Gabriel bullshit. I was gonna meet people, maybe some like me, but at least people who wouldn't treat me like a freak. People who understood the world was *complex.* And then . . . there she was."

"Trissiny never treated you like a freak," Toby said gently. "She was startled, *once,* when she found out you're a demonblood. Honestly, I think half of that was her being upset because she'd accidentally hurt you."

"I *know!*" Gabriel thew up his hands, splashing them both. "And *this* is why I've avoided talking about it, because there's no way not to be reminded what an utter dumbshit I've been about the whole thing. She just . . . She gave me that *look,* and all I could see was every other fucking person in Tiraas who'd looked at me that way. Except it was at the University, my second chance, where I thought things would be better . . . And it was a freaking paladin of Avei. Probably exactly the person they'd send to put me down if they found an excuse to. I overreacted." He slumped down in the water, so low that he made ripples when he spoke. "Holy fuck, did I overreact."

"Have you said any of this to her?" Toby asked.

Gabe snorted, causing a minor splash. "I'm terrified to even bring up the topic. I'm just trying to be *nice* to her, for all the good that's doing me. I just want . . . peace, with her. No more drama. It's easier if she's not getting riled up with more recrimination, y'know? I was the angry dumbass, so I'll be conciliatory and eventually it'll all go away."

"Half of diplomacy is understanding the other person's perspective. Avenists don't generally care much about *nice*, Gabe. But they're reasonable. You basically have her as a captive audience when you're doing those dishes, right? Just . . . try opening up like you did just now. Let her see you have *reasons*, even if they aren't good ones. Right now, I bet all she sees in you is a berserk demonblood who thinks he's funny."

"Excuse me, I'm fucking *hilarious*," Gabriel said with deep dignity.

"Yup!" Rafe grinned. "Now if you could just pull it off when you're *trying* to, you might get laid by something that has a pulse."

"Go fuck your— Wait a second. Juniper doesn't have a *pulse*?"

"Boy," the professor said, shaking his head, "you have the observational skills of a deaf cave bat."

"Oh, give me a break, I was distracted by the . . . Well, you've seen them."

"Indeed, I may have to give you that one."

"Really, it's no trouble," Fross said nervously. "I don't mind at all."

"And I appreciate that, Fross," Trissiny replied patiently. "Regardless, we should set a watch. It's an important habit to be in, when camping out in potentially hostile territory."

"Oh, come *on*," Ruda groaned. "Why the hell are you so allergic to anything being *easy*?"

"Because *life* is not easy," the paladin said sharply. "This is a training exercise—its purpose is to prepare us to deal with the real world. How often do you expect to have a party member who doesn't need sleep on a long mission?"

"Trissiny is correct," Shaeine said smoothly as Ruda opened her mouth to object again. "Posting watch is an important habit to acquire. And we *are* on training maneuvers, for all intents and purposes."

Ruda thew up her hands. "Fine, what-the-fuck-ever. Wake me when it's my turn, I guess." She turned and stomped over to one of the tents, leaving the rest of the freshman class behind. Rafe was already in the boys' tent, snoring a touch too loudly to be believable.

Everyone was much refreshed after a long soak in the hot springs, but most were still tired from the day's hiking—and butchering. Glancing around at her classmates, who were mostly standing near their three tents clustered around a campfire in the upper crater of the volcanic formation, Trissiny could plainly see the weariness in many of them. Shaeine, as usual, was all but unreadable, and Toby had divine strength to draw on, but the others were visibly drooping—even Juniper. She, of course, was hardly even tired.

"I'll take first watch, then," she said, giving the rest of them a smile. "Sleep well, but . . . if you can, not too deeply. The Golden Sea's odd geography may protect us, but in normal territory a campfire on top of a hill like this will be visible for miles in every direction. It isn't improbable that we'll have visitors of some kind before dawn."

"And on *that* cheery note," Gabriel muttered, turning and dragging himself toward the tent from which the snores were emanating. "Good news—sounds like we'll have that 'don't sleep deeply' thing down. Without even trying." Toby laughed, following him in.

The crater itself was uneven, the rim of stone surrounding it even more so. On the side opposite from their approach—the uphill side, closer to the center of the Sea—it rose to a steep lip that almost qualified as an outcropping. Trissiny, no longer in armor but carrying her sword and shield, climbed this, taking up her perch as her classmates retreated into their tents. She noticed with some gratitude that

Teal and Shaeine had joined Ruda, leaving the other tent for her and Juniper. And Fross, of course, should she want to take advantage.

That seemed unlikely; the pixie was more interested in keeping company with the only other member of the party who was staying awake.

"Fross," she said some minutes later, which she spent slowly scanning the horizon for signs of movement and her companion spent buzzing about with no apparent aim, "I don't mean to be rude . . ."

The pixie came to an instant halt, hovering right in front of her. "Are you mad at me?"

"What?" Trissiny blinked, taken aback. "No. Why would I be?"

"Oh. It's just that . . . Well, I've kinda noticed a pattern when somebody says 'I don't mean to be rude' or 'not to be rude' or 'sorry if this is rude' or anything along those lines, that whatever comes next is usually pretty rude. So, uh, I'm still having kind of a hard time untangling the colloquialisms around here, but I figure if you're about to say something rude I've done something to make you mad."

Trissiny stayed silent for a moment, digesting that, then had to smile. "That is actually pretty perceptive. It . . . probably doesn't mean they're *mad*, per se. People can be hostile for a lot of different reasons. Most are fairly silly, and it's honestly best to brush them off unless they're actually threatening you."

"I don't . . . Man, that makes *no* sense. Social interactions aren't a zero-sum game. I mean, that's just not how it *works*."

"That's people for you," Trissiny said wryly.

"So, uh . . . why were you wanting to be hostile?"

"Oh!" She clapped a hand to her forehead. "I'm sorry, Fross, I didn't mean to give you the wrong impression . . . I'm not hostile. I actually just wanted to ask you something and didn't want to hurt your feelings because I'm not sure if it would or not."

"Oh!" The pixie buzzed around in a rapid circle. "Oh, that's okay, then, that's not actually rude at all! Go ahead, you can ask me whatever and if I don't like it I can tell you so we don't have to have the awkwardness again, 'kay?"

"Deal," Trissiny said with a smile. "That being established . . . is it possible for you to turn down your glow a little? You're sort of wrecking my night vision."

The pixie vibrated in midair for a moment. ". . . aw, man, I'm so sorry. I didn't even think about . . . I mean, I'd read about how human eyes work; I did all my research before coming here . . . Gosh, that's embarrassing. Um, yeah, I can repress a bit, but . . ."

"But?" Trissiny prompted after a silent moment.

"Well . . . I don't want to be rude."

She laughed. "I will try not to take offense."

"Is it, uh, okay if I sit on your shoulder? See, it's kinda hard to stay aloft with my magic dimmed, and I try not to be on the ground as a matter of policy. *That* is a recipe for getting stepped on. Also, there's snakes and rats and stuff in the grass, and getting eaten is really annoying."

"I don't mind that at all," Trissiny assured her, still grinning.

"Great!"

She zipped over to alight on Trissiny's shoulder, momentarily making the problem of night vision even worse. Almost immediately, however, her white glow dimmed, then vanished entirely, leaving Trissiny able to study her classmate up close for the first time.

Fross was about three inches tall, and . . . *fuzzy*. She looked something like an anthropomorphic moth, her humanoid figure coated in white down that glittered like snow in the starlight, with reddish highlights where it caught even the glow of the distant campfire. Her eyes were (proportionately) enormous black jewels that dominated her head, leaving no room for anything else on her face but a thin little mouth and two arched, fuzzy moth antennae. From her back sprang four wings, long and narrow like a dragonfly's, but without the network of veins. In fact, they were all but invisible except for their frosted edges. They buzzed in short bursts, apparently unwilling to be still even when Fross wasn't flying.

She was also very cold. Trissiny quickly began to develop a numb spot on her shoulder. Despite thinking fondly of her metal pauldrons, she found herself reluctant to dislodge the fairy. A paladin's life was sacrifice after all.

"While we're sharing stuff, I have a question," the pixie said, sitting down and folding her arms around her knees.

"Go ahead," Trissiny replied, slowly turning to scan the empty horizon.

"Why don't you like Gabriel?"

She was silent for a moment. "Everybody doesn't have to get along," she said finally. "I don't want conflict with Gabriel. I don't really want to interact with him at all."

"Yeah, I kinda got that, I'm just confused about why. I mean, he tries *so hard* to be nice to you. I don't understand what's going on with you two. I guess it's not really my business, you don't have to explain. I'm just trying . . . I mean, there's so much about human relationships I don't get. I want to understand as much as possible, that's all."

"Gabriel . . . is annoying. And he's a fool."

"Well, yes. He's a lot like Ruda, which is an opposite thing. You keep trying to give her a chance and she keeps being mean. I don't understand what the difference is."

Trissiny stared hard at a fixed point in the distance, forgetting for the moment to turn her head and scan. "The difference is that Ruda, at the end of the day, is only human. Whatever her bloodline or responsibilities, she's one woman and there's a stark limit to the amount of damage she can cause. Gabriel is part *demon*. If he can't control himself, the harm he could potentially do is . . . staggering."

"Yes, well, I mean, sure, but . . . that's a lot of us, right? You and Toby are both pretty powerful. Shaeine the same way, you're all connected to gods. Don't even get me started on the mess Teal could make with that demon she's got, and Juniper . . . Well, Juniper's pretty much a force of nature. I read up on hethelax demons, and . . . I don't see why Gabe's so dangerous, really. He's only a half-blood, and even full hethelaxi aren't any stronger than a human, and they don't have any magic. They're just really, really hard to stop or kill, so of course it's really hard to contain them if they go into a berserk mode."

"That's just it, they're berserker demons. The others . . . and myself . . . have basically understandable motivations. Without *incredible* self-control, Gabriel can be set off and cause untold havoc."

"So . . . doesn't it make more sense to encourage him when he's obviously trying so hard?"

Trissiny glared at the horizon, refusing to look at the pixie. "It's not that simple, Fross."

"Why?"

"Because . . . some things are just not as simple as it seems like they should be."

"Yeah, well, okay, but . . . *Why?*"

The paladin sighed slowly. "Because the world . . . is imperfect."

Fross buzzed her wings once before speaking softly. "No, it's not."

"Pardon?"

"The world *is* perfect. It's exactly what it was meant to be, whatever that is. If it seems wrong . . . maybe you're expecting something from it that it was never designed to give."

Trissiny found herself nodding. "Maybe I am, at that."

They lapsed into silence for a moment before Fross spoke again.

"Also, I *really* don't think you understand Juniper's motivations. I know I pretty much don't, but . . . She looks pretty human, yeah, but she doesn't think like one. At all."

"I've been getting that impression more and more."

Teal relieved her without having to be awakened. Trissiny was initially unsure about leaving Teal on watch—the bard was likeable and making progress in their sparring sessions, but she'd grown up in the very lap of luxury, never having to work or struggle for anything. However, as Trissiny headed toward her tent, the blossoming of flames behind her meant that Teal's other half was taking over. Trissiny lengthened her step. She really did not want to have a conversation with Vadrieny . . . but at least the demon could be trusted not to nod off.

In her bedroll, she stared at the ceiling of the tent for a long time.

CHAPTER 7

Professor Tellwyrn's office door opened without warning.
"Knock, knock!" Principia sang, leaning inside with a cheery smile.

Tellwyrn stared at her over the rims of her spectacles for a moment, one hand still holding a quill poised above the papers on her desk. "Oh, this had *better* be good," she said finally. "It won't be, but it had better."

"Don't be such a grouch," Principia replied, sliding in and shutting the door behind her. "We used to get along so well! Remember?"

"I remember paying you to do things you were going to do anyway to people I wanted you to do them to instead of the general public."

"Uh . . ." She blinked. "You lost me about half—"

"I *do* know the basics of running a con, Prin. Trying to establish an emotional connection with your mark is amateur stuff. I'm very nearly offended; don't I deserve the top of your game? Anyway," she went on more loudly as the other elf opened her mouth to object, "you would be wise to say your piece before my tolerance wears out. You are specifically *not* supposed to be on my campus."

"Yeah, well, there's a difference between the letter of the law and the *spirit* of the law," Principia said, edging closer to the desk. "We both know why you don't want me around, and she's not even *on* campus right now."

"The fact that you know this isn't helping your case. Spit it out, Prin."

She sidled closer, letting the smile fade from her face. "I need your help."

"Interesting. I'm leaning heavily toward 'no.'"

"You haven't even—"

"And it is not in my interests to even. I know how you operate; it's not as if you're terribly complicated. Whatever you may or may not be up to right now, I *know* your ultimate goal at this University, and you're not getting that. *Engaging* with you is just a way for you to work a fingernail into some crack."

"Arachne," she said somberly, "I'll give you my word that I'm not working any angle. I won't swear that I might not change my mind and try to take advantage in the future . . . we both know me too well for that to be believable . . . but if you really think I'm nothing but self-interest, then I promise you that's all this is. I might be in *real* trouble here. I'm asking for your help."

"I have every confidence that you'll manage to weasel your way out of whatever you're into. Probably the same way you got into it in the first place."

They locked eyes, Principia glaring, Tellwyrn impassive. Finally, Prin heaved a sigh and shrugged.

"Well, if that's how it's going to be . . . I guess I'll go throw myself out, then."

"Oh, that won't be necessary," Tellwyrn said sweetly.

"All right, you're down for two doubloons on the drow, despite my earnest advice."

"Hey, I like me an underdog! Comes down to it, they're the ones who fight hardest."

"Whatever you say, Wilson. Ox, are you *sure* you want the dryad?"

"Positive," the big man rumbled. "Put three doubloons on her."

Hiram Taft, the owner of the town bank, shook his head and chortled even as he jotted down Ox's name on the grid inscribed on the parchment rolled out between them. The men were clustered around an upturned barrel on the shaded front of the sheriff's office. Sheriff Sanders himself stood at the edge of the sidewalk with his back to them, working a toothpick and watching the comings and goings in the street.

"Well, I hate to take your money, Ox—"

"The gods frown on lies, Hiram."

"—but if that's the way you want it. Mind you, I'd have much stronger opinions about the green girl if I was twenty years younger, but there ain't no way she's a match for my demon."

"'Your' demon," Sanders grunted, not turning around.

"That's cause I've read my Imperial Army encounter manual," Ox rumbled. "Dryads are classified as a sapient monster race, neutral alignment, fae/divine origin. Threat level of *eight*. I like my odds."

"If you're sure, then!"

"I have half a mind to go to Mayor Cleese," Sanders said, "or the council, or Father Laws. Hell, or Miz Cratchley. *Somebody* who'll slap a ban on this foolishness so I can toss you galoots in a cell."

"Aw, don't be a spoilsport, Sam, it's harmless fun," Taft said jovially. "And who knows, the pool might actually pay out this year! You know there was a scrap between the Avenist and that half-demon boy already."

"The pool has never paid out, and *will* never pay out," Sanders grunted. "It'll all go to the church fund like always, and you can all be damn glad of that. If the pool ever pays out, it'll mean the freshmen have *actually* started takin' blades to each other. And *that* will only happen if the whole place up there dissolves into complete anarchy, in which case this town is likely to be razed to its foundations."

"What's the harm, then?"

The sheriff shook his head. "I live in fear of the day Tellwyrn finds out about this annual pool of yours. Dunno whether she'd knock all your heads together or join in. Frankly, I'm not sure which idea spooks me more."

A muted *pop* sounded a few yards away, expelling a puff of air that forced Taft to lunge after his suddenly airborne parchment grid. In the middle of the street, at the epicenter of the disturbance, Principia Locke appeared from midair, about two feet off the ground. She landed with catlike grace, peering about in startlement for a moment, then a scowl fell across her features.

"Oh, you smarmy *bitch*."

"Prin!" Sanders shouted, straightening up with his errant hat in hand. It took him all of one second to do the math on this situation. "You wanna tell me *why* you were up there pestering Professor Tellwyrn?"

"Ah, ah, ah," she scolded, wagging a finger at him as she approached from the street. "Just as soon as somebody passes a law against me visiting old friends, that'll be your business. Till then, you can just butt out."

"Hmph," he grunted, folding his arms and leaning against one of the vertical wooden beams holding up the awning. "On your head be it, then. I have it on *very* good authority that Tellwyrn does not like you at all."

"Really? I hadn't noticed. Ooh, hey, are you guys doing the annual pool? Put me down for three on the Hand of Avei."

"Hah!" Taft chortled, grinning. "Any other year, sure, but you do know there's a bona fide *demon* up there now? You've got no chance." He did, however, mark her name and wager down on the appropriate spot.

"I like my odds. You whippersnappers may not remember what the world was like when paladins were running around willy-nilly, but *I've* seen the Silver Legions in action." She leaned forward, peering over the map; three sets of eyes shifted momentarily to her low-cut bodice. "I see Ox is shafting you out of an honest ten doubloons, Hiram."

"Bah! I have faith in my demon, even if she is attached to a bard."

"Uh huh. I take it nobody's informed you that demons are critically weak against high-level fae?"

". . . wait, what?"

"Yup!" she said cheerfully. "Their magic just peters out, like a fire underwater. That's why witches are almost as good as priests against warlocks. Your demon isn't gonna do squat against that dryad."

"That . . . you . . . *Ox*! You cheating bastard!"

"No takebacks," Ox said smugly.

Sanders shook his head, still not looking at them. Instead, he glanced up the street at the mountain, wondering at the source of the bad feeling he suddenly had.

Bishop Darling ascended a broad marble staircase with a red-and-gold rug cascading down its center, nodding to the two holy legionaries keeping watch over the door at the top.

They were clearly showpieces, their armor and halberds both gilded, lacquered, and generally ornate to the point of uselessness. Under any other Archpope, Darling might have suspected they were only to be kept for show. Justinian, though, had not gone to the trouble of obtaining unprecedented permission for a Church military arm because he liked to look at shiny things. What *was* his game, then?

Darling pulled open one of the great gilded oak doors himself, stepping into the Archpope's private meeting room and letting the guards close it behind him. Four people were present; Darling initially ignored all but one.

"Your Holiness," he murmured, kneeling and pressing his lips to the proffered ring, a thick gold band with an absurdly sized round-cut diamond, within which an ankh symbol glowed with the golden light of the gods.

Archpope Justinian was well over six feet in height, with broad shoulders that suggested a more athletic lifestyle than his ecclesiastical duties required. In his later middle years but still handsome, he wore his brown hair a touch longer than was fashionable, with a neat goatee surrounding his square chin. Two wings of gray swept back from his temples, with a matching pair of thin stripes in his beard, all as precise as if painted on; the only lines of experience on his face suggested a lifetime spent smiling. Though his office traditionally involved rich, fur-lined robes, glittering jewels, and a truly massive crown, Justinian wore the simple black surcoat of a Church priest, with a white tabard emblazoned with the Church's ankh symbol in gold. Only that and his ring announced his office. His humility had done much to endear him to the people.

"Rise, my friend," Justinian said with a kind smile, and Darling did so. The Archpope radiated power and calm in a way that had nothing to do with any divine energies. As a student of body language and theatrics himself, Darling always felt he was in the presence of a master when he met with Justinian.

"I apologize for my tardiness, your Holiness," he said humbly, finally glancing over at the others in the room. Three fellow bishops—people he knew, but not well.

"Nonsense, you arrived well before the stated time," the Archpope replied, turning to stride back to his thronelike seat at the head of the table. Darling followed.

"It's all relative, your Holiness. If everybody else is already here, clearly I'm late."

"What makes you think *everybody* who's coming has arrived?" asked the slim, dark-haired woman nearest him, smiling faintly.

"Everyone *important*, then," he said with a wink. She gave him a raised eyebrow, but the other woman at the table laughed obligingly.

He glanced over them swiftly as he sat, noting that they were all regarding each other with the same wary curiosity. This was not a group accustomed to meeting together. They were all acquainted, but not close; many of the Church's constituent religions did not get along, and not all of its bishops liked to socialize.

Lean and sharp-featured, with a coppery Tiraan complexion and a dominant nose that didn't spoil her looks, Basra Syrinx wore the traditional white robes of a bishop, as did they all, with a brooch in the shape of Avei's golden eagle pinned at the shoulder to identify her cult. Darling knew relatively little of her, personally, but nothing he'd heard suggested that the empress's assessment—sneaky, mean, and less than devout—was inaccurate. Directly opposite him sat Branwen Snowe, a woman who was strikingly beautiful in a way that she clearly was well aware of and spent effort on. That was actually unusual for disciples of Izara, but her fiery auburn hair had been wound into an elaborate knot that had certainly taken time and probably needed help, and she actually wore cosmetics. Skillfully enough that they might not be apparent to everyone, but Darling knew a thing or two about disguises. The fourth bishop present, Andros Varanus, was a follower of Shaath and truly looked the part. With his thick beard, untamed black hair, and deep, glaring eyes, he looked out of place in the sumptuous surroundings and uncomfortable in his white robe. Doubtless he'd have preferred to be in furs, as his cult considered proper for a huntsman.

"Since you mention it," said the Archpope, smiling serenely at them from the head of the table, "everyone invited is now here, and as such, we may begin discussing our business. My friends, I have selected the four of you according to very particular criteria. Despite what you may believe, it has little to do with your various efforts to acquire my political favor."

As one, they stiffened slightly, like youths caught out in some mischief, urgently wanting to protest, but not sure how to do so without challenging an authority figure and making the situation worse.

"There is neither shame nor condemnation in it," Justinian said gently, his kind smile unwavering. "You were all sent here by your various cults in recognition of your skill at the great game of politics. There are few within the Church who do not play that game, and none at or near your rank who fail to play it skillfully. I have no shortage of clever operators at my disposal. What I need from you ... What I believe you are uniquely suited to provide is something different entirely." He folded his hands before him, leaning forward and somehow holding all four of their gazes without moving his eyes. "Faith."

"I do not lack faith in my god," Varanus said in a tone that was perilously close to a growl. "Nor do any of my people. The faithless are not suffered in Shaath's cult."

"Faith is a decision," replied the Archpope smoothly. "It is a choice of alignment, a determination to believe a given thing regardless of what evidence presents itself." He paused, his smile widening as he watched them glance uncertainly at one another. To hear the leader of the Church give voice to what was beginning to sound like agnosticism put them all off-balance. "Faith is perhaps the most *crucial* aspect of human existence. We have faith that our loved ones will not betray us, that our government will shelter us, that our partners in trade will deal fairly with us . . . that our gods will succor us. And no matter how many times each of these disappoints that faith, we *hold* to it. Because without it, we are nothing. We would be eternally at each other's throats, trusting no one, never able to rest. Faith, friends, makes all human endeavors possible. It is the one thing that binds us together while all our other impulses seek to rend us apart.

"My concern is not the depth or sincerity of the faith you have in your individual gods, or in me. No, I have gathered the four of you, specifically, because of the *nature* of the faith you hold. After all, one does not have faith in a spouse or parent the same way that one has in a deity. I have watched all my bishops closely, and selected the four of you on one basis." He lowered his hands to his lap and leaned back in his great chair, eyes roving across their faces. "You understand that the gods . . . are *people*. And as such, they are far from perfect."

Absolute stillness reigned in the room. For excruciatingly drawn-out seconds, the bishops stared at their Archpope in consternation, afraid even to glance at each other.

It was Darling who finally broke the spell. "I feel like the only safe thing I can do here is take a pratfall to cut the tension."

Branwen tittered nervously; Andros gave him a scathing look. Basra was still staring fixedly at the Archpope.

Justinian, for his part, nodded, still smiling. "In point of fact, Antonio has the right of it. Before the gods, what are mere creatures such as we? We dance for their amusement. I do not mean to suggest that we attempt to elevate ourselves above our station. On the contrary," he went on, leaning forward and gazing at them intensely, "it is my belief that we serve the Pantheon better by acknowledging their limitations. By not expecting them to tend to every little thing that takes place on the mortal plane. There are matters which are ours, their servants, to address, so that they can be about the business of holding up the firmament and maintaining the order of the world." Slowly, he panned his gaze around the table, meeting each of their eyes in turn. "One of these matters, which I have called you together to attend to, concerns the Black Wreath."

Darling felt a shiver begin at the base of his skull and travel slowly down the whole length of his spine. Too much coincidence . . . too many people pointing him in this one direction, the same direction he'd set out to search on his own, first. Or had he? Was he being moved by the gods—his, or others? How *much* did Justinian know? Or Eleanora?

The possibilities grew more disturbing the more he wondered. He felt . . . elated. The game was *on*.

"That, of all things, would seem to be the gods' concern," Basra said slowly.

"It is an easy mistake to make, Basra," Justinian replied. "*Elilial* most certainly is a threat for the Pantheon to address. The *Wreath*, however, are mortal men and women . . . like ourselves. What power they have is the gift of a deity."

"Like ourselves," Andros said, his eyes narrowed in thought.

"Just so." The Archpope nodded. "And they are becoming more active in recent days. The Church's capacity to contend directly with such threats is growing, of course."

"We saw the new guards," Branwen commented.

"Indeed. However, some wars are not meant to be fought by armies. Some *cannot* be fought thus. That is why I've assembled you."

"I assume I am missing something," Basra commented, "if you intend the four of us to *fight* the Black Wreath."

"Not directly, or in its entirety, nor all at once," Justinian replied. "As I said, I chose you based on mindset, on your willingness to act in necessity and not be excessively bound by the traditions of your own faiths. Your willingness to see members of other cults as colleagues rather than rivals. Unfortunately, the *lack* of that same willingness still chokes some divisions of the Universal Church. Despite my selection of you on that criterion alone, I see the providential hand of the gods in the array of skills before me. Warrior, hunter, thief, persuader. I believe you were guided to this task by the Pantheon themselves."

There came another brief silence, while they all studied each other speculatively.

"Intrigue," Branwen said at last. "You are talking about espionage, not combat."

"Just so. We will begin with specific, individual missions, pursuing certain leads that have come to my attention, and work up from there. Elilial, in the end, is distinct from our gods by circumstance, not nature. Whatever leadership she provides the Wreath, she is not running every aspect of its actions, any more than your own gods direct every step you take." A note of wry humor entered his voice. "If my own bishops can manage to trip each other up in the halls of this very cathedral, how much more effective will four of you prove against a single target?"

"What target?" asked Basra.

"Small ones, at first. By necessity. But eventually . . . You will do what Imperial Intelligence, what centuries of counteraction by the various individual cults of the Pantheon, have failed to do." The Archpope smiled. "For in the end, what is a faith without a high priest?"

The sparse crowd in the square was drifting toward and around Ale & Wenches in preparation for the traditional lunch rush, and Principia let herself be carried along with the throng after she stepped out of the scrolltower office. Her eyes darted across the people present, seeking out navy blue uniforms and paying little attention to those who didn't have them. In this, she was quickly disappointed, and then chagrined by her lack of attentiveness when a hand closed around her upper arm.

"Heard you ran into a mite of trouble up there on the mountain," Jeremiah Shook said mildly, smiling down at her.

"Oh, how people love their gossip in this town," she replied dryly.

"Every town, as I understand it. The smaller, the gossipier." He glanced about quickly at the idlers and strollers in the square, and she quashed an urge to smack him upside the head. Nobody was paying them any attention; the surest way to *attract* attention was to act like there was something more going on than two people pausing for a chat. "Now, you wouldn't have gone and blown our business here, would you? Maybe counting on Tellwyrn to protect you from . . . the consequences?"

Principia gave him her most scathing look. "No, *Thumper*, Tellwyrn is not aware that you are sniffing around her business. Know how you can tell? Because your ass isn't *dead*. I was just . . . ruling out a possibility. I didn't really think it would pan out, but it had to be tried, and now I can focus on more likely prospects."

"And now she knows to watch you," he said, his voice gaining an unmistakable threat, though he kept it too low to be overheard.

"She *always* knows to watch me. Now, duckling, she's watching for the wrong *thing*. She thinks I'm running some kind of con on her. So she'll keep me at arm's length and feel smug about it, while I can maneuver around more *reliable* sources of information without having to worry about her overhearing something awkward. This isn't my first rodeo, y'know," she added, smirking.

"What reliable sources?" he asked curtly.

"Gonna start with those three soldiers the empire sent over. They come to town for meals and booze. Getting intel out of sloshed soldiers is like taking candy from three big, tipsy babies."

"Those three tipsy babies are at the heart of all this," Thumper warned. "Be careful not to get *too* clever, Keys. This is not a mission you want to blow." As he spoke, he kept his hand on her arm, but began moving his thumb up and down in a soft, caressing motion.

"Aw, are you worried about little ol' me?" she asked sweetly, reaching up to pat him on the cheek. "That's so thoughtful of you. Tell me, since you're clearly the expert, exactly how clever is it safe for me to be?"

"That," he said quietly, "is too clever. Don't push me, Keys."

Principia let her smile drop. "Look, wiseass, you can be in charge and as threatening as you want. But if you want this job to succeed, don't forget who the expert is. You want me to work?" She gripped his wrist and extricated her arm from his grasp. "Then let me *work*. Tricks will get his info, if there's anything to get. If there's not, I'll get verification of that. And *you*, meanwhile, need to not get under my feet."

He allowed her to remove his hand. "Fine, then. When are you going to corner the boys?"

"I was hoping to see them in town for lunch, but no dice today, it seems. I'll keep trying that, but according to the local scuttlebutt they're only *reliably* here in the evenings. My next night off is in three days; I'll spend it at A&W chatting them up if nothing better comes along in the meantime."

"Your next night off?" He raised his eyebrows incredulously. "Are you seriously confusing your bullshit job slinging drinks at that rundown little rathole with what's actually *important* here?"

"That bullshit job is my cover," she said, forcing herself to moderate her tone. They were already pushing the boundaries of polite conversation; it wouldn't do to attract any further interest. "Without that, I've got no reason to loiter around this town, and then I *can't* do the real job. And the Saloon is not a rathole."

"Keys, you're going native." He shook his head. "It's almost tragic, a fine little piece like you, wasted on this dust bunny of a town. Fine, three days, then. I expect to have some good news waiting for me on the morning of the fourth."

"Oh, I will be *sure* not to disappoint," she simpered.

"Good girl," he said condescendingly, reaching up to pat her on the head.

Principia smiled broadly, showing more teeth than was necessary, and turned on her heel, flouncing off down the street. Jeremiah stood for a long moment and watched her go.

Behind him and high above, the orb atop the scrolltower began to flash, sending out a message.

CHAPTER 8

The house in Hamlet had once been owned by a prosperous merchant, somebody who'd made it good in the cattle trade. Cattle were really the only trade worth bothering in out here; the village wasn't close enough to the Golden Sea to have any commerce from passing adventurers. It was two stories tall, which was positively grandiose for this little town, though its simple white paint and utter lack of adornment was almost shockingly plain to those accustomed to the grandeur and grime of Tiraas. There was even a white picket fence. Basra had yet to run out of jokes about that.

The four bishops had taken time, after arriving, to freshen up and settle in. It wasn't a large house, so Basra and Branwen ended up sharing a room. Darling, who had been feeling out his traveling companions during their exhausting journey, was not sure how well that was going to go; he didn't see those two becoming friends, but hopefully they were both professional enough not to snipe at each other. Branwen's habit of flirting with every man she met seemed to antagonize Basra, but fortunately, the Avenist expressed her antagonism through smug superiority, rather than outright hostility. He had ensconced himself in a tiny servant's room, which was plenty adequate for his purposes, leaving Andros the other main bedroom.

Thoughtful neighbors had left them a pie and several congenial notes. The rental of the house had been undertaken by the Church through a real estate broker in Tiraas; nobody was supposed to know anything about it, but such things worked differently in little towns. The locals were an almost comically straightforward lot, failing utterly to conceal their curiosity about the new strangers in town behind a facade of friendliness.

The four of them did not in any way resemble a family. They were all in fancy civilian garb rather than bishops' robes or the trappings of their respective cults. Andros was as awkward stuffed into his starched collar as a bear in a tutu, and Basra was decidedly unstylish, having flatly refused to wear a dress, but overall they were not a distinctive or memorable group—or wouldn't have been, in Tiraas. Just well-to-do travelers, not worthy of particular notice, but here, that fact alone drew attention. That was the idea.

Clothing aside, Darling was tall, lean, and blond, Andros tall, burly, and dark-haired, with a wild beard and wild eyes. Branwen was similarly pale, but short and curvy, with reddish hair and blue eyes; Basra had an olive Tiraan complexion and a lean build. Speculation was bound to run rampant as to their identities and business.

Darling and Branwen had immediately taken over the handling of nosy neighbors, both of them being specialists in people skills; Basra's sense of humor would likely not go over well in this town, and Andros didn't seem capable of making a good impression on anyone. They also, without discussing it, began collaborating on moderating with the others and keeping the tension in the group as low as they could. It didn't help that none of them really liked one another that much. Andros, in particular, was still sullen and smarting over Darling having been placed in charge of their expedition.

For his part, Darling was out of his element. He was a creature of the city and hardly knew what to do with himself in a little flyspeck town like Hamlet; not to mention, he was concerned about leaving his two brand-new apprentices behind in Tiraas. Price would keep an eye on them and he'd set up training for them with other senior Guild members, but considering who (and what) those two were . . . being worried seemed sensible. He had reason to be tense.

He wondered what worries the other three had left behind, that were now weighing on them. None in the group were particularly inclined to open up.

Dinner was terse, though they were in a somewhat better frame of mind by that point in the evening, and even more so after a meal. A full belly did wonders for one's disposition. At least the discomfort of the trip from Tiraas to Hamlet had taught them a thing or two about dealing with each other. Three of the religions represented in their group had deep doctrinal conflicts, and Darling's cult had a complex relationship with Basra's, to say the least. Still, they managed to be civil, which gave him hope.

Now, finally, night had fallen and they were ready to get down to the business at hand.

"The house is secure," Andros growled, descending the steep wooden steps to join the others in the basement. It wasn't a hostile tone; his normal speaking voice was a growl. "I've placed wards and charms at all entrances. I will know if anyone approaches."

"We're hunting the Black Wreath," Basra chided. "The whole problem with them is that they can slip through—"

"I will *know*," Andros repeated sharply, "if anyone approaches. The Wreath's stealth works like an animal's camouflage. We may not notice them in the wild, but when they step into one of *my* traps, it will go off."

"Are you *sure* . . ."

"Let's assume he's sure, and that he's right," Darling said from the opposite side of the room, where he was studying an open spellbook by the light of the oil lamp that was the room's sole illumination. "Have a little faith in your partners, Bas! Either we're all competent and trustworthy in our respective fields, or we're all about to be excruciatingly dead." He looked up, grinning toothily at her. "Me, I prefer to be an optimist."

"Antonio," she replied, "at some point in your youth, someone allowed you to gain the impression that you're funny. That person owes a great debt to the world."

"Oh, like I've never heard that one before."

"I have a *very* bad feeling about this," Branwen said. Her voice took on a sharper tone as Basra opened her mouth to comment. "*Yes*, I know I've said that already, and *yes*, I know my reasons for it are painfully obvious. I believe it bears repeating, nonetheless. There are *so* many ways this can go horribly wrong."

"Go upstairs and tend to the kitchen if you're frightened," Andros said, staring at her. He might have been glaring, or that might just have been what his face looked like. "This is the work of men."

"Okay, let's please agree not to start up with that," Darling said soothingly. "We're already a setup for a punchline as it is: an Izarite, a Shaathist, an Avenist, and an Eserite walk into a basement to cast a spell circle, eh? I think it'd be a very good idea to avoid topics that we *know* are just going to lead to arguments." The huntsman grunted. Darling chose to take that as acquiescence.

"How's this?" Branwen asked, stepping back from the circle she had just finished laboriously drawing on the floor in a selection of three different colored powders. Darling picked up the book in one hand and the lamp in the other, crossing over to her and studying her handiwork.

"Excellent! Matches the diagram exactly."

"Is this *really* all it's going to take?" Basra asked skeptically. "It seems like there should be something . . . more. Just lines on the ground aren't going to do much."

"This is powdered dragon bone, blessed by the Archpope himself in the Hall of the Pantheon," Darling said absently, pacing around the circle and comparing it to the diagram despite his pronouncement that it was correct. It *looked* right, but he shared the women's nervousness. They were meddling with serious forces here; there was no such thing as too much caution. "Fae and divine energies in considerable strength. That makes up for a lot; most practitioners would need a more elaborate circle to compensate for the lack of raw power. The glyphs provide the arcane boost we need, and as for the rest . . . Well, we're coming to that. Anyone else care to double-check us, or shall we proceed?"

"Just get on with it," Andros growled.

"Jolly good. Basra, how're we coming along?"

"Oh, please, I've been done for twenty minutes."

"Smashing! Let's have a look!"

She crossed over to him, giving the circle a wide berth, and laid five pieces of parchment out on the upturned wooden crate he was using as an impromptu desk. Darling, with the same excessive care he'd given to the circle, laboriously checked each line against the illustrations in the book. He couldn't read what was written—that language wasn't spoken natively by anyone on this plane—but he could check the marks against each other.

"It looks good to me," he said at last. "Branwen, come have a look, please?"

"Oh, honestly, you don't think I—"

"Basra," he interrupted, "I have the *utmost* faith in your penmanship. But when it comes to this, I am going to be unreasonably, excessively cautious, and I won't apologize for that."

"Fair enough," she said with a faint smirk, crossing her arms.

"I agree," said Branwen, peering at the book and the marked parchments. "If we *must* do this, let's do it as carefully as possible. The markings match the book as far as I can tell."

"Good. Andros, wanna quadruple-check us?"

Andros grunted.

". . . so, no, then? All right." Darling carefully stacked the papers up in the proper order and handed them back to Basra. "Each needs to be laid in one of those triangular glyphs spaced around the edge of the circle, in order. If we were *speaking* the spell, it would be one continuous thing, but none of us can pronounce any of this gobbledygook, so timing is going to be a factor. The actual incantation is supposed to take just under a minute, so . . . give it a slow count of ten between them."

"Got it," she said crisply, moving over to the circle. "Everyone ready?"

"No," said Branwen. "Do it."

Pausing only to grin at her, Basra bent and carefully laid the first parchment in place.

It was fortunate that she moved her fingers so adroitly, as it immediately burst into flame. The parchment burned with a painfully unnatural green fire, putting off neither smoke nor heat. The lines of powder on the floor began to glow, luminosity spreading out from that glyph like dampness through cloth, petering out about halfway to the point of reaching either of the next glyphs along the edge.

Basra's timing was good. She set down the second, and the effect repeated itself; the slowly creeping illumination reached the same flat light from the other direction and doubled in intensity, two glyphs now alight, lines of brightness stretching between them.

They didn't quite hold their breath as she stepped smoothly around the circle, laying down each piece of the spell in turn, but the tension in the room was palpable, increasing with each added component of the spell and subsequent increase in light level. Basra set the final parchment in place and immediately backed away. By unspoken plan, they had placed themselves in the four corners of the chamber, encircling the now fully illuminated spell circle.

As it burst into a brighter illumination than before and the five rune-marked parchments erupted in puffs of greenish flame, they reached for the divine light in unison. The glow filled the room with a much brighter illumination than the oil lamp could emit. Light coruscated against an invisible cylinder of protection cast upward by the spell circle, golden sparks marking out a line where the power of the gods was held back from a small piece of territory that now belonged to something else.

It rose up slowly from below, as though the dirt floor were fluid and it was breaching the surface, gasping for breath. The thing writhed in obvious discomfort at its passage, sliding headfirst up into the chamber over the long course of a minute. It was lifted bodily off the ground momentarily after breaking through, then fell back, its feet landing on the packed earth.

Everything about it was . . . wrong. It was humanoid, but could never have passed for human. There were the horns, the spiny wings, the lashing, barb-tipped tail and oddly gray-blue complexion, but more than that, it was simply shaped wrong. Too lean, too long. Its skull was grotesquely elongated, its facial features likewise; its limbs were spindly, its torso scrawny and skeletal. For feet it had birdlike claws, balancing upright on only two large toes; its hands were far too large for even its peculiar frame, dangling from bony wrists like overfed spiders. It was, somehow, the subtler inhumanities in its appearance that were truly disturbing, more than the ostentatious ones. Most disturbing of all were its eyes—its plain, gray, apparently human eyes, set in that unnatural face.

It flexed its wings once, wincing when they sparked against the borders of the containing circle, then folded them around itself rather like a cape, concealing its figure. All it wore beneath them were tightly-fitted scraps of leather that looked reptilian in origin and concealed little of its emaciated flesh. Tilting its head in apparent curiosity, it turned in a slow circle, studying the four priests who had summoned it.

"Well," the demon said at last. "*This* is different."

CHAPTER 9

Ruda yawned hugely as she descended the rocky incline to the plain below. The chilly gray of predawn lingered in the sheltered area she was headed for, where the rocky outcropping cast a long shadow; everywhere else, the endless expanse of tallgrass blazed red and gold with the sunrise. She'd paused to admire the scene briefly, but Zaruda Punaji had seen her share of sunrises. What was going on below was far more interesting.

Yawning again, she flopped down on a low, flat lump of stone next to Shaeine and watched Trissiny and Teal exercising on the area of flattened grass they'd already created with their exertions. The paladin was dressed but not armored or armed—her gear sat nearby—and she looked as alert and energetic as if she'd just spent an uninterrupted night in a luxurious feather bed. Ruda didn't know how the hell that girl always looked in top shape, but it was maddening. Teal was no longer visibly groggy, as they'd been at it for a good ten minutes already, but her movements were stiff and showed weariness.

They weren't actually sparring, but drilling. Punches, first with one hand then the other—from the shoulder, from the waist, overhand, underhand. Twenty repetitions of each while Trissiny called out a cadence and corrected the other girl's form.

"I dunno how the hell you can stand that," Ruda said when the paladin called a rest and Teal flexed her spine, grimacing. "The same damn thing over and over. That's not fighting, it's *homework*."

"You repeat motions until your body knows them," Trissiny said, her voice thick with patience that made Ruda want to club her. "Till you don't have to think about every move you make in a fight, because a real fight won't give you the luxury. The point of the *homework* is to get them down perfectly, so that when they're needed, they will *be* perfect."

"Bah. You want to learn to fight, you go out and fucking *fight*. You can talk about form and stance and technique till you pass out, but when it comes down to it, what matters is that you have the *will* to fuck somebody up." She removed her hat, dropping it next to Trissiny's armor, and grinned. "People who've never been in an actual scrap don't realize just how big a deal that is. A person who's right in the head doesn't want to inflict pain. You're drilling to fight *right*, when the truth is that fighting *well* means being just a little bit . . . wrong."

"I think it's interesting that Professor Ezzaniel's never had us spar with each other," Trissiny replied coolly. "Don't you?"

"I always thought that was a pretty good idea," Teal commented, slightly out of breath.

"Why," Ruda drawled. "You afraid of learning there's a pirate-shaped hole in our fancy-ass *technique*?"

"If you'll recall," the paladin replied evenly, "we tested this once. Or rather, you did."

Ruda was on her feet before she decided to be. "Are you saying you want a rematch?"

"Ladies," Shaeine said firmly, "let's please be civil."

"I agree," Trissiny said, nodding at her. "We're just here to practice. If you don't mind learning some pure technique, Zaruda, you're welcome to join us."

"Do I fucking look like I need your help?"

"Yes."

She bounded off the rock and stomped over to stand inches from Trissiny. Immediately she regretted this decision; the other girl was a head taller, and Ruda had to crane her neck to make eye contact. The hell she was going to back down, though. "Where I come from, that's a challenge."

"Yes, it is a challenge," Trissiny replied, still insufferably calm. "I'm not interested in a real battle with you, Ruda, because that would be unfair even if we were unquestionably equal in skill. I have powers at my command that you just can't contend with. But again, we are here to *practice*. If you're willing, I'd like to see what you can show me."

Ruda took the excuse of thrusting a finger into her face to step back. "No magic, no weapons."

"Agreed."

She unbuckled her belt and threw it to one side, rapier and all, and instantly lunged forward, driving a fist at Trissiny's midsection.

Trissiny spun to one side, slapping her arm away and sending Ruda stumbling past her. She wheeled around, lashing out again and following up with a flurry of punches; the taller girl ducked and dodged, deflecting blows with precise little motions when evasion wasn't possible. It took only a scant few moments of this before Ruda could positively taste the rage on the back of her tongue.

"Fucking fight *back*, you bitch!" she screamed, swinging a wild haymaker at the paladin's jaw.

Trissiny grabbed her wrist, then her upper arm with the other hand, and flipped her neatly overhead. Ruda slammed into the ground on her back, hard enough that she saw spots and momentarily lost the ability to breathe. When her senses swam back into focus, the first thing she became aware of was Trissiny's foot on her neck.

It was withdrawn immediately, but as far as Ruda was concerned, the damage was done.

She lay there, gasping, and squeezed her eyes shut, forcing back tears and a sob of pure, undiluted frustration. The *hell* she was going to show that kind of weakness here.

"You're sloppy," Trissiny said inexorably. "You let anger drive your movements, which makes you predictable. You have little fine control or even awareness of your body."

"Shut the fuck up," Ruda hissed. All of this she'd heard from Ezzaniel.

Trissiny just sat down in the grass beside her. "And not *one* of those things is a fault of yours," she said. Ruda kept her eyes closed, recovering her breath as the paladin continued. "You've got bad habits, that's all. You're clearly an experienced fighter, Ruda. That ferocity you were talking about is there; if you'd just *practice*, solidify the technique, you'd be an absolute terror." She sighed. "And I'd really like to work with you on it, but I feel like you take it as an insult that I know something you don't."

"I take it as an insult," Ruda growled, "that you think you're *better* than me."

"I'm better *at* something than you, which is a whole different thing. Once when I was fed up with being smacked around by the older girls training me, I asked my instructor how long it would take before I'd be considered a master. She laughed at me and said a master is whoever's been working at it long enough to have *failed* more times than you've tried."

A long silence stretched out, and Ruda eventually opened her eyes. Trissiny was watching her face.

"It seems to me we each know some things the other doesn't," she said gently. "We're students. It's not a contest. I'm willing to teach you, Ruda, and I don't think it'd make me weaker to learn from you. If anything, it would make us both stronger."

Ruda groaned and threw an arm over her eyes. "There you go, doing that paladin thing again. How do you just pull wisdom out of your ass like that?"

"Because a lot of women who know more about the world than I ever will spent a lot of time stuffing it up there. I've got quite a backlog at this point."

"Well, *that* was a mental image I didn't fucking need."

Trissiny laughed lightly. "Well, the offer stands. Teal and I do this every morning before breakfast; we'd both love to have you join. I would *really* appreciate it, though, if you didn't call me a bitch."

Ruda grunted as she sat up, seizing gratefully on the change of topic. "Yeah, what's your deal with that, anyway? I thought you were just making an issue of it to get under Tellwyrn's skin."

"I don't need a reason to antagonize Tellwyrn," she said wryly. "I just dislike gendered insults."

"Gendered? So fucking what? Most of the people I've called bitches were men. Hell, that makes it sting harder." She grinned, but the corners of Trissiny's mouth turned down.

"Exactly, it's meant to hit harder. Did you ever pause to think about *why*?"

"Because no man likes to have it pointed out that he's being a pussy?"

Trissiny drew in a breath slowly through her nose. "So calling a man weak is one thing, but calling him weak and *feminine* is even worse? Don't you see the implication? It's a statement that womanhood is a disadvantage. Call someone an idiot, a jerk, or whatever else, and you're making a personal statement about them. Call them a *bitch*, and you make it about all women."

Ruda frowned, then stood, dusting off her pants. "Well . . . shit. I was all ready to just blow you off like I usually do, but . . . fuck me if that doesn't actually make some sense."

"I do my best," Trissiny said dryly, rising also.

"*Fuck.* I *liked* calling people 'bitch.' Now I'm gonna have this in the back of my head every time."

"Or," she suggested, "you could not do it."

"Don't rush me, prissy britches. You can belittle my fighting technique, but if you take away my cussing, I'll turn to dust and blow away. What's next, cutting off my booze supply?"

"I wouldn't dare," she said, deadpan.

"Damn right, you wouldn't." Ruda turned around and scowled. "And what the fuck are *you* two grinning at?"

"I'm not grinning," Shaeine said mildly. Sitting beside her on the rock, Teal only grinned wider.

"Morning, everybody," Gabriel said, stumbling sleepily down from the rock and plodding toward them. "I'm almost afraid to even ask how the hell you're all so chipper at this disgusting hour. Hey, Ruda, how're—"

He broke off as Ruda slapped him hard across the face.

"That's Ms. Punaji, *asshole*. I care about that shit now." She cackled gleefully as she snatched up her sword belt and hat, and swaggered back toward their camp.

Gabriel, suddenly wide awake, stared after her with a hand held to the side of his face. "What the *hell*?!" he screeched, turning around, then scowled as his gaze fell on Trissiny. "This is *your* doing!"

"Well," she said, hiding a smile while she retrieved her sword and shield, "it's a start."

"CENTAUR!"

Their heads snapped up in unison at the shout. Juniper was standing on the rim of the crater above, waving to get their attention. Once everyone was looking, she pointed down and to the side, at an area hidden from their view by the rocky slope.

Ruda and Trissiny immediately set off at a run, but they had to navigate around a long arm of the rock formation too steep to climb over with any speed, painfully aware that any four-legged enemy would be long gone by the time they got there. Fortunately, not everyone in the group had the same problem.

Teal erupted upward in a burst of flame, and an instant later Vadrieny was banking over the rocks and diving to the plain beyond, folding her blazing wings around herself as she fell.

Trissiny had longer legs; she pulled ahead despite Ruda taking the inside track around the rocky outcrop. They had to sprint across an open area between that and another long extension of stone; ahead, flashes of orange were just visible over it from Vadrieny's wings. Juniper bounded down the incline ahead of them, then yelped as she lost her footing and went tumbling the rest of the way. They didn't slow to help her; she might not be the most agile member of the party, but she was one of the most durable. Behind them, Gabriel and Shaeine brought up a distant rear.

Ruda was lagging behind and putting too much breath into running even to curse about it by the time Trissiny rounded the next stone barrier and skidded to a halt, taking stock.

The centaur was exactly as she'd always heard them described: a horse with a man's torso sprouting from where its neck should be.

He had wild, bushy hair, and she caught glimpses of a full beard, despite him being faced away from her and trying to escape. Draped over his back was a collection of bags such as a packhorse would carry, with two spears and bristling quivers of arrows visible among his inventory. Geometric designs were tattooed onto his human skin, and appeared to have been *branded* into his hindquarters.

Vadrieny was blocking his frantic efforts to escape. The demon was far more agile and had the advantage of flight; no matter which way he wheeled, she swiftly placed herself in front of him, snarling and flexing her talons. She didn't seem to be attacking, for whatever reason, but was effectively holding him in place.

It was enough.

Ruda charged past her, and Trissiny burst into motion on her heels; the paladin went right and the pirate left. At their approach, the centaur whirled to face them, throwing all his weight onto his front legs for a moment to lash out with his powerful back hooves at Vadrieny. In one hand, he held the broken half of a bow; those hooves seemed to be his only functional weapons.

The maneuver cost him. Vadrieny hopped nimbly back out of his range, but the rearing kick gave the two humans time to close in. Before he could get his footing firmly back, Trissiny dropped to a crouch mid-run, skidding on the grass, and slashed at one foreleg with her full strength. The crack of breaking bone was clearly audible.

With a cry of agony, the centaur stumbled drunkenly to one side, his left front leg out of commission. He brought up the broken half of his bow to club Trissiny; she raised her shield, but before the blow could fall, Ruda reached him and drove the tip of her rapier into his upraised underarm.

From there, it took only a few more slashes and hits to subdue the centaur; finally, the tip of Ruda's sword pressed into his throat seemed to convince him to cease struggling. He glared pure hatred at them, chest heaving with exertion, but making no more aggressive moves.

They had matters pretty much under control by the time the others arrived. Fross got there first, buzzing around the felled centaur in frantic circles. Juniper, Gabe, and Shaeine all came staggering up as a group, the former brushing gravel out of her hair and the other two out of breath. Toby and Professor Rafe were the last to arrive; they had been forced to pick their way down the steeper side of the rock formation to avoid going all the way around.

"What the fuck was *that*?" Ruda demanded as soon as relative calm had descended, scowling at Vadrieny. "You could've finished this fucker off easy."

"Had we been alone, I would have," the demon said, meeting her glare. "But as it was, you were on hand to deal with him. Teal does *not* like it when we hurt people." Having said her piece, she withdrew, flames fading and claws withdrawing to leave Teal standing in her place, looking pale and shaken.

"This'll be a scout," Rafe noted, looking more focused than they'd ever seen him before. "Obviously, we can't let him take word of us back to his . . . group."

"Herd?" Gabriel suggested.

"They'll be curious if he doesn't come back at all," Trissiny warned.

"Yeah," Rafe said, nodding, "but that buys us some time. And they may not. There's no shortage of dangerous crap in the Golden Sea; we've had a pretty gentle time of it, largely because we haven't been screwing around with it. You remember what Ansheh said? Centaurs navigate by twisting the Sea to take them where they want to go. It tends to drop the nastiest stuff it has on them in retaliation. I bet they lose scouts all the time."

"So what do we do with this guy, then?" Juniper asked, stepping up close to the kneeling centaur despite hisses of warning from her classmates. "Should we . . . I dunno, interrogate him for information?"

"*What* information?" Gabriel asked. "The Sea shifts around, and *we* can't make it take us anyplace useful. Knowing where his herd is doesn't do us much good when we can't even know where *we* are."

"So he's not really good for anything, then?" she asked, turning her back to the centaur to face the group.

"Gabe's got the right of it," said Rafe. "Even if we could make him cooperate . . . Well, there's just not much of any use we could learn from him."

"This is a problem!" Fross cried, buzzing around in a tizzy. "Cause we can't really take him with us, and we can't afford to leave him here, and imperial law governing the treatment of prisoners—"

"Meh," Juniper said dismissively, then turned around and smacked the centaur hard in the face. With a sickening *crunch* of pulverized vertebrae, his head was wrenched backward to hang over his spine. He spasmed violently, toppling to one side, legs twitching.

"What the *fuck*?!" Ruda bellowed, barely leaping back out of the way in time. Other voices of shock and protest joined her.

"What?" Juniper looked around at them, apparently baffled. "What's the problem? What else were we gonna do with him?"

"You don't just *kill* a *prisoner*!" Ruda snarled.

"Why *not*? He's only a prisoner if we want to keep him one, right? And we didn't! He was an enemy combatant." The dryad shrugged, frowning around at them. "I don't know what you're all so upset about."

"*That* is what we're upset about," Toby said quietly. "It's important to treat beaten foes with *mercy*, Juniper. That's what separates us from the animals."

"No," she shot back, scowling, "what separates you from the animals is that you burn up resources you don't need doing things that don't contribute to your survival. I've gotta say, this sounds like more of that. Mercy, indeed. The poor thing couldn't even walk anymore."

"That's *not* the *point*!" Ruda shouted. "Yeah, mercy indeed! If someone weaker than you is under your power, you don't fucking *abuse* it!"

"That doesn't make *any* sense!" the dryad retorted, growing increasingly irate. "*None* of you are making any sense! If something wants to kill you, you kill it back, *first*, otherwise you die! I don't *get* why this is so hard for you all to understand! How has your species survived this long if you don't grasp the most basic—"

"All right, enough," said Rafe.

"But she—"

"*Enough*!" They all reared back from the unfamiliar crack of command in his voice. Rafe moderated his tone somewhat, but his expression was still much more resolute than they were used to seeing on him.

"Kids . . . don't argue moral philosophy with fae. Okay? Juniper simply doesn't think the same way the rest of us do. You wanna have this talk, that's great, but do it *later*, when you have time to go around in circles and everybody's not riding an adrenaline high. And Juno, hon, I love you, but don't *do* shit like that, all right? There are rules we have to respect. If you don't know them, let the people who do take the lead. 'Kay?"

"All right," she said in a small voice.

Gabriel cleared his throat. "Well. I was kinda hoping to have another dip in the springs before we left, since we'll probably never see this place again, but . . . I've suddenly got a feeling it would be in our best interests to get the hell out of here."

"No shit," Ruda grunted, wiping blood from her sword with a handful of tallgrass stalks.

"Right," said Rafe, rubbing his hands together and looking a bit more like himself. "Time to break up camp, my little cabbages. I'll get all our crap packed away. Gabe, Ruda, I'm putting you in charge of cleaning up this guy."

"Fuckin' *ew*." Grimacing, Ruda rubbed her hands on her coat as if she could already feel the blood.

"Wait! Are we allowed to do that?" Fross asked shrilly. "We don't know their burial customs! We could be messing up his spirit or something! Isn't it bad enough we killed him?"

"'Scuse me, but *we* didn't kill him," Ruda said.

"Fross, if he'd been here with more of his group, he would have murdered us and looted our corpses," Trissiny said firmly. "In fact, his goal was probably to go *get* more of his friends so they could do just that."

"But what does that have to do with their funerary rites?!" Fross chimed, zipping back and forth in agitation.

"I think what Trissiny means to say," Gabriel said, "if she'll pardon me for presuming, is that we don't give a fuck about their funerary rites. There are enemies who are treated with respect, and then there's *these* guys. Let him rot." Trissiny nodded grudgingly at him.

"O-okay," the pixie said uncertainly. By her continued darting back and forth and soft undercurrent of jangling chimes, she wasn't much reassured.

"Great!" said Rafe cheerfully. "Since we've got that cleared up, I'm gonna give you guys some protective gloves and vials of solution to dispose of him."

"What, some kind of potion that'll make him invisible or something, so the other centaurs can't track him?"

"Yes, Gabriel, just so, in the sense that it's basically a virulent acid which will reduce him to biodegradable goo. Also, don't get any on your skin. Even with two paladins, a cleric, and a dryad on hand, I'm not sure we're packing enough healing to straighten that out."

"Have I mentioned yet today how much I hate your class, Professor?"

"That's the spirit, Punaji! Ten points!"

"*Seriously*, fuck you."

"Right, while they're doing that, I've got a subtler solution for the rest of you to apply to the bottoms of your feet. Also, the hems of any robes, skirts, or anything else that'll be trailing along the ground. It will prevent us from leaving any tracks. I'm not sure it's *possible* for us to be tracked in the Golden Sea, but I'm not taking any risks with something like this. Here, Toby, pass these out. Now if I could just get a hand breaking down the tents, I'll go stuff the rest of our campsite down my pants and we can get movin'. Oh, Fross," he added more somberly, "I'm afraid I don't have anything to conceal pixie tracks. For the good of the group, you'll need to be left behind."

"*What?!*" she squealed. "But that— How?! I don't— It doesn't— What does that—"

"*Don't* make fun of her, you addled degenerate!" Trissiny snapped. "Fross, ignore him. He's trying, at the most inappropriate possible time, to make a joke. We're not leaving anybody behind."

"Okay. Okay. All right." Muttering softly to herself, the pixie darted over to flutter around behind Trissiny.

As they all split up, heading off to their various tasks, Juniper stayed put for a minute, looking down at the fallen centaur, then back after the departing members of the group. She sighed heavily. "I just don't *understand*."

CHAPTER 10

The law came knocking a little after lunch the next day. Fortunately, it was Darling who answered the door. This was not happenstance; the thought of Basra or Andros trying to deal with an imperial marshal without blowing their whole operation made him break out in a cold sweat.

"Afternoon," the man on the step said politely when Darling opened the door, tipping his hat. "I'm Marshal Ross. How're you folks enjoyin' your stay?"

"Splendidly, thanks!" Darling said cheerfully, his mind already racing ahead. He'd prepared for this as best he could, knowing it was coming. "After the big city, Hamlet is a remarkably friendly place."

"By and large, I find that's so," the marshal said agreeably. "I've only lived here a few years myself, but it's easy to settle in. I wonder, though, how much you know about the history of our little town?"

Darling bit back a snide comment; Hamlet was a picturesque but utterly stereotypical frontier town of not more than three hundred people, all plank buildings and dirt streets, which couldn't have been here longer than the empire's push to the very edge of the Golden Sea sixty years ago. He wasn't sure "history" was the right word. Luckily, Marshal Ross went on without waiting for a response.

"We've had a recent spate of pretty big trouble for such a little place," he said, hooking his thumbs into his belt, "which is all the harder to bear because this *is* such a quiet town ordinarily. The demon attack four years ago cost us one of the brightest young spirits any of us knew... June'd be twenty this summer." He sighed heavily before going on. "Then, an uncomfortably short span of days ago, a good half dozen townsfolk, neighbors and friends all, got themselves outed as Black Wreath cultists and took their own lives. The shock from *that* hasn't even properly started to fade yet. What I mean to say is, we're all a little edgy about the strange and unexpected around here."

He glanced past Darling, who half turned his head to follow his gaze. Branwen was visible in the kitchen, singing as she puttered around the stove. Honestly, she was settling into her role with a little too much enthusiasm to be feigned; he was starting to wonder if she harbored a secret desire to be a housewife. Closer to hand, though, was Andros in the living room. He had a thick book open and had been reading, but was now staring unblinking at the conversation taking place at the door. The huge, hairy, keen-eyed man had never yet managed to look at someone without glaring.

"Four rich folks who are clearly not related renting out the old Moorville house and then settling in on no business in particular... Well, that's strange and unexpected."

"Is this an official visit, then, Marshal?" Darling asked mildly.

He shook his head. "As of this moment, this is me stopping by for a friendly chat. I'd love nothing more than some assurance I won't need to make an official visit."

"Wonderful! Maybe you wouldn't mind taking a little stroll with me, Marshal? I've seen the sights, but it's always good to have an experienced guide along."

The man nodded slowly. "Maybe that wouldn't be a bad idea."

Darling thought rapidly as they stepped down from the porch and out into the street. This was complicated by the Archpope's firm orders that they not reveal their affiliation with the Church. He didn't want to outright lie to a man who had a direct line to Imperial Command. Between the proliferation of the scrolltower network and the imperial bureaucracy itself, the marshal could get confirmation or disproof of any story Darling told him within a few days. Long enough for them to finish their business and go . . . maybe.

"I can see how it'd be hard for us to slip in and out unnoticed," he said lightly once they were out in the street. In fact, the main street of Hamlet terminated directly at the front gate of their rented house. Darling would have preferred something a lot more circumspect, but apparently it was the only available space adequate for their needs.

"Old man Moorville had quite the opinion of himself," the marshal said, strolling along beside him. "To be fair, he did work his way up from ranch hand to cattle baron without stepping on any more faces than he had to, and it's thanks to his herds that we even have a town. Always very particular about getting the proper respect, though. Had to have his house right there where everybody had to see it . . . And then when he got rich enough to envy the lords and ladies of the home province, well, a two-story wooden house just wasn't good enough anymore, so off he went to join them. To speak the plain truth, he makes a better neighbor when he's a thousand miles away."

Darling laughed obligingly.

The marshal gave him a keen sidelong look. "So, what brings you to his old home, then?"

"My name is Antonio Darling," he said. "I'm a member of a council tasked with overseeing imperial security at the highest level."

"Omnu's *balls*," the marshal groaned. "I thought the empire was done stomping around here."

"Oh, don't ask me," Darling said easily, "I'm on vacation." It was true, technically; he'd left notice with the Church and the council and everyone that he'd be gone for a week. The Church, of course, already knew (and he'd been more forthright with Tricks and the Guild), but there was merit in leaving the proper paper trail.

"On vacation," Marshal Ross said flatly, "in Hamlet."

"Yes, just some friends and I taking a little time away from the rigors of city life to enjoy the local scenery. We have *no* official business here whatsoever."

"And unofficial business?"

He was silent for a moment as they strolled along, apparently gathering his thoughts. Truthfully, it was just for dramatic effect; his thoughts were never ungathered.

"I understand you met Professor Tellwyrn." This got a noncommittal grunt, so he pressed on. "What's she like? I've always wondered."

"Quite frankly? Scary. She... has her moments, though."

Most people might have missed the faint color rising in Ross's cheeks and the deliberate way he avoided the other man's gaze, but Darling analyzed people the way most people breathed, and he found himself forced to repress his amusement. *Why, Arachne, you sly dog.*

"So she shows up, pokes around the town for half a day, outs and then kills a bunch of cultists, and then takes off the next morning, having left the impression of shock and awe she usually does. Am I more or less right?"

"More... or less."

He nodded. "It's hard to analyze the motives and methods of people like that. You can never put it completely out of your head how *beyond* you they are... which makes it tricky to see their weaknesses, unless you go looking for them. The weakness is always there, though, if you do. In Arachne Tellwyrn's case, it's her over reliance on brute-force tactics."

The marshal made no reply, but glanced at him again, showing his attention. Darling went on in the same blithe tone. "I'm not saying she's unintelligent, because that clearly isn't true. But she's the most powerful known wizard by a wide margin, not to mention a more than competent fighter, and those are the traits she uses the most. Her plans are bluntly straightforward, and subtler things... slip her notice. Like, for example, the rest of the Black Wreath in this town."

At that, Marshal Ross came to a stop and turned to face him, glaring. They were right in front of the town's general store; Darling glanced about at the people passing by, who were failing to conceal their interest in the two. "It sure does get hot out here on the plains," he said lightly. "You wouldn't happen to know someplace shady we could continue this chat?"

Ross glanced about, too, clearly taking note of the townsfolk and imagining the result of having this particular discussion in their listening vicinity. He jerked his head to the right and set off again, Darling trailing along behind.

They came to the town jail a few doors down, marked by a hand-painted sign and the imperial flag. Ross led the way inside, where a young man was lounging behind a desk, smoking a cigarette and reading a magazine.

"Rusty, take a little walk," the marshal said curtly. The youth looked up at him, then at Darling—who grinned cheerily—then stood up and slipped outside without a word. Ross closed the front door, then the one opposite it, which led to a hallway lined by cell bars. They were left in a narrow front office, sparsely furnished with battered wooden chairs, a big desk, and behind that a wall full of dented file cabinets. Ross stepped around behind the desk and seated himself, setting his hat atop a cabinet.

"So what," he asked grimly, "makes the empire think there are still Black Wreath in this town after Tellwyrn cleared them out? And why the hell didn't all the other imperial agents who've been through here in the last two months say or do anything about it?"

"Oh, I wouldn't presume to know what the empire thinks about anything," Darling replied, pulling over a ladderback chair and seating himself. "I'm just a guy on vacation, remember? But, hypothetically, think about it. Wreath cultists are ninety percent dumb, ordinary folks who like feeling naughty but have no idea what they're screwing around with. Maybe one or two in an entire cell will be actual diabolists . . . Not to mention they keep their numbers low in a given area for obvious reasons like blending in. There's a *lot* about the Wreath cell in Hamlet that was strange. There were too many, for one thing, they had been supplied with dwarven technology that even the empire is only just beginning to implement, every last one of them was willing to sacrifice themselves . . . That's not the general run of cultist nonsense. Those were people on a *mission*, one for which they'd trained and been equipped."

"I'm still not hearing how this adds up to there being more of them."

"If you were running a cell of well-trained, well-equipped agents, Marshal, would you throw *all* of them at the first problem to rear its head?" He gave that a silent moment to sink in, watching Ross's face grow longer. "I see two scenarios, depending on whether they knew who Tellwyrn was when they struck. Either they didn't, and she was just some elf needing to be silenced, in which case excessive force wasn't needed and would have risked drawing attention, or they *did*, and would never have gambled the lives of every agent they had against her. Hell, I'm leaning toward the former; the Wreath has tended to give her a wide berth when they know she's coming. She and Elilial have a history."

"They didn't know," Ross said curtly. Darling nodded.

"Then . . . It hardly makes sense to assume they're all gone, then, does it?"

"Son of a *bitch!*" The man slammed a fist down on his desk. "Those people were *friends*. Neighbors, at the very least. Now you're telling me that even more of *my* townsfolk are . . ."

"I'm telling you it's likely," Darling said evenly. "More than that, I'm hardly in a position to know."

"I don't know how much more this town can take," the marshal said gloomily, his anger of a moment ago dissipating rapidly; though, even as he slumped in his chair, a spark of a glare ignited behind his eyes, directed at Darling. "I'm sure as hell not gonna thank you for bringing more trouble to my town."

"I haven't brought anything. Either the trouble's here, or it's not. If it's not, well . . . My friends and I will spend a relaxing few days enjoying the peace and quiet before we have to head back to our various dull office jobs. If it *is* . . . I have a suspicion our vacation will be interrupted very soon."

The marshal dragged a hand over his face, staring glumly into the distance. "Fuck."

"You said you weren't from here, originally," Darling said mildly. "I wonder if that means you'd have friends from other parts of the empire? The sort of friends who are unquestionably loyal to their emperor, and have wands. You may want to pass along a recommendation from me:

It's a good time of year to take a week or so off, and Hamlet is a surprisingly pleasant spot to spend some free time."

"You're suggesting men like that are going to come in handy soon."

"Men like that *always* come in handy," Darling said, smiling disarmingly. "I just have a hunch that pretty soon Hamlet's Black Wreath problem will be over, one way or another."

For some reason, that didn't seem to make the marshal happy.

Hearing raised voices even through the door, Darling quickened his pace at the porch, hustling inside. The scene within didn't surprise him.

Basra and Andros were less than a foot apart, staring each other down. The hulking Shaathist was physically the more intimidating, but even though she had to crane her neck to meet his gaze, Basra didn't look remotely cowed. In fact, she grinned wickedly into his glare.

"Antonio," Branwen said in obvious relief, standing in the doorway to the kitchen. "What happened is—"

"Thanks, love, but I know what happened."

"What, you were lurking just outside?" Basra said, turning her grin on him. Something about her eyes was just unsettling. "Naughty, naughty."

"No," Darling replied evenly, "but I'm acquainted with you two, and neither of you are full of surprises. Bas, go check on our guest."

Her grin widened. "What's the magic word?"

"*Now.*" The grin vanished from her face; he pushed on before she could make another remark. "Have I ever given you a direct order before? Honestly, Bas, usually I can trust you to see what needs doing and do it without having to be told. If you're going to act like a child, however, I will *speak* to you like one. That, or we can go back to the previous option, which I liked better. Your call."

She stared at him for a long moment through narrowed eyes, then turned on her heel and flounced off through the kitchen, shouldering Branwen aside.

"As for you," Darling said to Andros, who glared mutely at him, "same goes. You're a grown-ass man, Andros; have some basic self-control. If you don't respond to her needling, she'll get bored and quit doing it."

"I will *not* be treated with disrespect by that *woman*," he growled.

"Yeah, you probably will be. Look at it this way: Getting a rise out of you is Basra's way of asserting dominance. If you don't let her goad you, she can't win."

"Where I'm from, we have ways of dealing with women who won't learn their place," the huntsman rumbled, but his tone was more subdued. After two days, Darling was growing used to the subtle gradients of his growling and snarling, and interpreted this as evidence that Andros had at least absorbed his message. Hopefully it would stick.

"How did it go with the marshal?" Branwen asked brightly.

"Well enough," he said. "I managed to deflect his attention without revealing anything. He's under the impression that we're here on imperial business, so nobody do anything to rock the boat." In truth, he'd somewhat exceeded his mandate in making suggestions as strong as he had, but Darling was the expert in navigating social and political tensions; that was why he'd been placed in charge. This would all be so much easier—and quicker—if they could just reveal that they were agents of the Church, but he had his orders.

The reason behind that particular order was a puzzle he was still teasing out.

"I knew you'd take care of it," she said warmly, gazing up at him with limpid eyes. Andros snorted loudly and returned to his seat and his book.

"That's what I do, pet," Darling replied cheerfully, chucking her under the chin as he slipped past her into the kitchen, and getting a flirtatious giggle in return.

The solitude and close confines were wearing on all of them. It wasn't Branwen or even Andros who were causing most of the trouble, though, which frankly surprised him. Despite Andros's generally surly demeanor and the fact that his cult had deep doctrinal conflicts with all of theirs, the huntsman was mostly content to be left to himself, working through the surprisingly substantial library that came with the furnished house. Basra, however, was pushing her luck. Where Branwen dealt with stress by baking and Andros by retreating into himself, Basra did so by picking at people until she got a reaction.

The door to the cellar swung open and the Avenist herself stepped out, giving him an ironic look. "Our boy's snug as a proverbial bug in a rug; no problems with the circle. Same as it's been every time previously."

"Smashing. I believe I'll go have a look."

"I literally *just*—"

"Yes," he said soothingly, "and I don't doubt your assessment. But we've been looking in on him at half-hour intervals for nearly a whole day now. Sshitherossz are trickster demons; I don't want him getting a handle on any consistent pattern he can try to manipulate."

"Oh, please," she scoffed. "What could he possibly manipulate from inside that circle?"

"I can't imagine, and that's what spooks me. The first step to getting outmaneuvered by a demon is letting yourself believe it's not dangerous. Be right back."

He shut the door behind him as he stepped into the gloom of the cellar, as per their established house rule. Despite Andros's wards and the general unlikeliness of any of the locals barging in here, there was no limit to the hell that would break loose if anybody found out they were keeping a demon in the basement. Some things were simply not to be risked.

The only light now came from the glowing circle. It was adequate to navigate the room, though the effect was eerie.

"What's this?" the occupant of the circle asked wryly, not getting up from his seat on the ground. "Two for one? Why, I'm downright flattered! Oh, it's just the poncy one, though. I was hoping for that chesty redhead again, but eh . . . You're not bad." He grinned viciously and made a twirling motion with one clawed finger. "Spin for me; let me get a good look."

Darling made a show of pacing around the circle slowly, studying it. Despite being made of fine powder that should be easily disturbed by the faintest breeze, it was intact and unchanged. Once imbued with the kind of magic that coursed through it, it took on a solid integrity of its own. Not that he couldn't wreck the whole thing with a carelessly placed foot, of course.

"I think you're the one they all hate the most," the Sshitherossz went on airily. "Ah, the burdens of leadership! I wonder how long it'll be before they—" He broke off as Darling burst out laughing.

"Oh, please. Really? 'They're all plotting against you?' I'm almost insulted. Tell you what, skippy, you can go back to sitting alone in the dark and think about your tactics. Next time I come down here, I want to hear some *quality* manipulation." He turned his back on the creature and began ascending the ladder.

"What do you *want?*" the demon snarled, its calm facade shattering. It bounded upright, slamming both fists against the invisible barrier and causing them to spark. "Who the fuck summons a demon and doesn't *do* anything with him? Damn it, don't just leave me *sitting* in here!"

Darling paused at the top of the ladder and turned to wink at him before climbing out and shutting the door. Behind, the creature cursed him at the top of its lungs. He didn't need to speak its infernal language to recognize cursing.

"Ooh, cookies! Ow!" He rubbed his knuckles, staring reproachfully at Branwen as she waggled the spoon with which she'd rapped them.

"You let those cool or you'll just burn yourself. You can wait fifteen minutes, Antonio."

"Ah, how we suffer." He sighed. Standing in the doorway to the kitchen, Basra snorted.

"If I were going to complain—"

"You? Perish the thought."

"—I wouldn't start with the cookies. We're all going nuts here, Antonio. How much longer are we just going to sit on our hands?"

"I'm giving it three days," he said. "It's a nice round number."

"Three is *not* a round number."

"A significant one, then. Any practicing diabolists in this town would have been aware of the summoning when we cast it. That'll give them time to organize and investigate. They'll be keeping their senses alert and the circle doesn't block scrying, so they'll know the creature is still on the premises. If we haven't been approached, one way or another, within three days, we'll give up this spot and try our luck at the next attack site."

"I don't understand why we didn't start with the one where the Falconer girl was taken," she said. "Nobody ever found the cultists in that region, but they've got to be there. They *succeeded*, which means they're the best of the lot, the most likely to be useful."

"And the most likely to be dangerous," Branwen murmured, working her spoon in a bowl full of batter. Gods above, was she baking something *again*?

"That," Darling said, nodding, "plus the fact that they succeeded changes the game. Vadrieny was looked over by several actual deities, in addition to Church priests, and her amnesia appears to be genuine. We want to move *very* carefully in areas where we may trip over whatever strings still tie her to Hell. The Church is assuming that the deaths of the other six archdemons means the Wreath failed to provide adequate hosts, and that Vadrieny's trauma is more of the same. However, it's not impossible that her memories are meant to be restored later."

Basra grinned crookedly. "All the more reason to set that off *now*, rather than wait for them to be ready. Let the demon be Tellwyrn's problem; I wish I could be there to take bets."

"You're a bloodthirsty little thing, aren'cha?"

Her grin widened. "Watch who you're calling 'little.'"

"Oh," he assured her, smiling calmly, "I am."

In the dead of night, the door creaked. A slim crack of illumination opened at the top of the steep steps, though between the darkness of the silent house and the burning circle in the basement, the difference was barely noticeable. A dark shape blotted out the light in the crack for a moment, then the door eased the rest of the way open, and it stepped down onto the stairs.

She was a plump woman in her middle years, clad in a simple dress suitable for a farmwife, clutching a candleholder on which stood a single unlit taper. Her broad, plain face was clenched in a mask of suspicion; she peered carefully around the dark cellar, not reacting to the spell circle or its occupant.

It was a nearly empty room. Aside from the circle, there was only an upturned shipping crate against the far wall with one of the kitchen chairs dragged over beside it, and an oversized armoire against the right wall from the steps, its glossy finish and ornate carvings incongruous in the plain, dusty basement. Apparently satisfied with what she saw, she began descending the stairs.

"It's a traaaa-aap," the demon sang, grinning at her.

"Silence," she hissed, pausing on the upper steps to glance back through the open kitchen door. "Where are your masters?"

"In Hell," he replied with a chuckle. "In about three seconds when you're feeling *really* stupid, remember I did warn you."

"Wh—" She broke off with a cry, receiving a hard shove from behind, and tumbled forward down the steps.

"*Careful*," Darling protested, popping into view as he deactivated his invisibility charm. "We need people able to answer questions! That means with unbroken necks." There came a characteristic grunt from Andros at the top of the stairs.

"Oh, she's fine," Basra said dismissively, likewise appearing in the opposite corner and striding over to the fallen woman. Branwen joined them from the back of the room.

"Oh, hey, it's Mrs. Harkley!" Basra said cheerfully, having grabbed a fistful of the woman's hair and wrenched her head back to reveal her face. With her other hand, she had adroitly twisted one of her captive's arms and was effortlessly holding her down. "You remember, the nice lady who brought us the cherry pie? Come to borrow a cup of sugar, neighbor?" She grinned far too broadly. "We'll forgive you the late hour. I'm sure you have *lots* of fascinating things to tell us."

"I'll tell you *nothing*!" Mrs. Harkley spat.

"You're mistaken," Basra said gleefully. "And I'm disappointed. What, no attempts to dissemble? You heard a noise and were investigating, fearing for our safety? You're not even gonna *try*? Come on, there are traditions to this game! It's no fun if you won't play."

The woman spat a word in a harsh, guttural language, and the darkness around her intensified, then solidified, forming into spikes.

Just as quickly, they shattered and disintegrated as all four priests blazed with divine light, driving every shadow from the room.

"Hey!" the demon protested, shielding his eyes with an oversized hand. "Do you mind? Do you *know* what time it is? People are trying to sleep here!"

"All right, that's enough of that nonsense out of you," Darling said lightly, crouching beside Mrs. Harkley's head on the floor and meeting her dumbfounded stare. "I don't suppose you'd like to be helpful and tell us how many of your cell are still in this town?"

Her expression of shock melted into one of pure stubbornness. She clamped her lips firmly shut.

"Ah well, it was worth a try." With a regretful sigh, he stood, brushing off his knees. "Into the box she goes, ladies."

"You think I'm afraid of you?" Mrs. Harkley spat. "You're not the first clerics who came to this town looking for trouble. There's more trouble here for you than you can handle."

"You should worry about the trouble *elsewhere*," Darling informed her. "Nobody here will harm you."

"Aw..."

"*Nobody*," he repeated firmly, giving Basra a flat look. "No, we're just going to put you on ice, so to speak, till we're ready to transport you back home. The people who'll be asking the questions are *very* good at getting answers."

"The others will come for me!" she shrieked, unable to keep the panic out of her voice.

"Of course they will, duckling," he said soothingly. "Really, I'm not being sarcastic—I fully believe your friends will come. And unless they're a lot smarter than *you* are, we'll be returning to Tiraas with a full set."

CHAPTER 11

He stepped calmly from the Rail caravan and looked around, resting the butt of his staff on the stone platform. Around him rose Last Rock, a collection of plain stone buildings that weren't old but would not have looked out of place in a bygone era. Aside from the modern dress of the people passing by, and the scrolltower perched at one edge of the square, it could have been a painting of a medieval village.

To his right, another man weakly extracted himself from another caravan, clutching the edge of its door for support briefly before wobbling out onto the platform. Listing from a combination of dizziness and a limp—probably freshly acquired—he stumbled toward the tavern at one side of the square, its sign proclaiming it the Ale & Wenches.

He snorted. Pretentious. The kind of name designed to sucker in fools who went treasure hunting in the Golden Sea and called themselves "adventurers," as though they were dungeon delvers of old.

"Made the trip all right?"

He looked to the left, finding himself approached by a towering, burly man with an impressive mustache in an old, faded Imperial Army coat. His expression was solicitous, but stern.

"Well enough," he said easily. Tucking his staff into the crook of one arm, he reached into his coat and pulled out a small cigar case, carefully selected a cigarillo, and lit it by tapping the end against the head of his staff, this whole display giving the big man time to look him over carefully. He knew the way of these small towns.

His appearance, as he was well aware, invited scrutiny. The tan leather duster he wore was old, scarred, and even burnt in places, as was his matching flat-brimmed hat. Around his neck was a sweat-stained bandana, and his boots, though of fine quality, had been with him long enough to bear their own scars, too deep to be healed with polish. Beneath all that, though, his suit, while also dusty and rumpled from travel, was presentable. Much as it galled him to admit it, his age was an asset. Nobody seemed to expect trouble from a well-lined face framed by steely gray whiskers.

"I think that other fellow came off it a bit worse than I," he said mildly, jerking his head toward the man who was even now limping through the A&W's doors.

The big man had fixed his eyes on the lighting of the cigarillo with a faint frown, but apparently decided he passed muster. "That's Jethro; he comes through here every couple weeks. Works with some bank in Tiraas, has some business with the University. After a whiskey he'll be good as new. I'm Ox. Welcome to Last Rock, stranger."

"McGraw." Clenching the cigarillo between his teeth, he took the proffered hand and shook it firmly. "Good to know you."

The crack of the Rail reigniting its transit matrix sounded; a static buzz washed over them, and his arcane senses were momentarily blinded by the activation of complex, powerful enchantments so close in proximity. It passed quickly, though, as the caravan accelerated away and was soon lost to view.

"Damn fool contraption," Ox grunted. "I dunno why the empire lets people ride those things. They kill a couple dozen a year, as I understand it."

"Control," McGraw said simply, puffing at his cigarillo. Ox raised an eyebrow. "I was around when the Rails were new, got to ride in some of the very first caravans. They had safety harnesses.

The cargo cars still do—all kinds of straps and buckles to hold things steady. Despite what the empire likes to say, those things were *not* meant to move troops. They were for moving adventurers, specifically to the frontier."

"Never heard that," said Ox, frowning.

"Suppose, friend, you're in charge of running some rats through a maze. You want 'em to go a specific way, get 'em to the end where you want 'em. Now what's a better use of your energies—trying to herd and heckle each one along, or move the walls such that they naturally lead where you want?" He glanced over at his new acquaintance; Ox was studying him more closely now, his eyes narrowed. He grinned, teeth clutching his cigarillo. "The world is run by a certain kind of men, my friend. Be it the crowned kings of old or the bureaucrats of today, they're well-fed men in expensive suits, who have no idea what it means to risk your neck and bust your ass workin' for a living. To governments, rats in a maze is all we are. The empire was modernizing, moving from a chaotic, loot-based economy to one of systems, structures, and laws. Shunting off the well-armed loners to the last place guaranteed to grind 'em up en masse served two purposes—getting *them* out of society, and helping to push back the frontiers as far as they can *be* pushed, so society has room to expand. Thus, crazy rattletrap Rails, fit for those willing to risk their necks, but sure to discourage the saner, calmer breed who they want to stay in the cities and pay their taxes. It was . . . elegant, really."

"That's . . . an interesting theory," Ox said noncommittally when he finished.

He shrugged. "And I may be wrong. Wouldn't be the first time. A funny thing, though . . . There are hardly any adventures or adventurers left these days. Lo and behold, the Rails are getting upgraded. The ones serving the interior provinces are downright comfy now, safe as your mother's arms. Last I heard, the schedule they're on, even these frontier lines will have full safety features within two years."

"Well, whatever the empire's motives, *that* I can get behind. All I know is, these Rail cars are insane. Sooner they get straightened out, the better."

"On that we can agree."

"What brings you to Last Rock?"

"Oh, I'm just stopping in on my way elsewhere," he said easily. "I heard a friend of mine might be loitering in this town and thought I'd see if I could catch him. Name of Shook? Greasy-lookin' fellow, cheap suit . . . Ostensibly a salesman, but I'll lay odds he's not been seen trying to sell jack shit to anybody."

"I know him," Ox replied slowly. His increasingly serious expression told McGraw this was, indeed, the place. "He don't cause any trouble, just hangs around the A&W, playing cards and drinkin'. Seems to be an acquaintance of Prin's."

"Prin? That wouldn't be Principia Locke? Brunette wood elf?"

"You know Prin, too?" Now, Ox looked downright leery.

"Only by reputation. We have acquaintances in common, you might say."

"You're not reassurin' me, McGraw. Shook's not good for much that I can see, but like I said, he's no trouble. Prin's another matter. I'm not sure Last Rock needs any more of her 'friends' moving in."

"Oh, don't worry none about me," McGraw said, grinning around his cigarillo. "Like I said, I don't aim to be here long. Just to pay my respects, and then I'll be on my way. You attached to the law in this town, by any chance?"

"There's no budget for a paid deputy," Ox rumbled, "but I help out Sheriff Sanders when help's needed. I live on a pension; I've got the free time."

"That's good to hear, friend, good to hear. Do give the sheriff my regards, won't you?" He puffed smoke contentedly for a moment, jabbing his cigarillo in the direction of the A&W. "How're the accommodations over yonder?"

"Clean. Food's good, whiskey's . . . plentiful. Ain't a quiet place, though; that's the common watering hole for the University kids and every wannabe hero who passes through on the way in or out of the Sea."

"Perfect. I believe I'll arrange a bed for the night. These old bones don't look forward to another Rail ride any sooner than they have to."

"I'll let the sheriff know you're in town, then," Ox said firmly. There was no mistaking the warning in his tone. McGraw just smiled at him. "Do that, friend. Perhaps I'll see you around."

No one had ever accused the Ale & Wenches of false advertising. There *was* ale, technically, though frontier tastes being as they were, the A&W did more business in whiskey and beer. As for the other part, the serving girls did indeed dress in medieval-style attire, prominently featuring low-bodiced peasant dresses and blouses. There was also invariably at least one burly man with a cudgel and a wand on duty, but they rarely had time to step in, even when the need arose. In a town the size of Last Rock, every one of those girls was the daughter of someone's friend or neighbor. The University kids knew to treat them politely; out-of-towners seldom had to be told twice.

Despite the way expectations thus yielded to the reality of modern life, the A&W remained a perennial favorite of the students and the would-be heroes who passed through town, because it played perfectly to their fantasies. The fairy lamps illuminating the common room were of the flickery old style rather than steadier modern versions, and they were housed behind yellow-tinted glass that made their light resemble that of torches. Maps, hunting trophies, and old, well-used, bladed weapons decorated the walls, and the room itself was of rough timber and plaster with fieldstone accents, just like the illustrations of taverns in modern books full of old stories.

Principia loved it here.

She didn't push the swinging doors open and stand in them—aside from being mindful of the cliche, it wasn't her habit to be the center of attention unless a specific con required it. Usually there was better hunting to be had in blending in. But she did, as usual, slip to one side of the doors and treat herself to a moment of soaking in the ambiance. This was just like old times. The Age of Adventures was already stumbling toward its slow end by the time she'd started her career, but she was still old enough to have been in a few adventurer bars—the *real* ones. Those were some of her happiest memories.

But that was then, this was now, and she was on a particularly unforgiving deadline. The reminder of her straits soured some of her nostalgic pleasure, and she narrowed her focus to the night's business.

It was after sundown on a Friday, and the A&W was predictably busy, but she had no trouble zeroing in on her targets; they were ensconced at the largest table in the place. The three privates stood out in their navy blue army uniforms, and were keeping company with a couple of the more exotic University kids. Chase and Tanq blended in as they would in any group of miscellaneous humans, but Hildred, a honey-blond dwarf girl, and especially Natchua made for a more distinctive sight. There was a card game in progress, as well as tankards and pitchers and platters of the A&W's simple but good finger food.

Prin took a moment to consider her approach. She needed those boys' interest, and first impressions were vitally important.

"Hey! PRIN!" Chase waved at her, grinning delightedly. "Perfect timing, get that perky butt over here!"

Her sly smile wasn't entirely faked. Once in a while, fortune *did* favor her.

She threaded her way nimbly through the crowd, pulled out a chair between two of the soldiers and plopped down. "What's this, then, you started without me? Now my feelings are hurt. Somebody better buy me something to compensate."

"Something shiny or something alcoholic?" Tanq asked with a grin.

"That'll do for a start!"

She received a smiling greeting from Hildred and a glare from Natchua, which she knew by now not to take personally. It *wasn't* personal, and wasn't even the usual hostility that drow often held toward surface elves and vice versa; Natchua was simply, as usual, trying for the "brooding badass" look, and, as usual, managing only to come off as surly. The three soldier boys all eyed Prin with interest.

"Well, hello," she purred at them. "I don't believe you've had the pleasure."

"Not so far," said the swarthy one to her right, grinning. "Am I going to?"

"*I* haven't," Chase complained. "Rumor has it that makes me the only one in town."

"Funny thing is," she said airily, setting a stack of copper coins on the table, "he keeps saying things like that to me, and yet appears to think he's going to get somewhere. Deal me in."

"I am very stupid," Chase agreed, nodding solemnly. "This is known."

It was a good group to work. Chase and Rook, the soldier with the olive complexion, were jokers and talkers, keeping conversation going. Finchley, Hildred, and Tanq were quieter, but affable; Natchua and Moriarty were too sullen and stiff, respectively, to contribute much, but that was fine. A group that size would have been chaos with everybody talking over each other. Prin could apply her charm in chaos—she could apply it anywhere, but chaos was less than ideal.

A few hands and a pitcher of beer were enough for her to get the measure of her targets. Moriarty she dismissed as a prospect to leverage. Not that she couldn't do it, but guys like him required a lot of effort and very particular tactics, which she had neither time nor inclination to pursue. Finchley and Rook were likelier prospects, though their personalities demanded such different approaches that she wouldn't really be able to work both at one time. Luckily, she'd placed herself right between them at the table, and both kept giving her eyes of interest. Prin didn't devote great time or attention to her looks; sometimes, in company like this, being an elf was all it took.

Half an hour after sitting down, she'd settled on Rook as her best prospect, as he was clearly the more careless of them. Getting useful intel on Tellwyrn out of him here, now, during a loud poker game, wasn't really an option, but she had plenty of room to strike up a rapport to be leveraged later. This couldn't all be done in one night.

Hopefully that would be enough to keep Thumper off her for a while longer.

She had just gotten down to a seriously, slowly escalating campaign of subtle touches and flirtatious glances when a man stepped up to their table.

"Evenin', folks," he said, tipping his hat politely. "This a closed game or can an old wanderer join in? Ain't had a good round of cards in far too long."

"Glad to have you, stranger!" Chase said cheerily without waiting to get anybody else's opinion. "I don't mind taking your money if you don't mind donating."

"Much obliged." The old man pulled over an unoccupied chair from a nearby table and seated himself beside Hildred.

"Another hand like that last one, Chase, and you'll be out of it for the night," Tanq warned.

"Nonsense, I'll just tap into my reserves."

"You asked us not to let you do that. Remember?"

"Oh, I say lots of things. You should always listen to what I'm saying *now*. Past me was naive and innocent, and future me will probably be drunk."

Prin appraised the new arrival silently. He had the dark complexion of a Westerner and was clearly well along in years. The ragged old coat and hat gave off a certain impression, but the staff gave another one entirely. That was no mass-produced soldier's weapon, but an old, hand crafted object polished to a dull glow, surmounted by a short obelisk of smoky quartz in an asymmetrical iron setting. There was no clicker, or any mechanism to activate it, meaning its owner did so mentally. Even from across the table she could feel the haze of arcane energy around the thing and its owner.

He caught her looking and nodded politely, giving her a small smile. She returned an equally stiff one.

Their game resumed mostly unchanged. The stranger, who gave his name simply as McGraw, was on the quieter side, or at least seemed so in comparison with some of the others at the table, though he wasn't shy about joking along, and quickly endeared himself to the party by paying for his own drinks rather than partaking of what was already on hand. Principia let him be, pursuing her own game, which was also going well. Finchley seemed a bit put out at the lack of her attention, but Rook was clearly quite interested.

She felt a little wistful, in truth. It was a good night—food, drink, noise, and the company of friends and cheerful strangers. It would have been nice to simply enjoy it.

McGraw caught the elbow of a serving girl the next time his tankard was empty, beckoning her closer, and murmured a message into her ear along with his order. She smiled, nodded, and gave him a pat on the shoulder as she straightened, then trotted off. Prin seemed to be the only one paying attention to this exchange; again, he caught her looking, acknowledging her with that private little smile.

"What is it you do, McGraw?" Chase asked without looking up from his cards.

"For starters, I take coin from smug kids who try to distract me from considering my bets."

Chase laughed in response to that. "Well, that must keep you busy. I was just curious—you've got sort of the look of an adventurer, but most of those around here are, ah . . ."

"Younger?" McGraw said dryly. "By a good thirty years' minimum, I'd say, yeah. Heh, been a while since anybody accused me of having 'the look.' Guess it clings to a man."

"So you *were* an adventurer, then?" Natchua asked, giving him what she probably thought was a piercing look. It made her look nauseous. Not for the first time, Principia felt an urge to pull the girl aside and give her a few pointers on acting.

"One of the last," McGraw mused, staring down at his cards without really focusing on them. "When I was your age, a body could still make an actual living roaming about, slaying monsters, and looting ruins. Not as good of one as previous generations, of course . . . Even then, the end had already begun, so to speak. The times sure are changin' . . . I had a couple of good scores, though, enough to set me up. Good thing, too, since there ain't much room for my kind in the world of today."

"I wish you'd explain that to Professor Tellwyrn," Hildred commented, taking a sip of her beer. "I think she's trying to train us up for a new Age of Adventures, sometimes."

"With regrets, little lady, I'll leave you to deal with that on your own," McGraw said with a wry smile, tipping his hat to her. "I managed to have a full career without bein' in a room with Arachne Tellwyrn or any of her ilk, and I'm long past being foolish enough to be disappointed by it. Anyhow, I fold, and I'll have to wish you kids good night." Grunting softly, he rose from his chair, leaning for a moment on his staff. "Get to be my age, you find yourself heading to bed at decent hours whether you want to or not. Enjoy my coin, kids, and thanks for the game."

"Cheers!" Chase said, suiting the words with a lifted mug, which he then drained.

McGraw looked directly across the table at Principia. "Actually, if I could borrow you for a moment, Miss Keys? Won't take long."

She did not freeze like a startled rabbit, nor allow any emotion to show on her face except mild confusion. She was too old, too practiced, and too *good* for that. "Wh—is that me?" she asked blankly. "I think you have me confused with somebody else."

"I might, at that," he said agreeably. "Wouldn't be the first time. I'd be mighty grateful if you'd spare a moment to correct me, lest I waste an evening barkin' up the wrong tree."

"Eh . . . sure, I'll sit this hand out." She leaned over to Rook with a smile, placing a friendly hand on his arm. "I'll be right back. Don't let Chase steal my coins."

"Shock! Outrage! I would never!"

"Cause you can't *reach* 'em from over there."

"Precisely!"

She stepped smoothly around the table and wrapped herself around McGraw's free arm, simpering up at him. Keep your enemies closer; that applied double to casters. Besides, she might ignite a spark of jealousy in Rook that she could make use of later. "So," she said at a good volume as she led him away, mostly for the benefit of the group, "tell me about this *clearly* attractive and talented acquaintance of yours. You know, I believe I've been approached by friends of every dark-haired elf on the continent; we really do all look alike to some people! I wonder what she would say."

"I'm curious to find that out myself," he said more quietly, gently steering them toward the only remotely private spot in the common room, a relatively shady nook under the stairs of the second-floor balcony. He had clearly identified it in advance, and timed his approach for a moment when there was nobody in there having a quick grope. That, plus the fact that the arm coiled up in hers was corded with lean muscle belying his apparent age, made her consider him a bit more carefully. This one was more than he appeared.

"If you will indulge me in wasting a bit of your time, ma'am, in the interest of not repeating myself, I'd like to wait for—ah, never mind! Speak of the devil."

Rounding the bottom of the steps into their shadowy alcove stepped the last person she wanted to see at that moment.

"Why, Jeremiah," Prin said coolly, "I was *specifically* not expecting to see you this evening."

"Always a pleasure, Miss Locke," Shook replied dryly. "I was just informed by one of the girls that a patron was asking after me down here? You look to have found him."

"Indeed, at least we're all gathered," McGraw said agreeably, gently disengaging himself from Principia. "My apologies for interrupting your respective evenings. It was a bit of a bother to follow you all the way from Tiraas, Mr. Shook, and regretfully, I didn't manage in time to grab a word with you on the way. Regardless, and you may well call me a relic of an older age for this, which would be fair enough, but I feel if you're going to kill somebody, you owe it to 'em to look 'em in the eyes first. Seems to me what little nobility there was in battle went out of it when we moved from blades and armor to magic bursts from a hundred yards away."

They both stared at him blankly for a moment. Prin eased a step away from him. ". . . I'm sorry, I think I must've misheard you."

"That's one of the great peculiarities common to all sapient beings, I find," McGraw said, reaching into his coat to pull out a thin cigar case. As he continued speaking, he withdrew a cigarillo, lit it by pressing the tip against the quartz head of his staff, and tucked the case away. "I had an acquaintance some years ago . . . well, a friend, really, as best as men like myself can reckon such things . . . with the given name of Bell. No matter how clearly he enunciated, upon introducing himself to just about *anyone*, he'd get back a 'Nice to meet you, Bill!'" He puffed calmly at the cigarillo for a moment. "Now, nobody thought this over and decided to change his name for him . . . I reckon none even decided on a conscious level that they'd misheard and corrected it. It's a thing that happens quicker than thought. Our fickle brains look for patterns, for the familiar. They see somethin' outside their register of what makes sense, well, they just erase it and substitute something more comfortable. Thus, a man named Bell gets called Bill. Likewise, a man who states his intention to kill the other party in a civilized conversation *must* have been misheard. Why not? The way we're accustomed to treating each other, well, it just doesn't make a damn lick of sense. My apologies for the language, ma'am," he added, tipping his hat to her.

"Oh, good," Prin said sourly. "He's a talker."

McGraw laughed at that. "Apologies for that, too. Afraid at my age, I've already kicked the bad habits I'm going to and made peace with the rest."

"Just to be clear," Shook said softly, "you *are* talking about killing us?"

"Well, her, specifically. Things bein' as they are, it's likely to end up being you, too, 'less you decide to keep well enough out of it."

"Now why would you want to go and do a thing like that?" the enforcer asked, still in that mild tone. His hands, though, had curled in on themselves, obviously (to the trained eye) preparing to access the knives hidden up his sleeves.

"I don't concern myself with the likes of 'why,'" McGraw said, puffing away. "Ain't a wise thing to ask about, nor a safe thing to know. Once the money's paid, I proceed with the job. I will say, as I've been authorized to do so, that the Thieves' Guild has stepped on toes that ought not to've been stepped on. A rival cult would very much like to see the end of whatever specific business *you* two are sniffing around after, in the most absolute manner possible. Hence, here I am." He spread his hands in a gesture that was half shrug, as though amused by the vagaries of life.

"What cult?" Shook asked tersely. McGraw just gave him a long look. ". . . right."

"This is insane," Principia protested, backing up again. "If you intend to murder someone, you don't *announce* it to them ahead of time."

"Indeed, assassination must come from the shadows, right?" He shook his head. "That's just the way it's done. I wonder how many people a year die from seein' what they expect to, 'stead of what's right in front of 'em."

"You're in the middle of a crowded bar *full* of witnesses, most of whom would love nothing better than to jump into a fight and play hero. And *threatening* murder is itself a crime under imperial law! All we have to do is go to the sheriff and you'll be in a cell faster than you can finish that foul-smelling cigar."

"You make an awful lot of presumptions concerning what I do or don't care about," he replied calmly. "Yes, you could, indeed, go to the sheriff, at which point the matter would be your word against mine. That can be a dicey thing, when one's an outsider in these little towns. Folks are more inclined to believe what's familiar and comfortable to them, as I think I've mentioned recently. Course, matters become different when the familiar faces are the town's two shiftiest residents. *My* blank slate looks a lot more attractive in that situation, I think. And I happen to find the smell soothing."

"You can't just—"

"My apologies for cuttin' you off, ma'am, but it's been a long day and I really would prefer to move this along. There are a couple ways this can proceed. Best of all for me is that you try to get the jump on me. Thank the gods for self-defense laws; they've allowed me to put down more than a few targets in public without appearin' so much as suspicious."

"You're assuming we can't take you," Shook snarled.

"Why, yes," McGraw said mildly. "It appears I am assuming that. Slightly less advantageous to me is that you try to flee the town, get yourselves lost in the Golden Sea, or the more mundane prairie in the opposite direction. Killing you out of sight of civilization is similarly clean. Just as a word of warning, though, if either of you puts a foot near the scrolltower office or a Rail car, you'll be dead before the second foot comes down."

"You can't watch us *all* the time, you know!"

"You think not, miss?" he asked in that same tone of calm. "Down the list to the less preferable alternatives, you could just sit on your hands and wait till I've got no choice but to act. I have a generous timetable, but I don't aim to fool around in this town more than a few days. Or, you could attempt to enlist help. It'd have to be help of the illicit sort, since the law won't be too kindly disposed toward a couple members of the Thieves' Guild."

"You can't possibly prove—"

"That is actually a lot less challenging than you Eserites like to believe. Most people simply don't bother."

"That's because being a member of the Guild is *not* against the law!"

"Just so, ma'am," he said agreeably. "But it sure doesn't make the law more favorably inclined toward you. And if you optimistically assume you'll be around to continue your operations after I leave town, well, it'd complicate your life considerably to be outed. So, what's it to be, then? Care to do me a favor and start this right now?"

He puffed placidly on his cigarillo, watching them. Principia glanced sidelong at Shook; she wasn't armed, and wasn't much use in a fight anyway. The enforcer was glaring pure fury at McGraw, every line of his frame rigid. He remained silent, though, and made no movement toward the other man. Whatever his prowess in hand-to-hand combat, it didn't take much wit to see that they were dealing with a mage. The way to attack one of those was *not* from the front, when they were expecting it.

"Pity," McGraw mused after the silence had stretched out for a few moments. "But circumstances being as they are, I can hardly fault you for being less than accommodating. No offense is taken, I assure you. Well, in that case, I'll bid you good night."

He stepped forward twice, until his way was blocked by Shook, who still stood tensely, glaring at him.

"'Scuse me," McGraw said politely. He received only a murderous stare in reply. After a moment, he grinned around his cigarillo and shifted sideways to slip around the enforcer. "Be seein' you two real soon," he said amiably as he turned to mount the stairs.

They stood in silence, listening to the sound of his footsteps above, until they grew too distant to be audible over the babble of cheerful noise in the tavern.

CHAPTER 12

"Why can't they just look like the illustrations in the book?" Trissiny complained.

"I guess the plants just don't feel a need to conform to your expectations," Toby said, smiling. "Maybe Juniper could carry a complaint to Naiya for you?"

"Actually, that would be a *really* bad idea," Juniper called from a few yards away. "She doesn't have a lot of patience for complainers."

Trissiny just grumbled, staring at the sad, little cluster of leaves in her hand, wondering whether to pick it and add it to her collection. "I can't tell if this is a twisted, undernourished specimen or just . . . not a *versithorae*."

"Rafe did say those wouldn't be as common," Gabriel said, craning his neck around Toby to peer at her. "I mean, look how thick the brush is around here. Stands to reason there's been no burning for a while. *Versithorae* like ash."

With a sigh, Trissiny plucked the scraggly little plant and pressed it into the small book Rafe had issued for the purpose. "Well, whatever, I'm counting it. If I'm wrong, the worst thing that'll happen is I get a poor grade in herbalism. I've yet to hear someone explain why I should care about that."

Gabriel laughed; she ignored him, turning toward another clump of brush in search of the next item on her list.

The Sea had dropped an interesting geographical feature into their path, and Rafe had not hesitated to make homework of it. A crater, deep but sloping gently due to its considerable width, sat in the floor of the prairie, its lip surrounded by a rim of thick trees that made it look like a patch of jungle when approached from the outside. Within, however, the broad bowl was filled with bushes and lush grasses, around a small, almost perfectly circular lake in the center. After having seen nothing but miles and miles of amber tallgrass, the various shades of green were a relief for the senses.

They had paused to enjoy the little oasis, but Rafe had also set them to collecting and identifying plant samples, as he had at the last such feature they'd encountered, which was a near perfect opposite of this one—a steep, rounded hill rising out of the prairie, covered with towering trees. Two days after their brush with the centaur at the hot springs, they had seen no other signs of intelligent life and were beginning to relax a little.

Everyone remained in sight of each other, which wasn't hard; the underbrush wasn't as tall as the tallgrass, and the sloping geography of the crater made everything visible from any point within. They'd wandered off into smaller groups, though. Only Rafe was by himself, apparently asleep on the shore of the lake. Teal and Shaeine were prowling up near the lip of the crater, where the shade of the trees was more comfortable for the drow. Ruda was making methodical progress through a swath of brush with her list in hand, Fross buzzing about her head to help spot plants, and Juniper ranging widely around them—and doing more goofing off than work, or at least so it appeared to the others. Much like her performance their first day in the University's greenhouse, she seemed delighted to meet every plant she came across and was determined to introduce herself to each of them. The last group was mostly quiet and somewhat more tense. Trissiny and Gabriel had both gravitated toward Toby, but were scarcely inclined to talk to each other.

Trissiny knelt to rummage beneath a bush, looking for the shade-loving, ground-cover plants near the bottom of her list. Behind her, Toby nudged Gabriel with an elbow, then jerked his head significantly in her direction. Gabe grimaced, shaking his head emphatically; Toby bopped him gently on the forehead. With a sigh, the half demon took a hesitant step toward her, squaring his shoulders as if about to march into a dragon's den.

"So," he said with forced lightness, "I keep forgetting to mention it, Trissiny, but I think we know one of your relatives."

"*What*?!" She shot upright and spun so abruptly that Gabe staggered backward, raising his hands to ward her off. Her expression was a blend of shock and disbelief.

"I . . . uh . . . I . . . A teacher!" he stammered, still backpedaling. "At our school, growing up . . . There was a Ms. Avelea who taught history. I liked her a lot better than Tellwyrn."

"*Oh*." Trissiny relaxed, and then, disconcertingly, chuckled. "Oh. You startled me for a moment."

"I, um, noticed. Sorry? I . . . think I've missed something."

She shook her head, still smiling ruefully. "Avelea is the surname given to orphans raised by the Sisters of Avei. So, in a sense . . . Yes, your teacher would be my sister, as we all are. I doubt I've met her, though. Hardly any of us with the name share even a drop of blood."

"Oh," he said, then grimaced. "So that . . . *Oh*. So when I talked about your relatives out of nowhere, that probably sounded like . . ."

"Like more of what I generally expect from you," she replied, turning back to the bush.

"Um . . . sorry. I didn't realize . . ."

"No harm done." Trissiny spoke without turning around, her voice somewhat muffled by the foliage. "Or meant, I'm sure."

"I wouldn't have *deliberately* pushed a button like that," he said, sounding lame even to himself. "I was just . . . trying to be friendly."

"Okay."

Gabriel sighed again, staring at her back. He turned to face Toby, shrugging. Toby rolled his eyes and made a shooing gesture in Trissiny's direction, getting another emphatic headshake in reply.

"Guys?" Juniper eased up out of a nearby stand of broad-leafed grass, in which she'd been crouching. Her voice was pitched lower than usual. "Trissiny? Stand up slowly and come over here."

"Why? What's up?"

"You're being stalked. I'm gonna try to put myself between—"

She spun mid-sentence and leaped to one side as an enormous shape exploded out of a nearby copse of bushes, lunging at Gabriel. Juniper collided with it in midair; she brought a hand down on the animal's head, eliciting a howl of protest, and they both crashed to the ground, immediately springing apart.

It was a cat—that much was obvious—though the thing was the size of a horse. Its tawny coat made for poor camouflage in the green crater, but would have suited it ideally out among the tallgrass of the prairie. Most alarmingly, it had two colossal fangs protruding from its upper mouth, each the length of a human forearm. The cat rolled to its feet immediately, glaring at Juniper, but did not lunge at her again, even though she was slower to regain her balance. With the two of them standing so close together, it seemed absurd that her weight could have been enough to slow the creature, much less knock it down.

Toby and Trissiny both burst alight, golden radiance flaring up around them, and sending Gabriel staggering away, retching in pain. Trissiny drew her blade, but didn't even have time to step around Juniper to face the cat.

Vadrieny landed beside them with a *thump*, having hit the ground hard from a steep dive. The great cat whirled to face her, but the demon extended her burning wings to their full extent, flexed her talons, and screamed.

Gabriel and Juniper both backed away, clutching at their ears in pain; only the two paladins seemed protected. The sound was abominable, a protracted shriek, somewhat like the cry of a hawk but filled with an impossible fury that clawed at the brain, and with a shrill resonance like nails on a blackboard.

The cat flattened its ears back against its skull, dropping to the ground. It stared at Vadrieny for a mere second before turning and bounding away with a howl of protest. Within moments, it had ascended to the rim of trees and vanished beyond the crater.

It took the sudden silence following the demon's cry for the group to realize just how noisy the crater had been before. Insects, birds, and frogs from the lake had all filled the air with the sounds of life; now, dead silence descended, broken only by the faint voice of the wind. And then by Gabriel.

"What the *hell* was that?!"

"Smilodon," said Ruda, having just made it there. Her sword was out, but she was simply staring after the departing animal, letting the blade trail among the grass. "Damn . . . Never thought I'd see something like that. We got a skeleton of one back home, but they're supposed to be extinct."

"Like centaurs," said Trissiny.

"Triss, would you mind awfully turning down the glow a bit?" Gabriel asked. He was standing a good fifteen feet from her, but still wincing at the light she was putting off. Toby had extinguished his as soon as the cat had departed. She turned her head to regard him silently for a moment, but then allowed the light to wink out. "Thanks."

"There's lots of supposedly extinct stuff still bopping around in the Golden Sea," Professor Rafe said brightly, arriving along with Shaeine. "The thing *I* wonder about is what it was doing here! Do you guys see any prey animals? Cause I sure don't."

"Oh, it probably just came to drink," said Juniper. "I don't guess there are a lot of sources of fresh water out here. Actually . . . it is sort of puzzling how a predator that size lives in the Sea. Aside from those bison, we haven't seen a lot of animals big enough to support him."

"Maybe the Sea takes them where they need to go," Gabe suggested. "And on the subject of *going*, I'm of the opinion that the charm has gone out of this place."

"Oh, please, you heard the tree lady," Ruda said, grinning. "The big kitty's gone, probably a hundred miles away on a Sea shift by now. We're safer here."

"Nonsense! We move on!" Rafe declared, pointing dramatically at the rim of the crater. "Everybody pack up your samples and lace up your boots; we've tarried plenty long enough! We've been going mostly uphill, deeper into the Sea, and not getting much action except for the odd bit of pretty scenery. From now on, we travel . . . SIDEWAYS!"

With this declaration, he marched off, heading for the edge of the crater. After exchanging a round of significant glances, the students began trailing after him.

"Was that more joking?" Fross asked uncertainly. "Because I'm not wearing boots."

"For purposes of this discussion, sure, he was joking," Ruda said. "But don't repeat any jokes you hear from Rafe, they'll just make you sound like a fucking idiot. Gods know they do him."

"I was starting to figure that part out anyway, but thank you."

"Now that you brought it up, I'm really curious about how something that size makes a living out here," Gabriel mused as they walked. "It could probably bring down a bison pretty easily, but they travel in *big* groups."

"We brought one down easy enough," said Ruda.

"Um, no, *we* didn't," Fross corrected. "Juniper did. And no animal would attack a dryad unless it was mentally damaged. You saw how even the smilodon didn't jump after her even after she hit it."

"Maybe we're just a rare delicacy, then," Gabriel said lightly. "I wonder what human tastes like."

"It might be best," Trissiny said without turning around to look at him, "if *you* in particular didn't wonder about things like that out loud."

"A lot like pig," said Juniper, who was in the lead of the group. "Or . . . I guess you'd call it pork when you're eating it. Which is *really* funny when you think about it! There's, like, no resemblance at all. Maybe humans and pigs evolved from the same kind of animal?"

She continued blithely on in Professor Rafe's tracks, apparently unaware that the entire group had come to a stop and were staring at her back.

"Wait, so . . . how does she know what humans taste like?"

Ruda sighed. "Welcome to the conversation, Fross."

"Thanks! I'm still confused, though."

"You're probably better off."

Sometime after noon, they encountered other travelers for the first time.

Rafe, walking at the head of the group, as usual, was the first to spot them. Trissiny, following his pointing finger, discerned them immediately, but it was some minutes before the others could make anything out beyond a faint smudge of dust thrown into the air. Two covered wagons, pulled by oxen, were coming directly toward them, heading downhill and thus to the edge of the Sea. Moving east as they were, the students could likely have avoided the other party entirely by continuing on their way, but by consensus the group stopped to meet them.

They had plenty of time to arrange themselves and watch the others approach. The occupants of the second wagon were hidden by the first, but those driving the lead wagon were visible—a man and a woman, both human, and both dressed in typical frontier style, in denim trousers and plain buttoned shirts. He was blond and fair, as was pretty common among frontier towns, with a ten-gallon hat shielding him from the sun; she was dark-haired and had a swarthy Tiraan complexion. Both carried staves, which they raised and aimed at the students when they drew close.

Trissiny and Toby both glowed subtly, probably not enough to be noticeable in the sunlight, but ready to throw up divine shields at need. Standing just behind them, Shaeine drew on her own power, a silver luminescence rising around her hands, which were folded behind her back.

The wagons rumbled to a halt, their occupants surveying the nine of them warily. Toby cleared his throat, opening his mouth to speak.

"BEHOLD!" Rafe bellowed, grinning maniacally and throwing his arms wide. Toby sighed.

"Yeah, we see you," said the woman, shifting her staff to aim it at him in particular. "Weren't expecting to meet any other adventurers, specially not on foot at this time of day. The sun's not— Holy fuck, is that a drow?"

Toby cleared his throat. "We don't mean you any harm. I don't begrudge you holding weapons, this being dangerous territory and all, but would you mind not pointing them at my friends?"

"I mind a little," said the man. His expression remained cold, and his staff remained aimed at Trissiny, who he had clearly decided was the most obvious threat. "I see you've got a Sister along, which is a little reassuring. Fact remains, though, it's been years since there was loot in any quantity to be found in the Sea. Most reliable way to strike it rich out here is to rob somebody else who's already done the heavy digging. It ain't wise for us to be too friendly toward strangers."

"Ooh, you looted something good? Nice!" Ruda grinned widely. "What'd ya get?"

Both of them shifted, aiming their staves at her. "Don't see how it's any of your business," the man said grimly.

"If I may?" Gabriel stepped forward. "We don't want or need your loot. We are on a glorious quest to wander around the prairie like idiots for an indeterminate amount of time until *this* headcase over here decides we can go home." He jerked a thumb at Rafe, who grinned delightedly.

The pair eyed him, then glanced at each other. The woman relaxed and raised her staff to point at the sky. "Ah, I see. Kids from Tellwyrn's University, then?"

"I'm a little troubled by how obvious that apparently is," said Teal.

"That's another matter," said the man, also lifting his weapon. "Sorry for the rude welcome. Can't be too careful out here."

"No harm done," Toby said, smiling. "It's a good idea to be cautious, especially in a place like this. Have you run into much trouble?"

"Not of the kind that's likely to be roaming around makin' a pest of itself," the man replied, then leaned over to spit to the side. "We did come across some ruins down in a canyon . . . Full o' monsters, but a fairly decent haul for the effort. You'll forgive me if I don't give you directions."

"Of course," Toby replied equably. "It wouldn't do us much good anyway; I doubt the way there still exists. Or if it does, it leads somewhere else by now."

"True enough."

"I should warn you that there are centaurs on the move," Toby went on more seriously. "The Golden Sea being what it is, there's no telling how close they might be. But we encountered a lone scout, which we killed, and met an elf who said there's an entire group of as many as sixty still in this general region. If . . . we're still in that general region. It's hard to say."

The man and woman exchanged a long, serious look.

"That's troubling news," she said slowly. "The Sea doesn't commonly shift by a large amount at one time . . . except that sometimes it does; but if you've seen something, it's likely to stay in your general area until you do some serious walking. When was this?"

"Two days ago."

"We appreciate the warning," said the man, tipping his hat to them. "Not much to be done about it except keep our eyes out and weapons up, but . . . forewarned is forearmed, as they say."

"Of course," he replied. "I wouldn't want anybody to wander into them by mistake."

"You'll pardon us if we don't hang around to chat, but with this news especially, we're eager to get outta the Sea and back to somewhere we can start spending our haul."

"Of course," Toby said again. "Thanks for talking with us."

"Mm," the man said noncommittally, and flicked his reins. He tugged the brim of his hat again as the oxen started moving. "Y'all take care."

They stood aside to let the tiny wagon train pass. Driving the second cart was a blond man with subtly pointed ears, doubtless a half elf, with a much scruffier man beside him, both also holding staves. They nodded to the students in passing, but didn't offer a word of greeting.

"So," Ruda said thoughtfully, "ruins. Wonder what our odds are of finding those?"

"Dismal," said Rafe cheerily. "But worry not, my little chickens! It's the Golden Sea after all. We're sure to find something rewardingly deadly, if we only persevere and have *faith*!"

"Seriously," said Gabe. "Is there a medical term for what's wrong with you?"

"It's called *genius*, y'little hellbug. All right, that's enough lollygaggin'. ONWARD TO FUCKING GLORY!"

Given the lack of general interest in the Sea's terrain—amber waves of grain were scenic and all, but got old quickly when there was nothing else to see—when the students found anything interesting, they made a beeline for it. Thus, when a canyon opened up before them, the group headed into it without a second thought. It began as a little dip in the level of the plain, but the tallgrass quickly faded away, yielding to gravel and dusty rock, with increasingly tall stone walls to either side.

"And what happens if there's no convenient exit at the other end of this?" Gabriel asked after they had hiked deep enough into the ravine that the entrance was no longer visible behind them.

"Then we backtrack!" Rafe said cheerfully. "Anyhow, these things often have side branches, so don't assume the exit's in a straight line ahead. Besides, odds are good we'll find something cool! Most of the interesting stuff in the Sea is attached to some anomaly in the geography. Once in a while you *do* find things just sitting around on the prairie, but odds are much better within the hills and canyons and whatnot."

"That guy on the wagon said they found ruins and treasure in a canyon," Ruda commented, gesticulating vaguely with a half-consumed bottle of whiskey. "Think this might be it?"

"Not likely," said Toby. "He also said that canyon was full of monsters."

"I don't think we've gone deep enough into this one yet to determine what it might be full of," Trissiny added. "In hindsight, I wish I'd thought to ask him exactly what kind of 'monsters' they were."

Teal stopped short, raising her head. "Something . . . Does anyone else hear that?"

"What?" Rafe paused, looking back at her. "I don't, and my hearing is *exceptional*."

"Hoofbeats," Shaeine said tersely.

The others glanced at one another, but before anybody could voice a question, the sound grew loud enough to be audible to everyone. Nervously, the group pulled together and by silent consensus pressed themselves against the canyon wall. The noise grew until it was obviously right above them.

"Could be bison," Gabriel said. "Or wild horses. Unicorns . . ."

A long, whooping shout echoed from above, followed by answering yells in a language none of them understood. The steady drum of hooves all moving in unison changed tempo, fading into the more chaotic noise of creatures stomping about in one place.

". . . with riders?" Gabe suggested weakly.

"Fross," Trissiny said very quietly, "would you mind having a look?"

The pixie didn't reply verbally, but zipped straight upward to the rim of the canyon. Her glow, already hard to spot in the bright sunlight, dimmed further. Seconds later, she shot back down to rejoin them. Nobody was surprised when she said exactly what they did not want to hear.

"Centaurs."

CHAPTER 13

"How many, approximately?" Trissiny asked very quietly.

"Approximately fifty-one," Fross replied. "They're . . . I'm not sure what they're doing. Milling around, listening to a big female who's giving orders."

On cue, the whole group paused and looked up at the rim of the canyon. Amid all the stamping and shouting, there was indeed one recurring voice which, while deep, might have been feminine. It certainly sounded authoritative.

Trissiny glanced around at her companions; they were a knot of tight, nervous faces. Only Shaeine looked truly calm, but apparently Narisians were trained for that from the cradle. Rising onto her tiptoes to look over their heads, Trissiny scanned their environs. Nothing ideal jumped out at her, but she did spot something serviceable.

"This way, everyone," she said, gently pushing between Toby and Ruda to lead the way up the canyon. "Quiet as you can."

A few yards ahead was a deep alcove in the base of the canyon, protected by an overhang of rock. It was barely out of the midday sun, not deep enough to qualify as a proper cave, but it'd shield them from view if any of those above happened to glance over the edge. Following Trissiny, they filed in and huddled together; Fross descended to Juniper's shoulder, dimming her glow almost completely.

"What do we do?" Gabriel hissed, his voice verging on panic. "Can we run? Hide in here?"

"We're sitting ducks down here," Ruda replied in a similar tone.

"What do you think, Trissiny?" Toby's tone was deliberately calm. It seemed to ground the others; again, everyone looked expectantly at Trissiny.

"Whatever they're doing up there, they don't seem to be leaving." She kept her tone calm and her voice low; a level headed commander could do a lot to maintain order among frightened troops, and much as some of them might have resented her taking charge, it seemed to work. "Whether they're settling in to camp or planning to move along the rim of the canyon for a place to cross, they're likely to send scouts down here."

"I think horse legs would have trouble with those cliffs," Juniper said.

"The way *we* came in isn't that far behind, and we don't know how many other paths up or down there may be. Best to plan on having to engage them. Listen, I think we can take them."

"Are you off your *nut?*" Ruda hissed furiously. "I love a good fight as much as the next girl, but we're talking six-to-one odds against us!"

"As Professor Tellwyrn pointed out, we heavily outclass most threats, Ruda. That's *why* all of us are at her crazy school instead of somewhere reasonable. There was a narrow spot a bit behind us where we can make a stand—"

"You can't seriously think—"

"*Listen* to me," Trissiny said urgently, struggling to keep her voice low. Goddess, give her patience; this lack of order and discipline would be the thing that got them killed, if anything did. For a wonder, Ruda shut her mouth, glaring. "Centaurs are more of a raider than a warrior culture. Like all bullies, they're cowards at heart; once they lose a few fighters without inflicting any losses on us, they'll back off and avoid us thereafter. If we run, though, they will pursue. This isn't going to end until we fight them off."

"What the hell makes you think we can inflict losses without taking any?" Gabriel snapped, barely remembering to keep his voice low. "Or that even if we somehow do, it'll scare them off?"

"I've had to study every known culture that practices diabolism, *and* the tactics of every enemy the Sisters of Avei have fought. *Believe* me, my education has covered centaurs."

"Look around at us," she continued. "Vadrieny, Juniper, and Gabriel are incredibly resistant to damage, and two of the three can hit *very* hard, regardless of their level of martial skill. We can add me to that list, as long as I'm calling on Avei's power. That's our front line. Ruda's nimble and has a long reach with that rapier; she makes an ideal backup to cut down any enemies who manage to get through the first four, which is possible, as we'll need to spread ourselves a bit to cover the canyon even at the narrow spot. Fross provides ranged magic attacks, and she'll be virtually impossible to hit with any returned fire. Toby can heal injuries on the fly with Omnu's blessings, and Shaeine's magic shield will be perfect to protect us from arrow fire from the rim of the canyon. And Rafe . . ." She looked over at him for a moment. ". . . is a professor of the Ultimate University; he's bound to be good for something."

"Finally, some proper respect," he said smugly.

"We can *do* this," Trissiny insisted, ignoring him. "Just hold them for a few minutes, inflict a few losses, and make it plain that we are not easy prey."

They all stared at her for a moment, faces creased in near identical expressions of worry, silently listening to the sounds from up above. Whatever the centaurs were doing, they hadn't left; the way sound echoed in the canyon, it was impossible to tell what direction they were moving in, but they were clearly staying in the same general vicinity. One by one, the students tore their eyes from Trissiny's resolute face to glance around at each other.

"We'll decide as a group," she said quietly, "but remember, we don't have *time*. They'll start scouting any minute, if scouts aren't already on the way. There's no luxury of debate or long thought here."

"Fuck it, Shiny Boots here knows her tactics," said Ruda, nodding to her. "I say we stand and fight." Trissiny felt a rush of unexpected warmth toward her roommate at the endorsement.

"I'm sorry, but . . . I don't want anything to do with any battle," Teal said softly. "Not if there's any other way." Beside her, Shaeine nodded.

"The only unequivocal victory in battle is a battle that is avoided completely," said the drow. "I doubt we can negotiate with these creatures, but I also cannot believe escape is impossible, given the terrain."

"Professor Tellwyrn *specifically* told us to listen to Trissiny in a combat situation!" Fross said, her wings buzzing in agitation, though she was still perched on Juniper's shoulder. "She knows the most about it, and she has a good plan. We should do that!"

Juniper nodded. "That one guy wasn't so tough, and we weren't really using all our resources against him. I've never seen organized fighting the way humans do it; we should try that, since Triss has a strategy and everything."

"I can't support violent action, not when there's a possibility of avoiding it," Toby said gravely. "Sorry, Triss." She nodded to him, keeping her expression even with some effort. His rejection stung especially hard. Even though she knew the reason—Omnu was a god of peace. Even though she also knew why his opinion mattered so much, which made her feel foolish to boot. This was no time to be nursing a crush.

"I hope nobody thinks I'm selfish about this," said Gabriel, "but I *really* don't like that this idea puts me on the front lines. I mean, if centaurs are big diabolists or whatever, I'm guessing they don't have many clerics, so nothing they've got is actually going to *hurt* me. But let's face it, I kinda suck at fighting. I feel like this is gonna lead to me being the reason one of you gets hurt. That's . . ." He swallowed. "I say we run."

Everyone turned to look at Professor Rafe. For all that Tellwyrn had insisted he wasn't in charge or responsible for their safety, he was part of the group, and now was in a position to cast a tie-breaking vote.

"Let it never be said that Professor Rafe retreated from a fight," he said solemnly. "All things considered, though, I think this is a good time to charge slowly and as quietly as possible in the opposite direction from the enemy. Avelea has a good strategy; we'll do that if it comes to a scrap. But we're better off making that plan B and trying to get away from all this horseshit. Fair?"

Trissiny slowly drew in a deep breath, nodding her acknowledgment along with the others. She shoved aside frustration—and a certain amount of hurt—to be dealt with properly in prayer, later. For now, she still had to get these people out of danger. And no matter that they were apparently turning down her advice, she still deemed it her responsibility. The Hands of Avei existed to protect those who needed it.

"Right," she said, briskly but quietly. "Keep the noise to a minimum. Try to hug the canyon wall to make us less visible, and *absolutely* no divine or infernal magic; diabolists will sense either immediately. That means no transforming, Teal. I'll take point. Juniper, bring up the rear, please. Quick and quiet, people. Let's move."

She slipped out of their little alcove and set off down the edge of the canyon. Walking as close as she could to the wall and placing each foot as quietly as possible without sacrificing haste, she tried to set an example for the others. It was frustrating, though unsurprising, how much noise they made, even though she was the only one in armor. Trissiny reminded herself that nobody else likely had training in operations like this, and the centaurs probably couldn't hear them anyway over the noise they were making up above.

No matter how quickly the students moved, they didn't get out of range of the noise from overhead. Given their focus on quiet, they were not making great time and hadn't been moving long, but even so, the fact that they weren't leaving the centaurs behind grew increasingly alarming. Either they were galloping up and down the *whole* length of the canyon, or at least a very large stretch of it, or the group was moving more or less along with the University group. So far, there was nothing to indicate they'd been spotted, just galloping and whooping.

Trissiny looked back, smiling encouragingly at the others, who were looking as tense and drawn as she felt, and apparently not coping with it as well. Not for the first time, Trissiny felt homesick for the abbey and her Sisters-in-training, women she could trust to know how to behave in a hostile situation. Much as she wanted to trust in her fellow classmates, she wasn't at all sure how several of them would react to the pressure. She generally couldn't predict how the two fae would react to anything at all . . . Shaeine would keep cool, and probably Toby, but Teal was *way* out of her comfort zone, and Gabriel . . . was generally hopeless. To say nothing of Rafe, who didn't run on any kind of coherent logic.

Her right hand, which she was using to pad along the wall as she went, waved emptily at her next step and she paused, turning back around. She had come to a gap in the wall, which she'd failed to see coming up due to how narrow it was; it had looked like nothing more than a crack when approached from the side. She held up a hand to signal the others to stop, studying the space. It was very roughly the size and shape of a door in an average human house, though the upper edge was angled crazily and the left side bowed inward. Its edges were as rounded as every other stone in the canyon by exposure to the elements, but something about the regularity of it tugged at her mind.

"It's out of place," Rafe whispered, having broken formation to come up beside her. "See? Any time something happens to the rock due to natural geological forces, there are signs of it all around. Fallen rocks, cracks leading into each other. There's no debris under this, and there are no cracks at all around it. It's old now, but this was *cut*. By someone intelligent."

"Could it be centaurs?" Gabriel asked in a hushed voice from just behind them.

Trissiny shook her head. "Look at the size of it, they couldn't get through. It's too short . . . and possibly too narrow."

"There's no animal life anywhere around here," said Juniper, joining them. "Seems pretty deep, though. Fross?"

The pixie zipped forward and into the opening before Trissiny could warn her not to. Her icy glow illuminated a corridor that, though rough, was unquestionably too square to have occurred naturally. "There's . . . something," she said, coming back to the entrance. "It's not arcane or nature magic, and it's not strong. Hard to identify . . . It's like a faded, old echo of a spell."

"Infernal?" asked Teal from behind them.

"I don't sense anything like that," Trissiny said, "though it's a little hard to tell; there are definitely warlocks up above, and that might be throwing me off. Toby?"

"I don't think so." He joined the growing cluster around the opening. "No, I'm pretty sure there's nothing like that in there, at least not within the range of my senses."

"Okay, so . . . empty cave, made by people, too small for centaurs to follow us in, no animals or bad juju. Why the fuck are we just standing around instead of getting *in* there, then?" Ruda demanded.

"Because this is too convenient," said Gabriel, getting several nods of agreement.

"Convenient or no, I say we take it," said Trissiny. "We're not getting any farther away from them. If they're not following us deliberately, the chances of them noticing us get higher the longer this goes on. We can wait in there till they pass us by, and if they *do* find where we've gone . . . this gap is very defensible. I think I could hold it by myself, even."

So saying, she ducked inside, having decided after the last episode that the surest way to get this group to comply with sense was not to offer them an alternative. What she wouldn't give for a functioning chain of command . . .

Fross bobbed alongside her, providing ample light that didn't require Trissiny to call on divine energy. Aside from the fact that it seemed somehow sacrilegious to use the power of the gods given to her to heal the innocent and strike down the wicked as a lamp, Gabriel's presence in the group complicated the matter further.

The floor ascended gently as they went. Trissiny had to wonder if this was leading toward an exit onto the prairie, in which case they were heading straight for a centaur encounter unless the tunnel was extremely long. It didn't get quite that far, however. About the time the floor of the tunnel reached the height of the upper edge of its outer door, it abruptly evened off and turned sharply to the right. She paused at this point to give the others a chance to regather, noting that Shaeine had lit herself with a silver glow, which seemed to be causing Gabriel, who was right in front of her, no distress.

Now, the magical light put off by Fross and Shaeine was their only illumination. Fortunately, this next leg of the corridor wasn't quite as long. After only a few dozen steps it terminated in an arched doorway, much more evenly cut than the exterior opening, which opened into a much broader chamber. Three steps led down from the door to the ground inside. Trissiny descended carefully, scanning the space for any signs of trouble.

There was none; she had the strong impression that no one and nothing had been here for a very long time, and not just because her boots made significant prints in the otherwise undisturbed layer of dust on the floor. There was a heaviness, a gravitas to the chamber, that was something more than just her emotional response to entering a dark, empty space.

"Fross?"

"Yeah?"

"That feeling you mentioned outside, about something vague in here . . . Is it stronger here?"

"Ohhhh, yeah. You feel it, too, now?"

"I think so. Do you think it's dangerous?"

Fross didn't answer for a moment, zipping back and forth in the air just above Trissiny's head. "I don't . . . think so. But I've got the impression it's sort of . . . barely . . . maybe . . . conscious."

Trissiny nodded slowly. But she neither felt nor saw anything she could interpret as a threat, and stepped aside to let the others gather in the chamber.

The impressiveness of its size was partly an illusion due to the cramped tunnel through which they'd reached it. All in all, the space was smaller than the chapel back at the University; high by the standards of an average house, but she could have reached the ceiling by extending one arm overhead and hopping. It was maybe fifteen feet wide and a little more than twice that in length, with the doorway standing on one of the short sides. Small enough that their relatively modest light sources touched the far wall and their group made the near end seem rather crowded once they'd all crowded inside.

Along every visible inch of the walls were crude paintings. Done in dull colors, mostly reds and blues, with brown and black lines, they seemed to depict scenes of battle, with figures mostly on horseback but sometimes afoot, brandishing a variety of weapons. The lower parts of them weren't completely visible, due to an assortment of actual weapons lining the walls along the floor. Axes and swords were present, but the most commonly represented were spears, some decorated near the head with brightly colored feathers, now faded and scraggly with age. Bows and bundles of arrows were also present in abundance. Most of these were stored in large clay jars decorated with more paintings similar to those on the walls, but quite a few were also stacked in baskets or on wooden racks. The jars and racks were mostly intact and the weapons generally in decent shape, but some of the baskets had broken apart to dump their contents onto the floor, and in several places arrows were scattered in heaps where the thongs holding them together had broken.

Occupying pride of place in the chamber, however, was a huge, oblong slab of stone, apparently having been carved out of the living rock. A precise line ran all the way around it, where the upper piece, about a foot thick, was apparently detachable, resting on top. It was set far back enough that they had room to gather near the steps, and of roughly the same proportions as the long chamber itself. Though devoid of any decoration, either carved or painted, it was unquestionably a sarcophagus.

"Whoa," Teal said softly.

"This place should be treated with respect," said Shaeine, echoing what they all felt.

"It couldn't be . . ." Professor Rafe shouldered past the group, frowning with uncharacteristic intensity at the wall paintings. "Could it? I think . . . Surely not; it's not possible. But . . ." Picking his way carefully around jars and over piles of arrows, he followed along one side of the room, scanning the wall paintings as if reading a story, though there were no words in any language. "It might be . . . I don't believe it. It really . . .

I think . . ." He came back toward them, still carefully watching the paintings as though they might have changed in the last few seconds, his expression one of growing awe. "My gods, I do believe it is!"

"I think he's trying to communicate," said Gabriel.

"Guys!" Rafe turned to face them directly, his face practically shining with joy. "I think this is the tomb of Horsebutt the Enemy!"

Gabriel sighed. "Never mind."

"Wait . . . are you serious?" Teal stepped down from the doorway, frowning at the walls. "How can you possibly tell that?"

"Look at the pictograms! See, there's no actual writing, but these look *exactly* like Stalweiss tomb decorations, which, come on, how many Eastern barbarians would be buried in the Golden Sea?"

"But . . . really?" Teal began slowly retracing Rafe's steps, frowning intently at the paintings. "It's obviously a battle . . . But *the* Horsebutt? What are the odds?"

"Wait, what?" Gabriel said sharply.

"Like I said, who *else*?"

"It does seem to strain the bounds of coincidence," Trissiny said frowning. "At the same time, the Sea moves unpredictably, but not necessarily randomly. If our steps are being guided toward some purpose . . . Perhaps. And Rafe is right, they do look like early Shaathist battle paintings. No one touch the walls; if they're done in the traditional ash pigments, they could be very fragile."

"I almost can't believe it!" Rafe spun dizzily in a circle, grinning madly at every inch of the tomb. "Arachne would chew her foot off with envy! Horsebutt's tomb!"

"Are you guys pranking me?" Gabriel demanded shrilly. "Because this is *not* the time!"

Trissiny frowned at him. "Have you *seriously* never heard of Horsebutt the Enemy?"

"Stop *saying* that! It can't possibly be a name!"

"I haven't, either," Toby said more quietly.

"Um, you guys went to an imperial public school, right?" Teal said hesitantly.

Gabriel scowled at her. "What of it?"

"It's just that . . . Horsebutt's campaign against the empire was basically the last act of the Enchanter Wars. That whole business has been covered up and changed in retrospect by so many different factions that even the historians aren't exactly sure what happened . . ."

"I guess you haven't gotten to that in Arachne's class yet," Rafe said absently, still ogling the tomb paintings avidly. "She was ass-deep in the whole thing."

". . . yeah, well, anyway, nobody came out of it looking good, and the Tiraan Empire ended up looking worse than most. In fact, by most accounts the empire itself was nearly broken. I've heard some versions where it *was* overthrown, and then got pieced back together after the fact. Point being, most official imperial sources hush it all up pretty hard."

"I'd hush it up, too, if I got my ass kicked by somebody named Horsebutt," Gabriel scoffed.

"If it helps you," Teal said, grinning, "his name in the original language was Heshenaad."

"Yes. That helps. Let's *please* say that from now on."

"Yeah, especially considering we're maybe standing in the guy's fucking *tomb*, and our resident pixie wizard thinks there's some kind of mojo still working here," Ruda said sharply. "Might not hurt if everybody showed a little goddamn *respect*."

There was a momentary silence while they considered that.

Teal cleared her throat. "Anyhow . . . Heshenaad was actually an honor name given to him when he distinguished himself in battle. The Stalweiss, uh, have different ideas about respect than we do."

"Boy, that's for damn sure," said Rafe, turning back toward them and grinning. "Just because the Easterners decide you're hot shit doesn't mean you can go around calling yourself by whatever honor name they give you. Arachne's practically a demigod over there, and you should hear what they call her. Teal, don't wander off!"

"There's no *off* to wander to!" Teal protested, picking her way carefully toward the shadowed back of the tomb. "I just wanna look at the paintings . . ." Her voice trailed off as she rounded the end of the sarcophagus, gazing up raptly at the walls. Shaeine went after her, carefully holding the hem of her robe up out of the piles of arrows and taking her silver glow along, leaving Fross's light the only illumination for the rest of them.

"Wait, what do they call Professor Tellwyrn?" Ruda asked, grinning.

Rafe winced. "Um... I don't remember. Ask Chase when we get home; he loves to share embarrassing stories."

"Anyway," Trissiny said firmly, "Horsebutt—"

"*Heshenaad!*" Gabriel insisted.

"—the Enemy was a Stalweiss cavalry leader who pillaged his way across imperial territory from the Stalrange to the Golden Sea, where he effectively trapped himself. Indirectly, he's responsible for reuniting the fragments of the empire, giving the factions a common enemy and a reason to rally together again under the restored emperor. Some historians think he might have been manipulated into his campaign for exactly that reason. He actually survived within the Sea itself for nearly ten years, which made him a *severe* threat, as no one knew where he'd strike. Even he didn't; his raiders would just come out of the Sea at whatever random point it spat them out, then vanish back into it. He's the reason the empire has such a solid military infrastructure around the frontier, even now."

"Hm," said Toby thoughtfully. "Sounds like he did the empire quite a few favors, then, however unintentionally."

Trissiny nodded. "That's why he's remembered as *the* Enemy. At the time he lived, an enemy was exactly what the empire needed, something to band together against. If not for him... the continent might be a patchwork of kingdoms again, like in the Age of Adventures. No empire, no Church, likely no Rail or telescroll networks, even if humanity still had the chance to develop those enchantments..."

"How'd he die?" Gabriel asked, looking interested in spite of himself.

"Nobody knows." She shook her head. "He was always guaranteed to lose what had become a war of attrition. His forces took losses with every raid, with no way to get reinforcements from the Stalrange, and their successful attacks grew fewer and farther between as the empire moved more resources to the frontier; at the same time it was developing better weapons. That was about the time the earliest battlestaves and wands were used by the Imperial Army. He was also doubtless losing forces to centaurs and whatever else lives in the Sea . . . Some thought he must have a fortress out here, but since his tomb is in a ravine in the middle of nowhere, it seems more likely they were just living nomadically, like the centaurs and plains elves. A decade after his horde made it to the Sea, their attacks just . . . trailed off. Eventually it was assumed that he'd died, but no one ever learned how." She turned slowly in place, looking around at the tomb. "People have been hunting for his tomb for all the usual reasons. Everyone figured a great raider would be buried with fabulous riches or something. All I see are weapons, though . . ."

"Yeah, riches," said Ruda firmly. "He was laid to rest with what his culture considered important. The things that *matter* to a warrior. All this stuff would have been sacred to the Stalweiss, therefore nobody is touching a fucking *thing*. You don't fuck around with a great man's resting place."

Though there was enough airflow from the open door that the air in the tomb didn't seem poisonous or even very stale, it had been dead still the whole time they were present, only the tiny breeze of their passing stirred the dust on the floor. As she spoke, however, there came a short, faint gust of wind, ruffling Ruda's coat and blowing back the few strands of her hair that had come loose from her braid. Her eyes widened slightly; the others shifted away from her.

"I think he likes you," Fross noted.

Rafe cleared his throat. "Ah, yeah, anyway, everybody get a good look; who knows when anyone will see this place again, if ever. But yes, let's be *respectful*. The last thing we need on top of our other problems is to incur the Curse of Horsebutt."

"Why is this my life?" Gabriel asked of the ceiling.

"What Ruda and Trissiny said goes. Don't touch the paintings, don't take any souvenirs. In fact, just don't mess with the weaponry at all. *Meanwhile*, we've got more immediate problems." Rafe cut his eyes toward the now-dark opening to the passage beyond. "With apologies to our host, we're gonna have to park it here for a little while. Somebody can scout down near the door and keep an ear out; we better not try to leave until our friends up there have moved on, and there's no telling how long *that'll* take."

"It better not be too long," Gabriel muttered. "That whole 'respect' thing is gonna get a hell of a lot harder as soon as somebody needs to take a piss."

"Good gods, don't even joke," Rafe groaned. "We'll . . . figure something out. Somebody can check the canyon, see if there's a convenient . . . uh, spot . . . near the entrance. Whatever happens, we're staying the hell put until it's safe. If it comes down to it, I'd rather stay put here with Heshenaad than go back and explain to Taath K'varr how I got you lot killed."

"Wait, what?" Coming back around the sarcophagus the other way, Teal stopped suddenly and frowned at him, apparently having caught only the last part of that. "Who's a golden bitch?"

There was one beat of silence, and then Ruda collapsed onto the steps, howling with laughter.

"Great," Rafe said dourly. "You wanna put a cork in it, Punaji? That's probably echoing all the way to the—"

He cut off, and so did she, as a heavy thudding began all around them. They all jerked to attention, staring wide-eyed at each other. The noise was relatively faint, as though heard from a distance or through a thick barrier, but it seemed to resonate unnaturally in the very air around them. It appeared to be coming mostly from the ceiling, to judge by the tiny streams of dust that fell with each pound, but echoed sharply from the tunnel.

"Is that who I think it is?" Teal asked wanly.

"Centaur war drums," said Trissiny, unconsciously gripping her sword.

Gabriel gulped. "*Please* tell me they're having a square dance."

"*War* drums, Gabe," she said tersely. "Those are magical. They're a *weapon*; they only use them in the presence of enemies."

"Then . . ." Toby trailed off, staring at her.

She nodded. "Either they've found somebody to fight up there . . . or they know we're here."

CHAPTER 14

One of the fringe benefits of being an old man in less than pristine garb was that he was commonly left to enjoy his meals in peace. The A&W was somewhat less rowdy during the midday meal than it had been the night before, but a hubbub of conversation still filled the room, and more tables were full than otherwise. McGraw had found a seat at an unoccupied circular table in the corner, and so far had been left to enjoy it alone. The waitress had just delivered his plate of sausages and potatoes, and he was looking forward to a quiet meal, unless the wards he'd set warned of Principia or Shook making for the scrolltower.

She moved fast. Scarcely had the sudden hush of an attention-grabbing arrival fallen over the common room when Arachne Tellwyrn pulled out a chair and sat down across from him.

That, McGraw reflected wryly, was what he got for boasting of a perfect record. The very next day, there it went.

"Ma'am," he said politely. "Pardon me for not standing; you kinda snuck up on me there. Can I offer you a bite to eat? My treat."

"To be frank, I only bother to fence and dance about with pleasantries when my sparring partner exceeds a certain level of significance," she said, folding her hands on the table and staring at him over the rims of her spectacles. "Don't take offense; there are very few individuals who make the cut, and most of them refuse to have anything to do with me anyway. So I'll come to the point, McGraw—what the hell are you doing in Last Rock?"

He chewed a bite of sausage carefully, weighing his options. Her commentary suited her reputation—blunt, aggressive, and heavy-handed. McGraw didn't much care for needless confrontation, himself, but he knew when trying to deflect would cause more harm than good.

"I've been employed by an outside party," he said calmly after swallowing, "to remove Principia Locke from Last Rock." Past her, he noted those three soldier boys making a brave but inept try at looking imposing. Sheriff Sanders pulled it off much better, lounging against the wall by the door. Tellwyrn wouldn't have felt the need to bring her own posse to confront the likes of him . . . No, this was the other way around. Somebody had warned the sheriff about him, and Sanders had called in the big wands.

"Define 'remove,'" Tellwyrn said flatly.

"The young lady is under the impression that I'm here to kill her. I'd take it as a professional courtesy if you didn't correct her."

The elf raised an eyebrow. "Then you're not, in fact, after her head?"

"At this stage in my career, it'd be pretty hypocritical to balk at a little homicide," he said, carefully maintaining his calm tone, despite the ratcheting tension in the room. Around them, other patrons were steadily finding excuses to cut short their lunches and go elsewhere. Nobody was obviously within earshot. "But no, killing is very seldom necessary, and certainly not my first choice of method in a civilized place like this. Ain't like the old days," he went on reminiscently, stirring potatoes around his plate with his fork. "Seems nowadays, nobody's so inconsequential that a whole mess of paperwork doesn't ensue when they turn up dead. I do hate dealin' with lawyers."

"But as long as Prin thinks you've got a contract on her life, she's likely to go and do something rash . . . which will make it that much easier to chase her out of Last Rock." She nodded approvingly. "Elegant. I like it. Provided, of course, that you're not lying to me."

McGraw finished chewing a bite of potato and swallowed. "Granted, you've no reason to take me at my word. Let me assure you, ma'am, that if I *am* lying, I'm well aware I'd be gambling my life on the outcome. You can trust me to proceed with all due restraint."

"Well, that's something, I suppose. I will be frank, then. It would suit me admirably to have Principia out of this town and out of my hair. I can't say I'd shed any tears if that involved her death, but I agree that cleaner methods are usually preferable."

"Mm. I'm less inclined to be careful around her buddy, Mr. Shook," he mused. "Been listening to the local scuttlebutt . . . Honestly, a man like that is better off removed from the mortal coil."

"Which brings me to a point of concern," she said flatly. "I neither run this town nor enforce the law in it. Generally speaking, the citizens of Last Rock do not need, nor would they appreciate, my help in seeing to their business. I do, however, have an ancillary interest in the doings of the town, for obvious reasons. So, let me establish my ground rules: If you cause such a degree of collateral damage that my help is requested to come down here and deal with it, I kill you. If any of your actions result in harm to my University or any of my students, I may or may not kill you, but I *guarantee* you will have ample time to repent your mistakes before that final judgment is made. Anything else you get up to is between you, the law, and whoever you do it to. Understood?"

McGraw calmly carried on eating, swallowing another bite as she finished speaking. Many years of practice kept his expression even as ever, despite the unaccustomed frisson of fear that passed through him. It wasn't often he had been so baldly threatened by someone who could unquestionably back up their bluster. "Seems quite reasonable, ma'am. As I said, I don't aim to do anything that'll run afoul of your rules, but a little extra motivation never hurts."

"Glad we understand each other," she replied, standing up to leave.

"I was recently reminded," McGraw said mildly, "that making threats of murder are, in fact, grounds for imprisonment under imperial law." He glanced over at Sheriff Sanders, who was still lounging by the door, too obviously not looking at them to be unaware of every detail of the conversation.

Tellwyrn gave him a condescending smile. "That's adorable."

Gathering up her uniformed entourage with a peremptory gesture, she swept out as suddenly as she'd arrived, leaving behind only Sanders, who calmly straightened up and wandered over toward the bar in search of a drink.

McGraw chuckled to himself, and tucked back into his lunch.

Tazlith made a show of frowning in contemplation as she examined the amulets behind the glass barrier of their display case, hoping the shopkeeper would interpret her expression as a sign she was carefully weighing the pros and cons of each enchantment, as they were described on the accompanying labels. In truth, she was weighing the pros and cons against what remained of her money purse.

She'd been sold on the idea that stocking up on equipment back home in Calderaas was foolish, when things were bound to be cheaper out on the frontier. Last Rock, however, did most of its commerce in the hopes and dreams of people like herself, and she was finding that the pendulum swung the opposite direction. Not by very much, but weaponry and enchanted gear was proving to be a touch pricier than she'd seen it advertised in the city. Foodstuffs, at least, were cheaper, whatever sense that made. Economics was over her head.

Occupied with her grim thoughts, her general disappointment with the way reality was sullying her excitement at setting off into the Golden Sea, and her efforts to look as upstanding as possible—the shopkeeper's patience with her browsing had visibly begun to fray—she didn't realize she had been approached until the man cleared his throat softly.

Tazlith jumped and immediately flushed with embarrassment. Great, *very* heroic. Luckily, he wasn't laughing at her, though she was hardly delighted to meet the guy with the oily hair and cheap suit who she'd caught checking out her butt yesterday in the tavern.

"Can I help you?" she asked in her unfriendliest tone. Had she been interested in ending up as some jerk's bedwarmer, the prospects had been better in Calderaas.

"Depends, ma'am," he said. Well, at least he was polite, and seemed to have less trouble keeping eye contact than some men. "You'll doubtless find this a presumptuous question, for which I apologize in advance." Oh, great, here it was. "Are you one of those adventurers in it for the fortune and glory . . . or more the storybook-inspired type? Looking to right wrongs and smite evil, that kinda thing?"

She frowned at him. This was a setup to an insult or a scam, she just knew it . . . and to her embarrassment, a flutter of hope stirred deep inside her. "What's it to you?"

"I'm just hoping it's the latter, is all. Fraid I don't have a lot of budget to hire on muscle, but there's somethin' bad 'bout to unfold in this town. Someone who aims serious harm to a good friend of mine, and needs to be stopped. If you require fair payment for your time, I'll have to leave you to your shopping . . ." Jeremiah Shook smiled, and maybe it was Tazlith's own repressed dreams that did it, but suddenly he looked a lot less crooked. ". . . but if you have plans to be a hero, it may be that only you can help."

CHAPTER 15

"There's nobody out there now," Fross reported, buzzing back into the hall, "but there are horse tracks all over. Centaur tracks, actually, I'm assuming. Also . . . our tracks, which I guess explains how they found us."

"Stupid," Trissiny muttered. "I should've thought of that. Rafe even has that stuff which hides footprints . . ."

"Then we're *all* equally stupid," Toby said firmly, "and there's no point in dwelling on it or casting blame. Let's deal with our current situation."

They had moved into the last stretch of hall, leaving the tomb itself, by unanimous agreement. Whatever the spirit of Horsebutt may have thought of them, it simply didn't feel right to anybody to loiter in someone's final resting place. Juniper had seemed somewhat nonplussed at this, but had followed the group without comment.

"My original plan stands, then," said Trissiny, nodding. "Matters are slightly different now that they've had a chance to prepare for us, but the canyon remains a good place to hold off a charge. Shaeine, can you put a shield over us to cover while we get in position?"

"Now, hold on," Rafe protested. "I'm not about to sign off on you kids going to *war*. Waiting the bastards out seems like a better strategy, since they can't get in here. We've got plenty of food for a few days."

"We are *not* equipped for a siege," she said firmly. "They can hunt and gather up there, quite apart from whatever provisions they have. *We* don't even have water. Plus there's the immediate issue of sanitation."

"Actually, I can fix that," he said brightly. "For a day at least; it's not wise to take back-to-back doses, that can mess up your body chemistry. But a quick sip and you'll all be fully self-contained biological vessels for the duration!"

"Fucking *ew*," Ruda muttered.

"*Plus*," Trissiny went on patiently, "there is the *immediate* matter of the drums."

They all paused to glance upward. The drumming was muted by rock and distance, but hadn't let up in the last half hour.

"Do you remember me saying those drums were a weapon?" she continued. "Specifically, they are warlock tools. The war drums induce a state of bloodlust in those already steeped in infernal magic, and create unnatural fear in all others. Stealing emotional energy, in essence, trading our poise for their power. They severely demoralize a foe while strengthening the centaurs themselves."

"I can deal with that," said Toby. "The aura of calm is Omnu's most basic gift to his followers. It should neutralize their advantage completely."

"That's great, as far as it goes. But I'm not as much concerned about fear among the rest of us as the drums' effect on those *already steeped in infernal magic*." She turned to stare significantly at Gabriel, the others following her gaze.

"I'm fine," he said hoarsely, and completely unconvincingly. He was hunched over and breathing hard, as if winded, and refused to lift his head to make eye contact with anyone.

"Oh . . . shit," said Ruda.

"I'm *fine*," Gabriel snapped.

"Gabriel," said Trissiny quietly, "look at me."

"I don't need your—"

"*Look at me!*" she barked. He jerked his head up, meeting her gaze. His eyes were completely black.

"Toby," said Trissiny calmly, "your aura of calm is divine in nature. It will hurt him if you use it. Do you think it would have a calming effect, even so? Are you willing to subject him to constant pain if it does? And how long can that possibly work, even in the best-case scenario?" She shook her head. "We can't stay here. The longer we wait, the more worn out and vulnerable we become. We have to *deal* with our enemy, and in this situation that means striking first."

Juniper, who had been crouched against the wall nearest the exit tunnel, stood up, walked over to Gabriel, and wrapped her arms around him from behind, resting her head on his shoulder. He took a deep, shuddering gasp, then straightened slightly. The darkness receded somewhat from the edges of his eyes. "Oh . . . wow. That's actually better. What did you do?"

"Cuddled you," she replied, not moving.

"Juniper is a very high-ranking fae," said Shaeine. "Fairy magic neutralizes infernal magic. We have not covered the Circles of Interaction in Professor Yornhaldt's class yet, but that much is common knowledge. Have you any active spells you can use, Juniper?"

The dryad shook her head, rubbing her cheek against Gabriel's shoulder. "I can neutralize poisons, that's it. Nothing . . . y'know, flashy."

"It's better, though," said Gabe, then actually grinned faintly. "And I can't say I mind. This is cozy."

"That's because I have *very* nice breasts," Juniper said matter-of-factly. "I know how you like it when they're touching you."

"And that buys us some time, at least," Trissiny said, her impatience beginning to leak into her voice. "But it doesn't change our situation!"

"She's right," said Ruda. "We're just gonna get weaker if we try to wait this out; they've got all the advantage. With apologies to our resident pacifists, there's a time when you just gotta go out there and fuck somebody up. It's that time, people."

"All right, hold up," said Rafe firmly. His tone and expression were so different from his normal slack-jawed insouciance that they all looked over at him in surprise. "There's more to a situation than fight or huddle. *Fleeing* is also a good option."

"Those are *centaurs*," Trissiny exclaimed. "They run like horses!"

"I didn't say we should challenge them to a footrace. There's such a thing as subterfuge, though. All we've gotta do is create a little confusion, and I think I know how."

"And then what? Wait till they run us down again?"

"I was thinking more about making sure they're in no position to do that. And frankly, Triss, maybe you should acknowledge your own bias. It's not so hard to conceive that the Hand of War is more inclined to a combative solution, is it?"

"Um, I don't see how this is anything but a combative situation," Fross interjected. "Those aren't creatures we can negotiate with. Even *I've* read enough about centaurs to know that. This is almost certain to come to a fight one way or another, and if everyone will *please* remember, Professor Tellwyrn specifically said we should listen to Trissiny if a fight happens!"

"She is not *here*," Rafe said sharply, "and while we're on the subject, let me tell you about Professor Tellwyrn. She believes in testing people, *hard*. I would even say cruelly. If she were leading this expedition and you went too long without stumbling into something life-threatening, she would damn well go find or *create* something life-threatening for you to deal with, just to see how you did. *However*, she would also stand watch over the proceedings and make sure nobody actually died. End of the day, testing is all well and good, but what matters is getting you kids home alive, and I'm making a decision here. Fifty bloodthirsty centaurs is not an academic exercise, it's a *threat*. The trip's over, we're getting the hell out of this."

"Fine!" Trissiny said sharply. "But you still haven't presented a solid case against *fighting them off*! We *have* the capacity."

"Maybe," he replied. "Maybe not. If you're right and we tried it, well, great. If you're *wrong*, then we wouldn't find out until somebody was dead or maimed." He panned a stare across the whole group. "Going to battle is something you do only when it's necessary. If I can present a solid plan that'll get us out if this without it *becoming* necessary, will you guys agree to go along?"

Nobody answered him; they all turned to look at Trissiny. She folded her arms. "Fine. Let's hear it."

"All right. Step one: We have to evacuate our demonfolk before those drums get to them. Vadrieny can fly and carry someone—she needs to take Gabe and get out of range, pronto. She can make it back to Last Rock pretty quick at her flight speed." He turned to Teal and said, "Tell Arachne what's going on and try to get help in case it's needed."

"I don't . . . think . . . the drums are working on Vadrieny," Teal said hesitantly. "I don't feel anything . . . *She* doesn't feel anything."

"She's a whole other class of demon, Teal," Rafe said, still uncharacteristically solemn. "A dozen orders of magnitude beyond a half-hethelax; she'll be resistant to tampering. That might mean the drums just won't work, or that they don't work as well . . . Or maybe that they won't work as *quickly* and the effects will hit all at once later. Frankly, that's a risk we can't take. If Vadrieny goes berserk . . . Two paladins, a cleric, and a dryad aren't going to cut it. She'll demolish us."

Teal folded her arms around herself and looked downward but didn't offer him any argument.

"If that's the case," Toby said slowly, "how many can she carry? I doubt she could take us *all* out, but . . . she's got two hands."

"Nope," said Ruda. Toby blinked at her.

"Nope?"

"Nope." The pirate shook her head. "Nobody else'll go. Think what we got here—three light-wielding types, right? Any of you willing to bug out and leave the rest of us to the centaurs?" She raised an eyebrow, glancing around at them. "Didn't think so. You can add *me* to that list. I'd never be able to look my papa in the eye if I ditched crewmates in a battle."

"That still leaves Juniper," Gabe said, placing a hand over one of the dryad's, where it pressed against his heart.

"Nuh uh." Ruda shook her head again. "She couldn't even *fly* carrying Juniper. Fae and demon magic, remember? Vadrieny doesn't actually have a body, she's using Teal's. So when she . . . y'know, comes out, that's all magic. It's a spell effect. It won't even *work* if she's so much as touching a dryad."

There was a moment's silence while they digested this.

"That's . . . very insightful, Ruda," Toby said slowly.

Ruda grinned sardonically. "Ooh, look, pirate girl has a *brain*. Stop the fuckin' presses."

"So, that's settled," Rafe said, drawing their attention back. "Demon-touched safely out of the picture, all we have to do is throw the centaurs into confusion and get ourselves the hell out."

"I'm *still* waiting to hear how you intend to do that."

He grinned. "Wait no longer, then, Trissiny. I think even *you'll* like this."

"Are you people *insane*!?" the man in the cell shrieked. "What are you *doing*? How?!"

"I see you're still in a mood," Darling said solemnly. "That's fine, I'll come back later."

"Of course I'm still in a mood, you fucking imbecile! You were just here a minute ago!"

"All right, well, good chat," he said cheerily, waving his fingers at the three inmates. "You kids be good, now!"

Whistling jauntily—just to irritate them, because he was not inclined to be the bigger person, as a rule—Darling bounced up the steps to the doors of the jail. Aside from the elaborately carved oak door, it looked like any other prison on the inside—stone floors, torchlight, iron bars separating cramped cells. When he slipped out, though, shutting the door behind him on the newest prisoner's ranting, he was left standing in front of the elaborately carved wardrobe set up in the little house's basement.

"Have fun eyeballing your little collection?" the demon said snidely from within his circle. Darling just strode past him, still whistling.

That wardrobe had certainly cost more than a comparably sized prison would have to build. The enchantments on it were state of the art, and the power source running it was an enchanted crystal of the sort the archwizards of old had spent lifetimes creating and went to war to steal from each other. The use of pocket dimensions for storage—even of people—wasn't anything new, but time within this prison was frozen except when a person bearing one of the control runes entered. Thus, the four prisoners had scarcely had time to get their bearings, even two days later. With the bishops checking on them every hour and not staying long, the first captive, Mrs. Harkley, had only been there a few minutes by her own reckoning. As it must have looked to the prisoners like their captors were cycling in and out immediately on one another's heels, not to mention that the three from the previous night had been collected right behind Harkley, it surely wouldn't take them long to figure out the basics of their situation.

What troubled Darling was how this thing had come to be given to them for their mission. It had been delivered shortly after their arrival in the town, with no explanation beyond a description of its function and directions for its use. Such incredibly advanced enchantment was the kind of toy he'd expect Imperial Intelligence to have in its possession, but everything they carried had been provided by the Church, which historically didn't work very much with arcane magic. Had Justinian established a group of enchanters or mages under the Church's aegis? Had they somehow appropriated imperial property? If so, was it with the empire's cooperation? Every question spun off into more questions; the only thing he could be certain of was that the extra dimensional wardrobe showed the Archpope's resources to be well beyond what he had imagined.

That, needless to say, was disturbing.

He emerged into the kitchen to find it quieter than when he'd left. Branwen's mixing bowl was sitting on the counter, still full of batter and with her spoon stuck in, but the stove was cool. Darling frowned, unease tingling at the back of his neck.

"Everything all right?" he asked, stepping into the living room.

"Doesn't look like it," Basra replied. She and Andros were by the front windows, holding up the curtains to peer out. Branwen stood near the kitchen door, wringing her hands; she gave him a tense smile as he entered.

"The town is too quiet," Andros rumbled. "It's only just sundown; there should still be people about. The street is deserted."

Darling frowned, striding across the room to join him. Sure enough, Hamlet appeared to be a ghost town. He half expected an iconic tumbleweed to blow across the road. "You suspect our Wreath friends?"

"Who else?"

"This may be their last gasp," said Basra thoughtfully. "Given the size of the town and the sheer number of those Tellwyrn took out, there can't have been many left. Strategically speaking . . . They sent one to investigate our demon, let a night pass after she turned up missing, then dispatched three with more obviously hostile intentions." She turned to look at him, frowning. "I'd thought that might be the end of them . . . If it wasn't, though, we might be about to see the last, desperate act of whoever's left."

"Good," Andros growled. "I'll be glad to see the end of this nonsense."

"How's our perimeter, Andros?" Darling asked.

"Intact. My wards and traps have not been approached."

"Mm. Anyone sense any magic at play? Anything that might make the townspeople up and leave?"

"No," said Basra, "for whatever that's worth. We'd sense open infernal magic, but what makes the Wreath more dangerous than hedge warlocks is Elilial's gift of stealth. They can hide even from the gods."

"I don't sense *anything*," Branwen said fretfully, "even stretching my mind out to its furthest extent. There should be . . . a buzz, a background noise of people's desires and passions. There's nothing. It's like the townspeople are all asleep."

"Or gone," Andros growled.

"Right." Darling stepped back. "Everybody, gear up. Seems likely something's about to go down; it's not going to take us by surprise. Charms on, weapons at hand, in position. Andros, you're on point. Let us know the instant anything gets too close."

For a wonder, Andros didn't give him any backtalk. He and Branwen turned and retreated to their rooms to gather their things; Basra remained on watch until they returned, then she and Darling did the same.

He could feel it in the very air now. Not something magical, or something tangible, but a tension. A feeling weighing on the back of his neck that this was all finally coming to a head.

He hoped they were ready for it.

In the end, they didn't need Andros's wards. Their enemy approached openly as the sun fell over the silent town.

Three figures in cowled, gray robes stepped up to the front gate of the house and paused. The one in the middle drew back a hand, then hurled it forward as though throwing a ball. At the gesture, the four bishops felt a spike of diabolic energy and the middle section of the white picket fence exploded into splinters.

"Classy," Basra snorted.

She stood beside the door; the rest of them were positioned throughout the living room, all four wearing their invisibility charms. They watched through the windows as the three attacking Wreath cultists strode forward onto the lawn and paused again.

Once more there came a huge swelling of infernal energy, though this time the cultists weren't visibly doing anything but standing there. Immediately, however, the gathering shadows rippled around them like disturbed water, and two additional figures appeared between them.

A serpentine creature wound itself around the cultist on the far left; the length of a python and twice as thick around the chest, its horse like skull contained a flickering green flame that blazed through its open mouth and apparently empty eye sockets, casting an eerie glow along its glossy black scales. Between the middle and right figures, a creature appeared that was the size and roughly the dimensions of a dog. It had enormous, burly forelegs, like a gorilla, and a long snout bristling with teeth, reminiscent of an alligator. With neither fur nor scales along much of its frame, it had preposterously oversized claws on each foot, and spiky plates of bone lining its spine.

Their familiars summoned, the cultists lowered their hoods. Even in the falling light, their features were clearly visible, as were their grimly resolute expressions. Darling couldn't see his fellow bishops, but he suspected he wasn't the only one who reared back in surprise.

They were *children*.

Well, teenagers, anyway. The boy on the right, the one who rested a hand on the hellhound's back, couldn't have been thirteen. On the opposite side was a girl maybe a year or two older, if that, with the taller boy in the center just barely old enough to lie his way into the army.

Darling held position, though internally he was reeling. Was this the Wreath's plan? Send someone they'd be reluctant to harm? He had to acknowledge that if that was their game, it was a good one; he wasn't at all sure he had the stomach to use force against kids that young. What disturbed him more, however, was his certainty that at least one, and probably two, of his compatriots *did*.

The three started forward as one, their demons in tow, but stopped just short of the stairs, uncertainty registering on their faces, when Basra silently opened the door. She was still invisible; they stared warily at the suddenly empty space for a moment before the tallest youth, the one in the middle, set his jaw and stepped forward again. Taking his cue, the others came, too, visibly regathering their courage.

The youngest boy snapped his fingers and pointed at the door; the hellhound let out a hoarse grunt and lunged forward, barreling through.

Basra lashed out with her sword, neatly beheading the demon as it charged past. It plowed into the stairs, already beginning to crumble to ash and letting off gouts of sulfurous smoke before it had stopped twitching. The boy who commanded it emitted one short cry of shock. Basra's invisibility charm failed, though, its arcane power source probably disrupted by the burst of released infernal energy.

"Oh, come on," Basra said, standing in the door and grinning at them. "You're not even trying."

The smirk vanished from her face when all three of them pulled out wands and took aim. Basra barely dived out of the line of fire before lightning bolts ripped through the front of the house, blasting the door off its hinges, taking out a chunk of its frame and punching a hole in the staircase.

The serpentine demon lunged forward, flying without the benefit of wings, and spat a gout of green fire at her. Basra, cursing, erupted in golden radiance and swiped at the creature with her sword. She was quick and precise, but the girl spun through the air with unnatural agility, evading every strike. Basra was forced to retreat through the door to the downstairs bedroom to evade another round of wandfire as the two older kids pushed inside, forcing her back.

Then Andros switched off his own invisibility charm. He had a bow ready with an arrow nocked; in one smooth motion, he drew back and let it fly, and this time it was the Wreath kids who were forced to dive aside. He hadn't aimed at them, however; the arrow thunked into the lintel above the shattered door, and an eerie blue radiance rose from it. All at once the temperature plummeted in the room. Flakes of actual snow began to appear from the ceiling, flung about by the winds that suddenly sprang up. With the blessing of Shaath suddenly upon the house, its internal weather became a facsimile of that in the frigid Stalrange, contrasting painfully with the heat of the plains. The kids found snow driven into their eyes by winds that whipped their ill-fitting gray robes about, as though seeking to tear them right off.

They barely had time to react to this before Andros tossed aside his bow, pulled out a pair of wands, and returned fire. Darling noted with relief that he was aiming to keep them separated and on their toes, not to kill. Even so, every shot blasted a hole in the wooden walls of the house, except those which pulverized furniture instead. Only the frigid winds kept the place from catching fire.

Branwen flickered into view, already wreathed in a golden glow, but whatever she'd planned to do, her sudden appearance only made her a target. She barely formed a divine shield in time to absorb a blast from a wand aimed by the youngest boy.

One of Andros's wandshots clipped the snake demon, sending it careening into the wall with an unnatural screech that grated painfully on the ears. Branwen immediately directed a blast of pure light at it, pinning it against the wall long enough for the huntsman to level both his wands and unleash a barrage that reduced the creature to ash and that section of wall to kindling.

Meanwhile, the girl finally took aim at the blessed arrow with her own wand, blasting it to oblivion and taking the upper half of the doorframe down with it, causing a section of wall adjacent to the front door to tumble outward, unsupported.

In the sudden absence of howling winds, the house groaned alarmingly.

Darling wasn't paying attention to this. The last one still invisible, he was staring at Branwen. For a moment, something had flickered through her golden aura, disturbing it at the moment when it was weakest, when she was directing more power at the snake demon. He glanced around; Basra was still in the other room, apparently the target of the wandshots the tallest boy was firing in that direction, and Andros was in a momentary standoff with the other two. Three warlocks . . . two demons. There was no way these kids had conjured familiars of that caliber on their own . . .

He darted over to Branwen, placing a hand on her back and hoping she didn't jump in startlement. She didn't react at all, in fact. Of course, Izarite priests were empaths; she'd probably sensed his approach.

"Give me ten seconds," he murmured, "then drop your aura."

Darling scuttled back from her, hoping his message was received and accepted; she had the presence of mind not to give away his position by acknowledging it verbally. Sure enough, ten seconds later, she turned to face the two kids in the corner, letting the glow around herself wink out and placing a shield of light between their wands and Andros.

He watched her back intently. A moment . . . Wait for it . . . Could he have been wrong? No, there . . . the faintest distortion.

Darling lunged forward, snatching a heavy pewter candlestick from the mantle. He brought it down with all his strength, apparently into midair; by sheer luck or the favor of Eserion, it was a dead hit. The succubus popped into visibility as the chunk of pewter was slammed down on her skull. With stealth now a lost cause, he finally nixed his charm, dropping the candlestick and reaching out to grab the demon by the hair as she crumpled. With his other hand, he whipped out his belt knife and drove it into her back, then viciously yanked the blade out sideways, splattering the floorboards with black ichor. The demon crumpled to the ground, putrefying as her body began to dissolve into rancid charcoal.

Gods in the sky, a succubus. Not even a warlock would be crazy enough to give teenagers access to a succubus. This was all wrong.

With the younger two distracted, the tall boy was suddenly alone and found himself in the sights of both Andros's wands. He turned, wide-eyed, raising his own weapon at the huntsman.

Basra whipped around the corner, commanding his attention again, but before he could swivel his wand back around to aim at her, she drove her sword into his belly just below the ribs.

"*Andy!*" the girl shrieked in anguish. The boy dropped his wand, gaping at Basra, who winked at him, then yanked her weapon free. He crumpled soundlessly.

"Damn it!" Darling swore.

"You *didn't* need to do that!" Branwen exclaimed, rushing to the fallen boy's side. Her shield over the other two winked out, but Andros immediately swiveled both his wands to cover them.

"Drop the weapons," he snarled. Both kids, tears pouring down their faces, did so.

Meanwhile, Basra was wiping blood from her short sword with a piece of curtain that had been badly scorched by wandshots. Her eyes flicked between Darling and Branwen, narrowing. "I don't tell you two how to pick pockets or suck dicks. Do *not* tell me how to end a fight."

Branwen had placed her hands over the boy's wound. While light blazed around her, Darling eased over to the other two and collected their wands. Stepping back, he peered critically around the room.

The stairs had been pulverized, the front door was completely gone . . . Holes had been blasted in all four walls and the ceiling, and most of the furniture was nothing but scraps of kindling and scorched fabric. He winced at the sight of all those books, burned to ash and fragments, their pieces strewn about by Shaath's winds. The entire front of the room was more open space than wall at this point. "Something tells me we're not getting our security deposit back," he said.

"Still too quiet out there," Andros grunted, then raised one wand to point directly at the girl's face. "You. Explain."

She tore her eyes from the spectacle of Branwen trying to heal her fallen friend. Tears still ran down her face, but the glare she directed at Andros was pure hatred. She answered, however, her voice thick with barely controlled emotion. "It's a spell. The elders set it up long ago in case we needed to . . . to . . ." She paused, swallowing down a lump in her throat. "Everyone's asleep, but they're fine. They'll wake up fine. *We* don't harm innocents," she spat.

Andros grunted. "How many more of you?"

"We're *it*, moron!" the younger boy said shrilly. "Do you think they'd send *kids* after you? There's nobody else *left*. You killed our *parents*, you bastard! We called up their familiars and came t-t-to . . ." He trailed off, squeezing his eyes shut, and choked back a sob. The girl wrapped both her arms around his thin shoulders.

"To what?" Basra asked dryly. "Get revenge? Well done."

"Enough," Darling said sharply. Turning to the kids, he moderated his tone. "Nobody's been killed, no thanks to you. Your parents, if that's who paid us an unannounced visit last night, are fine. They're about to go to Tiraas, but the good news is you'll be going, too. Branwen, how's it look?"

She had just let the glow around her fade, and sat back on her heels, looking exhausted. "I'm *really* not a healer. I think . . . I think he's stable. But it's not a *good* stable . . . He's lost blood, which I can't do anything about. Might be in shock, too."

"Right . . ." Darling looked around again at the destroyed house, the eerily silent street, their beaten and traumatized underage foes. "Well, then, not only is our mission accomplished, but I think we're about to be very unwelcome in this town. Time to be moving along. Andros, Branwen, get these three into the cells. The stasis should keep the lad stable until we can get him to an actual healer. Basra, we're done with the . . . thing . . . in the basement. Be so kind as to kill it."

"*Excellent*," she said, already grinning and fondling her sword lovingly as she shouldered past Andros into the kitchen.

"I'm going to make a break for the scrolltower office while the town's asleep," Darling said, already starting for the door. "We can't take that wardrobe on the Rail; we'll need transport out of here as quick as possible. Andros, I don't anticipate more trouble, but keep everything stable here till I get back."

The huntsman nodded to him. Confident this situation was as under control as it could be, Darling exited through the gaping hole roughly where the front door had been and bounded down the steps.

Hamlet was downright creepy like this. The last redness of sunset had faded while they were occupied shooting up the house, but even in the darkness, the town felt *dead* in a way that no town should. He had an irrational thought that the residents might not be merely asleep, and made a mental note to double-check on them—or at least some of them—once his immediate errand was complete. Gods knew they'd have time while they waited for a coach to get out here.

It happened faster than he could react.

One instant he was disturbingly alone in the silent town, the next, the moon-cast shadows seemed to blossom all around him, spitting out half a dozen figures. All but one of them wore ash-gray robes.

Darling skidded to a stop, completely encircled. Directly in front of him, a man in a dapper white suit and matching boater hat stepped forward. His face was dark brown, homely, and brightened by an amiable smile.

"Evenin'," he said lightly, tugging the brim of his hat. "It's Sweet, isn't it? I do believe you have something of mine." That mild-mannered grin widened, and the cultists began to close in. "Well . . . something of my Lady's, that is."

"Ah," said Darling mildly, glancing around. No gaps to exploit. "Well, you know how it is, one picks things up. What are you missing, exactly?"

"Four members of my cult." The man's smile faded into grimness. "And their children."

CHAPTER 16

"We ready, then?" asked Rafe brightly. Trissiny repressed a sigh. They weren't ready; she did not have a good opinion of this plan, but the others had overruled her. Again.

"It's a little unwieldy," said Fross, drifting slightly to one side before catching herself. "The featherweight oil's working, though. I don't think I'll have any trouble carrying it at speed."

"Just be careful not to spill it. At least, not before it's time to."

"Yes, I *know*, Professor."

She looked very odd with a cobbled-together tray of bottles and glass vials suspended from her, swaying gently back and forth. Fross appeared to be able to handle the weight, but the students were nonetheless keeping their distance, knowing what was in those bottles.

"I *still* don't like that we pillaged Horsebutt's grave goods to make that," Ruda grumbled. "It's not respectful."

"We just took a few arrows to make the frame," said Gabe tersely. He still had Juniper wrapped around him, and was still clearly feeling the effects of the war drums. The rest of them were mostly okay, thanks to time spent in Toby's calming aura. "Just be glad Rafe had so much spider silk in that belt or we'd have been truly fucked."

"Still doesn't feel right," she said. "I left some food and ale, but . . . I dunno if that's what he'd like. Don't need an angry ghost coming after us."

"Well, he was a barbarian warlord," Teal said. "What else would he like? We could leave some coins?"

"Hmph. Simple things, practical things. Food, drink, loot, and girls. Oh," Ruda said, grinning suddenly. "Maybe I could strip down, lie on his tomb, and jill myself off a couple times. Bet he'd get a kick out of that."

"Okay," Gabriel said after a moment's stunned pause. "Two questions. Would that actually work, and if so, can I watch?"

"It actually might," said Rafe, "and no, that seems like the kind of thing for which Trissiny would stab you."

They all shifted their eyes to look at her. Trissiny glanced back and forth around the group, then shrugged irritably. "What? You're expecting me to argue?"

"Horsebutt will have to be content with Ruda's offering and our apologies," Rafe said firmly. "I don't think we can afford to waste much more time here. Fross? You're up."

"Wish me luck!" the pixie chirped, then drifted toward the doorway of the canyon. She was moving without apparent strain, but much slower than usual. There was a collective indrawing of breath as she came perilously close to clipping the stone doorframe with her makeshift basket, but she corrected and made it out into open air without trouble. From there, she ascended rapidly out of sight. There came no immediate outcry from the centaurs; she had clearly followed the instructions to move outside their range of view.

"Right," said Rafe. "Demons, your turn."

Juniper gave Gabe a quick kiss on the cheek, squeezed him once, and then let him go, backing away. Immediately, the blackness in his eyes expanded to fill them completely, and he hunched forward, features twisting as he fought the artificial rage induced by the centaurs' infernal magic.

Teal shifted without a word; even with her wings folded tightly against her back, Vadrieny's blazing presence was overwhelming in the cramped tunnel. She stalked forward, talons crunching on the gravel-strewn floor, the others pressing themselves against the wall to get out of her path, and laid one clawed hand on Gabriel's shoulder.

"Right," Rafe repeated. "Good. Now that you're here and the moment is upon us, Vadrieny, I want you to grab Ruda, too."

"What?" Ruda said shrilly.

"She's the most vulnerable of those left, with no magic of her own," the professor continued inexorably. "Get her to safety. The rest of us can cope."

"Fuck you!" Ruda snarled, grasping at her rapier. "I'm not leaving my friends like that!"

"This isn't up for discussion," he said sharply. "Vadrieny—"

"Not happening," said the demon curtly.

Rafe boggled at her for a moment, then scowled. "Look, this is in the best—"

"*You* look." She pointed one wicked claw at him, glaring. "Ruda *fights*. She stands by her friends. Loyalty and valor—those aren't just values, that's who and what she *is*. Maybe someday, Rafe, someone will strip away *your* identity, and then you'll understand why you don't *do* that to a person. Ready to go, Gabriel?"

"As I'll ever be," he rasped, lifting his eyes to look helplessly at the others. "Guys, I . . . I'm sorry. I wish . . ."

"It's *all right*, Gabe," Toby said firmly. "Get to safety. Get Tellwyrn; that's the best thing you can do for us now."

Gabriel had time to nod once before Vadrieny steered him firmly out of the tunnel, one arm wrapped around his chest, and took off with a mighty beat of her wings. They were instantly lost to sight, but there came a whooping from above as the centaurs spotted the glowing demon passing.

"We are going to *talk* about this, you and me," Ruda said grimly, glaring at Rafe.

"Can't wait," he muttered.

"Is there even the slightest chance of Tellwyrn coming to help?" Trissiny asked quietly.

"Not really, no." Rafe shook his head. "She may be the biggest, baddest mage alive, but the Golden Sea . . . Even *gods* have had trouble navigating in here. Teleporting into the Sea is completely random. Traveling by foot or by air isn't much better unless you're going toward the edge. Nope, we'd best not count on any backup arriving."

She nodded, unsurprised, and drew her sword.

Toby shifted uncomfortably. "How long do you think it'll take Fross... Oh. That must be her."

The sounds from above erupted into utter cacophony. The drums, mercifully, stopped. The centaurs' hollering abruptly increased tenfold in volume and intensity, many of the shouts becoming outright screams, and the sound of hoofbeats thundered about even more erratically than when they had first arrived.

Fross's collection of bottles had been a hodgepodge of disruptive compounds Rafe had been carrying. Hallucinogens and fear inducers, plus a bottle of pure elemental wind to spread the effects around as much as possible. A few bottled shades, barely intelligent shadow elementals, which would rush around in a mad panic in the absence of specific orders; he had bemoaned the loss of those, but they would be just the push needed to scatter the suddenly drugged and terrified centaurs.

"Ahh." Rafe grinned fiendishly, rubbing his hands. "I do love it when a plan comes together. Confusion and chaos, kids. This is why you don't screw with the alchemist!"

"Time for us to move," Trissiny said curtly, stepping out into the canyon.

Afternoon was fading above; it was already deep twilight within the canyon, only the reddish sky still showing any signs of light. The gloom was less disturbing than the chaos from the plains. No matter that the centaurs were enemies of the worst kind, hearing them screaming in abject terror was not pleasant for anyone.

The others filed out behind her, quiet as possible; Trissiny barely waited for them to exit the passage before setting off back the way they had come.

It was a tense, macabre reenactment of their journey into the canyon in the first place. Again, the centaurs were galloping about without plan or purpose, but this time they were obviously suffering utter havoc, rather than exulting in high spirits. Here and there, sounds of fighting broke out as the potion-addled brutes turned on each other. This time, too, it was dark, and growing darker by the moment; Shaeine carefully tucked her black glasses into their case and then into her robes. As before, though, the students made their progress as carefully and quietly as they could without sacrificing too much speed.

With a horrible scream, a centaur pitched over the rim of the canyon above, striking the ground with a massive *thud*, mangled by the snapping of limbs. She lay there, kicking with broken legs and shrieking nonstop until Trissiny darted forward and beheaded the creature with a quick stroke.

The others stared at her, wide-eyed, as she returned to the group. Shaeine, though, nodded once in understanding. In that instance, the tactically sound thing was also the only kindness she could have offered. Neither of them could have healed those injuries, even if they'd wanted to.

"Hug the wall, just like we did on the way in," she said, pitching her voice only loud enough to be audible amid the carnage. "If any more fall off, they'll hopefully overshoot us. We *don't* want to be landed on."

She resumed her place in the lead, setting off. They followed again with only the slightest hesitation.

For all that the trip back started much worse than the trip out had been, it gradually got better. The centaurs grew more scattered, and this time the group actually managed to leave them behind; they had apparently made their camp above the tomb to wait for the students to emerge. They made much better time, too, moving with a purpose and a somewhat diminished need for stealth. In what seemed like relatively short order, the canyon walls shortened enough that they had to hunch to hide beneath them, which they did; distant or no, the centaurs were still audibly present, still making a constant din of screams and occasional crashes.

Trissiny called a halt; this was where they were meant to rendezvous with Fross, and there was no sign of her. She knew to head downhill, which would lead reliably to Last Rock, if she became separated, but Trissiny very much hoped it didn't come to that. They wouldn't know their missing classmate's fate until they got back to the University in that case, and if Fross didn't turn up there, they'd have no realistic prospect of mounting a rescue.

At least it was finally growing dark enough to see stars. The pixie would be much easier to spot against a black sky.

"Everybody catch your breath," she said quietly. "When Fross finds us, we're going to move as quickly as we can, straight downhill. Once we're out on the open plain, stealth is not going to be a possibility. We'll do our best to get out of range of the centaurs, and if any of them catch up, we'll have to fight."

"How long does that stuff last, Professor?" asked Toby.

"Should keep 'em completely out of commission for most of the night! I don't brew halfway, sonny boy."

"And after that they'll have a hard time regrouping. They'll have wounded to tend to, and whatever supplies they were carrying were almost certainly damaged in the chaos." Trissiny nodded grudgingly. "It'll mean a very exhausting night, but I'd say odds are decent that if we make good time, we won't have to deal—"

It had been perfectly still; none of them had realized anyone was there. But abruptly, a centaur burst upright out of the tallgrass not twenty yards away, where he had apparently been lying on his side. Trissiny spun to face him, and for an instant they locked eyes. His face was twisted by panic, but not reduced to witlessness. She saw him see her. See all of them.

He raised a horn to his lips and blew a series of sharp blasts, galloping back along the rim of the canyon toward whatever was left of the main herd.

"All right," said Rafe, "which one of you forgot to make an offering to Arseface, the god of irony?"

"Never mind," said Trissiny. "We have to move. Those who are so inclined, say a prayer of guidance for Fross, but do it while we run."

She suited the words with action, setting out at a sharp pace after doing a quick visual scan to identify the direction in which the prairie gently sloped. The others immediately followed; to her frustration,

Trissiny had to moderate her pace somewhat. Clearly, she was the only one accustomed to prolonged running.

In fairness, it hardly mattered. There was no way they were going to outrun centaurs.

For a good ten minutes it seemed they actually might; it was at least that long before the sounds behind them became organized. Trissiny skidded to a halt, though, when the hunting horns rose. At least three separate tones. She turned back to face their pursuers. They were merely a line of indistinct shapes in the darkness, but even at this distance, she felt the faint prickling of diabolic magic at work.

"Stop," she said firmly. Juniper leaned forward, bracing her hands on her knees; Shaeine was also out of breath. "Everyone catch your breath as best you can; we don't want to face this overtired. Toby, can you ease everyone's weariness?"

"I have been," he replied, then grimaced apologetically. "Except . . . it won't work on Juniper; divine magic's not helpful for fae. Sorry, June."

"'S'fine," the dryad said, waving him off. She straightened slowly with an odd cracking sound, like twigs snapping. She wasn't panting; she wasn't, Trissiny realized, breathing at all, but her body language clearly showed fatigue.

"Are you all right, June?" she asked.

"Yup. Just let me . . . limber up a bit." Juniper rolled her neck and shook out her arms. "I'm not really used to running. I'll be fine."

"Good. When they get close enough to attack, I want you on point. Be out in front and take down whatever they send at you."

"Can do," the dryad said grimly, stepping forward to position herself between the group and the rapidly approaching centaurs.

"Shaeine, support her initially with your shields until the battle closes and Ruda and I advance to her position. I want Juniper to take the first hits; use your best judgment about what's too much for her to take."

"Why's that, exactly?" Ruda demanded.

"Psychological warfare," Trissiny said, keeping her eye on the enemy. They had slowed their advance, forming into a more even line. That was not the behavior of people hopped up on alchemical terror drugs. Either the potions had missed a few, or they had a way to counteract them. It was barely more than a dozen, though, which was much better than facing the full horde of fifty. "They'll open with arrows, spears, and/or infernal magic. Juniper's impervious to diabolism. She's also our most durable member and can take a few hits. I want them to see their opening salvo fail to make a dent on a pretty girl in a short dress before we proceed to carving them up. June, as soon as you feel you've had enough, start backing up, and Ruda and I will move in and take the front. Then focus on recovering until you feel ready to rejoin the fight."

"Got it." The dryad smiled brightly at her. "You know, you're actually really good at this!"

"This is what I've trained for my whole life," the paladin said flatly.

"And me?" Rafe asked. Trissiny repressed the first comment that came to mind. Thanks to him and his nonsense, she was conducting this battle without their two most impervious members—one of whom was also their hardest hitter—not to mention their ranged magic support. This was not the time, though; you didn't berate your troops right before an engagement if you wanted them fighting at their best.

"Unless you've got a weapon, hang back. Since holy magic won't heal Juniper, and I'd rather she not waste her energy, use any applicable potions you've still got to support her."

"Right y-o!"

"What, no special instructions for me?" Ruda asked grinning.

Trissiny shook her head. "Your job is to kill things. I don't think you need supervision."

The pirate laughed. "Once in a while, roomie, you say something that makes me think we just might learn to get along."

"Here we go," Trissiny said firmly as the centaurs let out simultaneous blasts on three hunting horns. "Stand firm and show them just what they're messing with, people."

The centaurs—fourteen of them—formed a cohesive line fifty yards distant. At their center was a female who stood head and shoulders taller than any of the others, wearing a headdress of antlers and carrying a long staff surmounted by a collection of grinning skulls. Even from this distance, Trissiny could feel the demonic magic radiating from her.

One trotted forward, a male—the same one, she realized, who'd spotted them and sounded the alarm. He made a diagonal pass across the distance between the two groups, studying them. She saw the moment when he realized they had no bows, wands, or spears—a savage grin broke across his features, and he wheeled about, charging forward. Directly at Juniper.

The dryad had stepped forward, placing a good six yards between herself and the other students, and stood there, watching him come. He eyed her up and down with a leer, even as he rapidly closed with her. Not slowing in the slightest, he reangled himself to pass perpendicular to the battle lines, reaching out to grab a fistful of Juniper's hair in passing.

He might as well have grabbed a tree.

The centaur emitted a pained squawk as he was brought up short, flopping onto his side, his legs going out from under him. Juniper very calmly raised her own leg and kicked him right under the chin.

With a disturbing *pop*, his head went sailing back the way he had come, striking the ground and bouncing toward the other centaurs. It vanished into the tallgrass before reaching them.

With a howl of rage, another female broke from the centaur lines and charged forward, this one brandishing a staff somewhat less elaborate than that wielded by their leader. She gesticulated with this as she came, sending a huge, roughly bird-shaped patch of shadow careening straight at Juniper.

It struck the dryad and vanished.

The charging centaur's yells only grew more furious. She launched two more of the shadow-birds, each of which simply petered out upon making contact; the second one, Juniper actually swatted out of the air, grinning.

Her smugness vanished when the warlock changed tactics, hurling a fireball. The dryad yelped, diving frantically out of the way. The spell impacted the ground just beyond where she had been, igniting the tallgrass. Juniper rolled to her feet and lunged away from it in a panic, even as the rest of the students were forced back from the growing blaze, Rafe fishing frantically in his belt for something to put it out.

The centaur warlock brandished her staff again, grinning triumphantly and calling another ball of fire into being. Her own victorious expression was snuffed out when a translucent silver wall sprang into existence right in front of her. Moving too fast to stop, she slammed into it at full speed with a hideous *crunch* and staggered backward, then fell to the ground, stunned.

"Good work, Shaeine!" Trissiny shouted. "Everyone, regroup! Back away from the fire. Juniper, this way! Don't get separated!"

The centaurs had begun to move forward at a walk, the leader brandishing her skull staff overhead. The students were in disarray, despite Trissiny's efforts to regather them; the fire was taking hold admirably in the dry tallgrass, spreading fast and unpredictably.

And then, out of nowhere, a blast of frigid wind ripped across the space between them, accompanied an instant later by a brutal splattering of sleet. In seconds, the fire was gone and a swath of scorched tallgrass glistened under a thin coating of ice.

"Hi, guys!" Fross sang, zipping into their midst. "What'd I miss?"

"Fross!" Trissiny shouted in relief. "Thank the goddess! I was afraid they'd caught you. Can you discourage them while we pull back together? *Elemental* magic only; they may be able to turn arcane spells against you."

"Excuse me, I'm an arcane sciences major. I *know* my Circles of Interaction. Hey, four-legged assholes! BEHOLD!"

From the tiny point of white light that was the pixie sprang forward an unthinkable torrent of magic. A wave of wind rippled across the plain, drawing the centaurs up short; in its wake came dozens of icicles, spraying across them without pattern. They let out cries of surprise and pain; some of those shafts of ice were sharp enough to pierce flesh. A few halfhearted bursts of fire cut swaths into the ice storm, but after less than half a minute, the centaurs broke formation and wheeled about, galloping away in full retreat.

"They grow up so fast," Rafe sniffled.

"Is everybody all right?" Trissiny asked as they finally managed to regroup.

"Peachy keen! I'm . . . Whoo, head rush . . ." Fross chimed weakly, and dropped suddenly from the air. Shaeine dived forward to catch her in her cupped hands.

"Fross!" Toby said in alarm.

"She's okay," Juniper assured them, peering down at the spent pixie, "just exhausted. Pixies are basically *made* of magic; she can't exactly run out, but she can dip so low she's got no energy left for stuff like flying and talking. Here, give her to me, your fingers'll get frostbite." Tenderly taking Fross from Shaeine, she set the pixie atop her head, nestling her into her thatch of green hair. "There. That was a *lot* of power to be throwing around at once. She'll be okay in a few hours."

"So we can't expect her to do that again anytime soon?" Rafe said, glancing back the way the centaurs had gone.

"Better not," Juniper replied. "Honestly, I think she might try, but she'll just burn herself out again. It's not . . . *unsafe*. Like I said, pixie magic is pretty much bottomless. But there's a limit to how much she can hold at one time."

"So she needs to regenerate," said Trissiny, "and we need to move. I don't think we can afford to assume they've had enough."

"What would you guess are the odds?" Toby asked as they fell into step behind her. She didn't try to lead them at a run this time; she'd chivvy them into a faster pace eventually, but for now, Fross wasn't the only one needing to regather her strength.

"Depends on too many factors we can't really understand," she replied. "Mostly down to their culture and the psychology of that big one who was leading."

"It comes down to this," said Ruda. "They're raiders. We've just embarrassed them twice; they can't have that. The leader can't have it; it'll be cutting into her authority. If we scared them badly enough, she may not be able to whip them back into fighting shape to come after us. Otherwise, they definitely will."

"Their apparent leader, in addition to being an abnormally large specimen, was clearly a warlock of notable power," said Shaeine. "It is difficult to imagine that they are more frightened of us than they are of her."

Toby closed his eyes and drew in a deep breath. "So you're saying..."

"We're saying," Trissiny said grimly, "it is going to be a *long* night. Walk faster."

There were few things more brutally exhausting than a long fighting retreat, as they soon learned.

The centaurs did not give up. The students managed to kill a few with each engagement, but the overall trend in their numbers was in the opposite direction as they gathered more of their scattered herd. The students suffered only minor wounds, easily mended with three light wielders and an alchemist in their group, but they were leaning heavily on Toby's gifts and Rafe's concoctions to keep their energy up. Nobody knew exactly where the tipping point would be, but they were all well aware that magic and alchemy were not long-term substitutes for rest, especially when they were alternating constant running with short bursts of grueling violence.

The first time the centaurs charged again, a swift counter charge by Trissiny and Ruda smashed their lines, throwing them into disarray. Despite their disadvantages in number and size, the two humans were wreathed in healing light from Toby and mobile barriers provided by Shaeine; the centaurs very quickly grew tired of fighting indestructible little pests who darted into their midst wielding cold steel, and broke away to regroup.

Thereafter, they abandoned their strategy of using numbers and weight, preferring to make passes from a safe distance, firing arrows and spells. Shaeine continued to shield the group from projectiles, and Fross, by that point, had recovered enough to retaliate with ice bolts; though, at Juniper and Trissiny's insistence, she carefully paced herself. Even Rafe managed to be helpful, hurling vials that unleashed fire, poison, blasts of wind, glue, and all manner of effects. Any lone centaurs who wandered too close to the group were taken down brutally by Juniper; the couple of times small knots of them tried to charge, those who slipped past the dryad were cut down by the two swordswomen.

This long engagement stretched for over an hour before the students, faltering with weariness, changed their own tactics. As yet another column galloped past, readying their bows, Fross zipped overhead to blast them with wind and snow from the other side, herding them closer to the group, while at the same time Shaeine slammed a shield into place, boxing them in. Ruda, Trissiny, and Juniper waded into the mix, wreaking devastation, until the centaurs broke completely and scattered, beaten and demoralized.

One group, anyway. There always seemed to be more trickling back into the herd to replenish their numbers, even as the students grew weaker and more weary.

In the aftermath of the failure of their last charge, the centaurs attempted to regroup into battle lines, as they had in the first place, but were sent into full retreat when Toby burst into radiance with an intensity that lit up the prairie like high noon. Throwing his arm forward, he sent his own aura rushing at them, a small mobile sun. In its wake, Trissiny could feel the crawling miasma of infernal magic burned away. The centaurs finally retreated out of their line of sight.

"Sorry, Shaeine," Toby said ruefully.

"No apologies necessary," she replied, rubbing at her eyes. "I would appreciate a word of warning next time, however."

"There's . . . there's not gonna be a next time," he said. "I can't manage that again. Guys . . . I'm nearing the point of burnout here. If we don't do something to stop this soon . . ." He let the thought trail off. It wasn't really necessary to finish it.

The light of the gods was infinite in scope and depth, but there were stark limits to how much of it mortal flesh could safely channel. "Burnout" was not a euphemism; clerics who drew too deeply on divine power tended to literally combust. Some deities cut off their followers before it got to that point. Avei, trusting her soldiers to recognize the battle in which they would die, did not. Trissiny wasn't feeling the warning twinges of heat herself, but she had been relying more on muscle while Toby was using divine magic entirely.

"It will be as the gods will," she said grimly, bringing up the rear of the party.

"That's just fuckin' wonderful, that is," Ruda growled, trudging along just in front of them. "What a fucking miserable place to die. No proper body of water within miles."

"We're not going to—" Trissiny broke off her reassurance as Juniper abruptly collapsed.

"June!" Ruda shouted, rushing over to her and kneeling at the dryad's side. "Oh, fuck . . . she's not breathing!"

"She *doesn't* breathe," said Rafe, coming over beside her. "Not the way we do, anyhow. You won't find a pulse, either. See, her skin's warm. Dryads go all wooden when they die; she's fine."

"I think 'fine' might be an overly optimistic description of someone who has just fallen unconscious," said Shaeine. Indeed, Ruda's shaking and patting was getting no response at all from the dryad.

"All right," Rafe said grimly, hooking his hands under Juniper's shoulders. "We'll have to—OW! My back! Holy fuck, she weighs a literal *ton*!"

"Metaphysical properties of a tree, remember?" said Trissiny. "That's how she's been shrugging off all those hits. I guess if she's not conscious to control it, she gets more . . . tree like."

"I've never seen a tree faint before," Toby said worriedly.

"I bet if you ever saw a tree run cross-country as long as Juniper just has, you'd see it faint," Trissiny replied.

"I'm pretty sure that's it exactly," Fross said, buzzing about their heads in a tizzy. "Dryads are *really* strong and very durable but they aren't perfect; everybody's got their weaknesses. Fire's very bad for them, and they're really meant to be kinda stationary. Oh, man, what are we gonna do? We can't let her die. Naiya would massacre everybody within a mile."

"No one is letting anyone die," Trissiny said firmly. "Rafe can carry her."

"Are you out of your—"

"Featherweight oil!" she snapped. "Surely you didn't use all of it making that absurd basket?"

He blinked at her. "Oh. Huh. That's actually a pretty good idea. Right on . . . Sorry about this, Juno, but I'm going to have to lather you a bit," he said, turning back to the fallen dryad and reaching into one of his belt pouches.

Trissiny scanned the horizon. On this flat terrain the centaurs *really* shouldn't have been able to get out of their view so quickly, especially when they were up the incline, slight as it was. Perhaps the Golden Sea had shifted them away . . . But then, how did they keep following? Ansheh had said they had ways of controlling, or at least influencing, the Sea's changes up to a point.

In the end, logic only went so far; Trissiny was a creature of faith. They were still out there. They were still coming. She could feel it.

Her fellow students were in sorry shape. Fross seemed to have recovered from her previous exhaustion and was buzzing around Rafe, chattering something about dryads at high speed. Ruda and Shaeine were both sitting in the grass, the pirate looking absolutely worn out. The drow was poised as ever, but even her slim shoulders were slumped with fatigue. Toby had kept his feet, but his face was drawn tight with exhaustion.

Trissiny wasn't tired. She had always had more stamina than the other girls she'd trained with; now, with the goddess supporting her, she was still good to keep going. The others, though, weren't going to last much longer.

"Toby," she said quietly, "a word?"

He looked up, glanced over at the others, and nodded, allowing her to lead him a few yards away. Still plenty close enough for Shaeine to hear, but it couldn't be helped.

"I need you to look after everyone," she said quietly. "Keep them safe, and keep them moving. Do not stop until dawn at the earliest, and even then, not until the Sea gives you something defensible to camp in."

"Triss, no," he said sharply. "I know what you're driving at, and you can forget it. We stick together."

"*That* ship has sailed," she retorted. "We should have made our stand when we had the full group together. Everyone's on their last legs; they *can't* keep doing this. Look at me. *I* can."

"But—"

"I wasn't trained for diplomacy, so I hope you'll forgive my bluntness," she said fiercely. "You are *holding me back*. None of you can fight in anything approaching my league, with the exception of Ruda, who doesn't have any magic supporting her. Having to ride herd on all of you is crippling me. If I can get into the middle of the centaurs, call on everything Avei will give me, go *all out* . . . Well, only the gods know what will happen, but it will be a very different game. All I need to do is take out the leader, I think."

"And the others? How will you get back, even if you win? And how can you *possibly* win? Trissiny, think about this, you can't seriously—"

"A paladin's life is sacrifice," she said coldly. "With all due respect, Tobias, I suggest you get used to it." He reared back, staring at her as if she'd slapped him, and a stabbing pain shot through her heart. "This is what I do," she said more gently. "This is what I *am*. I fight. I protect. *You* nourish and support. These are the roles our gods called us to, Toby. You have to let me do this." He just stared at her, anguish suppressing the weariness on his face. She reached up and gently placed a hand on his shoulder. "I *know* I'm asking a lot, and I'm sorry. But I need you to get the others moving, make *them* accept this, and get them home, and *safe*. Can you do it?"

He closed his eyes for a long moment, then nodded, swallowing heavily. "I guess I'll have to," he said miserably, opening his eyes to look at her again. There was a strained moment between them, and then, suddenly, Toby wrapped her into a hug, squeezing fiercely despite the way her armor had to be digging into his skin. "Omnu light your path, Hand of Avei," he whispered fiercely, then kissed her on the forehead. It tingled nearly as much as the gentle warmth of Omnu's blessing did, settling over her.

A blush suffused her features as she finally, reluctantly pulled back; Trissiny devoutly hoped none of what she was feeling was visible on her face. Of all the silly things, at a time like this ... having the tingles over a boy. Mother Narny would either laugh at her or box her ears.

Suddenly, she realized that Shaeine was right there. The drow reached up to place one hand gently on Trissiny's cheek, and she felt another light sensation ripple through her like a gentle breeze.

"Wisdom guide your steps, Sister," the priestess said quietly, "and bring you safely back to us." She stepped back three times, bowed deeply, and turned back to the others.

Trissiny swallowed, forced herself to meet Toby's gaze, and nodded to him. "Go. Now. I don't know how much time I can buy you."

Turning her back on them was easier than facing them. She wasn't made for heartfelt goodbyes and awkward embraces. She was the Hand of Avei, a creature of justice, of *war*. Among the torrent of emotions spiraling through her was a rising sense of purpose. Certainty.

Trissiny strode forward, alone, toward the enemy, while her friends resumed their retreat behind her, and found that for the first time in days, she was finally calm.

CHAPTER 17

Principia was just finishing up, settling her reagents back into place on her worktable, when a sharp knock came at her door. Thanks to the escalating stresses of the last few days, her usual equanimity was frayed. She started violently, then had to move quickly to prevent the vial of glittering powder from spilling, even as she slid it back into its holder. Who the *hell* would be bothering her in the middle of the night?

The door to her attic apartment swung open before she could even call out that she was busy, and Shook strode in. She scowled, putting the cork back on the vial.

"By all means, come *in*," Prin snapped. "Make yourself at home."

"Much obliged," he said easily, his eyes flicking over her in that skin-crawling way he had. She was reasonably sure he wasn't even all that attracted to her. That just made it worse. "While you've been hiding away in your room, I've been getting things set up to get your hide out of this mess intact. Principia, meet our newest ally."

Shook stepped aside to admit possibly the most ridiculous person Prin had ever seen.

She was human, an ethnic Tiraan, with the dark hair, olive complexion, and narrow face. Most eye-catching, however, was her costume—impractically tight pants, boots with two-inch *heels*, and a low-cut, sleeveless, midriff-baring top, every inch of the whole thing in black leather. An absolutely idiotic number of knives were bedecked around her in various places, which made them far from practical to grasp, their sheaths stitched into the outfit itself. The only remotely useful thing she was wearing was a fairly typical belt with two holstered wands, which clearly had come separately. It was dyed a different shade of black and looked out of place.

"What," Principia demanded, "are you supposed to be?"

The girl frowned at her. "Name's Tazlith; I'm an adventurer. And I'm here to help you."

"Uh huh." Prin leaned back, exaggeratedly eyeing her up and down. "An adventurer dressed as *what*?"

"Be nice, Prin," Shook reproved her gently. With Tazlith behind him, his face was hidden from her, and he didn't trouble to conceal his amusement.

"Oh, I'm nice. All peaches and sunshine, that's me. By the way, it's pronounced *tasleef*."

The "adventurer" narrowed her eyes, color rising in her cheeks. "I know how to say my own name, thanks."

"It's elvish for 'arrow,'" Prin explained to Shook. "I guess it'd come out *tazlith* if you've got a thick Tiraan accent, like this one does. I *know* your parents weren't daft enough to call you that. Unless the outfit is an heirloom."

"I really don't need to be here, you know," Tazlith snapped. "If you want to deal with your problems alone—"

"Girls, girls!" Shook said soothingly. "Please! You're both pretty. Taz, understand the kind of strain Principia's under; a rather legendary wand slinger's in town after her head. You'd be grouchy, too. And Prin, Taz has a point—she's helping us for not nearly enough material compensation, out of the desire to do a good deed. I think it'd be appropriate if you were a little more gracious about it."

"Sorry," Prin said ungraciously. "You're right, I'm pretty damn tense. And I don't see how gathering up stray adventurers is going to help; have you *heard* the rumors about this guy, McGraw? You're probably just gonna get the poor girl killed."

"I know what I'm doing," Tazlith said curtly, tucking her thumbs into her belt and adopting what she probably thought was a cocky pose.

"Anyway," Shook interjected, "I don't intend to just throw people at this guy like pies at a clown. We're still refining a strategy, but when it comes down to it, no matter the quality of everyone's equipment or skill, taking out a contract on one elf is a very different thing from facing a whole adventuring party. I highly doubt this guy's badass enough to start something that'll end with the town being shot up. Quite apart from what the law will say, he's pretty much done for if he makes enough of a stink to coax Tellwyrn down off her mountain."

"We're *all* done for if anybody makes that kind of stink," Principia groaned.

Shook nodded. "Exactly. Which is why I aim to persuade him not to do it. Taz here has been in town a couple weeks and knows some people. She's already gathered one other and has leads on more."

"Heroes," Tazlith said, nodding solemnly, "or those who have the inclination. Much better than hiring mercenaries; you want people who're in it because it's *right*, not because they're looking to make a quick doubloon."

Principia had to concentrate hard on repressing her response to this absolutely idiotic statement. Of *course* people in it for the money were better; someone who expected to make a living at something had an immediate need to be *good* at it.

"Yes. Well." She smiled toothily. "Thank you for your assistance, Tazlith. I apologize for any snide things I've said, and likely will in the future."

"She's kind of a bitch," Shook said agreeably, nodding.

"I'd argue with that, but the record's against me. Would you mind if I had a word with Jeremiah in private?"

"Of course." The wretched girl glanced back and forth between them and smirked faintly. "Take all the time you need." Principia wasn't sure whether she wanted to scream or punch somebody, but at least Tazlith stepped out into the stairwell, pulling the attic door shut behind her.

She rounded on Shook, but he spoke up before she could get a word out. "So, how'm I doin'? I never was much for running cons, but I think it's going rather well. Doubtless you've already found a whole laundry list of things I could be doing better."

"You seem to have it in hand," she said grudgingly. Laundry list indeed. As if she were fool enough to poke holes in his brittle ego, knowing how he reacted to that. "Of course, you couldn't have picked a better target. Manipulating people who are desperate to believe something is downright unfair. But . . . seriously? You're gonna send *that* up against McGraw?"

"Not too bright, is she?" he said, grinning. "No, I don't aim to make this a war. It's just like I said: The hope is to put up a spectacle that'll persuade McGraw to step more lightly, *without* involving Tellwyrn or anyone else who'll overturn the whole cart. If it *does* come down to a fight, though, I want him wasting his spells on Taz and her dumbass friends, not us. It's a shameful waste of a nice pair of tits, but them's the breaks. While that's going on, he'll be vulnerable, and that's what I came to speak with you about." He nodded toward her workstation, on which were laid out her glittering enchanting dusts, imbued inks, and the various tools of their use. "What've you got?"

She gave him a grudging look but turned to gesture at a row of bronze rings laid out on the table. "Some basic boosts. Luck, protection, constitution . . ."

"Really?" He twisted his features disdainfully. "That's it? That's crap straight out of a museum."

"No," she said wryly, "the museum pieces would be gold and set with gems. Yeah, they're the oldest, most basic enchantments, and that's about all you can plan on. Modern enchantment is all about specific, reliable effects, which works great for making enchanted objects, but if you want to enhance the attributes of a *person*, you have to be vague, or run the risk of messing them up. People are complicated."

"Hm." He stepped over to the table, running a fingertip over the row of rings, and she tensed, fighting the urge to chase him away from her work. "I guess it'll have to do, then. Can you gear up Taz and her buddies?"

"Excuse me?" Prin said incredulously. "*Gear up?* Does this *look* like a production line to you? *This* took me all day. I'm a hobbyist; I make some pocket change on the side because this town is such a steel market. You want a pile of adventure-grade enchantments, you're gonna have to go *buy* some."

"Shame," he murmured, stepping away from the table. Shook raised his eyes to her face, and she had the distinct impression of something greasy being dragged along her skin. "Well, that's not in the budget. I guess they'll just have to trust their luck."

"Mm-hmm." She folded her arms. "Anything else you wanted?"

He watched her silently for a moment that stretched long enough to be awkward.

"You're wondering why I bother," he said finally. "I don't really expect you to like me, Keys. Hell, though you dug yourself into this whole mess, I'll freely acknowledge you've got some just cause to look unkindly on me. But you can trust that I'm quite sincere. I'm not gonna let anything happen to you if it's in my power to prevent it."

He stared at her, the hint of a grin hovering about his lips, until she finally had to ask. "Why?"

"Because I'm responsible for this mission, and for you. You may be a poor resource, but for the time being, you're mine." He reached up to brush the backs of his knuckles across her cheek, smiling faintly; her skin crawled so much it was all she could do not to physically shiver. "I don't *like* it when people mess with my things."

"Your friend out there's probably wondering what we're doing," she said coldly. He laughed.

"Yeah, yeah. Wouldn't want the young'uns to get the wrong idea. You just sit tight for now, doll, and let me take care of this."

He briefly but very deliberately flicked his gaze over her body once more, then turned and walked to the door. Shook stepped out and shut it gently behind himself without looking at her again.

She stood there silently, regathering her calm. It took a few minutes.

The cultists' faces were well hidden, but the man in the suit wore an expression which clearly said he meant business.

"I'm going to take it upon myself to assume you're here in the capacity of your role as imperial advisor, Mr. Darling," he said amiably. His tone was light, his posture relaxed, but those eyes were hard as flint. This was a man worth taking seriously, one who knew that roaring and gnashing teeth weren't nearly as impressive as some liked to think. "There is . . . an *understanding*. Most of the cults of the other gods know it—excepting yours, of course, as Eserion isn't much for waging war, even against my Lady. Over the last century we've even hammered the lesson into the Church, somewhat laboriously. It's a good system. Peaceable, functional."

He put on a mild, slightly lopsided smile, taking a step closer to Darling. His steps were smooth, slow, precise, and somewhat exaggerated; with his long limbs, in that white suit, he put Darling in mind of a wading stork. "The Wreath guard this world against demonkind, you see. You could say we have an affinity with the children of Hell; we know, better than most, that they can't be allowed to run amok on this plane. *As such*, other cultists—even the Sisters of Avei—don't jump on our backs when we are cleaning up a demon problem. And they most *definitely* do not abuse our willingness to be helpful by *using* a demon to coax us out. You're hardly the first to think of that trick, my boy. The rest simply know better."

"Well, this is just downright embarrassing," Darling said genially. He kept his own face cheerful and posture relaxed, concealing the frantic racing of his thoughts. That explained the Archpope's insistence that they not identify themselves as agents of the Church; posing as imperials gave them plausible deniability if they were breaking some kind of treaty. "There are customs? Rules, even? I feel like I've showed up at a party and nobody told me it's fancy dress." But why hadn't Darling and the others been informed of this up front? What was Justinian playing at?

"Speaking more generally," the man in the suit went on, his smile growing brittle, "I think it's considered bad form anywhere to go after an opponent's kids. That's the kind of conflict you don't want to escalate; it gets *real* ugly, real fast."

"Now, I'll have to demur, there," Darling replied, holding up one finger. "Those precocious little sprouts came at *us*. I'm pretty sure they put the town to sleep and conjured up Mommy and Daddy's demon companions, too."

"Well, little ones grow up pretty fast out here on the frontier," the man said with a grin, tucking his hands into the pockets of his coat. His movements were languid, graceful. "They *also* had the forethought to call for aid; wading right into your little nest of vipers was a somewhat less intelligent move, I'll grant. Course, matters look different if you put yourself in their shoes. Bunch of outsiders from Tiraas come swaggering into town and kill your parents? You'd be a bit excitable, too."

"I'm reasonably sure you're already aware nobody's been killed," Darling replied. "By the way, sir, it seems you have me at a disadvantage. Aside from the obvious, I mean," he added, turning his head to wink at one of the cowled cultists.

"Why, I do most humbly apologize!" The man swept off his hat, revealing a shiny bald pate, and executed an elaborate bow. "Embras Mogul, at your service. I'm sorry we aren't meeting under more cordial circumstances."

"Ah, well, we go where the gods dictate," Darling said lightly. Could this be Elilial's high priest? If so, he had a name and a face, which put the Archpope's plans, *and* his own, miles ahead of where he'd expected this night's events to lead. Could he advance the one without aiding the other? At any rate, even if this wasn't the one, he was clearly high enough in the organization not to be bound by their dress code.

"Yes, they're good at . . . dictating, aren't they?" Mogul replied, straightening and replacing his hat. "In honor of our new acquaintance, and in recognition of your relative inexperience in this business, Darling, I'm going to let you off with a proverbial slap on the wrist. Obviously, I'll need my people back, especially those kids. The demon, too. Aside from that, you and your little compatriots are free to go, with my blessing. Provided they behave themselves."

Darling was spared having to form an answer to this by the opening of the saloon's door.

Marshal Ross stepped out and crossed the board sidewalk at an even pace, as though he hadn't a care in the world. By the time he'd descended to the street and turned to face the gathering of Wreath cultists and Darling, the two nearest Embras Mogul had drawn wands from within their robes.

"Welcome to Hamlet," the marshal said flatly. His hand hovered at his sides, near but not grasping his wands. "It's usually a friendlier place, but *someone* appears to have put my townsfolk to sleep."

"Present company excepted, I note," Mogul replied, his tone as even as ever.

"Present company and more."

Figures rose from the rooftops around them. Two men in denim and leather, each carrying staves, stepped out from behind the sign on the general store's flat roof across the street. Another, aging and with a gray-streaked beard, knelt on the edge of the saloon's overhanging porch roof, carrying a pair of wands. A middle-aged woman in a threadbare Imperial Army coat hopped from concealment into the rungs of the iron lattice scrolltower, balancing adroitly and keeping both hands on her staff. All of their weapons were aimed at the group in the street. Darling had to admire their positioning; they had the cultists neatly positioned to be cut to pieces by crossfire without accidentally firing on each other. Unfortunately, he was in the center of the kill zone.

"There ain't a town on the frontier that doesn't keep at least one practicing witch in business. Casting town-wide infernal magic ain't a smart move, if you intend to keep a low profile; my girl knew exactly who to wake up and how. *Legally*," the marshal drawled, "I suppose I oughta arrest you. Seems like you could spare me some paperwork, though, if you decline to drop those fucking wands in the next ten seconds."

"It's Ross, isn't it?" asked Mogul politely. "Jackson Towerwell always spoke of you in the highest terms. Marshal, we're both civilized men, and I presume that we are both followed by more of the same. You don't want your town shot to bits, and I don't want any of my people cut down. How about, instead of that, you and I reach an accord?"

"Mm." Ross tilted his head downward so his eyes were concealed by the brim of his hat. "Mr. Mogul, was it? Mind if I ask you a question?"

"But of course," said Embras, bowing with an elegant flourish of his hands. "Glad to be of service in any way I can."

Ross lifted his head again, and the look in his eyes was beyond ice, beyond fury. "Did you offer to 'reach an accord' with June Witwill?"

For one breath, everything was still.

Ironically, it was Darling who started the action—by diving to one side and throwing his arms over his head. He didn't quite fit under the boardwalk, so he smashed himself against it, squishing down as small as possible, while the whole street dissolved in lightning and hellfire.

Eserion didn't encourage his followers to draw on divine light, as a rule. Members of his Guild were meant to rely on their wits and their skills; that was the whole point of their faith. The god of thieves was out to set an example, not solve people's problems for them. Darling had used more divine magic in the last week than in his entire previous career, what with one thing and another.

Oddly, this thought sat in the forefront of his mind as he crept, inchworm-like, along the edge of the sidewalk, glowing with an intensity of held light that was the closest he could manage to a divine shield. It wouldn't stop a wandshot, but would certainly discourage any demons that might have been summoned in the vicinity.

He didn't risk looking up until he came to the corner of the saloon, but he could clearly hear the *snap* of thunderbolts, as well as the crashes and screams that marked their impacts. The air buzzed with static electricity and reeked of ozone and sulfur.

Finally reaching the corner, Darling bounded up and somersaulted around the edge of the building, keeping himself as low as possible. He pressed himself against the wall, very carefully peeking out.

Three bodies lay in the street, two in gray robes, one where it had fallen from the roof of the general store. The firefight continued, though Ross's posse were exchanging blasts with opponents now out of his field of view down the street. Retreating? Were these cultists local, or had they come in with Embras? Whatever the case, they'd sure made a mess of the town. Every building in sight bore scorch marks and outright holes where they'd been blasted by wands. Plus, there was that stink of sulfur hanging in the air; someone had summoned something.

Obviously, his original plan to get to the scrolltower office was off the table. He needed to get back to the house, regroup with the others, make sure all the prisoners were secure and the demon taken care of. Equally obvious, he wasn't going back up the main street. He'd stick out like a sore thumb, and no place in this town was out of wand range of any place else. All it'd take would be one Wreath with a grudge and a clear shot to put him down.

He reversed course, heading for the alley behind the saloon. Hamlet didn't have a lot of depth; there was nothing in town that he'd describe as a "street," aside from the main one, but behind the shops there were houses, stables, and a few other structures, enough to give him a little cover.

In theory, at least.

No sooner had Darling slipped around the corner into the wide alley that would carry him on a roundabout way back to the house than Embras Mogul stepped out of a perfectly flat shadow lying against a wall, followed by one of his robed cultists.

Darling skidded to a stop; no more than six feet separated them. The cultist was carrying a wand, pointed at him; Mogul appeared to be unarmed, but he wasn't about to dismiss the man as a threat.

"Well, this has all gone belly-up, hasn't it?" Embras said cheerfully.

"You said it," Darling replied in the same tone. "What *is* it about wands coming out that makes people stop using their brains?"

"Must be that fight-or-flight instinct everyone's always talking about. Ah, well; you'll note that I *did* try to do this the civilized way. As will your patron, if he happens to be watching."

"I like the civilized way. I was never in favor of abandoning it." He still clung to the glow of divine light. It wasn't likely to do him much good. "How about we try that again?"

"Alas," Embras replied with a mournful expression, "the good marshal's intervention has played hell with my timetable. Now it seems I'll have to content myself with making an *emphatic* statement to your superiors and bugging out. A disappointing outcome for everyone, but such is life."

Darling opened his mouth without knowing what he was even going to say—it was a good strategy, usually, as his mouth was a finely tuned machine that reliably figured out the proper course of action—but before it even became an issue, a shadow passed over the moon, accompanied by a rush of wind, and the demon which had been imprisoned in the basement landed on the roof of the tiny shed next to them.

"Hi, Boss," he said, grinning unpleasantly at Darling.

"Well, well," Mogul remarked, and for the first time there was an obvious note of strain beneath his affability. "Every time I turn around, this night just gets more interesting."

"Bad news, big man!" the demon said, turning its gaze to him. "By way of saving my own ass, I've cut a deal with my erstwhile captors. I have come to interfere with you, so as to assure this asshole here's escape!" He made a silly face, stretching his spiny wings to their fullest extent and waving his hands about over his head. "Grawr! Boo! Boogity, boogity! *Are you not distracted?!*"

Mogul pointed a finger at him and growled a word that was just barely a word, and the shadows around them swirled as though trying to take physical form, sweeping the demon off the shed and dragging it to the dirt floor of the alley. The shadow coalesced into black chains, dark as iron but less reflective, holding him to the ground by the wrists and ankles.

"Curses!" he declaimed. "Foiled again! Well, shucks, I keep finding myself in jail in this town," the demon said gleefully, turning to leer at Darling. "Ah, well! Can't say I didn't try. You might have a word with that ferret-faced chick of yours, though. She can't bargain worth a *crap*."

"All right, enough," Mogul said wearily. "You, hush, we'll get you home in just a minute. Brother, kindly *shoot* this—"

He broke off as the steel tip of a sword appeared from the center of his chest. An explosive grunt was driven from the cultist's mouth; face still concealed by his cowl, he lowered his head, staring down at the blade. Behind him, the air rippled as Basra Syrinx deactivated an invisibility charm, deftly plucking the wand from the man's suddenly limp fingers.

"Are you not distracted?" she said, grinning wickedly, and kicked the slumping cultist to the side, wrenching her sword free as he fell. She leveled the wand at Mogul's heart.

"Right," he said dryly. "Well. Looks like I owe you lot one. Until then!"

Lightning snapped straight through him, illuminating the alley for a split second, but he was already gone; it was as if he had turned to shadow, then was dispelled by the blaze.

Darling blinked rapidly to clear his vision. "Well, you sure have excellent timing."

"Andros would've come, too," she said lightly, "but neither of us thought leaving Branwen in charge of the prisoners alone was the best idea. I guess we all have our strengths and weaknesses. After all . . ." She turned to the demon, her grin broadening. "Apparently I can't bargain worth a crap."

"Hey, just a little drama to sell the story," he said, all bravado suddenly gone. The chains of shadow were steaming slightly as though coming apart, but continued to hold him, even as he tugged experimentally on them. "All's well that ends well, right? I mean . . . we had a deal."

"So we did! And it's now fulfilled." Basra stepped forward and drove her sword straight through his bony chest. She leaned in close, placing her face inches from his. "Avei thanks you for your service," she said sweetly. "Go, with her *blessing*." Light blazed along the blade, wrenching an impossibly shrill scream from the creature. For just a moment, golden radiance burned from his mouth and eyes, and just as quickly ceased.

Basra ripped her sword out sideways; the pieces of demon that were pulled loose more resembled charcoal than flesh. The smoking corpse flopped to the ground, already reeking of sulfur.

It was during this scene that Marshal Ross arrived, panting.

"Ah, there you are," Darling said brightly. "Got the rest of them rounded up?"

"Three dead," Ross said tersely, "four including this guy. The rest escaped. I've got no real way of tracking demon magic; Mavis is working on the spell keeping everybody asleep."

"Sounds like a wise choice of priorities," Darling agreed. "Honestly, I doubt it would matter, Marshal. We're not going to find them, I suspect."

The marshal straightened his back, setting his shoulders; the mantle of authority was all but visible as he pulled it back on. "Well. Seems you've had an interesting night."

"To be honest," Darling said ruefully, "I feel more as if it's had me. The good news is we'll be out of town just as quick as we can arrange transport from Tiraas, and we'll be taking the last of your Wreath problem with us."

"Do I wanna know who?"

"Legally, you're entitled. If you think it'll make you happy."

"I don't do this job because I want to be happy," he growled. "Right . . . Clyde took a bad hit, but Doc thinks he'll live. I'll round up the others and we'll help you finish up the last of your business."

"Thank you," Basra said sardonically, "but I think we can manage without your help. Just like we have been from the beginning."

"Bas," said Darling gently, "just because the man spoke politely doesn't mean he was asking."

"Well put," said Ross.

They allowed the marshal to take the lead on the way back to the ravaged house. It was still the most damaged structure in sight, much of its bottom floor having been ripped out—Darling hoped they could get themselves and their magic wardrobe out before the second floor came down—but after the shoot-out with the cultists, much of the town matched. Ross's scowl deepened with every step. It was hardly surprising that he'd take all this personally.

Darling was grateful for the silence; he desperately needed a chance to think. Much had been explained, but more questions had branched out from each answer. The next steps in this dance would have to be taken in Tiraas, where he intended to sus out more of the Archpope's plans before proceeding with his own.

He hoped, quite sincerely, that Hamlet had seen the end of its problem with demons and cultists. For him, though, this matter had just begun.

CHAPTER 18

Light encompassed Trissiny—her own energy, drawn from Avei, as well as the blessings of Omnu and Themynra laid upon her. Omnu granted peace, which was an ironic sensation under the circumstances, but she certainly appreciated the core of unshakable inner calm while she fought among two dozen foes, each more than three times her size. His blessing was also one of life and healing, which she also had cause to be thankful for, especially the first time she took a kick full in the chest from an equine hind leg. Her breastplate didn't so much as dent, its silvered steel having been a gift of the goddess, but she felt her ribs break and skin rupture, and then set themselves instantly right, with a pleasant tingling sensation.

Themynra, as Shaeine had said, was a goddess of judgment, and Trissiny was grateful for her assistance as well. She had been skeptical when told of the drow goddess's association with Avei, but in the heat of this melee, the matter began to make a great deal more sense. Her mind already held the knowledge she needed of martial arts and military tactics, but she found herself thinking faster and three steps further than usual, deducing where a strike would fall or an enemy would maneuver almost before they did.

She whirled among them, unable to reach higher than their equine backs, but nearly impossible for them to strike—and when they *did* land a hit, Trissiny was immediately back on her feet, unhurt. It was a battle of attrition, and while the centaurs might have expected to win since it had just been her, they were also facing off against the power of the gods.

It helped a lot that they could hardly see. Trissiny moved in a mobile blaze of light that blinded and confused them; they could either look right at her and accept momentary blindness and longer-term damage to their night vision, or look outward into the darkness and fall afoul of the rapidly dancing little human with the inhumanly precise sword.

That didn't mean she was going to win. Themynra's touch told her the odds, and Omnu gave her peace with it. Gods or no, she was an imperfect vessel for their power, and her enemies had power of their own.

After the first clashes, though, the warlocks had pulled back to let the warriors face her. Her divine light didn't effortlessly snuff out their spells the way Juniper's fae magic did, but rather reacted against it—violently. It was quickly proven that whatever sources they were drawing on, Trissiny's was stronger. Curses hurled at her rebounded or exploded at the outer edge of her aura; the two demons initially summoned to attack her had died excruciatingly within seconds, one bisected by her blade, the other struck insensate to the ground by a burst of radiance, to have her boot slam down on its throat. The third had taken one look at her and fled across the prairie, its shrieking warlock in pursuit.

Trissiny learned quickly that the best place to be was right in front of them. To the side, they could turn swiftly, using their bulk to knock her over; behind, she was in range of those mighty hindquarters. No blessing or healing would save her if a kick took her head off. She had gained some insight into why the barbarian lord, whose tomb had hosted her party, had been given his name—now that she knew firsthand which end of a horse was *not* to be messed with.

Too far back, and they sent arrows, spells, and javelins at her, which she had ways of dealing with, but that forced her to expend her energy with nothing to throw back at them. No, the sweet spot was right in front; they couldn't reach her with their hands, and she was quick enough to deflect their longer weapons on sword or shield. From that range, she could reach their human bellies with her blade, which seemed to hold *some* vital organs. They were most likely to rear up and slash at her with their hooves, which afforded her the chance to dodge beneath them and put her sword into their lower bodies. From there, it was somewhat tricky to disengage her blade and get away before being crushed under their falling weight, but the centaurs were only faster over long distances. Up close, she was the more nimble.

Three lay dead now, with half a dozen more still on their feet but bleeding or limping. Another four were alive but immobile; Trissiny had found that the creatures were just as vulnerable as horses once their legs were broken. Of those, only one had tried to continue the fight with bow and arrow and had subsequently lost a hand—a lesson in why one should not launch a ranged attack on a mobile foe when one could not run away.

She wasn't even tired, yet. It would come, though; she knew it. So far, she still didn't feel the burning sensation of divine overuse, despite the fact that she was using more than at any previous point in her life. That was coming, too, however. It wasn't a pretty way to die.

What would be, would be. Live, die, it hardly mattered. She was protecting her friends. She was the Hand of Avei. She *fought*.

Sword, shield, and boots were equally useful for breaking legs. Shield and aura both worked to deflect attacks. Her blade bit into flesh, her power pushed back against curses. Trissiny rolled under their legs, smashed their limbs, maneuvered them to collide with each other, slashed at them until their blood ran under her armor. Those who survived this night would remember Avei's wrath.

The blast of a hunting horn split the night. One long note, two short ones, a pause, and a final bleat. She didn't know their signals, but Trissiny suddenly found herself alone. The centaurs peeled away in every direction, flowing around her at a respectful distance to regroup.

She held her ready stance. Were they *retreating*? Had she convinced them they couldn't win this? She hadn't yet convinced herself of that... Then again, they were expecting easy prey; the fact that she was not might be enough to dissuade them.

A sudden fear chilled her as she watched them gather together. What if they just backed off and went *around* her, after her friends? She'd never catch up in time.

The centaurs, however, held their position, about fifty yards distant, except the nine lying wounded or dead on the battlefield. Thirteen still in their ranks, as best she could tell; they were milling about enough to confuse the matter.

Then, they parted, and their leader emerged from the throng.

She held her skull-staff in one hand and the hunting horn in the other. Stepping forward, she tossed the horn to one of her number and continued on at an even pace, alone, her gaze fixed on Trissiny.

The towering centaur came to a stop. Then, very deliberately, she raised her staff high over her head, and nodded once to the paladin.

For a moment, Trissiny felt only revulsion. A warlock among a tribe of warlocks, raiders, and the gods only knew what else was not worth treating as any kind of equal. That, she realized, was only her faith talking. And, in the end, there were some things which were about faith, and some that were about being a warrior.

Trissiny returned the salute in the Avenist fashion—sword hand over heart, blade vertical beside her face, and a shallow bow.

They lowered their weapons at the same moment.

The centaur broke into a canter, calling upon her power; shadowy forms, an inky purple against the night sky, began to circle above her like vultures over carrion. First one, then more, until they swirled above her head in a twisted vortex. As she accelerated into a full gallop, the skull head of her staff burst into sickly green flame.

Trissiny charged to meet her, shield forward, blade held out and ready to strike. Her aura intensified until the other centaurs couldn't look, her sword burning white with divine energy. A tone like the chime of an immense bronze bell rang across the prairie, and in the final sign of Avei's favor, golden eagle wings lit the air behind her, as if to lift her from the ground.

From the point where light and shadow met, the tallgrass was blasted flat for a quarter mile around.

The little hillock wasn't much in the way of shelter, but it was something, and in the endless flatness of the Golden Sea, something was plenty. Small, thorny bushes decorated it, interspersed with craggy little protrusions of rock. It had also held a few grouse, which were now roasting over the campfire. Not much else of interest was to be found, but the travelers had made the best use of it they could. With the hillock on one side and the two wagons drawn in a loose V formation, they formed a sheltered triangular nook, lit by their campfire.

The oxen were tethered outside the formation, and Jim sat atop the modest high point of the hillock, still plenty close enough to speak without shouting, keeping watch. The other three sat cross-legged on the ground around their campfire, laughing, chatting, and waiting for dinner.

"Somebody's coming," said Jim suddenly, standing up.

A hush fell over the group; Bella slipped a hand into her vest to grasp at one of the talismans hidden there.

"Trouble?" asked Lance tersely.

"Dammit, man, if I *knew*, I'd have said so. Shut up a minute and let me look."

Moving slowly so as not to create noise or cast dramatic shadows, Elroy leaned to one side, picking up his staff and Lance's, which he passed over; Lance accepted the weapon with a nod of thanks. Bella was fingering her amulet now, almost silently whispering an invocation of some kind. Lance had little understanding of witchcraft, but it seemed to involve almost as much muttering and superstition as he expected from clerics.

"It's those kids," said Jim, his tone more bemused than relieved. "The ones from the other day. Well . . . half of 'em, looks like."

"Tellwyrn's kids?" Bella asked, biting her lip. "Hell."

"Ain't likely to rob us, then," Lance mused. "How far?"

"Bout a hundred yards. Makin' right for us. No surprise there, what with the fire."

"You say there are fewer?"

"Yeah, I count . . . four. No, five; one's unconscious and being carried. They got some kinda floating glowball for light."

"Down part of their number and walkin' around in the middle of the night," said Lance, frowning in thought. "Sounds like trouble. Anything comin' after 'em?"

"Not that I can see. They ain't hurrying, either. Look plumb wore out to me. Kinda, y'know . . . trudging."

"All right. Hands near weapons, but until we get a sign otherwise, I'd say it'll pay to be neighborly."

"You sure?" Bella asked carefully.

"Tellwyrn ain't a good enemy to have. We'll be polite until a compelling reason not to pops up. Like I said, they ain't likely to mean us harm, and it sounds like they've had some trouble of their own."

She nodded slowly, Elroy doing the same. They waited in silence for the few minutes it took the students to reach their camp.

The short brown girl in the hat led the way, stepping through the gap between the wagons with naked steel in her hand. Lance's eyes flicked to the sword, and Elroy's hands tensed on his weapon. Her posture wasn't aggressive, though; the blade was practically dragging along the ground. She looked angry and tired, but relaxed slightly as her eyes widened in recognition.

"Oh, hey," she said. "It's *you* guys again."

"Evening," Lance said mildly. He glanced at her unsheathed weapon and came to one of the rapid decisions that had marked his career up to this point. "We weren't expecting to run into y'all again. It's not often that paths cross twice in the Golden Sea."

"Perhaps the gods brought us," said the tall, dark-skinned boy, gently pushing past her. "Sorry to barge in on you like this."

"Ain't no trouble," Lance replied. "Elroy, point that thing someplace else. Nobody here's bein' hostile. Sit a spell, neighbors. Food's not quite ready, but you're welcome to the fire. Unless I'm mistaken, there were more of you previously."

"We've had . . . a day," the boy said ruefully, glancing back as the last of his companions entered, the drow and the half-elven man, who was carrying the slumbering green-haired girl. "Thanks for the welcome. You're the first good news we've seen in quite a while."

"Centaurs?" asked Bella, tense.

"A good way behind us," said the boy, nodding. "But we've not seen them in hours. It looks like we lost them."

"Are you *sure?*" Elroy asked nervously.

"They are not stealthy creatures," said the drow, and Elroy started violently, twitching his staff in her direction. Thankfully, she ignored this. "I would have heard any pursuit. No, we've left them behind . . . though the price was steep."

"Then it sounds like you've more'n earned a little rest," Lance said solicitously as the four carefully arranged themselves to one side of the fire, Elroy having stood and circled around to stand between him and Bella. The blond main carefully laid out the green-haired girl to one side before seating himself. "Hell, I'm not gonna make you kids wait on this to finish cookin'. Bella, why don't you find something for our guests to eat? They look tuckered out. Hey, break out some of that special cornbread of yours."

The others twisted their heads around to look at him in obvious surprise. "The . . . *special* cornbread, Lance?" Bella asked uncertainly.

"Now, don't be stingy," he said with gentle reproof. "We're doin' okay for supplies, and you can have all the cornbread or whatever else you want once we get back to civilization. These kids need a little somethin' to pick 'em up after the day they've had."

"Sorry," she said, flushing. "I just . . . Yeah, sure, gimme a second."

She stood and stepped over toward one of the wagons, but reared back in surprise when a glowing silver ball zipped around from behind them. "Need a hand?" it asked in a bright, somewhat squeaky voice. "I'm getting good at carrying stuff!"

"Holy *shit,*" Bella whispered in awe. "You're a *pixie.*"

"Um . . . yes?" The pixie bobbed in place a couple of times. "We've met before, you know. I was there when we ran into you out on the prairie."

"You *were?* How did I not see that?"

"Oh, well, it's my coloration, I guess. I'm told I can be kinda hard to spot in broad daylight."

"I bet we've got all kinds of stories we can share," Lance said pointedly, "but we've got hungry guests, Bella."

"Ah. Yes, right." Grudgingly tearing her eyes from the pixie, she hopped up onto the wagon and vanished within. "Comin' right up."

The special cornbread was wrapped up in oilcloth, bound with some of Bella's charmed twine to keep it fresh. In short order, she had undone this and was passing around tin plates, breaking off chunks of bread for the students.

"Y'all go ahead and dig in," she said, smiling warmly. "You're welcome to some bird, too, when it's ready, but we can wait on that. Looks like you kids have had a hell of a day. Is your friend there all right?"

"She's just tired out," said the half elf, managing a weak grin, ". . . hopefully. We're not a hundred percent sure. She doesn't seem sick or injured, anyway."

The students accepted the offering of food with murmurs of thanks; only the boy tried to demur, insisting on sharing, but Bella was too gently persistent, and Lance managed to distract them by asking about their situation.

For all that the story was fairly straightforward, it seemed hard for them to get through. Toby, as he introduced himself, took the main role in laying it out, with occasional interruptions, mostly from Ruda and the professor. The drow remained silent, eating quietly, and Fross just sort of drifted about their heads, commenting little.

He was carving the birds by the time they were done and waved off their refusals with a smile as he refilled plates with fresh, fragrant grouse, in addition to passing shares around to his own people.

"So the long and the short of it is," he said carefully, "y'all have had one *hell* of a day."

"Few days," Ruda muttered, chewing. "This is really good cornbread."

"Bella's special recipe," he replied easily. "It's got beans baked right in—you probably noticed that—and a dusting of cinnamon on the top. Your ma's recipe, wasn't it?"

"No, Lance," she said, rolling her eyes. "It was Mother Gowan's, the woman who taught me the craft. Honestly, do you even hear words when I talk?"

"Depends on how much I've had to drink," he replied, grinning at her, then sobered, turning back to their guests. "At any rate, I'm glad to hear the rest of your crew aren't a total loss. Sounds like you managed to send 'em off to safety, at least. Well, except for the paladin girl. Reckon she's all right?"

An obvious pall fell over them. Ruda's features twisted into a virulent scowl and she glared into the fire, as though it had just insulted all her ancestors. Toby glanced down at Juniper, lying stretched out a safe distance from the fire, as if to reassure himself that they hadn't lost any more members of their group while he'd been talking.

"We hope and pray it is so," said Shaeine. "There seems little more we can do at this juncture."

Lance nodded. "That's life sometimes. You expect help from your University?"

"Yeah," Ruda said quickly, an edge to her tone. "Tellwyrn will know if anything happens to Triss. She'll take care of it." Toby glanced sidelong at her, uncertainty plain on his face, but he made no comment.

"Well, regardless, you kids are welcome to spend the night here," Lance continued. "We're headin' back to the edge of the Sea as quick as we can make it, and I gather you're planning the same?"

"We are," Toby said, nodding.

"Good, then there's no reason not to help each other out. We'll cover the watch tonight, since you're kind of under the weather."

"Not necessary, we'll gladly . . ." He yawned mid-sentence.

"So I see," Lance said dryly. "Tell you what, anybody still awake when it's time to change shifts can draw straws for it. Fair?"

"'s fair," Toby agreed, nodding again. He and the others were all visibly sleepy now, lulled by fatigue, the cozy fire, and a belly full of hot food. Shaeine had set her plate on the ground after nearly dropping it once, and Rafe was already stretched out on his back next to Juniper.

"We'll just see about gettin' squared away for the night, then," Bella said, rising with a smile and leaving her half-eaten plate of grouse. "You still want to help, Fross?"

"Oh! Uh, sure, what can I do?" The pixie fluttered curiously over to her. Bella smiled, clambering up onto the nearest wagon and reaching under the seat.

"Well, we always keep somebody on watch, as you can see. That's just basic common sense."

"Ooh! I can stay on watch, I don't need to sleep!"

"I know you don't," she replied, smiling, and pulled forth a lumpy knapsack. "But I was going to say, in addition to keeping a pair of eyes out, I always lay some simple protections on us and set a few wards for the evening."

"Wards? Oh! You're a witch!"

"Bingo!" Bella grinned. "So you see why I'm a little embarrassed. Imagine, a witch not noticing a pixie."

"Aw, shucks, don't worry about that. Human eyes aren't made for spotting white lights in broad daylight."

"Well, regardless, we're all together now, and that's what matters." She had set her sack on the wagon seat and was laying out items—old charms, bundles of herbs, bones, crystals, and a pint-sized glass jar with a lead stopper and swirling designs inked on the sides. "So, while I'm sure you're *very* talented at lifting things, maybe you can help me out with this instead?"

"Well . . . sure! I've never assisted a witch before; it should be interesting. I mean, where I was born we didn't really run into humans at all, but I'd heard about humans who used fae magic and I always thought that must be the most fascinating thing, so, yeah, I'd be glad to! Sorry if I ask too many questions; I don't know very much about the craft and I always love to learn new things."

"I don't mind at all," Bella said easily. She had tied a thin, silver chain around the upper rim of the lead stopper and laid two springs of dried herbs in the bottom of the wide-mouthed jar. "Here, let me show you. Can you come down here, please? Right by the jar."

The pixie obediently buzzed downward, doing a lap around the jar before settling on the wood next to it. "What am I looking for?"

"What I need you to do is very carefully infuse those dried leaves with just the *tiniest* bit of pure elemental magic. Careful not to overdo it; if they burn up, we'll have to start over."

"I dunno," Fross said nervously, "I've never tried that before."

"Don't you worry about a thing, darlin', I've got plenty more. A few false starts won't hurt us any. Here, try to get a straight shot; can you perch on the rim of the jar?"

"Easy-peasy!" She buzzed her wings once, bounding up onto the very edge of the jar's mouth. "Oh, I see your point, this thing's enchanted to bar magic."

"Exactly," Bella said, nodding, "the power only goes in and out through the mouth, that way I can control it. Now . . . let me walk you through it. Don't draw on any magic yet; just start by looking at the herbs."

"Check. I'm looking."

"Look *hard*. Really focus on them, get a feel for them. Let the herbs fill your awareness . . ."

Her wings buzzed briefly, but Fross made no reply, her light dimming slightly in concentration as she peered down at the bits of dried plant at the bottom.

"Very good," Bella cooed softly. "Nice and still. Hold that in your mind, and now . . ."

With a single motion, she knocked Fross forward with the lead stopper and then drove it firmly into the mouth of the jar, trapping the pixie inside. Quick as a cat, she snatched up a length of woven cord wrapped in an elaborate pattern of silver thread, winding it three times around the jar, and tied it off. Inside, Fross buzzed about frantically, though she barely had room to extend her wings. Her voice was reduced to meaningless squeaks by the thick glass.

"Ah!" Bella set the jar down on the wagon seat and shook her hands. "Cold!" She held them out toward the fire, but her savagely triumphant grin didn't so much waver.

"You about done, then?" Lance asked dryly.

"Oh, I am *so* done," she purred. "Got everything I ever wanted right here."

"Really? You were just supposed to put her out of commission. What do you want her for? What can you *possibly* do with a captive pixie?"

"What *can't* you do with a pixie?" she retorted gleefully. "She's a little bundle of *pure* elemental magic, endlessly self-replenishing. Doesn't need to eat, sleep, or breathe, and no matter how much power I pull from her, she'll produce more. Most witches only *dream* of binding a pixie! You almost never see them unless you go where they live, and then they'll mob you if you mess with one. Ohh, this is ten times better than that haul of jewels we found."

"Yeah, that's great and all," Elroy said skittishly. "Bella gets her little glow-toy and, meanwhile *we* just probably pissed off Arachne goddamn Tellwyrn. For what? I'll eat my boots if these kids have anything worth taking in their pockets." Gingerly, he reached out and nudged Toby with a toe. He and Ruda had slumped over backward and were now stretched out side by side, their feet toward the fire. Only Shaeine still sat up, but she was slouched heavily and just as deeply asleep.

Lance permitted himself a smug smile. And they'd told him bringing the special cornbread was a waste of time in the Golden Sea. Preparedness; that's why he was in charge. He stood up, stepped around the fire, bent down, and picked up Ruda's sword. "Have a look at this," he said mildly, holding it out toward Elroy.

"Oh, c'mon, *that*? Yeah, sure, the gems'll probably sell, but dammit, Lance, they ain't nothin' compared to what we're already hauling! How the hell was that worth the risk?"

"Don't assume the sparkly part is the most important part, dummy. Hey, Jim, come down here. Have a look at this."

Jim picked his way down the rocky slope and approached curiously, plate in hand and chewing. He froze, though, staring at the sword in the firelight, going wide-eyed. Lance could almost swear his elongated ears perked up slightly.

"Okay, what are we missing?" Bella asked, tearing her eyes away from the glowing bottle. Fross had iced over the interior, hiding herself from view.

"See how the light shines on it?" Lance said, slowly turning the sword to make the firelight gleam on the blade. "Not like steel, more like it's soaking up the light and glowing, right? This, lady and gents, is *mithril*. Honest-to-gods dwarven-cast mithril. Magically nonconductive and damn near indestructible. This blade would stop a wandshot; it'll be around long after the empire is dust." To demonstrate, he took the rapier's blade very carefully in both hands and attempted to flex it, to no effect. A length of steel that thin would have bent easily. "This here shaft of metal is worth three times our entire haul of jewels. Add to that the fancy handle, and this is a weapon that should belong to a prince or high priest."

"Damn," Elroy whispered. "What's that little girl doin' with it, then?"

"*That*, Elroy, is the best part." Lance grinned. "See that blue jewel on her forehead? She's Punaji—a pirate. The obvious answer to what a scruffy teenager is doing with a piece like this is that she *stole* it. That's what Punaji do. So whoever actually *paid* for this thing will be lookin' for her, not for us. That's assuming they ain't at the bottom of the Azure Sea with a slit throat.

"So our plan's the same—we head back to civilization and sell the jewels. *Now*, though, we reinvest some of the proceeds in, shall we say . . . gentrification. Proper outfits, introductions. It'll take some doin' to get into the right circles to sell this sword; can't just anybody afford something like this, even if we don't let it go for its full value, which we ain't gonna get. Even so, once all the effort's made, we just doubled the size of our haul, easy." He caressed the slender blade as lovingly as Bella was now fondling her bottle. "We are *made*. After this score, we can retire and live like lords until we get so tired of decadence we're ready to shuffle ourselves off the mortal coil."

"You are rather glossing over the complication of our . . . guests," Jim pointed out.

"Right," Lance said, drawing his attention from daydreams of wealth and idleness and back to the present. "That'll be an extra step or two, but nothing too onerous."

"Just slit their throats and be done with it," Jim said curtly.

Lance shook his head. "You heard the girl. They die, Tellwyrn knows. Wouldn't put it past that lady to have ways of keeping an eye on the life force of her students. I've heard stranger things about her."

"That sounded like a bluff to me."

"T'me, too, Jim. But given the *risk* involved, and the fact that we don't *need* to call that bluff, we won't." He nodded at Bella. "Our resident witch here can use that memory spell we laid on Lord Calwynth last year. We take 'em out of the Sea, find someplace *relatively* safe where they won't get immediately killed, lay the whammy on 'em and haul ass out of there. They'll wake up amnesiac, which'll slow 'em the hell down without calling Tellwyrn down on us."

"It's a good plan," Bella agreed. "No permanent harm, even, just for a humanitarian bonus. They'll get most of their memories back eventually, but not the ones most recent before the spell. So they won't ever know what happened or who to look for."

"Sounds foolproof," Jim said, narrowing his eyes. "I distrust foolproof. It never works out in practice."

"Well, there's *one* complication," Bella admitted. "Lance, I don't think my memory spell will work on the dryad."

"So . . . that's an actual dryad?" He let out a low whistle. "I sorta figured green hair was trendy in Tiraas these days. Kids'll do any dumb fucking thing to piss off their parents."

"Lance Rogers, any woman wandering around the Golden Sea dressed like *that* is either a dryad or about to be a corpse. Use your head for somethin' besides a hat stand. Look, I can bind her so she won't wake up; that's easy enough. We'll leave *her* someplace separate, somewhere in the Golden Sea. Animals won't mess with her, and the Sea is twisted by fae magic; she'll be right at home until Naiya sends somebody to wake her up. If she ever does. She ain't exactly the most attentive mother. But we sure as hell do *not* want to bring her any harm. A pissed-off Tellwyrn would be *nothing* compared to a pissed-off Naiya."

Elroy jumped in startlement at a sudden movement from Shaeine, but she was only tumbling over on her side, finally overbalancing. He grinned weakly at them. "Well. Um . . . sounds like a plan, then?"

"It does," Lance agreed. "And we'll get started on it first thing in the morning. We ain't more'n a day or two from the outer rim, if that. Bella, anyplace special we should look for to leave the dryad?"

"Anyplace'll do, in a pinch," she said, chewing her lip and staring thoughtfully down at Juniper. "Could just drop her in the middle of the prairie and it'd probably be fine . . . But someplace *meaningful* would be better. We should hold out for a grove, something that could be sacred to the fae. If we don't come across anything, we'll just ditch her, but showing a little respect will go a long way toward appeasing Naiya."

"She ain't gonna be mad about us putting the girl to sleep, then?" Elroy asked nervously.

"We *didn't* put her to sleep. I'm just gonna keep her that way. Which, in a roundabout way, is probably for her own good, if her so-called friends let her wear herself out running in the first place. Anyway, fae have very different sensibilities. Long as we don't do her active harm, we're not pickin' a fight."

"All right, then," said Lance. "I want *two* people on watch at all times tonight. One looking outside, and one keeping an eye on these kids. We don't want any surprises, and let's face it, Tellwyrn doesn't let just any jackass attend her school. It'll mean short sleep, but in three days this'll all be behind us, and we'll be on our way to wealth and privilege. Jim, you take a rest; Bella, you an' me'll have the first watch, since it looks like you're too busy gettin' cozy with your new pet pixie to sleep anyway."

"Aw, you know me so well."

As they talked, Ruda's hand twitched toward Toby, and viciously pinched the skin on the back of his wrist. His breathing didn't vary in the slightest.

She cracked an eye open a slit, to glance up at the four travelers, then immediately shut it as they dispersed, two into the wagons, the leader toward her and her companions. There she lay, limp and breathing deeply.

Waiting.

CHAPTER 19

McGraw began to have a fatalistic feeling about the day when he wasn't even allowed to finish breakfast. It wasn't that the food at the A&W was particularly sumptuous, or even that he could afford to give it his undivided attention. He always kept an eye and ear on his surroundings when out on a mission, and in this particular town he also had his mental senses attuned to the wards that would notify him of his quarry attempting to flee via Rail. It was *breakfast*, though. There were some things to which a man was simply entitled, things he took it amiss when someone interrupted them.

He had, as usual, chosen a seat in the front corner of the room, which afforded him a view out the windows and one of the inn's common room itself. After Tellwyrn's surprise visit, he'd also taken to keeping a weather eye on the door. As such, he of course noted the five figures assembling in the square outside, but didn't assign any particular attention to them until the one in the middle bellowed his name.

With a sigh, he glanced down at his plate of eggs, beans, and hash browns, currently half finished. The thought of just ignoring them crossed his mind, but with some regret he dismissed it. The sort of fool who stood outside a tavern yelling for someone to come out was the sort of fool who'd create an even more disruptive ruckus if they weren't obliged. He brought the bite currently sitting on his fork to his mouth and stood, carefully wiping his face and beard with his napkin, and strolled across the room to the bar while chewing.

He swallowed just before reaching the waitress currently minding the tavern and tipped his hat politely to her. "Mornin', miss. Just wanted to settle up here, in case I don't get the chance later." Smiling unthreateningly at her wary expression, he set a small stack of coins on the counter.

"That's . . . uh, that's well more than enough," the girl said carefully.

"I'm aware. Listen, those kids outside yelling in the street? If they're in a position to take advantage later, give 'em a round on me. They're likely to need it."

Nodding to her again, he turned and strode unhurriedly toward the door.

McGraw stepped outside and descended the short steps to the square, then came to a stop a couple of yards from the front of the tavern.

"Mornin'," he said politely, tipping his hat. "It's a mite early for it, don't you think? I don't suppose you kids would care to do this later."

Two of the five—the women—he recognized from the tavern and around town; they were by far the more distinctive. The more absurd, if he was to be honest. The one in the center who'd been yelling was the attractive young lady in the dramatic black leather that showed a distracting amount of skin. He'd done his best not to be distracted, of course. McGraw's policy was never to ogle a woman unless she specifically indicated that she wanted him to, and this one looked more the type to invite attention just so she could ream some poor fellow out for showing it. The other was a short, waifish, rather hollow-cheeked girl in sweltering black robes, clutching a staff of dark-stained hardwood. A magical staff, but not one that fired bolts of lightning at the press of a switch. No, it was a wizard's staff in the tradition of his own, an aid to spellcasting. For all that, he didn't perceive any arcane energies around her. A witch, then, or warlock? Either way, an amateur. People who meddled with either fairies *or* demons quickly learned to be serious and not waste time on such melodramatic touches as sweeping black robes and ornately carved staves, or they came to a swift and sticky end.

The men were slightly more respectable looking, with the exception of the mage, who was actually wearing hooded robes straight out of the last century. The man was middle-aged, at least, with a slight paunch and as much gray as brown in his beard; of all people, he ought to know better. Beside him stood a fellow who wasn't a cowboy but had dressed as one, his leather and denim attire brand-spanking new and embellished with needless embroidery, surmounted by a *white* ten-gallon hat. He also sported late-model wands holstered at his belt, over which his hands hovered menacingly. On the other side was a nervous-looking fellow in a plain suit, a bronze badge at his lapel marking him a cleric of Salyrene.

"*Justice*," said the girl in leather, self-importantly, "doesn't wait till it's convenient for you."

"Now, I might be mistaken," McGraw said mildly, "It wouldn't be the first time. But I was under the impression that justice in this town was the province of a nice fellow with a badge, who has the actual authority of the empire to hand it out."

"Our weapons are all the authority we need," sneered the "cowboy."

"That's no way to live, son," McGraw told him gravely. "It makes for a world that ain't fit for anybody to live *in*."

"There are things more important than the law," the girl in leather said sharply, clearly trying to steer the conversation back to herself. "Especially when assassins hide behind the law to do their dirty work."

"Was that directed at me?" he asked. "I didn't realize I was hiding behind anything."

"There are higher powers," intoned the girl in the black robe. She had a thin, strained voice. "Higher concerns. A great doom is coming; it is whispered on the wind in every corner of the world. Those who care to stand against the darkness must do so, ere it is too late."

"Kid," he said wearily, "*nobody* talks like that."

"Enough," snapped Leather. "We're not here to argue the point. *Any* point. We know what you're here for, Longshot McGraw, and it's not happening. I think you should leave town."

"If there's a problem with me minding my own business in this fair little burg, I believe I'll wait till I hear about it from an official source. Just as a point of curiosity, though, are you kids aware the people you're protecting are members of the Thieves' Guild?"

That caused a stir in their ranks. The girl in the leather narrowed her eyes; the cleric actually twitched as if startled, looking over at the leader as if for direction.

"So," said the mage with a smile, "you not only know who we're discussing, but that they need protection. Sounds like an admission to me."

"Well, it seems I'll have to grant you that one," McGraw said, chuckling ruefully. "Fairly caught. That's what happens when I don't get to finish my breakfast. What's your story, friend? Forgive my pointin' it out, but you don't seem to quite fit in among these whippersnappers."

"Rotscale," the other wizard replied, holding up an arm and pulling back the sleeve of his robe to show a long streak of black, hardened skin. "I've been to every cleric in Tiraas; they can't do a thing. The doctors say I've got two years, tops. Always wanted to be a hero, ever since I was a boy. Facing the prospect of actually dying in bed, well . . . A man reassesses what's naive and what's true."

"That, I can respect," McGraw said, nodding gravely. The other man nodded in return, his expression still calm and faintly amused.

"So what's it gonna be, McGraw?" asked the girl in the leather. "Are you gonna leave on your own terms? Or do we have to do this . . . the hard way?"

"Ideally," he replied calmly, "the outcome here is that I go back inside and finish my meal, and y'all cut this foolishness out and go get a real job. Ain't my policy to tell anybody how they oughta live, but I do wish you'd consider the consequences of your actions for people who aren't you. This here's an inhabited town." He nodded to the side, where a dozen or so townsfolk had gathered to watch the proceedings with great interest. "Anybody starts shootin', there's likely to be bystanders injured and *sure* to be property damage. Also, the way you've been carryin' on out here, I expect the sheriff to arrive any second, and as things stand, it ain't me who's aimin' to spend a night in the pokey."

That brought them up short. Some of the bluster leaked out of the leader; she glanced uncertainly around at the buildings and people nearby, while the cleric and the robed girl looked to her for guidance. The cowboy only stared at McGraw, a faint grin hovering around his mouth. That one was going to be trouble, no matter how this played out.

"All of this," McGraw went on, "is leaving aside that you poor saps have been suckered in by some authentically *bad people* to do their dirty work. So I'll turn your question back around on you, miss. You wanna step inside, have a seat, talk this out like civilized folk? Or would you prefer to do something foolish and get buried under the consequences of it? What's it gonna be?"

Watching from the shadows of a nearby alley, Thumper cursed softly to himself. Already it was all going wrong. All those damned kids had to do was be their stupid selves, and they couldn't even do *that* right. Even as he watched, he could see their resolve faltering.

As usual, he had to do everything himself.

He pulled a small hinged case from the inside pocket of his coat and flipped it open; inside were several vials from his potion kit. He might be a fake salesman, but the props provided for his cover were quite real, and he had taken the precaution of bringing several along in case they came in handy for today's work. Selecting one, he shut the case and tucked it away, flicked the cork off the vial with his thumb, and drank it down, grimacing at the bitter taste. Would it interfere with the functioning of alchemy to add some damn flavor?

At least it worked. In seconds, his own arms faded from view. Clothes and all, luckily. He'd read horror stories of adventurers caught in sticky situations when their invisibility elixirs had only concealed flesh, but thankfully modern alchemy was more reliable.

Shook was no sneak-thief, but he'd grown up on the streets of Tiraas and knew how to move quietly. For all that sneaking out in the open in broad daylight set his nerves jangling, he circled around the little tableau unfolding in the square without being spotted by any of the participants. He'd half expected McGraw to be able to see through the effects of the potion, but it seemed luck was with him.

Shook ghosted around behind the five would-be heroes, creeping up on the fool in the cowboy hat just as McGraw was finishing up his little speech. He was right about one thing—the sheriff would be here very soon. Thumper had singled out this guy when Tazlith had introduced him around to the posse she'd put together. He was aggressive, reckless, and exactly the sort of fellow who could be relied on to start trouble. Even if he didn't actually start it, nobody would have a hard time believing that he had.

As the five wannabes hesitated, glancing at each other, Thumper crouched, moved in closer, and then lunged. He grabbed one of the cowboy's hands with one of his and his wand with the other. The man cried out in surprise and tried to pull away, but Thumper was faster, stronger, and had the element of surprise. He mashed the wand against the man's hand, twisted it in the general direction of McGraw, and squeezed the clicker.

The shot missed, of course, cracking one of the wooden supports holding up the A&W's awning. That didn't matter; what mattered was that to those watching, it looked like the man had performed a quick draw and fired from the waist.

It had been a gamble; it would have backfired had his targets shown any introspection or reserve, but human nature didn't fail him. Once the shooting started, the thinking stopped.

McGraw hadn't been in the path of the wandshot, but he nevertheless threw up a shield, a sparkling blue sphere around himself which protected him from the shadowbolt hurled by the girl in the black robe. People screamed and ran in all directions. The cowboy had dropped his wand when Thumper let it go, and was looking around in confusion.

The sheriff would be there in seconds, surely.

Thumper was already on his way back into the alley.

Principia had chosen a good spot once she heard the shouting begin. For all the trouble-making types who came through Last Rock, few bothered to make use of the town's rooftops, which was almost a shame; the stone structures were extremely solid and their slate shingles kept in good repair. They also didn't transmit sound well, so as long as she stepped lightly, nobody knew she was making her way over their homes.

It helped that people never thought to look up.

The sloping roof of the general store had a conveniently placed chimney, from behind which she peeked down at the action in the square. She had marked the alley into which Shook had vanished prior to the action starting, and thus noted the faint disturbance of invisible footsteps in the dust heading toward the adventurers. It was, she had to acknowledge, a good effect. If not for elven eyes and the fact that she'd been watching specifically for something from that point of emergence, she would have missed it.

"You bastard," she murmured with a faint smile. He was nothing if not predictable.

Prin ducked lower as the first shot went off, hiding herself completely and thus losing her view of the action. There followed two more wandshots and the less distinctive sounds of spells being cast, then a lull. She peeked out again a moment later, taking stock of the scene.

McGraw had vanished. Unless one of those fool casters had managed to disintegrate him—about as likely as a sudden revelation that she was in line for the imperial throne—that meant he had moved to reclaim the advantage. The fact that she didn't know where he was . . . well, that could be all kinds of bad.

Tazlith was trying to rally her troops, who were varying degrees of frightened, confused, and pissed off. Principia decided none of this needed to be dealt with by her.

Moving lightly as a squirrel, she darted across the rooftops to the large house where she rented an attic, slipping neatly through her open window into her chambers. Even using her unconventional paths, nowhere in Last Rook took long to reach.

Prin shut the window behind herself, turned to her enchanting table... and froze. She darted over to the door—yes, it was open, the lock broken. Naturally Shook didn't have the skill, and probably also not the inclination, to pick a lock like a professional. She looked back to the table, where her row of carefully enchanted rings were missing.

"*Bastard*," she said with more feeling.

Right. Predictable.

Speaking of, at that moment her broken door pushed open and Longshot McGraw ducked inside.

"Ma'am," he said courteously, tugging the brim of his hat to her. "Pardon my intrusion, but it seems I need to move up my timetable considerably."

She stared at him for one silent moment before bolting.

Prin threw down an enchanted coin as she fled; its simple anti magic charm wouldn't have held against anything a wizard of McGraw's caliber threw at it deliberately, but it disrupted the stasis spell he tossed after her enough that she only felt a brief tugging sensation before she managed to dive through the still-open window.

She somersaulted midair and landed on her feet in a slide, shooting straight down the sloping roof tiles. In the alley below, she kicked off the far wall to blunt her momentum and rolled as she reached the ground, sprinting for the mouth of the alley.

McGraw's teleportation wasn't as tidy or potent as Tellwyrn's; his appearance was presaged by a split-second flash of blue light, giving Prin enough warning to skid to a stop rather than plow into him, and his reappearance came with a *crack* of energy and a static buzz that made her hair begin to stand up.

"It seems," he said conversationally as though nothing had just happened, "that your friend Mr. Shook has set a pack of ravenous puppies on me. I actually have to admire his cleverness; I'd feel quite bad if I brought harm to any of those silly kids, which hampers me more than a little. My feeling, though, is they'll maybe be a bit less trigger-happy if I show up again with you in tow. They *did* turn up to protect you from my depredations after all," he added with a grin.

Principia backed up two careful steps. "Why are you doing this?"

He shrugged. "The money's good."

"*That* is what I meant. Why? You could have apprentices . . . wealth, a life of comfort. You're ten times the mage any of those turkeys who go adventuring in the Sea are. Why *this*?"

McGraw tilted his head to one side, regarding her curiously for a moment before replying. "Short answer is, it's something to do."

"Seriously? That's *it*?"

"Miss, when you get to my age—"

"I'm at least *twice* your age."

"—you start to think about who you are and what you really want, whether you intend to or not. I stumbled into the adventuring life quite by accident and spent a couple decades moaning about it . . . but come time to retire, I found the thing I *truly* fear is . . . Well. Apprentices, wealth, comfort, and all the trappings of a staid life. Won't say I crave *adventure*, as such, just . . . not to be bored. Things like this suit me fine."

She crept back another step. "I could only wish I had your problems."

"I imagine my situation looks a fair bit better'n yours at this moment. Not that I'm not enjoying this discussion, ma'am, but I also am not a fool. We can carry on chatting while we walk, if you are so inclined." He leveled his staff at her and smiled politely. "This way, please."

Shook made a point of breathing hard as he dashed up to the adventurers, who were huddled together in the square. Townspeople had fled; they had the place effectively to themselves for the moment. Where the hell was that sheriff? It had been more than a couple of minutes already; Sanders had never been so slow to respond to a disturbance, at least not from what the locals had told him over the last few days. He'd had to wait for the counteragent to the invisibility elixir to take effect, and had been sure he'd come back to find his minions slugging it out with the law while their actual quarry slipped away. Well, odd as it was, he'd take it.

"Everybody all right?" He panted, doing his best to look concerned. "Damn, he moves fast. I didn't even have a chance to get in behind him."

"Jeremiah," Tazlith said with obvious relief, turning to him. "Marks says he was grabbed; somebody got his wand and made him shoot at McGraw."

"We are not of one mind on what to make of this story," said Lorrie, the warlock. "It seems terribly convenient for him. Terribly *inconvenient* for us."

"I didn't detect any invisible presence," the mage (whose name Shook hadn't troubled to learn) intoned pompously. It was all Shook could do not to roll his eyes.

"Dammit, I should've expected that," he said, putting on a rueful face.

"What?" said Tazlith. "What do you mean?"

"The whole point of this was to stand him down, *prevent* it coming to a fight, right? McGraw told me to my face he'd like nothing better than if I started the shooting so he could claim self-defense. If he realized we weren't going to oblige him, obviously he made it *seem* you were starting the fight."

"Can . . . can he do that?" Marks asked uncertainly.

"Man's a famous battlemage. Who can say *what* he can do?"

"It's an interesting theory."

They all spun toward the speaker in unison, those who had weapons raising them. Sheriff Sanders was striding toward them, his stare promising murder. With him came Ox Whipporwill . . . and the three imperial soldiers quartered at the University.

So *that's* what had taken him so long.

"I cannot recommend strongly enough that you lower those wands," Sanders said grimly. "Needless to say, a *thorough* investigation of everyone involved in this mess is forthcoming. If there's been magical meddling, we'll find out, one way or another. In the meantime, though, you are all coming down to the office with me. It'll look much better for you if I don't have to be assertive about it."

"All *we* wanted to do was protect that girl McGraw is after," Tazlith said stridently. "We'll cooperate in any way we can, but right now he is *still out there*, and so is she. We aren't the threat here. Do your *job*, Sheriff!"

Shook would have winced if her blustering didn't so perfectly suit his aim of deflecting the trouble toward herself. That was one of the top ten things you absolutely did *not* say to law enforcement.

"This ain't a conversation, miss," Sanders shot back, placing a hand on his own wand. "I am gonna repeat myself one more time, and after that I'll assume you're resisting. We are going—"

"Excuse me," said the robed mage, "but you should all see this."

They turned to look where he pointed, Sanders a second after the others as if expecting to be attacked from behind if he averted his eyes. It was no trap, though, at least not for them. McGraw and Principia were entering the empty square from the street beyond. She walked in front, stiffly, her hands balled into fists at her sides. The old wizard strolled behind her, staff resting over his shoulder, puffing idly on a cigarillo.

"Hello again," he said. "Ah, ah, ah, let's nobody go an' do something rash. There's been enough dust kicked up for one morning, I think. Seein' as how Ms. Locke and myself seem to be the source of all this commotion, we've talked it over amongst ourselves and decided the most responsible course of action is for us to remove ourselves from town till everything has a chance to settle down again."

"That true, Prin?" Sanders asked tersely.

She glared at him. "Of *course* it's not fucking true, you half-wit, I'm being kidnapped! *Do* something!"

McGraw shook his head. "Nobody around here can ever let me do anything the easy way," he said fatalistically. "Y'know, I believe I'm beginning to actively dislike this town."

"Feeling's mutual," Sanders said, drawing his wand. "Elias 'Longshot' McGraw, you're under arrest."

"If you consider the matter carefully," McGraw replied calmly, smiling, "I think you will find that I am not. As I was saying, Ms. Locke and I will be leaving the town now. I leave it to you and these lovely people to decide how much needs to get broken in the process, Sheriff."

"You are astronomically outnumbered, villain," the warlock intoned. "Submission is your only wise course." Around her, the others readied their weapons; wands and staves were aimed at him, and Tazlith drew a pair of throwing knives.

"It seems to me," McGraw said evenly, stepping up behind Principia so that he addressed them over her shoulder, "a show of force isn't appropriate in your situation. I'm assuming, of course, that you would rather Ms. Locke not get shot in the process. I might be wrong about that. Wouldn't be the first time."

"We fan out, take him from all angles," Shook said tersely. "He can't hide behind her skirts if he's encircled."

"Thank you for your input," Sanders said sarcastically.

"*What?*" Principia screeched, a note of hysteria entering her voice. "No shooting!"

"Do you *wanna* get hauled off into the prairie to be executed like a dog?" Shook replied. "Just keep your head down and try not to get shot."

"No! Fuck you, Shook! *No shooting!*"

"Prin—"

"Go to hell!" She was shrieking now, eyes wide in panic. "Nobody's taking shots in my direction just because *you* would rather I'm out of the picture! You stole my fucking enchanted rings and left me high and dry, you faked the shot at McGraw with that invisibility charm! This bullshit is entirely *your* fault!"

"Wait, you did *what?*" Tazlith said, whirling on him.

He glared at her. "This is not the time—"

"He's wearing rings," the robed man noted. "Rather a lot of them. I wondered about that."

"Seems I'm gonna need a bigger cell," Sanders said wearily. "Goddamn it, the middle of the street with weapons pointed in all directions is not the place for this. Everybody stop whatever the *hell* you're doing and stand down!"

"Y'all clearly have matters to discuss amongst yourselves," McGraw said cheerfully. "We'll just be heading—"

"No you don't!" Sanders raised his arm, aiming his wand right for McGraw and disregarding Principia's squeal of protest. "Nobody fucking moves!"

McGraw opened his mouth to reply, but cut off, his eyes widening as they shifted to look past the group. Immediately, he and Principia were wreathed in a sparkling sphere of transparent blue light. Two wandshots splashed against it, causing it to flicker and dim—Marks and one of the soldiers had apparently been spooked by the sudden spell effect.

"Hold your fire!" Sanders roared, to no effect.

McGraw pointed his staff at the ground between them; light flashed along its length, and an elaborate circular glyph appeared on the paving stones. Everyone backed rapidly away from it, Rook and Moriarty swiveling to point their weapons at the shape that began forming out of mist above it.

"What the fuck?" Marks moved one hand to aim at the figure, keeping his other wand pointed at McGraw and Principia.

"He summons something," said Lorrie, shifting her staff to rest in the crook of her arm and folding her hands together. "Two can play at this game."

"No!" Tazlith shouted, whirling on her. "Dammit, we *talked* about this! Do not bring that damn thing out; this'll *all* go to hell if you lose control of it!"

"An elemental!" exclaimed the mage as the mist coalesced into a figure. It wasn't even vaguely humanoid, though it had two arm-like protrusions. "How does an arcane wizard have access to a water elemental?!"

"Oh, *shit*." Sanders's outburst wasn't aimed at the elemental, however; he'd glanced over his shoulder, following McGraw's eyes.

"Shoot it!"

"Don't shoot it! Don't make it mad!"

"Will somebody do *something*?!"

CRACK!

The bolt of power that roared across the square, making all their hair stand up and momentarily blinding everyone, was nearly massive enough to suit a magical artillery shot. It struck the creature dead center; half its mass evaporated on the spot, the rest splashing harmlessly to the ground, apparently now inert.

The weapon that had fired it was clearly antique. Shorter than modern battlestaves and at least twice as thick, it was a throwback to the age when such enchanted weapons were a new invention borrowing from older sensibilities. Elaborately carved, decorated across its whole length with bands of silver and surmounted by a globe of glowing crystal, it looked like what an artist designing a cover for a penny dreadful might imagine an old-fashioned wizard's staff to be.

The person carrying it had made that perfect shot with the cumbersome weapon *one-handed*, using the other to prop herself up on one of her canes. She glared coldly at McGraw.

"*Shame* on you," said Mabel Cratchley.

With a *burble* and a huge gout of steam, the elemental rose up from the ground; it was smaller now, but clearly re-form itself.

This time, Marks, Lorrie, and the cleric dived away as Miz Cratchley blasted it again, Rook stumbling backward from the incredible force and falling on his rear. It made a smoking crater in the middle of the square where it struck.

The staff, too, was smoking now, though Miz Cratchley didn't pay it any mind, shifting her aim to McGraw.

"Don't do it!" Principia wailed, cowering back against him.

"Impressive shootin', ma'am," McGraw said, tipping his hat to her. At some point in the last minute he had dropped his cigarillo. "But there's a reason those old thunder busses were taken out of service. One more shot and the thing's likely to blow up."

"I've lived long enough," she replied, staring him down. "I'm ready to account for myself to the gods. Are you?"

McGraw stared back at her, apparently lacking an answer to that.

Before anybody could act or come up with something to say, there came a soft *pop* from right between the two groups, the effect rather underwhelming after the recent show of firepower. The effect on the group of the figure who materialized was another matter entirely.

"All right," Arachne Tellwyrn said flatly, "that's enough."

CHAPTER 20

"Oh, what the hell is this now?" Lance muttered. Ahead, Jim was already bringing the lead wagon to a stop. Between the gentle downward slope of the Sea and the height of the tallgrass, they hadn't seen what was coming until they were right on top of it. Or for that matter, maybe it hadn't been there before.

He hopped down from the wagon seat before it had even fully stopped moving. "Stay put," he said curtly to Bella when she began to rise, too. "And keep your eyes on those kids. I don't want any surprises at this point." Not pausing to see her reaction, he strode forward, around the other wagon, and approached Jim, who was standing on the ground as well.

"What do you think?" asked the half elf as Lance approached, panning his gaze around at the expanse of flat, rocky ground that had opened up before them. It looked like granite—uneven, marred by cracks, pits, and protrusions. "This'll play hell with the wagons. Won't be great for the oxen, either."

Lance cursed under his breath. "Can you see how far it extends?"

"Nope." Jim shook his head. "Not in front or to the sides. Of course, how big it objectively is has little to do with how long we'll be in it if we try to cross."

Lance glanced back at his own wagon, in which they had laid out the kids from Last Rock. "Bella reckons we can maybe keep 'em asleep a bit longer with her hoodoo, if it comes to that. The last thing we need is for our passengers to start waking up... That'll play bigger hell than anything this does to the wagons."

"Unless we throw a wheel, or lame an ox," said Jim, "in which case it'll all go to shit anyway."

Lance glared at the plain of stone, thinking. They were between the proverbial rock and an annoyingly literal hard place. "Risk damaging the wagons in the badlands, or risk getting lost as fuck and adding days to our trip if we try to go around. Both mean we have some angry and very dangerous people to deal with... Looks about the same level of risk to me either way, with more or less the same consequence. Unless you disagree."

Jim shook his head. "Sounds about right to me."

Lance heaved a sigh. "Then I say we go for the risk that gets us out of here quicker. Make sure everything's lashed down tight and let's move on. You best stay in front, I want your eyes findin' us the safest route."

The other man nodded mutely and climbed back up onto his wagon seat while Lance turned and walked back to Bella.

"I heard," she said. "Everything's secure back here, and it doesn't matter too much if the passengers get jostled a bit. The wagons were in good shape when we set out, and Elroy's been looking 'em over at every stop. We should be fine."

"Any chance of the bumpy ride waking our sleeping beauties?"

She grinned. "Not till dusk at the earliest, and even then they'll be too groggy to be useful for hours. Best we get a move on."

Jim's wagon was already moving, and Lance prompted the oxen to follow suit.

"Try not to distract me," Bella said, closing her eyes. "I'm gonna keep my attention on a little charm work, to help the wagons bear up under the abuse." Already she had to raise her voice to be heard under the aggressive rattle of wheels over uneven stone. Lance gave her a sidelong look, holding on to his seat.

"Shouldn't you have got out and laid that *on* the wheels before we started moving?"

"I don't actually know a *spell* that'd do that, though you can bet I'm gonna look one up after this. I'm just using general buffing magic. Strength, endurance, good fortune, all that. Remember what I said about distracting me?"

He grunted irritably, but fell silent. It wasn't worth arguing, especially when they had to nearly shout to be heard, not to mention devoting serious effort to holding on. The noise really was incredible; it seemed the entire wagon shuddered with each little jostle, and not all of the jostles were little. Jim set them on a weaving course that sought to avoid the worst of it, but there was simply no good ground. The stone itself made the wheels grate ominously as they passed over its flatter stretches, and seemed to delight in tossing little cracks and rocks under them.

In the shady back of the covered wagon, Ruda cracked an eye, surreptitiously studying their captors, even as she and the others were jostled roughly against each other. Neither were looking back at them, and the noise and shaking made the best cover she'd found thus far for any action. This was clearly the time.

It wasn't that simple, though. She could probably take out Lance and Bella, having the element of surprise as she did. The others would be another matter, though; they had staves. Ruda could grab one of those in this wagon, of course, but the best-case scenario was still a firefight, which would put her sleeping companions at serious risk, even if the enemy didn't deliberately target them.

Careful not to move too much—no telling when one of the bastards would glance back to check on them—she swept an eye around the interior of the wagon. She'd become quite familiar with the layout during the long morning. Two wooden chests were set against the right side of the wagon bed, with herself and her fellow captives laid out like logs filling the rest of the space. They were cargo; the rest of the adventurers' belongings, including nearly all their supplies, had been moved to the lead wagon and piled in to make room. Ruda was pressed between the chests and Toby; blessedly, nobody had been laid on top of her, though Juniper's legs half covered her own. The front end of the wagon held sealed barrels, lashed in place, and ahead of that was just the driver's seat. Her sword was tucked carefully between two barrels, its pommel barely visible; Bella kept the bottle containing Fross with her.

She lifted her eyes at a sharp rattle from above her head. The rear gate of the wagon was held in place by a long, thin iron bar which fit into metal fixtures attached to either wall of the bed. It was all one piece, meaning it could be conveniently rotated to open both sides of the latch and lower the gate with a single motion. As she watched, the wagon went over a bump and the latch nearest her jumped again, nearly coming loose.

Ruda glanced at the chests, back at the latch, then forward at the drivers. A plan fell into place. Well, the rough outlines of one, but she hadn't the luxury of time to dither and refine.

She lifted one hand and wrenched the latch open, then swiftly lowered her arm and shut her eyes. By the time the unfastened gate banged open, she gave no sign of ever having been awake.

"The hell was *that*?" Lance shouted. Bella said something in reply, her voice muffled beyond audibility. "Oh, fuck, the gate's popped open. Signal Jim to stop; I gotta grab that before something falls out."

He kept up a chorus of grunts and curses as he picked his way back across the bed, his efforts becoming easier when the wagon eased to a stop. Ruda barely managed not to make a sound when he overbalanced and stepped right on her stomach; it helped that it drove the breath right out of her. Growling, he clambered over her, finally, leaning over the end of the bed to grab the fallen gate, pull it back up, and reset the latch.

Ruda concentrated on her breathing, keeping it as deep and even as she could. That footprint was going to become a respectable bruise. It occupied plenty of her attention while orders were shouted and the wagons pulled forward again.

She had long since learned the value of patience. Ruda waited until she judged they'd been moving again for a good quarter of an hour, and then opened the gate again.

"Goddamn it!" Lance shouted from up ahead.

"Just *leave* it," Bella replied, raising her own voice to be heard over the racket. "The kids aren't gonna slide out and the trunks are too heavy."

"Those trunks are our *haul*, dammit! If one falls—"

"Too heavy," she repeated firmly. "If the latch has popped twice it'll just do it again. Unless you plan to balance back there and *hold* the damn thing shut, leave it."

"I can lash it shut!"

"With what, your belt? Elroy's got the rope up there with all the rest of the supplies. We'll deal with it when we stop next, let's not waste any more time with this."

He replied, but it was muted enough that Ruda couldn't make out his words, and anyway, it didn't result in the wagons stopping again, or him climbing back into the bed. Good, that was the easy part dealt with.

The trunk wasn't large, thank Naphthene, otherwise she'd never have managed, as it was full of rocks. Jewels, anyway. The bigger one, behind, held uncut stones salvaged from some kind of old mining operation the adventurers had found; the one closer to the back of the wagon contained their much smaller haul of cut and polished gems. Ruda wasn't clear on what exactly they'd found and didn't particularly care. All that mattered right now was that the trunk weighed far too damn much, and she couldn't risk getting herself into a proper position to shift it. She managed to hook her right hand around its end and *pulled*.

For the most part, it was reluctant to budge. It wasn't beyond her strength, but she was in a bad position and it was an uphill battle. The roughness of the ride actually helped; some of the worst bumps were bad enough to lift the trunk momentarily off the wagon bed, and in each of those little gaps she managed to tug it a few more inches.

Ruda kept one eye open and constantly on the seat up front. The two sitting there appeared to be having an argument, which was lucky. If not for their distraction, they would surely be keeping a closer eye on their cargo, and then she'd be in trouble.

The trunk inched past her head; she had to adjust the position of her arm to keep pulling. Surely the end of it had to be past the edge of the wagon bed . . .

Then they went over a particularly bad bump, the trunk actually bounced *off* the bed for a moment, landed in a slide, and overbalanced. It tumbled over the back, hitting the ground with a very satisfying *crunch* of breaking wood.

Not nearly so satisfying as Lance's cursing.

He brought the entire wagon train to a halt this time, calling the others back to survey the damage. Ruda hardly dared to breathe. The tension of her situation was actually a benefit, as she felt more than a small amount of pleasure at the situation of her captors, and this would be a bad moment to accidentally crack a smile.

"*Too heavy*," Lance snarled after a long, silent moment in which the four of them had stood there, staring down at the mess. The wagon had creaked forward a few yards before it could be brought to a stop, so they at least weren't standing right *over* Ruda and the others.

Bella sighed and didn't respond to his accusing tone. "What do you think? Can the box be salvaged?"

"Kindling," Jim said curtly. "And we don't have another."

"We got barrels . . ."

"None that aren't in *use*."

"Food, right?" said Lance. "We've got more'n we need. Dump some hardtack, just enough to make room for this. We'll be out of the Sea by the end of the day." Jim turned and trudged past without another word. "Elroy . . . clean this up. Just forget about the trunk. Gather up the gems in a pile, move 'em over there so we won't have to carry the barrel far once it's loaded. Oh, and when you're done with that, bring out some rope or something to lash down this *fucking* gate."

"Uh, the rope's all packed away," Elroy said nervously. "I mean, it's *under* a pile of—"

"Son of a *bitch*, can't *anything* go right today?"

There came a moment of silence, and then the *crunch* of boots on gravel, approaching the wagon.

"This is all awfully, *specifically* inconvenient," Lance remarked, standing right at the edge of the wagon bed.

"I'm tellin' you, they're out," Bella said from behind him. "The dryad's bound and the others aren't gonna be getting up anytime—" She broke off at the loud slap of a hand striking flesh.

Ruda managed not to tense, not to react at all, despite the rush of white-hot rage. Toby was laid with his feet toward the end of the wagon bed, as was Rafe. If that hand had hit a face, as it sounded, it was Shaeine's.

Her wondering came to a stop seconds later when a similar slap landed on her own cheek. Her head was knocked to the side by the force of it, cheekbone bouncing off the wooden floor. Ruda stayed limp, let herself roll with the blow, kept her face neutral. This wasn't the first time she'd played dead, under more pressure than even this. The University wasn't nearly the beginning of her training.

"Satisfied?" Bella asked dryly. "I really hope so. I'm sure the ride won't wake 'em up, but you're pushing it."

Lance grunted. "Come help me find the goddamn rope. Elroy, get to work. *Jim!*" he shouted, stalking away. "Where the fuck is that rope buried?"

Ruda listened to them move past, listened to Elroy's muttering and grunting as he bent and hauled handfuls of jewels over to pile them by the end of the wagon. He was loud enough to give her a clear idea what he was doing. She waited until the fourth trip, as he was turning away to go back for another batch.

After a long, nearly sleepless night, followed by a long trip in the bumpy back of a wagon, she was a solid knot of bruises, sore spots, and stiffness in general. Her whole body screamed in pain, rebelling at the speed with which she suddenly demanded that it move, which was just too damn bad. Ruda came upright, less smoothly than she would have liked but still her athletic self, lunged off the back of the wagon, and closed in on Elroy while yanking her boot knife free.

One hand over his mouth cut off his cry of surprise; with the other, she reached around and ripped the knife through his throat before he even knew what was happening. Ruda pushed him away, letting him flop to the ground, clutching at his ruined throat. Not dead yet, but that didn't matter; he was well and truly silent. She turned her back and crawled as swiftly and silently as she could manage into the wagon and over the prone forms of her friends.

Her luck continued to hold. Bella had had the sense to leave her prize behind while going forward to forage in the other wagon. Ruda had to hide herself behind the barrels, watching surreptitiously, and time her grab for when the three were all facing away, but when the moment came, she reached out quick as a striking snake and grabbed the bottle off the wagon seat. Hopefully Bella wasn't looking back to check on it every minute; as enamored as the woman was of her captive pixie, Ruda wouldn't have put it past her.

Ducking back down behind the barrels, she brought the jar to her face. It was still iced over completely on the inside, but the pixie's glow was visible nonetheless. "Fross, I'm gonna get you out. We're still in trouble here, so I need you to stay low, out of sight, and be *quiet*."

She ripped away the thin chain binding the bottle, set the tip of her knife into the lead stopper, and viciously levered it loose.

Fross could at least follow directions. She zipped out, immediately diving to the floor of the wagon, and managed to keep her voice low, despite the fury filling it. "I am just so *mad*!"

"Me, too," Ruda said tersely, having turned to face her other somnolent companions. "Fuck. That's two of us now, and one of them down, but these are still not odds I like. We've gotta protect the others, which is a major handicap . . ." Her eyes fell on the form of Juniper, who was wrapped in thin cords, decorated with little charms and bits of marked paper. "How do you unbind a dryad? Do you know enough about witchcraft to counter the spell?"

"Just rip the cords off; they're holding the magic."

"Cake." She sliced through them, careful not to nick the dryad, and pulled them aside. "C'mon, Juno, rise and shine."

The dryad made no response, even when Ruda leaned over to pat her roughly on the face. "Juniper! Up, girl, we need your help. *June!*" Finally, in desperation, she slapped her.

Nothing.

"She fell asleep, cause she was overtired, remember?" said Fross.

"Maybe she hasn't rested enough yet."

"Well, that's a shame, because she is out of time," Ruda said grimly. She reached forward between the barrels and grabbed the handle of her sword, tugging it out. ". . . doesn't breathe, no heartbeat. Fross, do dryads have vital organs at *all*?"

"How should *I* know?"

"Wh— You're a fairy, too, aren't you?"

Fross buzzed a complete orbit of her head in agitation. "There aren't more than three dozen dryads in the world, and they're all cozy with Naiya herself. This is like me asking you how the emperor takes his tea. You're both humans, aren't you?"

Ruda sighed. "All right, then, looks like I'll have to test a theory. Juno, I'm really sorry about this. If it turns out I'm wrong, I'll be really, *really* sorry."

She placed the tip of her rapier at a point just under Juniper's right breast, and before Fross could say anything, shoved down, impaling the dryad until the mithril blade bit into the wood below.

Juniper sat bolt upright, eyes flying open, drawing in a desperate gasp. The sword moved with her body, wrenched out of Ruda's hands, but that was fine, as she immediately clapped them both over Juniper's mouth.

"Welcome back," she said cheerfully. "Here's the short version. We've been kidnapped, everyone else is drugged and won't be awake for hours, and we're a few seconds from being in a major fight."

"You *stabbed* me!" Juniper said, disbelieving, when Ruda took her hands off her mouth.

"Yeah, sorry about that. I couldn't get you to wake up. Desperate times, desperate measures, all that shit. Are you . . . I mean, obviously you're not *okay*, but is this, like . . . debilitating?"

"It's a *hole* through my chest," the dryad grumbled, probing experimentally at the point where the sword entered. "It doesn't feel *good*."

"What I mean is, can you fight? Is it safe to pull the— Well, there you go," she finished as Juniper yanked the blade out and handed it to her. Streaked across its length, and oozing from the tiny wound, was a thick amber goo. Ruda wouldn't go quite so far as to taste it, but couldn't resist lifting the sword to have a sniff. She'd been taught about shipbuilding and repair from the cradle, and knew the smell of tree sap very well.

"Right," Juniper said grimly, dragging herself upright. "Kidnapped and drugged. If I *really* hated these guys, we could just let them do it and have to deal with Omnu, Tellwyrn, Naiya, and Blackbeard later."

"I'd rather take care of my own shit, thanks. Especially if it means I get to live. You, uh, all right there? You're moving a little stiffly."

"I'm exhausted," the dryad said shortly, "and recently stabbed. I'll cope. Oh, here's a dead guy," she noted, hopping down from the back of the wagon with Ruda and Fross right behind her. "Your doing? I'm kinda surprised; I was starting to think you humans were squeamish about everything."

"Pff, I killed my first man when I was *seven*. C'mon, there's three more to—"

"Hey, Elroy!" Lance bellowed. "Jim doesn't know where the rope is either, and we don't have all day to fuck around with this. Get over here and lend us a hand."

"Only three?" Juniper said grimly. "Easy enough."

"Wait!" Ruda exclaimed as the dryad stepped around the wagon to face the others, then winced at the storm of shouted curses that rose.

Above them came Bella's frantic voice. "Wait, no! No! *Don't shoot!*"

Too late.

A thunderclap ripped across the badlands, and a blast of energy struck Juniper right in the midsection, hurling her backward two yards.

Ruda clapped a hand over her mouth in horror. The lightning bolt had clipped the dryad right below the ribs, blasting a large chunk completely out of her body. Almost a third of her abdomen was gone, its edges seared black and smoking.

"You big—mean—*JERKS!*" Fross howled, taking to the air. In the next instant, a blizzard roared out of the clear sky, pounding the lead wagon with sleet and jagged shards of flying ice. The three remaining adventurers, Ruda saw as she stepped around to look, scrambled into its meager shelter to avoid the worst of it. They hadn't let go of their staves, though. Two more lightning bolts ripped out of the wagon, of course not getting anywhere near Fross, but sending Ruda diving back into cover. Such as it was.

One of those staves would rip apart a wood and canvas wagon, along with her sleeping friends inside. She cursed monotonously to herself; *now* the luck chose to desert her. This was *exactly* the situation she'd been trying to avoid.

A soft sound from her left caught Ruda's attention. Juniper was dragging herself laboriously up, staggering as she got to her feet. She listed slightly to the right, as if her torso couldn't quite hold itself up on that side. Finally she lifted her head, and even Fross fluttered back from her expression. There was no hint of the cheerful openness her face usually held.

"That," the dryad snarled, "really . . . *really* . . . HURT."

Then the earth split apart.

The lead wagon was tumbled onto its side as an enormous pillar of wood burst from the ground beneath it, sending shards of stone flying in every direction and causing the rocky ground to crack and shift for dozens of yards on all sides. As it grew from the very stone, the tree twisted itself over to one side, unfurling thorny, vine-like tentacles to wrap around the damaged wagon and rip it apart, sending the oxen fleeing, braying in terror. The pair yoked to the wagon containing the students tried to bolt, too, but were stopped by tangles of vines tethering them to the earth. There they stood, bellowing piteously.

The three adventurers were plucked from within the wreckage by thorny curls of vine and slammed to the ground, where more brambles twined around them, digging into flesh and holding them firmly captive. Lance's stream of cursing was cut off as a thick vine wrapped around his head, covering his mouth.

Juniper limped toward them, glaring. Seeing her approach, Bella frantically redoubled her struggles against the vines holding her down. "I told them not to shoot!" she babbled. "It's not my fault!"

The dryad wasn't moving smoothly enough to kneel with any particular grace; she more fell to one knee beside the bound woman. "It wasn't me!" Bella wailed. "I'm *sorry!*"

"Don't care," Juniper said curtly, drew back a fist, and slammed it straight through Bella's chest into the ground. The woman emitted a strangled croak that was all but drowned out by the sound of breaking bone and tearing flesh. Her body thrashed once, weakly, as Juniper yanked out a moist handful of meat studded with bits of ribs, and then fell still.

Actually, everything went comparatively quiet at that point. The sudden thorn tree, its work apparently done, had stopped growing. Fross settled on Ruda's shoulder; not minding the cold, the pirate turned her gaze from Juniper to the two bound men. Blood pooled beneath both of them, and neither was so much as twitching. Those vines had *very* large thorns.

"Guess that's one way to do it," Ruda said grudgingly. She glanced down at her sword; sheathing it wasn't going to be an option until she'd cleaned all that sap off. What a mess. A sudden, sickening *pop* caught her attention; she looked up again just in time to see Juniper tug the sleeve off Bella's arm, which she'd just pulled free from her body. "Ugh . . . Juno, *please* don't do that."

"What?" The dryad half turned to face her, scowling. "Oh, for the . . . You people and your nonsense. Look, I'm *sorry* about your funerary customs or whatever, but I have an actual, *real* problem. I'm exhausted and injured. I need protein and calcium and *mass*. I killed this, so I'm eating it. That's life. That's how it *works*."

"Whoa, whoa, easy there!" Ruda said soothingly, holding up her hands. "Sorry, knee-jerk reaction. You take care of yourself however you need to, hon."

"That's okay, I forgive you," Juniper said brightly, and just like that she was as cheerful as ever, despite the carnage around her and the burned chunk missing from her own body.

"By the way, I, uh . . . didn't know you could do that. Call up trees to fight for you."

"Oh, I can't," the dryad said offhandedly. "That wasn't me." She lifted the arm to her face and bit off the thumb, and Ruda instantly decided to find somewhere else to busy herself rather than continue that conversation.

"Did *you* know she could do that?" she asked Fross as she strode back to their wagon. The oxen now seemed as placid as ever, which struck her as odd, but what did she know about beasts of burden? Maybe it was something else Juniper did.

"She . . . That wasn't her. She told you that." Fross buzzed her wings somewhat weakly, and it occurred belatedly to Ruda that she might have exhausted herself again with that wild torrent of ice and wind. "Do you . . . You don't know much about dryads, do you?"

Ruda paced around to the back of the wagon and clambered up, bending down to check on the others. They were all still out, but breathing normally and she detected no wounds. "Fross, I'm from the sea. I can tell you exactly how to kill a mermaid, but why the hell would I know anything about dryads?"

The pixie emitted a soft chime that Ruda had learned to recognize as laughter. "Yeah, well . . . Let's just say that killing a dryad is an exceptionally bad idea. You, uh, didn't realize that Juniper's technically a demigoddess, then, I guess."

Ruda stopped short and looked over at Juniper, whom she could just see over the barrels out the front of the wagon. She immediately looked away again; the dryad was sitting amid the ruins of somebody, chewing busily and holding up two red, dripping handfuls.

"She . . . Are you serious?"

"I don't know if . . . I mean, probably not the way you're thinking. Dryads aren't a *species*; they don't reproduce. But, yeah, Naiya created each one individually. Some people call them daughters of Naiya, which is pretty much the relationship. So, yes, *never* kill a dryad."

"She wasn't killed," Ruda protested, jerking a thumb over her shoulder at Juniper. "There she is."

Fross buzzed her wings briefly. "Um, yeah. That's why. In the first place, it's pretty pointless; it doesn't exactly . . . take."

". . . oh."

"And in the second, very, *very* bad things happen to people who kill dryads. If nature itself is mad at you, well, you pretty much don't get to be alive anymore. As you just saw."

"Well, I'm learning all kinds of fascinating new shit today," she muttered, picking her way carefully back to the rear and sitting on the end of the wagon. "For future reference, Fross, that's the kind of information I'd *really* like to have about someone before I stab them."

"How was I supposed to know you were gonna do that?! I don't *usually* assume my friends are going to act like crazy people!"

Ruda grinned at that. "Well, it hasn't been a total wash. In fact, hell, I'd say we came out of this pretty good."

"Did you . . . I'm sorry if this is too personal, but did you *really* kill somebody when you were seven? That's, uh, that's pretty young for a human, isn't it?"

Ruda snorted. "Oh, that? Wasn't my idea. Some asshat assassin or thief or something broke into my father's fortress, and just happened to come in through my window. Punaji kids sleep with knives under their pillows. Fucker got blood on my teddy bear." She scowled. "I'm *still* pissed about that. Why, seven's not young for pixies?"

Fross chimed again. "I'm three years old."

". . . oh." She cleared her throat. "Well, anyway, as I was saying, we're doing pretty good. Obviously, I'd have been happier if June hadn't gotten hurt, but it looks like she's gonna be okay, with some rest and . . ." She glanced back at the dryad and winced, averting her eyes again. ". . . nutrition. The rest of our gang are having their beauty sleep. And, as a bonus, we scored a free wagon, two oxen, and a shitload of jewels!"

Fross buzzed down to the scattered gemstones, avoiding Elroy's cooling body, and then returned to the wagon. "Those, um, jewels . . . have blood on them."

Pulling a bottle of rum from the magic pockets within her coat, Ruda grinned, yanked the cork out with her teeth, and took a swig.

"And that, my beauty, makes 'em the only kind worth having."

CHAPTER 21

Tazlith's group exchanged a round of glances, Shook began creeping back to place them between himself and Tellwyrn, the three soldiers grinned in unison, McGraw very casually lowered his staff to point in the professor's general direction, and Principia said something in elvish that was, even to those who didn't understand the language, unmistakably a curse.

"I know what several of you are thinking," Tellwyrn said, "and the answer is no. This nonsense is at an end."

Marks raised one of his wands. "I think we can take—"

She gestured in his direction and he vanished with an audible *snap* of arcane energy. In his place a small terrier reappeared at about chest height, yelping when it fell to the ground.

"What the *hell*?" Tazlith exclaimed. "What did you *do*?"

"It's called a baleful polymorph," Tellwyrn said serenely. "I do not like repeating myself."

"You can't just *cast* a baleful polymorph!" said Lorrie, the warlock, her attempts at sententious diction gone in panic. "It takes a ritual circle, multiple spell foci, a *huge* power source . . ."

Ox cleared his throat. "That's Professor Tellwyrn."

"Oh," the warlock squeaked, and fell silent, edging behind Tazlith.

"There will be no more acts of violence or general disruptive behavior," Tellwyrn continued. "Those of you who are under arrest will go quietly with the sheriff; the rest of you get lost back to your own business."

"You wretched *witch*!" Miz Cratchley screeched, brandishing her still-smoking staff at Tellwyrn. "This is all *your* fault, *all* of it. This was a good, quiet town before *you* came along!"

"Except for Mabel, for whom we make allowances," Tellwyrn said, waving a hand. With a soft *pop*, Miz Cratchley disappeared.

Sanders cleared his throat. "Ah, if you don't mind my asking . . ."

"She's safely at her home," Tellwyrn said, "and that staff of hers is in your office. Not sure why I bother," she added, giving him an exasperated look, "since I know you're just going to give it back to her again."

"That staff is an heirloom," Sanders replied in the weary tone of a man who'd had this conversation once too often. "Her husband carried it in the emperor's service. It's also a valuable antique. She'd need to actually *hurt* someone with it before I can confiscate it."

"At least have the enchantment stripped off. She's gonna blow herself up one of these days, and then how will you feel?"

"The vintage enchantment is the better part of what *makes* it valuable. Damn it, Professor, some of us have to follow the law!"

"Seems you two could use a mite of privacy," McGraw said solicitously. "Shall we come back and finish this later?"

"Do you think you're funny, McGraw?" Tellwyrn asked, turning to face him. She extended an arm and pointed at Rook. "The boy in the scruffy uniform there, *he's* funny. *You* are a pain in the ass."

"Well, to be fair," said Rook cheerfully, "I'm also a pain in the ass."

"With regard to our understanding, ma'am," McGraw said politely, "I didn't start this, and I did my very best to prevent it getting out of hand. As I'm sure you are more than aware, reasoning with high-strung youths just ain't always feasible."

"Do you know what Zero Twenty means, McGraw?" Tellwyrn asked mildly.

He subtly tightened his grip on his staff. "I'm afraid I do, ma'am."

"If I may?" the mage with Tazlith said politely. He bowed when Tellwyrn turned to stare at him. "Mr. McGraw speaks truthfully. He made every effort to talk this down before someone intervened, apparently forcing one of Marks's wands to discharge. It is, by the way, quite an honor to meet you, Professor."

"Did they now," Tellwyrn said quietly. "That's *very* interesting." She shifted her eyes to look straight at Shook.

She wasn't the only one.

"Anybody who wants to make an accusation had best have more than hearsay backing them up," Shook said, glaring.

"Oh, really? Should I?" Tellwyrn grinned savagely. "And why is that, *precisely?*"

"If you don't mind, Professor," Sanders interjected, "I would prefer to handle this. After all, a fine, upstanding member of the Thieves' Guild like Mr. Shook here knows better than to resist arrest when he's fairly caught. Ain't that right, Jeremiah?"

Shook gave the sheriff a share of his furious stare, which appeared not to faze him in the slightest.

"It's true?" Tazlith whispered. She glanced down at Shook's hands; he tucked them back into his sleeves, but not fast enough. "You stole her rings, too? You said we were *protecting* her."

"Oh, shut up, you dimwitted sow," he snarled. "She'd be dead twice over by now if not for me."

"Everything was going *fine* until you blundered into town, dumbshit!" Principia snapped. "*Now* look. Good *fucking* job, *enforcer.*"

"Yup," Sanders said. "Looks like everybody's coming down to the office. Boys, if you don't mind, I'd appreciate your help a while longer."

"You kidding?" Rook replied, still wearing a grin. "This is *fantastic*! Most excitement we had at our last post was when they sent us a shipment of bad beans and Moriarty had the runs for a week. Well, until that thing we can't talk about." He staggered, having been elbowed hard from both sides by Finchley and Moriarty.

"Shook's getting charged," Sanders went on grimly, then pointed at Tazlith. "Also *you*, missy, since I know for a fact you're the organizer of this motley troupe. Whatever your intentions, you need to learn a thing or two about law and order, and why you *don't* take them into your own little hands." Tazlith looked absolutely stricken by the unfairness of it all; mouth hanging open, she couldn't even formulate a response. The sheriff continued, moving his pointing finger around at those assembled. "The rest of you . . . I'll wait till I've heard the whole story from all participants before I decide if it's worth charging anybody with anything. Um . . . and that fellow who's now a dog . . ." He glanced helplessly at Tellwyrn.

"He's fine," she said dismissively. "He'll revert in about an hour, none the worse for wear. You might give him some water, though. This climate is rough if you're wearing a fur coat."

Marks yapped furiously at her.

"And *her*?" Tazlith demanded shrilly, pointing at Principia. McGraw wasn't visibly aiming a weapon at her, but the elf still held herself as still and small as possible. "Apparently she's a thief, too!"

Sanders heaved a sigh. "Being a thief is a crime. Being a member of the Thieves' Guild is not."

"What?"

"The Guild is the organized cult of Eserion," Tellwyrn explained, smiling faintly. "You can't just outlaw the cult of a god of the Pantheon."

"And as *usual*," Sanders said in annoyance, "Prin is sitting pretty in the gray area between what I'm pretty sure she's done and what I can *prove* she did. Apparently, all she's guilty of is getting threatened, stolen from, and kidnapped."

"I would just like to say," Principia remarked, "fuck you all. Every last one of you in particular. I'm certain you each know exactly why."

"Which just leaves the man of the hour, here." Sanders turned to face McGraw directly. "Kidnapping. Threats of murder. That's more'n a slap on the wrist."

"With the greatest possible respect, Sheriff, you are something of a redundancy here," McGraw said politely, then tipped his hat in

Tellwyrn's direction. "Professor, I'd take it as a kindness if you could sus out just where we stand. Makes quite the difference with regard to what I do next."

She shrugged. "If you didn't cause the trouble, you didn't cause the trouble. You start messing with the sheriff and matters will be different, but if all the harm you've done is to Principia . . . Well, I did specifically exempt that from any promises of retribution, didn't I?"

"Wait," Prin said, stiffening. "You fucking *what*?"

"I told him I didn't care what he did to you," Tellwyrn replied, grinning nastily. "Are you surprised? Offended? Do you think that's in any way *unfair*? Grow up already, Prin."

"Oh, you absolute unutterable *bitch*!"

"My, my, gendered insults between women. And in public, no less! What would Trissiny think, I wonder?"

Principia fell silent, but her face went scarlet with rage.

"On the subject of gray areas," Sanders said, "out here on the frontier I sometimes have to make a decision between observing the letter of the law and keeping the general peace. If the good professor doesn't care to step in, and considering I don't fancy havin' a shootout with *you* in particular . . . And since I'm also not excessively perturbed by crimes committed exclusively against Miss Locke, here, I might be amenable to lettin' all this go."

"You *fucking WHAT*?" Principia screamed.

"I always appreciate reasonable exceptions to silly laws," McGraw said mildly, stepping around from behind the apoplectic elf. He held his arms wide, grinning disarmingly. "Course, I'm honor bound to point out that if you *did* choose to make an issue of this, and I *did* defend myself, well . . . I'm pretty sure that'd cross the line drawn by the esteemed professor here. Might be small consolation for having half of Last Rock leveled, but you could go down in history as the man who helped bring down Longshot McGraw."

Sanders strode forward, straight at him. McGraw didn't back down by so much as a step, and the sheriff didn't pause until his nose was a mere inch from the other man's. He kept his voice low, but in the sudden stillness, the mild wind of the prairie wasn't enough to prevent his words from being clearly heard by everyone present.

"Get the hell out of my town, McGraw."

They locked gazes for a long moment, utterly still. Then Longshot McGraw very deliberately stepped backward, nodding politely.

"Fair enough, Sheriff. D'you mind awfully if I loiter on the platform, there, till the next caravan arrives? It's a long stretch of nothin' between here and . . . well, anything at all. You get to be my age, and the thought of hiking through the prairie for weeks just ain't as exciting as it once was."

Sanders held his gaze for another long moment, then turned away. "Ox, me an' the boys'll take this lot down to the jail. Kindly stay here and make sure Mr. McGraw gets safely on the Rail. He so much as sneezes, blast him."

"Sheriff," Ox said, nodding grimly.

"Feh," Tellwyrn said, making a dismissive gesture with one hand. "Half the morning, wasted. If I have to come deal with this again, everybody dies." She vanished with a quiet *pop* of air rushing in to fill the space she had occupied.

"Least one good turn came outta this," Sanders remarked loudly to Finchley as he and the soldiers began herding Shook and the adventurers down the street at wand point. "Membership in the Thieves' Guild isn't a crime, but it does constitute probable cause. So much as a butter knife goes missing in this town from here on, an' I get to search Prin's rooms as a matter of course. Should make several things easier."

"Well," McGraw said ruefully, "this'll be a blot on the record, I suppose. Guess I'll have to go give back some money soon as I get to Tiraas." Turning to Principia, he tipped his hat politely. "Ma'am."

She watched him stroll over to the Rail platform and lounge against one of the pillars holding up the awning there, taking out a cigarillo and lighting it with his staff.

For a heartbeat, all was quiet.

Then Principia Locke threw back her head and let out a long, wordless scream.

Admestus Rafe swam slowly up through the most delicious dreams. As reality began to coalesce around him, he found it just as agreeable, full of splendid warmth and softness. He opened his eyes, finally, just as gentle lips were withdrawn from his own. For a second, all he was conscious of were the big brown eyes inches from his, and the warm, curvy weight resting across his body.

"Hey, it worked!" Juniper said cheerfully.

"*Waugh*!" Suddenly lucid, Rafe scrambled backward in panic, throwing her off. "No! Bad! *Student*! Arachne will eat my liver!"

"Mornin', sunshine!" Ruda said cheerfully from just above him.

He paused to take stock. They were in a covered wagon, trundling along; to judge by the light filtering through the openings, it was early afternoon. Fross flittered around the interior, Ruda sat on the driver's seat just behind his head, Juniper was . . . well, *right there*. Toby and Shaeine were still laid out, unconscious.

"I wasn't absolutely sure I could do it," Juniper said, then yawned hugely. "Haven't had much opportunity to practice, y'know? But that's, like, the *one* bit of active magic dryads can do. Poisons, maybe even some curses. I can sort of . . . take the harm into myself, neutralize the bad stuff."

"You can suck drugs out of people?" Fross chimed. "Neat!"

Ruda cackled. "Word around campus is she can suck the enchantment off a battlestaff."

Juniper yawned again. "It's not easy, though. Been a rough day . . . I'm gonna . . ." She listed over onto one side and curled up, asleep before she finished her sentence. For the first time Rafe realized there was a large hole in the side of her dress, its edges burned black, and the flesh underneath it appeared to be covered in some kind of bark.

"What *happened* to her?" he asked.

"She got shot," said Ruda.

Rafe bit back a curse. "Oh . . . *hell*. Who's dead?"

"Just the fuckers that did it. All's well that ends well an' all that shit."

"Whew . . . I guess Naiya was in an uncharacteristically reasonable mood. Last time I heard about somebody shooting a dryad, it was killer bees and wasps from one horizon to the other."

"Let me get you caught up," the pirate went on, still in that cheery tone. "The nice people who gave us dinner drugged us with magic cornbread. It was damn *good* cornbread, almost worth the drugs. Beans baked right in and a cinnamon glaze, I gotta remember that . . . Anyway, they were gonna steal our shit, dose us with memory-altering magic, and leave us somewhere. Except Fross, who was being made into a lamp."

"Excuse me, I'm an arcane sciences major! That bottle was only warded against fae magic. I would've gotten out *eventually*."

"Yeah, but not before the rest of us were goners. I *still* saved all our asses."

"That's right, you did!" She buzzed down to hover in front of Rafe's face. "She did! Ruda's very smart."

"Also good-looking and a goddamn terror in a fight," Ruda said merrily. "So yeah, yadda, yadda, yadda, they knocked us out, I'm awesome, and now here we are, and I get to make fun of you, Professor Big Heap Alchemist, for getting drugged by cornbread."

"I beg your pardon," he said stiffly, "but I'm a genius, not a deity. Do you know how *many* tasteless, odorless, and basically undetectable compounds can be cooked into food to knock people out? No, you don't, and neither do *I*, because that's just about the simplest thing there is to do."

"Oh, please," she said, grinning over her shoulder at him. "'Bella, get the *special cornbread*.' They might as well have been twirling their fucking mustaches. Honestly, how the hell any of you so much as buy breakfast without getting swindled outta your goddamn pants is beyond me."

"*You* ate it, too," he said irritably, getting up. It wasn't easy with the lurching progress of the wagon, but he needed to check on Toby and Shaeine.

"I was hungry, and I don't *get* drugged. Just one of the many benefits of being Punaji. It's pretty much *all* benefits, for the record."

"And how did you know they weren't going to just feed us poison, if you're so smart?"

"It's called *tactics*, chucklenuts. Trissiny might be the military expert, but when it comes to knocking people down an' taking their shit, we're in *my* territory. They had staves, see? Practically pointed at us. If I'd made a stink about the cornbread, they'd've just shot us. Contrariwise, the fact they *didn't* indicated they didn't want us dead. So I played along until an opportunity came up to turn the tables. Which, inevitably, it did, and here we are. You're fucking *welcome*, by the way."

"What, you want a medal? I'll see to it Tellwyrn passes you for the exercise, anyway."

"Eh, that'll do for a start," she said airily. "I expect everyone to go on at *length* about the glory that is me, by the way."

"You savor that, kiddo," he said, grinning. "Now you have a taste of what it's like to be Professor Rafe every day!"

Ruda's smile faded; she glanced back again. Rafe was bent over Toby, holding a small vial under his nose.

"Ooh, is that smelling salts?" Fross asked, fluttering close. "Will that wake him up?"

"No, no, I don't want to just pump drugs into them without knowing what we're dealing with. I'm just working out *what* they got dosed with. Then I can apply the right counter-agent without risking a bad interaction. Actually, could you fly a little closer? I need to watch how this changes color, and you're the only light in here."

"So," said Ruda, turning back to face forward again. "What's with you, anyway?"

"Me?" Fross asked.

"No, him."

"Nothing's with me," Rafe replied, showing signs of his old bluster returning. "Merely the extravagant and vigorous splendor that is my stock in trade!"

"Cut the bullshit. You spent most of last night practically silent. Well, talking about like a normal person does, which for you is practically silent. Then you got your ass drugged, and you can make excuses all you want, but we *both* know that's a sign you fucked up. I bet you'd have seen the trap coming if you'd been paying attention. So, spill."

They were quiet for a minute while he fiddled with his reagents. Fross buzzed around as if uncertain where she wanted to hover. Ruda didn't prompt him again, and had just about decided he wasn't going to answer when he finally did.

"We've lost students before, of course. C'mon, the *kind* of people Arachne recruits? You little bastards are one of the better-behaved freshman classes I've seen in a while. You just don't throw the empire's most powerful weirdos onto a campus together and then send them out against real-world threats three times a semester without having fatalities. But . . . *I've* never lost someone before. Having a student that I alone was personally responsible for get—" He broke off, stuffed a vial back into his belt pouch and took out another one, not looking at Ruda or Fross. "It's . . . something to deal with."

Ruda nodded slowly. "I think I get you. Man . . . I didn't even *like* her. But she was part of my crew, and . . . now we don't even know if she's gone or not. I'm still wondering if there's even anything I need to deal with, never mind how the fuck I'm actually *going* to deal."

"Yeah."

"So, get the fuck over it."

He twisted around to scowl at her. "Excuse me? Real sensitive, Punaji."

Ruda kept her face forward toward the horizon, but spoke loudly enough to be clearly heard. "That's what leadership means— everything is your fucking fault, and you don't *get* to whine about it. You just keep at it and do the job. Instead, you got into your little funk and walked all our asses right into a trap."

"If you'll recall," he said pointedly, "Professor Tellwyrn reminded everyone that I'm along on this little shindig in an observational capacity. I'm *not* the one giving orders."

"Bullshit. *That* went over the side when you shouted Trissiny down for doing *her* fucking job and giving us advice on dealing with the centaurs. Which, by the fucking way, was good fucking advice and we probably wouldn't be in all this shit if we'd just followed it. You *took* the job, so *do* the job."

He scowled and turned back toward Toby, gently lifting the boy's head and tipping a vial of thick fluid into his mouth. Seconds later, Toby coughed weakly, his eyelids beginning to flutter.

"Well, too late now," Ruda said lightly. "No sign of the mountain yet, but the kidnapping assholes thought they were gonna get to the edge of the Sea by the end of today. Fuck if *I* know; I'm just figuring they understood how this place works."

Rafe had no answer for her. He simply occupied himself tending to the others.

The mountain at Last Rock cast a long shadow. Unlike its sudden vanishing when they had first headed out into the Golden Sea, it appeared in a geographically normal fashion upon their return, giving the students hours to prepare themselves for their homecoming. It was hours spent mostly in conversation; even after everyone had been fully brought up to speed on events, they found comfort in just talking.

Consequently, it was a tired and quiet group who drew their captured wagon to a stop at the foot of the mountain.

Professor Tellwyrn stood alone, waiting for them.

Toby had been handling the oxen; Ruda didn't actually know anything about steering them, and had simply been sitting up front for the view, Juniper having given the beasts their instructions. He took time to stop and pat both animals as the others filed down from the wagon, Juniper still yawning and rubbing her eyes.

"Well?" Tellwyrn said simply when they had finally assembled in front of her.

"Teal," Shaeine said, "and Gabriel?"

"Are fine. In their respective rooms, as far as I know, worrying about *you* lot."

"We scored us a free wagon, and a small fortune in gemstones," Ruda said.

"Actually, not such a small fortune," Shaeine corrected.

"Whatever. It's our plunder, won fair and square. The two demony types get a cut, too. Everybody, otherwise I wouldn't feel right takin' my share. And *nobody* who has any sense better come between a pirate and her booty." She glared over at the others.

"Miss Punaji," Tellwyrn said wearily, "three of your classmates—including *you*—are heirs to massive fortunes and don't need gems. Two are paladins who have no attachment to worldly wealth, and two are fae who don't even participate in the economy."

"Everybody gets a share," Ruda repeated stubbornly. "Sell 'em, donate 'em, chuck 'em down a well. Fuck if I care."

"Right. Anything *else* you'd like to report?"

"Professor," Toby said quietly. "We . . . lost Trissiny."

"Really," she said dryly. "Have you checked your pockets?"

There was a moment of stunned silence before Ruda responded. "Is that a fucking *joke* to you?!"

"Pretty much," Tellwyrn replied glibly. "I assure you, Trissiny's fine and will be along presently."

"How can you *possibly* know that?" Toby demanded.

"I keep forgetting you kids grew up in an era without paladins. Have you heard about the Stand at Stavulheim?"

"One imperial legion held the city gates, alone, against an army of orcs for three days," Shaeine replied. "Though the relevance of it to this situation escapes me."

"The relevance is that *that* is the sanitized, politicized version taught by imperial historians. I was around then, and I can hardly blame them for changing it up, as the truth is a lot less believable. It was *two* Hands of Avei who did that. Two. Against two *thousand*. And you think Trissiny was felled by a handful of centaurs? Please.

"Quite apart from that," she went on, raising her voice over the comments that arose, "I am far from Avei's favorite person; I assure you, if her brand-new Hand had just gotten killed on one of my training exercises, we would be hearing about it. Also, she's right behind you."

They spun, Toby so quickly he nearly overbalanced, to look back at the Sea. Nobody was there.

"Are you just fucking with us now?" Ruda snarled, whirling back to glare at her, one hand falling to the hilt of her sword.

"A little," Tellwyrn said with a smile. "'Right' behind you may have been overstating it, but yes, she's on her way, and making much better time than you did. Should be here in minutes. Trust me, you don't argue with elven eyes."

"You wear *glasses!*" Ruda shouted.

"Meanwhile," Tellwyrn went on in a more grim tone, "we can discuss your performance, or lamentable lack thereof. To review: Upon being accosted by centaurs, your first move was to send your two most durable combatants away, hopelessly splitting your group and depriving the rest of their best defenders."

"The centaurs' war drums—"

"Miss Awarrion, do *not* interrupt me when I am chastising you. *Then*, you set out on a long, exhausting fighting retreat, with the inevitable result that your next most durable member—and also your best remaining counter to your opponents' infernal magic—collapsed from fatigue. Honestly, how could you possibly have thought a *tree nymph* would fare well on a cross-country run? And finally, you apparently sacrificed your last magically endowed fighter to the horde while the rest of you went blundering away to . . ." She trailed off, running her eyes over the wagon and oxen. ". . . all right, I have to admit, I'm baffled how you got to a wagon full of plunder from fleeing for your lives from centaurs. It promises to be a good story, though. Probably not enough to redeem your grade for the exercise, but something."

"Then how," Shaeine asked quietly, "did you know we lost Trissiny to the centaurs?"

Tellwyrn tilted her head forward to stare them down over the rims of her spectacles. "Because, despite the fact that I specifically *told* you to follow Trissiny's advice on combat matters, I know *she* didn't tell you to enact this utterly ham-brained plot. Which means you weren't listening to her. You know what a paladin does when the idiot civilians she's trying to protect refuse to see reason? She puts herself *between* them and whatever is out to get them. Ergo, here you are, sans paladin, and plus plunder. I doubt she'd have let you loot the corpses of whoever else you killed, either. Hello, Trissiny."

They whirled around again; this time, Toby *did* overbalance, landing on his rump in the grass and staring up at the spectacle approaching them.

It was as if they'd appeared out of a fold in the ground—which was probably close to the literal truth, the Golden Sea being what it was. The steed was absolutely massive and glossy white, an enormous, barrel-chested draft horse with a thick arched neck, blunt nose, and feathered hooves the size of dinner plates. He wore silver armor over his neck, face, and rump, and the golden-eagle sigil of Avei was worked into his breast collar. Sitting in the saddle, dwarfed by the huge horse, despite her height, was Trissiny. She was covered in grime and dried blood but appeared as alert and unharmed as when they'd last seen her.

"Professor," she said, nodding as she guided the steed to a halt next to them. For all his size, his hoof steps were eerily quiet. "Is everyone all right? I passed these travelers' other wagon a while back, and their bodies. It looked like they were eaten by wild animals."

"No, that was me," Juniper said brightly. "Hi, Triss! I'm glad you're okay!"

"Hi," the paladin said slowly. "... and you did that because...?"

"Oh, they drugged everybody and captured Fross and were going to rob and abandon us. And then they shot me."

"Ah." Trissiny nodded. "Very well, then. I'm just glad you all made it."

"We made it?" Ruda said, gaping at her. "You're glad *we* made it?! We—you were—we left you... How did... WHY THE FUCK DO YOU HAVE A HORSE?"

"Paladins get divine mounts," Tellwyrn said serenely. "Avei usually doesn't bequeath one until the Hand in question has proven herself in actual combat. I guess the centaurs were an adequate test."

"Less trouble than I expected, honestly," Trissiny said. "Once I killed their leader, the rest scattered."

"Yes, for all their size and ferocity, they really aren't militarily impressive. Which makes it all the sadder that you lot got yourselves routed by them. Honestly, if anybody important had been along to see that, it would go down in the annals of tactical incompetence. I can't believe you let them do this," she added directly to Trissiny.

The paladin raised an eyebrow. "Oh, so they have to *listen* to me, now? Splendid. I want everyone assembled on the main lawn at 6:00 a.m. for drill."

"You joke," Tellwyrn replied, "but after this debacle I'm half tempted to authorize that."

"You got," Ruda said slowly, as though trying to convince herself of it, "a fucking *horse*."

"His name's Arjen," Tellwyrn said helpfully.

"How do *you* know that?" Trissiny demanded.

"There's a limited number of celestial steeds in Avei's stable," the professor said cheerfully. "These creatures are *truly* immortal, not merely ageless like elves. If killed on this plane, they just return to their divine point of origin, ready to be summoned again. This fellow has served the Hands of Avei for millennia. We've met before," she added, raising a hand as if to pat Arjen's nose. He snorted disdainfully and twisted his head away. "See?" she said wryly.

"Arjen, is it," Trissiny murmured, leaning forward to pat his neck. He whickered softly.

"You know what?" Ruda said flatly. "I fucking hate you."

Trissiny sat bolt upright in her saddle, gaping at her in shock. "*What?*"

"Can you just for *once* not try to fucking show me up?" She clawed a bottle out of her coat and took a long swig. "But," she added, wiping her mouth on her sleeve, "I'm really glad you're not dead."

Trissiny stared at her, open-mouthed, unable to formulate a reply.

"All right, it's been great adventuring with you lot, but I've had enough," said the pirate. "Tellwyrn can tell us all how much we suck another time; I'm done with this horseshit. Anybody needs me, too fucking bad. I'm gonna be in town, and I will not be back till I've drunk my weight in the dilute piss water that passes for beer around here and screwed at least three local boys. Concurrently, if I can find enough of these hicks without too many goddamn hangups. Have a good fucking night, all."

Still drinking from her bottle, she stomped off in the direction of Last Rock.

"Don't get pregnant!" Tellwyrn called after her.

"Fuck you!"

"So!" Rafe said brightly. "How've things been back here?"

"Eh." Tellwyrn waved a hand dismissively. "Nothing ever happens in this town."

CHAPTER 22

Darling threw his bag to the parquet floor, shoved the door shut with his entire body, and then leaned heavily against it, closing his eyes and letting out a long, melodramatic sigh. For a much longer moment than usual he just leaned there, savoring the quiet and the dimness of his entryway.

He opened his eyes just in time to catch Price's disapproving look at the discarded bag of luggage before she returned her gaze to his, schooling her features. That was undoubtedly intentional; her timing in all matters was preternaturally precise.

"Welcome home, Your Grace," she said serenely. "I trust your trip was satisfactory?"

"A rousing success," he said with a sour grimace. "We got the Archpope *exactly* what he wanted, and a dash extra."

"I am sorry to hear it, Your Grace. Brandy and scones are prepared in the downstairs parlor."

"Bless you, Price," he replied, heaving himself fully upright and striding past her.

Naturally, she made a point of stopping to collect his luggage before attending him, but Darling had far more pressing things on his mind than Price's nitpicking, or scones, or even brandy, no matter how badly he felt the need for one.

The Wreath and the Archpope chased each other endlessly around in his head. Just who *was* Embras Mogul? It could be a false name, though Darling couldn't fathom a reason for such deceit since he had only hunches concerning the man's identity and purpose. Clearly he was highly ranked in the Wreath. Maybe Elilial's own high priest? Justinian seemed to think so, which brought him to the other question of just what the Archpope was up to with the little circle of bishops he'd assembled. They'd been sent there with oddly specific yet unexplained orders—why did it matter so much that they not identify themselves as agents of the Church? Not to mention that details of the Wreath's (alleged) understanding with the other cults had been withheld from him. Did all of *that* add up to enough to warrant the attention of the Wreath's high priest? What *did* it add up to?

Lost in his own mind, he had crossed half the parlor toward the table, on which the tray was set, before realizing the room wasn't unoccupied.

Price had no doubt enjoyed dressing the two elves. Their slim, modest, black frocks were of the very latest fashion for servants of the well-to-do, and he noted immediately that their demeanor much better suited the uniforms than last he'd seen them make the attempt. Both girls stood to one side of the room, expressions carefully blank and hands clasped demurely in front of them.

"Well, well!" he said. "You two look positively harmless; how delightful. I gather lessons have been going well?"

"Indeed, Your Grace," Fauna said softly. Clearly, Price had also drilled them on the separate forms of address for his different identities.

"The acting coaching has been most instructive," Flora added.

"Well, that's very good to hear," he said solemnly. "I'm afraid developments have gone quite sour on my end. It seems I'll have to terminate both your employment and your apprenticeships. It's a very good thing you've picked up the beginnings of another trade."

Neither of them reacted overtly, though the corner of Flora's eye twitched.

"If that is meant to be some manner of test," Fauna said, "Your Grace will have to do better. Orthilon has been giving us worse."

"On an hourly basis," Flora chimed in, with merely the faintest hint of asperity.

"For the last week."

"He has *quite* the imagination."

"Ooh, that's *perfect!*" Darling squealed, applauding with a girlish, fluttery motion of his hands. "So self-contained, with just the right soupçon of derision. And after only a week! Last time I saw you, I swear you couldn't have lied to a blind Omnist monk. You two are positively *gifted*! Don't worry, there's no way in Hell I'm letting such a pair of talents get away; you've got a place here as long as you want it." He crossed to the table and poured himself two fingers of brandy, feeling an almost paternal satisfaction at their pleased smiles. "That's something you'll have to watch for, by the way; people will set you up to reveal something, you'll spot the trap, and then when you're feeling good about yourself with your guard down, zing! There comes the *real* trap."

The smiles vanished; Fauna failed to repress the tiniest annoyed grimace before their blank masks settled again.

Darling flopped onto the settee just gently enough to avoid sloshing his brandy and took a sip. "Ah, that was so very needed. In seriousness, ladies, I hope it hasn't been too bad. It's intensive training, I know, but it's better than what practically any other apprentices get—which, by the way, is why you were asked not to mention it to them. I think you've a bit longer to go, but the last thing we want is for you to be burned out. We don't drill our learners into the ground like bloody Avenists around here. You're bearing up all right?"

"It's actually been kind of fun," Flora admitted, allowing her smile to creep back into place. "Exhausting, yes, but it's satisfying to learn something new."

"Satisfying to find out we're *good* at it," said Fauna, nodding. "And Orthilon isn't so bad. He's not gentle, but he seems to have a good instinct for knowing just how far to push. It only gets *really* annoying when he tries to play us against each other, but I think we've taught him not—" She broke off as Darling sat bolt upright, choking on his brandy.

"Against," he coughed, then cleared his throat and slammed the glass down on the coffee table. "Play us *against* each other! *Augh*!" He threw himself backward, grinding the heels of his hands into his eyes and kicking both feet in the air. "It was *right there* in front of me the whole damn time! I am so very, *very* stupid!"

"I'm sorry to hear that, Your Grace," Price intoned solemnly, entering the parlor empty-handed after having done something with his bag. He didn't actually know where in the house it lived. "Shall I arrange for a private tutor? Perhaps a stay in a sanatorium?"

"Fauna, you bloody little *genius*!" Darling bounded to his feet and across the room, seizing the surprised elf by the waist and spinning her around in the air twice. Fauna, to her credit, refrained from kicking him senseless, which was assuredly within her capabilities. She staggered slightly when he thunked her back down, but didn't seem annoyed, merely bemused. "That was exactly the clue I needed—I know what Justinian's doing! It was a false flag operation!"

He stared at them expectantly, grinning. Price raised an eyebrow; the elves exchanged one of those loaded glances of theirs.

"Sir?" Flora said hesitantly.

"*That's* why we weren't to reveal we were from the Church. I mean, it wouldn't be hard to find out who the four of us are, but all of us have other allegiances—individual cults, and all except Basra have worked for the empire in some capacity." He began to pace up and down the carpet. "Elilial made her move directly against the empire, but we *know* it was a diversionary measure, or the first stage in a more elaborate plan. The one simple thing about her is her goals are a foregone conclusion. She wants the Pantheon brought down, and has never done anything with anybody on the mortal plane that wasn't part of a scheme toward that end."

"Right," Fauna prompted when he fell momentarily silent.

Darling paused before the window, staring out while he formed swirling thoughts into sentences. "So the Church, being an extension of the gods, is definitely her enemy, and the empire is at least momentarily so. They should be allied against her. *But*! Not only does the Church have a central interest in thwarting Elilial, but *Justinian* has been angling for more political power since he took office, often against the empire itself."

"It's a triangle, then," Fauna said, frowning.

"Exactly! And Justinian is trying to fill in its third side! The Wreath has to know at least some details of their goddess's plan, but they probably have even less direct guidance from her than most cults do—she's usually not even on this plane of existence, so it's not like they can run to her for confirmation on every little thing. *They* know the empire isn't the real target, and the plan has to take the empire's inevitable responses into account—Elilial is definitely clever enough to lay a scheme that elaborate. But if the empire *appeared* to be escalating the conflict beyond what they expected, turning their sham war into a *real* one while Elilial has her fingers in some other pie . . ."

"Then the Wreath and the empire would be at each other's throats," Flora said, her eyes widening. "It's the oldest gambit in war—if you have two enemies, pit them against each other!"

"*Yes!*" Darling whirled to face them. "And so we were sent there, ordered not to reveal we were with the Church—and of *course* the empire is the only other logical culprit for such an action—and not told to respect the ceasefire in place. Escalation of hostilities, and both Wreath and empire would feel themselves the attacked party because *neither* was the one truly doing the attacking! Oh, Justinian, you magnificent *bastard!*"

"Then . . . everything's explained," Flora said slowly.

"*Nothing's* explained!" Darling crowed, throwing his arms wide. "I still don't know who that Wreath guy we met really is or what he was doing there. I don't know whether this little cabal Justinian's put together are trusted agents he can send into the field with incomplete intel or patsies he can afford to lose on a suicide mission, which means I don't know where I stand with him, and therefore I don't know what I can get away with or what I need to do with regard to him." He had to pause for breath. "I have no *fucking* clue what Elilial's plan actually *is*, much less how to begin unraveling it! This whole thing is an ungodly *mess!*"

"Congratulations, Your Grace," Price said serenely.

"Thank you!"

"His Grace is most at home under adverse circumstances," she explained to the elves, who looked more baffled by the minute. "He tends to wilt under serenity."

"I do know *one* thing, though, and that's enough to start," Darling went on, his maniacal grin fading to a grimmer, more cynical expression. "Ladies, it's early yet, but I'm afraid your talents are about to be called upon."

"Just tell us what you need." Instantly, all training forgotten, both were on point, with matching expressions that put him in mind of a pair of cats about to pounce.

"I hope everybody's feeling patriotic," he said, rubbing his hands together and grinning fiendishly. "Looks like we have to save the empire."

The first hints of a storm were blowing in, and the citizens of Puna Dara were out in force to greet it. Everything was tied down and secured, but while the inhabitants of most port cities would hide themselves away indoors when bad weather was coming, the Punaji became almost gleeful. There was a downright festive atmosphere in the streets, with knots of people standing around chatting excitedly, hawkers desperately peddling wares ahead of the downpour, which would shortly drive them into shelter, and knots of children racing about underfoot.

It wasn't a large city—it couldn't be, with essentially no farmland, framed on three sides by stark cliffs and the harbor on the fourth, its only sources of fresh water a few mountain springs. Positioned at the northeasternmost corner of the continent, Puna Dara was accessible by land only through ancient dwarven tunnels, wide enough for merchant trains and used by such, but most of the city's commerce was by sea.

There were a few mansions of the wealthy and privileged against the cliff walls, built high above their poorer neighbors and well back from the dangers of the ocean and its fickle winds—and fickle goddess—just as the wealthy and privileged set themselves up everywhere, and had for all of history. At the very edge of the water, however, jutting into the harbor itself, stood the Rock, the massive square fortress, where the family for whom Punaji was a name as well as an ethnicity had lived for centuries. They lived in the very teeth of the storm, always the first to launch themselves into the sea, and the last to retreat from it—which, to date, they *never* had. The Punaji were a fierce people, and demanded fierce rulers.

The Mermaid's Tail, like most of the structures in the city, was solidly built of stone and well able to withstand the onslaught of the elements, which was necessary as it was perched practically on the docks themselves.

The common room of the tavern was loud and stifling tonight, what with the press of people seeking shelter within, and the fact that the windows had been shuttered against the encroaching weather. The same carnival atmosphere reigned in the taproom as out in the streets. People talked, sang, joked, and drank, men and women alike in heavy boots and long greatcoats over baggy trousers and brightly colored blouses. It was a perfectly middle-of-the-road tavern—rough and rowdy enough that any sort of person might wander in and most would not look out of place, but not so much that one needed to worry about watching one's pockets, or back.

It was McGraw's favorite spot in the city. He always stayed here when he was in Puna Dara and preferred to conduct his business here if the other party was amenable. The staff knew him and had managed to get him his usual circular table in the corner under the stairs, despite the hefty crowd.

He much preferred to be seated out of the way, standing out as he did among the Punaji. His skin was as dark as theirs, but lacked the bronze undertone they had. Plus, they ran toward sharp features, while he was obviously a broad-nosed Westerner, and stood head and shoulders taller than most of them. His coat and broad hat suited their fashion up to a point, though the suit beneath was clearly imperial in style. It wasn't that he minded standing out, exactly, just that when one was meeting with a business partner, it paid not to draw attention. Especially given the kind of business he usually conducted.

The waitress brought him his order—a platter of fried squid with a dish of curry sauce, big enough for two. He thanked her with a smile, and she accepted her tip with a flirtatious wink—which was all part of the job—and a grin of authentic friendliness, which was not. Getting on the good side of serving girls was as simple as showing respect, tipping well, and not letting one's eyes or hands wander. It constantly amazed him how few men seemed to manage it.

McGraw had ordered for two and gently nursed his rum, nibbling now and then on the squid. Curry wasn't exactly his favorite thing, but he did love fried squid, and you just couldn't get it inland. For the most part, though, he steeled himself to leave it alone, along with the second glass beside the rum bottle. Wouldn't do to seem inhospitable. He didn't bother trying to scan the crowd; in this press of bodies, he'd never see anyone approach before they were right on top of him. So he waited, ready to offer a polite smile or a barrage of fireballs, depending on what came at him.

Thus, despite the lack of forewarning, he was not particularly startled when Principia Locke materialized from a tiny gap in the press of bodies and slid into the seat across from him.

"Ma'am," he said, raising his eyebrows. "Not that it ain't a pleasure, but this is a long way from where we last met."

"Oh, you can cut that out already," she said with a grin, pouring rum into the empty glass. "The job's over, and we are hell and gone from Last Rock. You can speak plainly."

"Of course," he said. "Pardon me, I figured it was safer to let you lead. You seemed determined to maintain the facade back at the town, even when we were alone."

"When a job involves both a thief and an archmage, I don't make assumptions about who's in a position to overhear what," she replied, pulling out a small leather bag and tossing it across the table. "Here you go, as agreed. Your performance was absolutely perfect."

"Thanks," he replied, catching it and tucking it inside his coat without bothering to count the coins within. "And I suppose that's a wise policy. Now, with regard to the *other* part of my payment we discussed?"

"Hmm?" Principia dragged a fried tentacle through the curry sauce and raised her eyebrows innocently at him. "If you'd care to inspect the bag, you'll find every copper accounted for."

McGraw had been at this too long to bother getting annoyed. Some folk just liked to drag things out and be difficult; it was usually easier to indulge than oppose them. "You were going to tell me how you managed, on such very short notice, to bust into my scrying mirror, despite all my wards, and send me a message. I've been pretty anxious to get my hands on that little bit of spellwork."

"Ah yes," she purred, then popped the bit of squid into her mouth, chewing smugly. Just to drag out the tension. McGraw waited, wearing a faint smile of amusement until she finished. "Well, as with most of a thief's best tricks, it was all about strategy and had little to do with fancy tools. I'm a fourth-rate enchantress; you have to know there's no way I could power through your magic."

"That was my presumption, yes. Hence my curiosity."

"The trick was that I'd set all that up far in advance, and it took the better part of a year. I'd been thinking I'd use you to get Arachne off my tail if things in Last Rock went sour. But then the Guild set Shook on me and I had more urgent concerns, so I had to blow my little failsafe."

McGraw shook his head ruefully. Of course; he really should have thought of that. Anybody could crack any ward given enough time and persistence, which was exactly why it was smart to change them up regularly. He did have the unfortunate habit of leaving his unmodified for far too long. At his age, the enthusiasm for attending to piddly menial tasks just wasn't there.

"So you were going to aim me at Tellwyrn?" he said mildly, letting the other matter drop. "That sounds downright . . . unfriendly."

"Oh, don't make faces at me," she said with a cheeky wink. "It's not as if I was plotting your demise. Honestly, there's not a damn thing I could've offered you that would make you do something as daft as try to take on Arachne in a head-to-head fight, correct?"

"You better believe it. I'm way past having pissing contests with dragons."

"Trust me, Arachne's not so hard." She chewed another bite of squid, face twisting in an annoyed grimace. "She isn't *subtle*. If you understand how she thinks and have the right leverage, it's fairly simple to distract her, or maneuver around her. I know her, and you could've provided the leverage. Not *now*, of course, since we've both gone and pissed her off. But those are the breaks."

"It does seem you burned a few bridges over the course of this business," he noted after taking a sip of his rum. "Feel free to shut me down if it ain't my place to ask, ma'am, but is it wise to turn on your Guild like that? I can't imagine they'd appreciate you bringin' in an outside contractor to get rid of one of their enforcers."

"No, that is pretty explicitly against the Guild's codes," she said wryly. "The penalties would be . . . significant. What the Guild doesn't know won't hurt me, though." Principia stared at her glass, her expression sobering. "I do enjoy my little pranks, and I'll be the first to admit I'm not one to respect authority unless there's something in it for me, but I've always been loyal to the Guild. Faithful. This . . . is a first for me, and I don't mind telling you it sits poorly. No matter how necessary it was."

"I didn't get the impression Mr. Shook was an easy fella to work with."

She laughed bitterly. "No, I decided he and I weren't going to develop a solid working relationship about the time he declared his intention to rape me into submission if I didn't get results fast enough."

McGraw straightened in his chair, all the humor draining from his expression instantly. "Is that . . . typical policy for the Thieves' Guild?"

"That's the best part." Principia lifted her eyes; her grin was utterly devoid of amusement. "Hell no, it isn't. Last time one of our members did anything like that, our chief enforcer bent him in half so he could suck his own dick, stuffed him in a barrel that way, and sent him over the Tira Falls. *But*, there is the issue of credibility. As I've mentioned, I'm a bit of a wild card and happily so. Shook, on the other hand, has built a career keeping his shittier tendencies in check when important people are looking, and hanging around the central offices of the Guild enough to have built up a solid rep." She shrugged fatalistically. "I had no way to win. If it came to his word against mine, I would've lost that by default. It was either turn on the Guild or let that asshole treat me like his personal . . ." She cut off, turning her head to the side to glare at nothing. "Well. Let's just say you were the lesser evil and leave it at that."

"I've been fairly called much worse things," he replied, taking a sip. "If my opinion holds any weight with you at all, ma'am, I'd say you handled the situation well. Truthfully, I was impressed by your ability to play a part. Ain't often I've had such a professional to work with."

"Ah, yes, the whole world knows of Longshot McGraw's weakness for pretty girls in peril." She turned back to him with a grin, her dour mood of the moment before apparently forgotten.

He coughed. "Yes. Well. S'pose it'd be disingenuous to deny it at this juncture in my career. Truth be told, I had it in mind to decline monetary compensation once we were settling up accounts . . . but there at the end, I *did* have to expend a very rare elemental evocation on your behalf. Had that sucker waiting for an emergency for years."

"Yes, Mabel has that effect on everybody's plans," she said wryly.

"Well, all things considered, I'm just happy to have been of—" He broke off in shock, feeling a slippered foot slowly slide up his calf under the table.

Principia had leaned her elbows on the tabletop, resting her chin on her interlaced fingers and batted her eyes coquettishly. "Well, drat. With everything all paid for, I can't use my line about thanking you *properly*. Now I have to be baldly forward like some kind of hussy."

McGraw coughed again, for the first time in a long while finding himself utterly at a loss. "I, uh . . . I don't . . . Ma'am, I'm not sure if . . ."

"You can call me Prin, you know," she purred. "There are, in fact, a *lot* of things you can call me. We can go over that at some length, if you want."

He gaped at her for a long moment, then jumped as her foot made contact with him again, even higher this time. Finally finding his tongue, McGraw decided to go with the simplest statement he could. "I am confused."

"Let me tell you something about good-looking boys," she said, still gazing up at him through her lashes. "By and large, that's all there is to them. It takes time and experience to make a man into something interesting . . . Experience of a kind that leaves its own mark. I learned a long time ago to look past a lined face; learned to appreciate the face itself. Give me *interesting* men; they're the only ones worth the effort."

"I, um. Just to be clear, and I don't mean to put you on the spot, but you are talking about . . ."

"Oh, Omnu's breath," she said, visibly amused. "Yes, Elias, I am offering to go to bed with you. Asking, even. If you're having trouble with that, you can assume I'm trying to trick or swindle you or something. You can keep a wand pointed at my head the whole time if you like . . . *That* I've not done for a while. Might add a certain spice."

"I'm . . . having a little trouble with this," he admitted frankly. "You're, uh . . . well, a strikingly attractive young lady. It's been a longer time than I care to acknowledge since any such found me worth . . . um, spending the time with."

"Well." She smiled, a catlike expression. "It's something to do."

McGraw had to laugh. "Well, then, Prin . . . There, you're speaking my language."

Heading up the stairs, they passed the waitress who had brought the platter. She grinned and winked at McGraw, laughing when he actually ducked his head bashfully, before heading back down to collect their dishes and sweep them off to the kitchen. Like any good waitress, she had seen the signs of a pair of customers about to leave and made sure she was on hand to clean up promptly. At least, that was what she'd planned to tell the tavern owner if he gave her an earful for loitering on the balcony right above them.

She swished into the kitchen, casually deposited the dishes, and made her way over to the corner where a boy of twelve sat on an upended barrel, shelling clams.

"Sanjay! How's my favorite brother?"

"Your favorite brother knows very well when you want something. You've gotta work on that subtlety, y'know."

"Fair enough," she said, grinning. "I need you to run down to the wharf master's office and carry a message to Rajur for me."

"Storm's coming," he said, finally lifting his gaze to hers and matching her grin. "And I'm not your errand boy, Lakshmi."

"Fine." She stepped closer, lowering her voice and dropping the smile. "I need you to go take a message to *Fang* from *Peepers*. It's urgent."

"Oh *ho*! That's another matter!" Sanjay's grin widened and he hopped down. "Sounds like it's worth some compensation, if you're gonna be dragging me into Guild business."

"Don't get smart with me, little brother; you will *always* owe me for changing your diapers." She leaned in closer, letting her smile return slowly. "There'll be compensation for everybody; enough rep for both me and Fang to move up the ranks, maybe even to sponsor you an apprenticeship. This is gonna go right to the Boss in Tiraas."

"That good?" He grinned up at her expectantly.

"That bad. It seems we have a traitor among us."

CHAPTER 23

The office door opened and Style entered, a quietly seething Jeremiah Shook on her heels. Despite his glower, he was self-possessed enough to shut the door behind them, while Style paced down the carpeted center of the room, past the rows of accountants' desks to come stand behind Trick's shoulder.

"Thumper!" he said genially, beckoning the man forward. "Good to see you back safely."

"Boss," Thumper replied, making an effort to get his expression under control. Well, the man had due cause to be upset. None of that, as far as Tricks knew, was directed at him. Still, on top of the failure of his job in Last Rock, it was always humiliating, having to be extracted from the clutches of the law by the Guild's attorneys. At least they'd gotten to Shook before he'd been handed over to the Avenists. The cults of Avei and Eserion had a . . . complicated relationship.

"First of all," Tricks said, "I want to reassure you up front that you're not being called down on the carpet. What happened in Last Rock was patently not your fault. You were dealing with a foe extremely well positioned and practiced at outmaneuvering opponents."

"We should deal with that asshole McGraw," Thumper said, all but snarling, his self-control fraying. "Our rep's on the line. We can't have people thinking they can spit in the Guild's face and walk away."

"All in good time," Tricks said mildly. "He's not the foe I was speaking of, however. One of our people in Puna Dara spotted McGraw less than a week after the events in question."

"Doing *what*?" Thumper demanded.

Tricks grinned, well aware that it was an unpleasant expression. "Having dinner," he said, "with Principia Locke. Apparently they went upstairs together afterward. Our agent heard enough of their conversation to confirm that Prin was the individual who hired McGraw to interfere in your operation."

For a moment, Thumper just stared at him, completely nonplussed. Then his eyes tracked to one side, then the other. Tricks could almost see him making connections, considering events in light of this new information. Slowly, his posture stiffened until the man was practically vibrating. Fists clenched at his sides, he failed to maintain the mask of calm, his face twisting with rage.

"That little. Fucking. *Whore*."

"Here's the thing," Tricks went on, feigning a casual air but watching Thumper carefully. The man was clearly on the verge of a complete blowup; it would be preferable if Style didn't have to beat him compliant. "That operation of hers? *Brilliant*. One of the more elegant cons I've seen, and that is saying something. If she'd just had you roughed up or killed, the Guild would have sent along another, more dangerous agent, escalating the stakes and the risk. No, she had to generate complete chaos, turn the whole mission into such a complete and utter tits-up-in-the-rhubarb *debacle* that we had no choice but to withdraw all our attentions from the town. That succeeded brilliantly. Any new arrivals in Last Rock for the next little while are going to be examined *very* carefully, both by the local law and likely by Tellwyrn, so we risk the identity of anyone we send back in there. And that leaves me in an awkward position. If it were anything simpler—going to the law, hiring an outside thug to take out a Guildmate—you know exactly what we'd do."

"Drag her ass back here and beat it purple," Shook snarled.

"For starters," Tricks said with a faint grin. "But the point of that is to demonstrate to all that the Guild is still in control, that we're not to be made fools of. In *this* case . . . Well, Thumper, we've been made right fools of, and no mistake, Keys made you and I look like complete idiots. Only reason she hasn't managed to make a mockery of the Guild itself is nobody outside this room knows the extent of what she pulled. And it's going to stay that way. You keep your mouth shut about this business, understand?"

Thumper forgot himself so far as to take a step forward, raising both fists. "You're actually going to let the little cunt get *away* with—"

"Settle," Style said quietly. Thumper stopped, collected himself, and nodded sharply, evidently not trusting himself to speak.

Style yelled, cursed, and generally blustered as a matter of course, but as her enforcers quickly learned, when she whispered, people tended to die.

"So," Tricks continued, "I'm giving you a little time off from your duties. It's going in the records as a suspension related to a recent failed job. Consider it a well-earned vacation."

Shook physically twitched as though struck. "You said," he replied, clinging to a frayed thread of restraint, "I wasn't to be punished."

"You're not," Tricks said gently. "It's like this, Thumper. I obviously cannot let Keys get away with turning on the Guild like this, and I cannot afford to spend any more resources going after her without further undercutting our credibility. If it comes down to it, I'll suck it up and chase her down with whatever we've got, but *first*, I'm going to hope for her to magically find herself back here under completely different circumstances so I can straighten her out and make it look like we were, all of us, in full control the whole time."

Thumper's sneer eloquently said what he thought of that. "And she'll come back here because . . . ?"

"Hypothetically speaking," Tricks said, "if an off-duty member of the Guild were to find and bring Keys here . . . Well, that person would gain quite a bit of rep for exposing and collaring a traitor when they weren't even supposed to be at work. Naturally, if there were any recent blemishes on such a person's record, they'd be quite overshadowed. Hell, I could probably see my way to removing such black marks entirely."

Slowly, visibly, Thumper grew calmer as understanding dawned on him. His face didn't quite relax completely, but there appeared something in his eyes that hinted at a very cruel sort of smile. "I see."

Tricks grinned. "Enjoy your vacation."

"You got it, Boss," Thumper said, nodding first to him and then to Style, then turned to go.

Tricks let him get the door open and start to step out before he said, "Oh, and Thumper."

He turned back to look warily at his two superiors. "Boss?"

"In this hypothetical scenario, anybody bringing Keys back here had better be mindful of the condition she's in. I can't make an example of a corpse."

"In this hypothetical scenario," Thumper replied, "I would know *exactly* how to teach an uppity bitch some humility." He nodded to them again, stepped out, and shut the door behind him.

Just like that, Tricks let the mask fall, slumping down in his chair and covering his eyes with a hand. "Ugh . . . what an absolute cock-up. I *still* can hardly believe all this, Style. Principia's disrespectful and ornery, but she's always been faithful to the Big Guy. I just . . . didn't see this coming. Before the end of this, I've really gotta find out what it is she wants so badly in Last Rock that she's willing to cross the Guild to get it."

"This is why I wish you'd let me deal with my enforcers directly," she replied. "Before sending Thumper off, I'd rather have spent some time finding out what he *did* to set her off that way. Yeah, I know my man. You can bet he did *something*. People don't just up and turn on their cult on a fucking whim."

He twisted around and leaned his head back to look up at her. "Do you think he tried to hand her off to the Wreath or something? To Tellwyrn?"

Style shook her head slowly, her expression troubled. "No . . . not that. Shook's stuffed to the skull with rage and he's got bad habits around women . . . Sweet tried to teach him some self-control and ended up just teaching him to repress, which has *not* been helpful. But the Guild is his whole life, even more than Prin. I can't see him betraying a member to our enemies."

"Then it doesn't matter what he did; it matters what she did about it," Tricks said firmly. "I will not have treason, Style. It's not to be tolerated. Anything else we can deal with, work around, forgive if need be. Anybody who turns on the Guild is an enemy, simple as that."

She drew in a deep breath and blew it out all at once. "You *really* think Thumper has a chance of collaring Prin in the wild? He's a knee-capper; she's a con woman, and a damn good one. She's already manipulated the hell out of him once."

"Of course not. He'll flush her out, though. Principia settled down in some nest with her defenses up is something I don't fancy trying to root out. Principia fleeing across the countryside with *that* asshole at her heels . . . Well, if we play this right, she might still be persuaded to come home voluntarily. After all, Thumper's not working on my orders here, now is he?"

Style shook her head. "Well, let's just hope this works out better than your *last* clever idea."

CHAPTER 24

Trissiny returned from her morning run looking forward to a shower. As much as she'd found showering ostentatious on her first arrival at the University, she'd come to enjoy the experience. It was certainly a more efficient way of getting clean than scrubbing. But upon opening the door to Clarke Tower—the freshman girls' dormitory—she had to stop just inside and take in the scene.

At first glance, everyone appeared to be having breakfast. Pancakes, in fact. There was a large, steaming platter of them set in the center of the coffee table, along with dishes of butter and syrup, and those present were holding laden plates and forks. Shaeine and Teal sat side by side on the sofa, Ruda and the house mother, Janis, in two of the chairs.

Something about the situation made the fine hairs on the back of Trissiny's neck stand up, however, and she knew very well to respect her intuition about danger. Indeed, on a second look, only Ruda appeared to be enjoying the meal. Teal and Shaeine were glassy-eyed and chewing slowly as if bespelled or drugged. Janis was holding a plate but not eating; her body language was tense, and upon Trissiny's entry she looked up at her, an incoherent plea in her eyes. It was a jarring contrast to the woman's normally jolly, maternal demeanor.

Reflexively, Trissiny reached for her sword.

"What's going on?" she asked tersely.

"Breakfast," said Shaeine with a broad smile so totally unlike her normally reserved demeanor that it sent chills down Trissiny's spine. "Have I mentioned how much I *love* imperial food? Sugar on *everything*." She swirled a forkful of pancake in syrup and stuck it in her mouth, Teal giggling beside her.

"I'm pretty sure they're okay," said Ruda, grabbing Trissiny's attention. "I'm keeping an eye on this and Janis hasn't eaten the food."

"*You're* eating the food!"

"Yeah, have you *noticed* I drink a barrel's worth of liquor a day and never so much as slur my speech? Mind-altering shit doesn't work on me." She glanced at the hallway door. "Like I said, I'm keeping an eye on this; didn't wanna start up a scrap when we've got two incapacitated crewmates—that's asking for somebody to get hurt. Sides, help's on the way. Glad you're here, though; it seems to be you she's after."

"What's . . . *Who* did—"

She broke off as Principia Locke bustled into the room from the direction of the kitchen, carrying another platter of pancakes. She looked eerily domestic, wearing a frilled apron and oven mitts. Her whole face lit up when she saw who was present.

"Trissiny! How wonderful, everyone's finally here. I'm so glad, dear; I've been waiting a long time to—"

"What have you done to my friends?" Trissiny demanded.

Prin clucked her tongue, coming forward to set down the pancakes on the coffee table. "I made them breakfast. Honestly, everyone's so *suspicious* when I do a nice turn, you'd think . . ." She trailed off at the rasp of Trissiny's sword coming out of its sheath.

"I am not going to indulge you in banter," the paladin said icily. "Something is clearly, *badly* amiss with them. You will explain this, or you're going head first out the nearest window."

The elf stared at her in silence for a moment, her expression neutral, then sighed softly. "They're fine. It's just a little charm to encourage peace and happiness; people pay good money to have it done to them. Wears off in an hour. Honestly, Trissiny, all I wanted was a chance to *talk* with you, but you're always surrounded by . . ." Her eyes cut back and forth around the room, and a scowl fell over her features. "All right, what happened to the dryad?"

"Went to get Tellwyrn," Ruda said cheerfully. "C'mon, you didn't expect using a fairy charm on a *dryad* would do anything but cheese her off? Be glad she didn't decide to deal with you herself; Juniper's tastes in breakfast don't run toward pancakes. These are really good, by the way."

Prin narrowed her eyes. "*You* are annoyingly lucid for someone who's supposed to be charmed."

"Yup. Let's see, you're clearly using witchcraft, so it runs on sympathy and symbolism . . . Something that clouds minds, but it'd almost have to be divine in origin to avoid tripping Triss and Shaeine's alarms . . . Ah!" She grinned broadly. "Sacramental wine in the pancake batter, right? I'm right, aren't I? Yeah, read about the Punaji curse sometime; see if you can guess where you fucked up."

The door to the tower flew open. A shrill whine just at the edge of human hearing sounded for a moment, and then with a sharp *pop* and a flash of light, something burst from above the doorframe and shot across the room, landing smoldering in Prin's new dish of pancakes. It was a silver horseshoe, slightly charred. Immediately, Shaeine and Teal straightened up, blinking, and the goofy smiles faded from their faces.

Professor Tellwyrn stepped inside, Juniper hovering behind her. Her expression promised murder.

"Well, aside from the obvious," Ruda added.

"Arachne," Janis said in obvious relief. "I could have fought her, but the girls . . ."

"You acted correctly, Janis," the professor said, her eyes on Prin. "Kindly make sure they're suffering no lingering effects."

Principia stared at Tellwyrn for half a second, then turned back to the paladin. "Trissiny, just—"

"*No*," Tellwyrn snarled. She stepped to one side, herding Juniper along with her, then pointed at Principia and gestured at the open door. With a yelp, Prin was yanked forward and hurled bodily outside.

Clarke Tower had taken a great deal of getting used to; the dorm was a prime example of both Tellwyrn's power and her eccentric tastes. The tower actually floated in the air off to one side of the mountain, connected to the campus by a narrow bridge with tall guard rails. Physically tossing someone out its door was a clear sign of contempt for their well-being.

Tellwyrn followed, Trissiny right on her heels, Juniper and Ruda bringing up the rear while Janis attended to a confused Shaeine and Teal. Principia landed on her feet on the bridge, skidding briefly but managing not to lose her balance, thanks to elven agility.

"*This* is too far," Tellwyrn said icily. "You were warned about this, Principia. By me, and by the Sisters of Avei. The fact that you chose to challenge *me* instead of *them* just goes to prove you've not developed any wisdom in the last twenty years."

"The Sisters didn't send her into the Golden Sea to face off against a centaur horde," Prin shot back, glaring. "*They* aren't trying to get her killed!"

"They will, though," Tellwyrn retorted. "No Hand of Avei has ever died in bed. Well, except Taslin of Madouris; somebody got her with some kind of flesh-dissolving poison. *Nasty* business. Which doesn't change the fact that *none* of this is any of your concern."

"What is going on?" Trissiny demanded.

"This will *always* be my concern, Arachne!"

"You gave up the right long ago," Tellwyrn said inexorably. "Deliberately. Now I have to decide what to do with—"

"She's *still my daughter*!" Principia shrieked, then fell silent, fists clenched at her sides.

The only sound was the constant wind that sighed over the bridge.

And then Trissiny laughed. "Oh, come on," she scoffed, "that's not even *believable*. I'm not an elf!"

No one answered her. Principia was staring at her with something like hunger, and Tellwyrn . . . The professor's face was carefully blank, not the expression of someone who'd just heard an easily debunked falsehood. Trissiny felt her smile drain away.

Prin opened her mouth, then glanced warily at Tellwyrn.

"Well, you've gone to all this trouble," Tellwyrn said, folding her arms. "Go on, say your piece. See if she thanks you."

"The ears are a recessive trait." Prin began with a careful eye on the professor, but turned her gaze to Trissiny as she spoke. "Your friend Rafe is the exception, not the rule. *Most* half-elves are basically just tall, lanky humans with incredible stamina and really good eyesight. Usually blond. Sound like anyone you know?"

She paused, as if for a response. Trissiny stared blankly at her, unsure whether she was experiencing a total lack of thoughts or simply too many at once for her to pick one out.

"You've probably already felt the effects, training with the Sisters," Principia went on, her tone gentle. "You have ten times the stamina of a pure human and don't need as much food, but you'll have had to work thrice as hard as any of the other girls to put on muscle."

"I . . ." Trissiny looked desperately at Tellwyrn, who was still watching Principia.

"It's a tree," Prin said, barely above a whisper. Trissiny looked back at her and she swallowed painfully before going on, still as softly. "The trissiny. It's . . . I don't know the Tanglish word. They aren't common on this continent. It literally means 'silk tree.' There was one in the grove where I grew up; I used to climb it as a child. It's one of the very few happy memories I have of home. Slim branches, leaves like fern fronds, and little pink puffball flowers in the spring—"

"A *mimosa*?" Trissiny burst out, horrified. There had been a mimosa tree on the grounds of the abbey at Viridill. A delicate, decorative thing that with absolutely zero practical use, it was a standing affront to Avenist sensibilities. It had been a gift from some Izarite temple, Mother Narny had said. The cults of Avei and Izara had deep doctrinal conflicts, and the Izarites were forever trying to mend the divide with such ill-considered presents.

Principia jerked back from her as if struck; her expression fell, and Trissiny realized she had let revulsion stand out plainly on her own features. If any of this were true . . . The fact that she might have been named after that *stupid* tree was the last straw.

Professor Tellwyrn heaved a sigh. "Well, there you go. Look how *happy* everyone is. Janis?"

"The girls are fine," the house mother reported from the doorway behind them. Her eyes were on Trissiny. Everyone's eyes were on her; she couldn't make herself meet anyone's gaze. "It's a harmless enough spell, but Shaeine is furious."

"You came onto my campus," Tellwyrn said grimly, turning back to Principia, "broke into a residential building, and laid a hostile enchantment on *my* students. I have killed people in *extravagant* ways for considerably less, and none of them had been warned to stay off my property beforehand. All things considered, though, I think it's more poetic to leave you to stew in the consequences of your selfishness, Prin. The Sisters of Avei will know you flouted their command before the day is out, and you'll find them a more reasonable enemy than I, but also far more persistent. Enjoy. But you're done in Last Rock. I want you out of this town within the hour, and if I *ever* see you on my campus again, I will personally send you to Hell."

"Yes, yes," Principia sneered, "the great Professor Tellwyrn hands out death like candy at a parade. We *know*."

"I'm not talking about killing you," Tellwyrn said with a cold smile. "Not directly. On the Acarnian subcontinent there is a hellgate which, though easily accessible from this side, opens thirty feet in the air above a phosphorous swamp on the infernal plane. The nearest exit point back to this dimension is more than fifty miles distant, in the hands of a major demon settlement on the Hellish side and blocked by an Avenist temple on the other. Cross me again and I will take you there, toss you through, and see if you can weasel your way out of *that*. In four years she'll be out from under my protection and you can decide whether your selfishness is worth further antagonizing the Sisterhood. Meanwhile, get out of my town."

"I'm already packed," Principia said grimly, looking at Trissiny again. The sadness in her eyes made Trissiny furious for some reason. "I just wanted her to know."

"Yeah, good job. Everybody's just so very happy. Feh." With a wave of Tellwyrn's hand and a quiet *pop* of air, the dark-haired elf vanished.

The silence that followed was painfully awkward.

"She . . . was lying, right?" Trissiny had to pause to swallow the lump in her throat. She could hear a note of pleading in her voice and hated herself for it, but couldn't hold it back. "Right?"

Tellwyrn sighed heavily, taking off her glasses to rub at her eyes with a thumb and forefinger. Every moment she didn't casually brush off Principia's claims was another damning affirmation of them. "I suppose we should talk, Trissiny. Let's go to my office."

"Oh, for fuck's sake, you are *not* dragging her across the goddamn campus at a time like this," Ruda exclaimed. "I'll help Janis clean up and you can have the room. How many thousands of years does it take you to grow some fucking sensitivity, woman?"

"Thanks, Ruda," Trissiny said, touched in spite of herself. Ruda grunted and waved her off, turning to head back inside.

"Hey, guys!" Fross zipped over to them from the gate to the main campus, coming to a stop in the middle of the bridge. "Wow, everybody's up early! You know this is Saturday, right?"

Ruda had been progressively decorating the whole time they'd lived there, and her side of the room was now draped in rugs and heavily embroidered throw pillows, the walls swathed with silken hangings and tapestries. At the foot of her bed was an old-fashioned treasure chest that looked like it belonged in an illustration in a penny dreadful, as well as a modern enchanted cold box in which she kept pints of frozen custard. A white bearskin rug, complete with mounted head and claws, was draped haphazardly over her bed. Trissiny's side of the room was as stark and spartan as when she'd moved in.

Tellwyrn stopped in the middle; she didn't seem to be terribly interested in either side, but frowned at the sharp line of demarcation between them.

Trissiny shut the door behind her, a touch more firmly than was necessary. "It's . . . true, then? That woman is my mother?"

The professor turned to face her, a distasteful grimace twisting her lips. "Trissiny, any imbecile can get knocked up, carry a child to term, and squeeze it out. Profound as the experience may seem when you're going through it, the fact that so many imbeciles *do* so is the only thing that explains the state of the world. Motherhood is another matter entirely."

"You're avoiding the question," Trissiny said in an accusing tone.

Tellwyrn shook her head. "I am *clarifying* the question, because you asked the wrong one. Now you listen to me: *Abbess Narnasia Darnassy* is your mother. *She* gave years of her life to loving you every minute, taught you everything you know about the world, formed you into a young woman capable of living on your own, and then let go to let you do it. *That* is what a mother is, and you have a damn fine one."

Trissiny nodded; the lump in her throat was too painful to speak around, but there was something sweet in it as well. Mother Narny had been responsible for all the girls at the abbey, trainees of every age from all backgrounds, as well as the seven other orphans who'd been raised alongside her, but Trissiny had never once felt that she lacked for care or attention. It was a timely and welcome reminder—and surprising, coming from Tellwyrn—and she resolved on the spot to let the abbess know how much she was appreciated the next time she had the chance to go home.

"With that said," Tellwyrn went on, suddenly sounding weary, "the answer to what you *meant* to ask is yes. You do owe half your blood to Principia Locke. Best have a seat, Trissiny," she added, suiting the suggestion by stepping over to sit down on Ruda's bed.

Trissiny pulled out her desk chair and seated herself, keeping silent for the moment, as she still didn't trust her voice not to waver, and also wasn't sure which of the questions roaring in her head to grasp at first.

"Principia," Tellwyrn began, "is selfish, clever, unburdened by moral scruples, and rather predictable despite her twisty way of thinking. I make a point to keep several such people in my address book; they're very useful to know. So it was that I happened to be acquainted with her about twenty years ago when she was pulling something particularly crafty with a rural noble house—which I won't bother to name, as it's not really material to the subject.

"She'd managed to initiate a fling with the eldest son of the family. I don't know how, and it doesn't particularly matter. As you probably know, and should if you don't, such things are taken very seriously by the nobility; the two things they love most are their comforts and their bloodlines, and there is thus always some contention when an aristocrat's prerogative to screw around with lowborn women creates the risk of producing bastard potential heirs. Matters are more serious still when non humans are involved; the rich do love exotic playthings, but a half-human member of the family is seen as a disgrace most houses would go well out of their way to cover up. Of course, all of this happens regularly, everywhere, but it's still something shameful. The wealthy and powerful, Trissiny, are weird.

"Alchemical contraceptives weren't common back then, but you can bet that the aristocracy had access to them, and even the most dissolute noble wastrels were heartily encouraged to make use of them. Principia's paramour most definitely did; he didn't lack for intelligence or ambition. That ended up being immaterial, however. Prin arranged things so that her status as the young noble's mistress was well known throughout the province, behaved herself with uncharacteristic good taste and charity, and actually managed to be somewhat well-thought-of. And then she got herself pregnant."

"You mean . . . I'm an aristocrat?" Trissiny said numbly.

Tellwyrn grimaced. "You wouldn't be even if the poor boy had been your father—House Whatever would go to great lengths to hush you up in that case. Anyhow, he wasn't; he was more careful than that. Prin went and found herself some other human in another district to take care of that little detail. It was a rather inspired little con, which was why I loitered in the area to watch how it played out. She couldn't *prove* anything and didn't need to; it was all about perception and insinuation, about the court of public opinion, not courts of law. She couldn't have won a paternity suit, but with some skillful manipulation of rumor, she placed the house in the position of having to be *nice* to her or risk a greater scandal than she'd already created. If their scion's pregnant mistress were made to up and disappear, there would've been an outcry. She effectively forced them to pay her off, make a show of how generous and understanding they were. And then, of course, she wisely removed herself from the region before the fickle public forgot the whole story and the much more vindictive nobility she had effectively blackmailed decided to correct her manners."

"That is *despicable*," Trissiny breathed.

"Yes," Tellwyrn said, grinning faintly, "but it was quite clever, and it worked. That, I assure you, was all that mattered to Principia. After that, she was only left with the inconvenience of actually *being* pregnant, and too far along to extinguish it gently. So . . . when you came along, she was very relieved when I offered to find you a home."

"You offered?" Trissiny said shrilly. "*You?*"

"That's a little more shock than I think the story warrants," Tellwyrn said wryly. "Yes, me. I didn't happen to have any reliable friends who'd have wanted a child at the time, and state-run orphanages have a tendency to be unspeakable hellholes. Of the cults who take in orphans . . . Well, it was just lucky you turned out to be a girl. The Sisters of Avei indoctrinate their youth just like anyone—obviously, I mean look at you—but they generally don't screw kids up too badly. And Narnasia had just taken over as abbess at the time; I knew she'd do very well by a foundling. It was part of why she was given the job."

"But you *hate* the Sisters!"

The professor rolled her eyes. "Other way round, Trissiny. I've never had an argument with the Sisters; it's *they* who hate *me*. I doubt they even remember why anymore, but Avei chose to take something I did a few centuries back more personally than it was meant, and let me tell you, nobody holds a grudge like an immortal."

"And of course, you're famous for rescuing orphaned babies from a life of drudgery," Trissiny said bitterly.

Tellwyrn gazed at her in silence for a long moment before replying. "I've had five children, Trissiny. All by human fathers. Four errors in judgment and one extremely extenuating circumstance. Not a bad record for a three-thousand-year career."

Trissiny blinked in startlement. "I . . . You . . . Really? Somehow . . . I can't see you raising a child."

"Omnu's breath, girl, I didn't *raise* them. Can you imagine how messed up someone would be with *me* as their primary moral example?"

"That's a great thing to hear from an educator."

"*You* kids are at least nominally adults. You are intellectually and morally formed; I'm simply teaching you how to *think* effectively. Creating a fully functioning person from whole cloth, as it were, is an entirely different matter. Trust me, I know my limitations." She sighed softly and glanced to the side. "So no, Trissiny, I don't make it a habit of gallivanting around the world rescuing orphans . . . but I happened to be there, and I have a soft spot for the half-elven offspring of horribly unfit mothers. Prin didn't want you, and I found it wasn't in me to just *leave* you there. So . . . here we are." She shrugged, smiling ironically. "If I hadn't intervened, you'd have been brought up as a small-time grifter. In the best-case scenario. In the other . . . I would like to think even Principia wouldn't have abandoned an inconvenient baby in a haystack somewhere, but if you asked me to look you in the eyes and swear to it, I'd have to balk."

"Here we are," Trissiny repeated in a whisper, staring at the floor. Slowly, she lifted her eyes. "She . . . Principia . . . She's a bad person, isn't she?"

"In all my years, after all the things I've done, for all that I've kept myself at the forefront of world events about half the time, I've met maybe a dozen *bad people*. Trissiny, most evil in the world is due to stupidity, ignorance, and laziness. Some is the work of the mentally ill; much results from the accidents of birth and culture that train people to see the world in irrational ways. Actually evil *people*, individuals who understand right and wrong and deliberately choose wrong, are vanishingly rare. For the most part, people do what seems best to them, and their moral failings are the extension of intellectual failings.

"Principia Locke is selfish, lazy, deceitful, irreverent, and gratuitously obstreperous, but there are much, *much* worse things a person can be. I can't tell you she's a good person to know, but she is not the sort of person you as a paladin are likely to be called on to chase down and bring to justice."

Trissiny nodded, lowering her eyes again. "I don't even know what to think about all this. What . . . What do you think I should do?"

"I think I'm the wrong person to ask," Tellwyrn said, her voice uncharacteristically gentle. "I'm here to help however I can, but in this case, you have better sources of support. I suggest talking to Avei, and to Narnasia when circumstances permit. I'll tell you this much: redemption is a real thing and the desire for it is downright commonplace. People *do* change, and the love for a child is a powerful motivator. You should know, however, that Principia brought you into the world as a *prop* for a con she was running, and after handing you off to me, the first time she evinced the slightest interest in your existence was when you were chosen by Avei to be her paladin. A week after the announcement, she turned up on the steps of the abbey, and Narnasia threw her bodily down the stairs."

"Mother Narny did that?" Trissiny said, shocked. The abbess had been a Silver Legionnaire in her youth, but now suffered arthritis and walked with a cane.

"She was *quite* irate, I understand. She also swallowed her pride enough to keep me informed, which was lucky, as the next thing Prin did was move to Last Rock. Avei determined you were to attend school here when you were old enough, almost as soon as she called you, though how *Prin* found out about that I've no idea. You may choose to forgive her or not, maybe even to let her be part of your life, but don't do so blindly. Remember her interest in you began when you became a person who'd be useful to know. If she *is* genuinely repentant, I strongly advise you to make her prove it before you come to any decisions."

Trissiny nodded slowly. ". . . I'm a half elf, then. I think I'm having the most trouble with that."

"If you've gone eighteen years without knowing that, it's not likely to break your stride now. You're lucky in that you can pass for human; most humans and an unfortunate lot of elves tend to shun half bloods. You're also the Hand of Avei, so nobody with a lick of sense is going to give you a hard time. Talk with Admestus if you have questions. I can explain the basics, but it'd all be very technical; he's actually lived them."

"Ugh." Trissiny made a face, and Tellwyrn laughed.

"Yes, I know. Remember what I said about people doing what makes sense to them? Rather than turning up your nose at his eccentricities, it would behoove you to wonder what motivates him to act that way."

"I'm . . . altogether surprised at how *you're* acting," Trissiny admitted, forcing herself to meet Tellwyrn's gaze.

"Why, because big bad Tellwyrn has a kind streak?" The elf shook her head. "If I had to guess at Avei's motivations in sending you here, I'd say she meant you to soften the black-and-white view of the world that growing up in what amounts to a convent has left you with. Nobody's all one or the other, Trissiny. Honestly, I'm probably the most straightforward person you will ever meet. If I confuse you, you are dramatically oversimplifying the world."

"Do you know who my father is?"

"No idea," Tellwyrn admitted. "Some human. He was a bit part in Principia's game; probably got the night of his life out of the blue and never had an inkling it resulted in consequences for anyone else. They never do. Let *me* ask a question: what kinds of interactions have you had with Prin since you got to town?"

Trissiny shook her head slowly. "Not much . . . She tried to give me a necklace once, but Sheriff Sanders chased her off. Well, actually gave it to me, I suppose."

"What?" Tellwyrn straightened up. "You have something she *gave* you?"

"She didn't give it directly to me," Trissiny explained. "She found Teal and Shaeine in town one night and gave it to them to pass along. I, uh . . . I was going to have someone look it over for enchantments, but . . . it slipped my mind."

"Slipped your mind. *Well*, now we know how she's been following your movements, at least. I was all set up to go hunting down whoever blabbed about centaurs." She rubbed her forehead. "Damn it, Trissiny, I can accept your priggishness as a result of upbringing, but you of *all* people should know to be more careful than this."

"You're right," Trissiny said, flushing. She opened her belt pouch and rummaged inside for the necklace; it took some doing, as the thing had slid under her first aid kit. "I've been kind of overwhelmed by this place, but that's a poor excuse. Here it is."

"And you've even been *carrying* it—" Tellwyrn broke off abruptly, staring at the necklace dangling from Trissiny's fingers. "That's a golden eagle."

"Uh . . . yes. I guess she thought it's the only kind of ornamentation I might want. Which is true; I didn't even want *this*, but the sigil . . ."

"The *sigil*." She snatched the necklace out of Trissiny's hand, staring at it. "Yes, there's a tracking charm . . . Oh, *hell*, Principia, what have you done?"

"What?" Trissiny stared at her, nonplussed. "I'm confused, what does that—"

"No time!" Tellwyrn said curtly, and then the room vanished.

Trissiny had never teleported before; the lack of sensation was disorienting. It seemed it should feel like *something*, but her room simply disappeared and the sheriff's office in Last Rock replaced it. She also materialized in a seated position and staggered to one knee, only her years of physical training warding off an embarrassing tumble to the floor. Tellwyrn, she noted with annoyance, had resorted herself in transit so that she appeared upright.

"Damn it!" Sheriff Sanders shouted, jerking backward from his desk so abruptly he caused a minor avalanche of papers. "Don't *do* that!"

"Where is Principia Locke?" Tellwyrn demanded. "Have you seen her today?"

"A few minutes ago," he grunted, resettling himself in his chair. "She popped out of midair and landed right there in the street. I kinda figured it was *your* doing."

"Which way did she go?"

"Hell if *I* know," he said. "I ain't her keeper, unless I can manage to actually *catch* her committing a crime for once. Home, I reckon."

Tellwyrn hissed a curse, and the world vanished again.

"Son of a *bitch*!" Sanders barked when they materialized; this time he was dumped to the floor, suddenly without the chair under him. He winced, looking up at Trissiny. "Ah . . . My apologies, ma'am."

Trissiny nodded abstractly to him, looking around. They were in a bare attic space containing nothing but a bed with an uncovered mattress and a battered old table and chair. "Where are we?"

"Prin's place," Sanders grunted, climbing to his feet. "Though it looks like she's skipped town. Well, for all that I couldn't help liking her a little, I've gotta say this'll make my job a mite easier."

"Trissiny," Tellwyrn said sharply, "do you sense anything? Anything demonic or otherwise evil?"

Trissiny frowned, panning her gaze around the bare, little room. "Nothing like that. Why? Are you expecting demons?"

"I would take it as a great kindness if *someone* would explain to me what's going on," Sanders said with visibly strained patience.

Tellwyrn held up the necklace, regarding it grimly. "This piece of jewelry has a tracking charm on it. She's been using it to keep tabs on Trissiny's movements."

"Well, that's a misdemeanor, if Ms. Avelea didn't consent to the surveillance," he said slowly. "I'm not sure I understand the urgency of all this, though."

"Sam, this is the sacred symbol of Avei! The gods aren't always paying attention to us—okay, hell, they aren't *often* paying attention. But to lay a charm on a holy sigil intended to surreptitiously track her Hand? Avei would damn well notice *that*."

"What are you saying?" Trissiny demanded.

"There are ways of hiding such things from the gods," Tellwyrn said grimly. "They're commonly used on idols, to prevent the deities in question from realizing that those worshiping them are . . . less than sincere. This is *Black Wreath* spellwork."

Silence held for a moment.

"Aw, Prin," Sanders groaned, dragging a hand over his face.

"It's probably not what you're thinking," Tellwyrn said. "Principia wouldn't join the Wreath."

"This looks pretty damning!" Trissiny retorted. A hollow sensation was opening up inside her; this was just too many revelations for this early in the morning.

"Pun not intended?" Tellwyrn actually smiled a little when Trissiny glared at her. "Two kinds of people join the Black Wreath—true believing fanatics eager to pull down the gods, and everyone else, most of whom just like feeling subversive and get squeamish when they realize what they've gotten into—if they ever do. Principia is too self-centered and too cynical to be in either group. However, I can *well* imagine her being brazen enough to con the Wreath out of some spellwork. Which leaves the very significant question of *what* she offered them in return and whether she came through on her end of the deal. I can see that going either way."

"That's assuming she's not *actually* a Wreath cultist," Trissiny added grimly. "A personality profile isn't evidence, Professor."

"Yes . . . in any case, she's certainly intelligent enough to foresee how this would play out when she broke into Clarke Tower," Tellwyrn said, beginning to pace. "Packed up and ready . . . an escape prepared. We won't catch her."

"She broke into . . ." Sanders trailed off, shaking his head. "What do you mean, we won't catch her? Are you Arachne Tellwyrn or not?"

"Legendary power does not connote omnipotence or infallibility," Tellwyrn said, still frowning into the distance. "Last person I met who thought it did was a god. I will forever cherish the look on his face when I killed him."

Trissiny and Sanders exchanged a wary look.

"City girl or not, she's still an elf. All she has to do is get lost in the tallgrass, and that is pretty much that. With even the basic enchantments she can use, she can deflect a tracking hound." Tellwyrn shook her head, coming to a stop and staring out the room's one window. "This goes way beyond Principia. Damn it . . . We need to find her. We aren't going to be the only ones trying, and depending on who gets there first, she may be silenced before anybody can get answers."

"By 'silenced,'" Trissiny said slowly, "you mean . . ."

"You know exactly what I mean."

She realized she was gripping the hilt of her sword. Whether for comfort or in anticipation of trouble, Trissiny couldn't have said, and it bothered her that she could make so little sense of her own thoughts. Whatever else was going on, they needed—*she* needed—to find Principia Locke. They needed answers.

And so did she.

ABOUT THE AUTHOR

D. D. Webb is the author of the Gods Are Bastards and Only Villains Do That series. A former bookseller of ten years, he enjoys writing fantasy stories, playing the violin, and being sad. Webb resides in the Pacific Northwest with two elderly cats.

≋ Podium

JOIN THE FELLOWSHIP
follow us on our socials

 podiumentertainment.com
 @podiumentertainment
 /podiumentertainment
 @podium_ent
 @podiumentertainment